Praise for *New York Times*
bestselling author Garth Nix:

SABRIEL

"Rich, complex, involving, hard to put down, this is excellent
high fantasy."—*Publishers Weekly* (starred review)

"*Sabriel* is a winner."
—Philip Pullman, author of *The Amber Spyglass*

"Nix has created an ingenious, icy world in the throes of
chaos. The action charges along at a gallop, imbued with an
encompassing sense of looming disaster. A page-turner for sure."
—ALA *Booklist* (starred review)

LIRAEL

"What makes *Lirael* a delight is the magic that Nix brings to
his story and to his characters. It is filled with twists and turns,
playful inventiveness and dark magic, and is sure to satisfy his
many readers."—*Locus*

"Readers who like their fantasy intense in action, magisterial
in scope, and apocalyptic in consequences will revel in every
word."—*Kirkus Reviews* (starred review)

ABHORSEN

"Thought-provoking fantasy."
—*Publishers Weekly* (starred review)

"Terror, courage, bitterness, love, desperation, and sacrifice
all swirl together in an apocalyptic climax. Breathtaking,
bittersweet, and utterly unforgettable."
—*Kirkus Reviews* (starred review)

ALSO BY GARTH NIX

Shade's Children
The Ragwitch
Across the Wall
One Beastly Beast
A Confusion of Princes

THE ABHORSEN TRILOGY
Sabriel
Lirael
Abhorsen

GARTH NIX

Lirael

DAUGHTER OF THE CLAYR

HARPER

An Imprint of HarperCollinsPublishers

Ginee Seo, my editor at HarperCollins, is owed many thanks for her
editorial advice, particularly for encouraging me to go back and tell
more of Lirael's story.

Lirael: Daughter of the Clayr

Library of Congress Cataloging-in-Publication Data
Nix, Garth.
   Lirael, daughter of the Clayr / Garth Nix.
      p.   cm.
   Summary: When a dangerous necromancer threatens to unleash a
long-buried evil, Lirael and Prince Sameth are drawn into a battle to
save the Old Kingdom and reveal their true destinies.
   ISBN 978-0-06-231556-4
   [1. Magic—Fiction. 2. Fantasy.] I. Title.
PZ7.N647Li 2001   00-059707
[Fic]—dc21   CIP
                                                        AC

Typography by Henrietta Stern
❖
14 15 16 17 18   LP/RRDH   10 9 8 7 6 5 4 3 2 1

Revised paperback edition, 2014

To Anna, my family and friends,
and to the memory of Bytenix (1986–1999),
the original Disreputable Dog

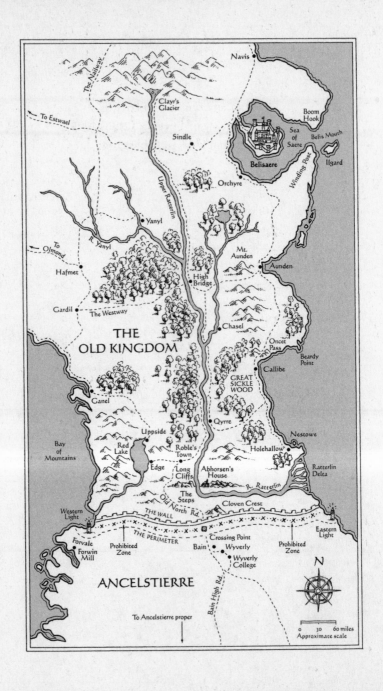

CONTENTS

Prologue 1

PART ONE 7

PART THREE 341

It was a hot, steamy summer, and the mosquitoes swarmed everywhere, from their breeding grounds in the rotten, reedy shores of the Red Lake up to the foothills of Mount Abed. Small, bright-eyed birds swooped among the clouds of insects, eating their fill. Above them, birds of prey circled, to devour the smaller birds in turn.

But there was one place near the Red Lake where no mosquito or bird flew, and no grass or living thing would grow. A low hill, little more than two miles from the eastern shore. A mound of close-packed dirt and stones, stark and strange amidst the wild grassland that surrounded it, and the green forest that climbed the nearby hills.

The mound had no name. If one had ever appeared on a map of the Old Kingdom, the map was long lost. There had once been farms nearby, but never closer than a league. Even when people had lived there, they would neither look at the strange hill nor speak of it. The nearest town now was Edge, a precarious settlement that had never seen better days but had not yet given up hope of them. The townsfolk of Edge knew it was wise to avoid the eastern shore of the Red Lake. Even the animals of the forest and the meadow shunned the area around the mound, as they instinctively stayed away from anyone who seemed to be going there.

Such as the man who stood on the fringe of the forest, where the hills melted into the lakeshore plain. A thin, balding man who wore a suit of leather armor that covered him from ankle to wrist, reinforced with plates of red-enameled metal at his neck and every joint. He carried a naked sword in his left hand, the blade balanced across his shoulder. His right hand rested against a leather bandolier worn diagonally across his chest. Seven pouches hung from the bandolier, the smallest no larger than a pillbox, the largest as big as his clenched fist. Wooden handles hung downwards out of the pouches. Black ebony handles, which his fingers crawled across like a spider along a wall.

Anyone who had been there to see would have known that the ebony handles belonged to bells, and that in turn would identify the man by kind, if not by name. A necromancer, he carried the seven bells of his dark art.

The man looked down at the mound for some time, noting that he was not the first to come there that day. At least two people stood on the bare hill, and there was a shimmer of heat in the air that suggested that other, less visible beings stood there, too.

The man considered waiting till dusk, but he knew he didn't have that choice. This was not his first visit to the mound. Power lay far beneath it, imprisoned deep within the earth. It had called him across the Kingdom, summoning him to its presence on this Midsummer's Day. It called him now, and he could not deny it.

Still, he retained enough pride and will to resist running the last half mile to the mound. It took all his strength, but when his boots touched the bare earth at the lip of the hill, it was with deliberation and no sign of haste.

One of the people there he knew, and expected. The old man, the last of the line that had served the thing that lay under the mound, acting as a channel for the power that kept it hidden from the gaze of the witches who saw everything in their cave of ice. The fact that the old man was the last, without some sniveling apprentice at his side, was reassuring. The time was coming when it need no longer hide beneath the earth.

The other person was unknown. A woman, or something that had once been a woman. She wore a mask of dull bronze, and the heavy furs of the Northern barbarians. Unnecessary, and uncomfortable, in this *weather . . . unless her skin felt something other than the sun. She wore several rings of bone upon her silk-gloved fingers.*

"You are Hedge," the stranger declared.

The man was surprised by the crackle of power in her speech. She was a Free Magic sorcerer, as he'd suspected, but a more powerful one than he could have guessed. She knew his name, or one of them—the least of his names, the one he had used most often in recent times. He, too, was a Free Magic sorcerer, as all necromancers had to be.

"A Servant of Kerrigor," continued the woman. "I see his brand upon your forehead, though your disguise is not without some skill."

Hedge shrugged, and touched what appeared to be a Charter mark on his forehead. It cracked in two and fell off like a broken scab, revealing an ugly scar that crawled and wriggled on his skin. "I carry the brand of Kerrigor," he replied evenly. "But Kerrigor is gone, bound by the Abhorsen and imprisoned these last fourteen years."

"You will serve me now," said the woman, in tones that brooked no argument. "Tell me how I may commune with the power that lies under this mound. It, too, will bend itself to my will."

Hedge bowed, hiding his grin. Was this not reminiscent of how he had come to the mound himself, in the days after Kerrigor's fall?

"There is a stone on the western side," he said, pointing with his sword. "Swing it aside, and you will see a narrow tunnel, striking sharply down. Follow the tunnel till the way is blocked by a slab of stone. At the foot of the stone, you will see water seeping through. Taste of the water, and you will perceive the power of which you speak."

He did not mention that the tunnel was his, the product of five years' toil, nor that the seeping water was the first visible sign of a struggle for freedom that had gone on for more than two thousand years.

The woman nodded, the thin line of pallid skin around the mask giving no hint of expression, as if the face behind it were as frozen as the metal. Then she turned aside and spoke a spell, white smoke gushing from the mouthpiece of the mask with every word. When she finished, two creatures rose up from where they'd lain at her feet, nearly invisible against the earth. Two impossibly thin, vaguely human things, with flesh of swiftly moving mist and bones of blue-white fire. Free Magic elementals, of the kind that humans called Hish.

Hedge watched them carefully and licked his lips. He could deal with one, but two might force him to reveal strengths best left veiled for the moment. The old man would be no help. Even now he just sat there, mumbling, a living conduit for some part of the power under the hill.

"If I do not return by nightfall," the woman said, "my servants will rend you asunder, flesh and spirit too, should you seek refuge in Death."

"I will wait here," Hedge replied, settling himself down on the raw earth. Now that he knew the Hish's instructions, they represented no threat. He laid down his sword and turned one ear to the mound, pressing it against the soil. He could hear the constant whisper of the power below, through all the layers of earth and stone, though his own thoughts and words could not penetrate the prison. Later, if it was necessary, he would go into the tunnel, drink of the water, and lay his mind open, sending his thoughts back along the finger-wide trickle that had broken through all seven thrice-spelled wards. Through silver, gold, and lead; rowan, ash, and oak; and the seventh ward of bone.

Hedge didn't bother to watch the woman go, or stir when he heard the sound of the great stone being rolled away, even though it was a feat beyond the strength of any normal man, or any number of normal men.

When the woman returned, Hedge was standing at the very center of the mound, looking south. The Hish stood near him, but made no move as their mistress climbed back up. The old man sat where he always had, still gibbering, though whether he spoke spells or nonsense, Hedge couldn't say. It was no magic he knew, though he felt the power of the hill in the old man's voice.

"I will serve," the woman said.

The arrogance, though not the power, was gone from her voice. Hedge saw the muscles in her neck spasm as she spoke the words. He smiled and raised his hand. "There are Charter Stones that have been raised too close to the hill. You will destroy them."

"I will," agreed the woman, lowering her head.

"You were a necromancer," continued Hedge. In years past, Kerrigor had drawn all the necromancers of the Kingdom to him, to serve as petty underlords. Most had perished, either in Kerrigor's fall or, in the years after, at the hands of the Abhorsen. Some survived still, but this woman had never been a Servant of Kerrigor.

"Long ago," said the woman.

Hedge felt the faint flicker of Life inside her, buried deep under the spell-coated furs and the bronze mask. She was old, this sorcerer, very, very old—not an advantage for a necromancer who must walk in Death. That cold river had a particular taste for those who had evaded its clutches beyond their given span of years.

"You will take up the bells again, for you will need many Dead for the work that lies ahead." Hedge unbuckled his own bandolier and handed it over cautiously, careful not to jar the bells into sound. For himself he had another set of the seven, taken from a lesser necromancer in the chaos following Kerrigor's defeat. There would be some risk retrieving them, for they lay in that main part of the Kingdom long since reclaimed by the King and his Abhorsen Queen. But he had no need of the bells for his immediate plans, and could not take them where he intended to go.

The woman took the bells but did not put on the bandolier. Instead, she stretched out her right hand, palm upwards. A tiny spark glinted there, a splinter of metal that shone with its own bright, white fire. Hedge held out his own hand, and the splinter leapt across, burying itself just under the skin, without drawing blood. Hedge held it up to his face, feeling the power in the metal. Then he slowly closed his fingers, and smiled.

It was not for him, this sliver of arcane metal. It was a seed, a seed that could be planted in many soils. Hedge had a particular purpose for it, a most fertile bed where it could grow to its full fruit. But it would likely be many years before he could plant it where it would do most harm.

"And you?" asked the woman. "What do you do?"

"I go south, Chlorr of the Mask," said Hedge, revealing that he knew her name—and much else besides. "South to Ancelstierre, across the Wall. The country of my birth, though in spirit I am no child of its powerless soil. I have much to do there, and even farther afield. But you will hear from me when I have need. Or if I hear news that is not to my liking."

He turned then, and walked off without further word. For a master need make no farewells to any of his servants.

PART ONE

THE OLD KINGDOM

Fourteenth Year of the Restoration
of King Touchstone I

Chapter One

AN ILL-FAVORED BIRTHDAY

DEEP WITHIN A dream, Lirael felt someone stroking her forehead. A gentle, soft touch, a cool hand upon her own fevered skin. She felt herself smile, enjoying the touch. Then the dream shifted, and her forehead wrinkled. The touch was no longer soft and loving, but rough and rasping. No longer cool, but hot, burning her—

She woke up. It took her a second to realize that she'd clawed the sheet away and had been lying facedown on the coarsely woven mattress cover. It was wool and very scratchy. Her pillow lay on the floor. The pillowcase had been torn off in the course of some nightmare and now hung from her chair.

Lirael looked around the small chamber, but there were no signs of any other nocturnal damage. Her simple wardrobe of dressed pine was upright, the dull steel latch still closed. The desk and chair still occupied the other corner. Her practice sword hung in its scabbard on the back of the door.

It must have been a relatively good night. Sometimes, in her nightmare-laced sleep, Lirael walked, talked, and wreaked havoc. But always only in her room. Her precious room. She couldn't bear to think what life would be like if she were forced to go back to family chambers.

She closed her eyes again and listened. All was silent, which meant that it must be long before the Waking Bell. The bell sounded at the same time every day, calling the Clayr out of their beds to join the new morning.

Lirael scrunched her eyes together more tightly and tried to go back to sleep. She wanted to regain the feel of that hand on her brow. That touch was the only thing she remembered of her mother. Not her face or her voice—just the touch of her cool hand.

She needed that touch desperately today. But Lirael's mother was long gone, taking the secret of Lirael's paternity with her. She had left when Lirael was five, without a word, without an explanation. There never was any explanation. Just the news of her death, a garbled message from the distant North that had arrived three days before Lirael's tenth birthday.

Once she had thought of that, there was no hope for sleep. As on every other morning, Lirael gave up trying to keep her eyes shut. She let them spring open and stared up at the ceiling for a few minutes. But the stone had not changed overnight. It was still grey and cold, with tiny flecks of pink.

A Charter mark for light glowed there too, warm and golden in the stone. It had shone brighter when Lirael had first awoken and grew brighter still as she swung her feet out and felt around with her toes for her half-shoes. The Clayr's halls were heated by the steam of hot springs and by magic, but the stone floor was always cold.

"Fourteen today," whispered Lirael. She had her half-shoes on, but made no move to rise. Ever since the message of her mother's death had come so close to her tenth birthday, all her birthdays had been harbingers of doom.

"Fourteen!" Lirael said again, the word laced with anguish. She was fourteen, and by the measure of the world outside the Clayr's Glacier, a woman. But here she must still wear the blue tunic of a child, for the Clayr marked the passage to adulthood not by age, but by the gift of the Sight.

Once again, Lirael closed her eyes, screwing them tight as she willed herself to See the future. Everyone else her age had the Sight. Many younger children already wore the white robe and the circlet of moonstones. It was unheard of not to have the Sight by fourteen.

Lirael opened her eyes, but she saw no vision. Just her simple room, slightly blurred by tears. She rubbed them away and got up.

"No mother, no father, no Sight," she said as she opened her wardrobe and took out a towel. It was a familiar litany. She said it often, though it always made her feel a terrible stab of sorrow in her stomach. It was like worrying a toothache with her tongue. It hurt, but she couldn't leave it alone. The wound was part of her now.

But perhaps one day soon, she would be summoned by the Voice of the Nine Day Watch. Then she would wake and say, "No mother, no father, but I have the Sight."

"I will have the Sight," Lirael muttered to herself as she eased open the door and tiptoed down the corridor to the baths. Charter marks brightened as she passed under them, bringing day from twilight. But all the other doors in the Hall of Youth remained shut. Once, Lirael would have knocked on them, laughing and calling the other orphans who lived there to an early bath.

But that was years ago. Before they had all gained the Sight.

That was also when Merell was Guardian of the Young, one who had governed her charges with a light hand. Lirael's own aunt Kirrith was Guardian now. If there was any noise, she would emerge from her room in her maroon-and-white-striped bathrobe, to order silence and respect for sleeping elders. She would make no special allowance for Lirael, either. Quite the reverse. Kirrith was the exact opposite of Lirael's mother, Arielle. She was all for rules and regulations, tradition and conformity.

Kirrith would never leave the Glacier to travel who knew where, only to return seven months gone with child. Lirael scowled at Kirrith's door. Not that Kirrith had ever told her that. Kirrith wouldn't talk about her younger sister. The little Lirael knew about her mother came from eavesdropping on her closer cousins' conversations. The ones during which they discussed what to do about a girl who so obviously didn't belong.

Lirael scowled again at that thought. The scowl didn't go away, even when she was scraping her face with pumice stone in the hot bath. Only the shock of the cold plunge in the long pool finally smoothed the lines away.

The lines came back, though, as Lirael combed her hair in the communal mirror in the changing room next to the cold pool. The mirror was a rectangle of silver steel, eight feet high and twelve feet wide, rather tarnished around the edges. Later in the morning it would be shared by up to eight of the fourteen orphans currently in the Hall of Youth.

Lirael hated sharing the mirror, because it made yet another difference more obvious. Most of the Clayr had brown skin that quickly tanned to a deep chestnut out on the glacier slopes, as well as bright blond hair and light eyes. In contrast Lirael stood out like a pallid weed among healthy flowers. Her white skin burnt instead of tanning, and she had dark eyes and even darker hair.

She knew she probably took after her father, whoever that had been. Arielle had never identified him, yet another shame for her suffering daughter to carry. The Clayr often bore children fathered by visiting men, but they didn't usually leave the Glacier to find them, and they made no secret of the fathers. And for some reason, they almost always had girls. Fair-haired, nut-brown girls with pale blue or green eyes.

Except for Lirael.

Alone in front of the mirror, Lirael could forget all that. She concentrated on combing her hair, forty-nine strokes to each side. She was feeling more hopeful. Perhaps this would be the day. A fourteenth birthday marked by the best possible present. The gift of the Sight.

Even so, Lirael had no desire to eat breakfast in the Middle Refectory. Most of the Clayr ate there, and she would have to sit at a table with girls three or even four years younger, sticking out like a thistle in a bed of well-tended flowers. A blue-clad thistle. Everyone else her age would be dressed in white, sitting at the tables of the crowned and acknowledged Clayr.

Instead, Lirael crossed two silent corridors and descended two stairways that spiraled in opposite directions, down to the Lower Refectory. This was where the traders ate, and the supplicants who came to ask the Clayr to look into their futures. The only Clayr here would be those on the kitchen or serving rosters.

Or almost the only Clayr. There was one other who Lirael hoped would come. The Voice of the Nine Day Watch. As she walked down the last steps, Lirael imagined the scene. The Voice striding down the main stairs, striking the gong, then stopping to make her announcement that the Nine Day Watch had Seen her—Seen Lirael—being crowned with the circlet of moonstones, had Seen her gaining the Sight at last.

The Lower Refectory wasn't very busy that morning. Only three of the sixty tables were occupied. Lirael went to a fourth, as far away from the others as possible, and drew out the bench. She preferred to sit alone, even when she was not among the Clayr.

Two of the tables were occupied by merchants, probably from Belisaere, talking loudly of the peppercorns, ginger, nutmeg, and cinnamon they had imported from the far North and hoped to sell to the Clayr. Their conversation about the quality and strength of their spices was all too evidently meant to be heard by the Clayr working in the kitchens.

Lirael sniffed the air. Their claims might even be true. The scent of cloves and nutmeg from the merchants' bags was very strong, but pleasant. Lirael took it as another good omen.

The third table was taken up by the merchants' guards. Even here, inside the Clayr's Glacier, they wore armored coats of interlocking scales and kept their scabbarded swords close by, under the benches. Obviously, they thought bandits or worse could easily follow the narrow path along the river gorge and force the gate that led to the Clayr's vast complex.

Of course, they would not have been able to see most of the defenses. The river path crawled with Charter marks of hiding and blinding, and under the flat paving stones there were sendings of beasts and warriors that would rise up at the slightest threat. The path also crossed the river no less than seven times, on slender bridges of ancient construction, apparently spun from stone. Easily defended bridges—with the river Ratterlin running below, deep enough and fast enough to keep any Dead from crossing.

Even here in the Lower Refectory there was Charter Magic lying dormant in the walls, and sendings that slept in the rough-hewn stone of floor and ceiling. Lirael could see the Charter marks, faint as they were, and puzzle out the spells they made up. The sendings were harder, because only the marks to trigger them were clear. Of course, there were clearly visible marks as well, the ones that shed light here and everywhere else within the Clayr's underground domain, bored into the rock of the mountain, next to the icy mass of the Glacier.

Lirael scanned the visitors' faces. Without helmets, their close-cropped hair made it easy to see that none had the Charter mark upon their foreheads. So they almost certainly couldn't see the magic that surrounded them. Instinctively, Lirael parted her own rather too-long hair and felt her mark. It pulsed lightly under her touch, and she felt the sense of connection, the feeling of belonging to the great Charter that described the world. At least she was something of a Charter Mage, even if she didn't have the Sight.

The merchants' guards should trust more in the Clayr's defenses, Lirael thought, looking at the armored men and women again. One of them saw her glance, and met her eyes for an instant, till she looked away. In that fleeting moment, she saw a young man, his head even more closely shaven than the others, so his scalp shone when it caught the light from the Charter marks in the ceiling.

Though she tried to ignore him, Lirael saw the guard get up and walk across, his scale coat too big for someone who would not see his real growth for several years. Lirael scowled as he approached, and turned her head away even more. Just because the Clayr did occasionally take lovers from amongst the visitors, some people thought that any of the Clayr visiting the Lower Refectory would be hunting for a man. This notion seemed particularly strong among young men of sixteen or thereabouts.

"Excuse me," said the guard. "May I sit here?"

Lirael nodded reluctantly, and he sat, a cascade of scales rattling down his chest in a slow waterfall of metal.

"I'm Barra," he said cheerfully. "Is this your first time here?"

"What?" asked Lirael, puzzled and shy. "In the Refectory?"

"No," said Barra, laughing and stretching his arms out to indicate a much larger vista. "Here. In the Clayr's Glacier. This is my second visit, so if you need someone to show you around . . .

though I guess your parents might trade here often?"

Lirael looked away again, feeling bright spots burn into her cheekbones. She tried to think of something to say, some snappy rejoinder, but all she could think was that even outsiders knew she wasn't really a Clayr. Even a stupid, undergrown, rattling clod like this one.

"What's your name?" asked Barra, oblivious to the blush and the terrible emptiness that had grown inside her.

Lirael swallowed and wet her lips, but no answer came. She felt as if she didn't have a name to give, or an identity at all. She couldn't even look at Barra because her eyes were full of tears, so she stared at the half-eaten pear on her plate instead.

"I just wanted to say hello," said Barra uneasily, as the silence stretched out between them.

Lirael nodded, and two tears fell on the pear. She didn't look up or try to wipe her eyes. Her arms felt as limp and useless as her voice.

"I'm sorry," Barra added as he clanked to his feet. Lirael watched him go back to his table, her eyes partly covered by a protective fall of hair. When he was a few feet away, one of the men said something, not loud enough to hear. Barra shrugged, and the men—and some of the women—burst into laughter.

"It's my birthday," Lirael whispered to her plate, her voice more full of tears than her eyes. "I must not cry on my birthday." She stood up and clumsily stepped over the bench, taking her plate and fork to the scullery hatch, being careful not to catch the eye of whichever first, second, or third cousin worked there.

She was still holding the plate when one of the Clayr came down the main stairs and struck with her metal-tipped wand the first of the seven gongs that stood on the bottom seven steps. Lirael froze, and everyone in the Refectory stopped talking as the Clayr descended, striking each gong in turn, the different notes of the gongs merging into one before they echoed away into silence.

At the bottom step, the Clayr stopped and held up her wand. Lirael's heart leapt inside her, while her stomach knotted in anxiety. It was exactly as she had imagined. So like it that she felt sure that it hadn't been imagination, but the onset of the Sight.

Sohrae, as her wand declared, was currently the Voice of the Nine Day Watch, the Voice who made the announcements when the Watch Saw something of public importance to the Clayr or the Kingdom. Most important, the Voice also announced when the Watch had Seen the girl who would be next to gain the Sight.

"Know one, know many," proclaimed Sohrae, her clear voice carrying to every corner of the Refectory and the kitchens and the scullery beyond. "The Nine Day Watch with great gladness announce that the Gift of Sight has Awoken in our sister . . ."

Sohrae took a breath to go on, and Lirael shut her eyes, knowing that Sohrae was about to say her name. It must, it must, it *must* be me, she thought. Two years later than everyone, and today my birthday. It has to—

"Annisele," intoned Sohrae. Then she turned and went up the stairs again, lightly striking the gongs, their sound a soft undercurrent to the talk that had resumed among the visitors.

Lirael opened her eyes. The world had not changed. She did not have the Sight. Everything would go on as it always had. Miserably.

"Can I have your plate, please?" asked the unseen cousin behind the scullery hatch. "Oh, Lirael! I thought you were a visitor. You'd better hurry back upstairs, dear. Annisele's

Awakening will start inside the hour. This is the Voice's last stop, you know. Whyever did you eat down here?"

Lirael didn't answer. She let the plate go and crossed the Refectory like a sleepwalker, her fingers listlessly brushing the table corners as she passed. All she could think of was Sohrae's voice, running over and over in her head.

"The gift of Sight has Awoken in our sister Annisele."

Annisele. Annisele would be the one to wear the white robe, to be crowned with the silver and moonstones, while Lirael once again would have to put on her best blue tunic, the uniform of a child. The tunic that no longer had a hem because it had been let out so many times. The tunic that was still too short.

Annisele had just turned eleven ten days ago. But her birthday would be nothing compared to this day, the day of her Awakening.

Birthdays *were* nothing, Lirael thought, as she mechanically put one foot in front of the other, up the six hundred steps from the Lower Refectory to the Westway, along that path for two hundred paces, and then up the hundred and two steps to the backdoor of the Hall of Youth. She counted every step, and looked no one in the eye. All she saw was the sweep of white robes and the flash of black-slippered feet, as all the Clayr rushed to the Great Hall to honor the latest girl to join the ranks of those who Saw the future.

By the time she reached her room, Lirael found that any small joy to be had from her birthday was gone. Extinguished, snuffed out like a candle. It was Annisele's day now, Lirael thought. She had to try to be happy for Annisele. She had to ignore the terrible sorrow that was welling up in her own heart.

Chapter Two

A FUTURE LOST

LIRAEL THREW HERSELF on her bed and tried to overcome her despair. She really should get dressed for Annisele's Awakening. But every time she started to get up, she felt unable to continue, and sat back down. For the moment, getting up was impossible. All she could do was relive the awful moment in the Lower Refectory when she had not heard her name. But she managed to wrestle her mind away from that, to think about the immediate future, not the past. Lirael made a decision. She wouldn't go to Annisele's Awakening.

It was unlikely anyone would really miss her, but there was a chance somebody might come to get her. This thought gave her enough strength to finally get off the bed and investigate hiding places. Under the bed was traditional, but the underside of Lirael's simple trestle bed was both cramped and very dusty, since she hadn't followed the standard cleaning routine properly for weeks.

She considered the wardrobe for a little while. But its spare, box-like shape and pine-plank construction made her think of it as an upended coffin. This was not a new thought for Lirael. She had always had what her cousins considered a morbid imagination. As a small child she had liked to playact dramatic death scenes from famous stories. She had stopped playacting years ago, but had never stopped thinking about death. Her own, in particular.

"Death," Lirael whispered, shivering to hear the word aloud. She said it again, a little louder. A simple word, a simple way to avoid all the things that plagued her. She could avoid Annisele's Awakening, but she probably couldn't avoid all the ones that would come after that.

If she killed herself, Lirael reasoned, she wouldn't have to watch girls increasingly younger than herself gaining the Sight. She wouldn't have to stand with a bunch of children in blue tunics. Children who all peeked at her under their lashes during the Awakening ceremony. Lirael knew that look and recognized the fear in it. They were afraid that they might be like her, doomed to lack the only thing that really mattered.

And she wouldn't have to put up with the Clayr who looked at her with pity. The ones who always stopped and asked how she was. As if mere words could describe how she felt. Or as if even if she had the words, Lirael could tell them what it was like to be fourteen and without the Sight.

"Death," Lirael whispered again, tasting the word on her tongue. What else was there for her? There had always been the hope that one day she would gain the Sight. But now she was fourteen. Who had ever heard of a Clayr Sightless at fourteen? Things had never seemed quite so desperate as they were today.

"It's the best thing to do," Lirael pronounced, as if she were informing a friend of a vital decision. Her voice sounded confident, but inside she wasn't so sure. Suicide wasn't something the Clayr did. Killing herself would be the final, terrible confirmation that she just didn't belong. It probably was the best thing. How would she actually do it? Lirael's eyes strayed to where her practice sword hung in its scabbard on the back of the door. It was blunt, soft steel. She could probably fall on its point, but that would lead to a very slow and painful death.

Besides, someone would almost certainly hear her screaming and get help.

There was probably a spell that would still her breath, dry up her lungs, and close her throat. But she wouldn't find that in the school texts, her workbook of Charter Magic, or the *Index of Charter Marks*, both of which lay on the desk a few paces away. She'd have to search the Great Library for such a spell, and that sort of magic would be locked away by charm and key.

That left two reasonably accessible means of ending it all: cold and height. "The glacier," whispered Lirael. That would be it, she decided. She would climb the Starmount Stair while everyone else was at Annisele's Awakening, and then throw herself onto the ice. Eventually, if anyone bothered to look, they would find her frozen, broken body—and then they would all realize how hard it was to be a Clayr without the Sight.

Tears filled her eyes as she imagined a great crowd silently watching as her body was carried through the Great Hall, the blue of her child's tunic transformed to white by the ice and snow encrusted upon it.

A knock at the door cut short her morbid daydream, and Lirael jumped up, relieved. The Nine Day Watch must have finally Seen her, for the first time ever. They'd Seen her climb out onto the glacier and go plunging down, so they'd sent someone to prevent that future, to tell her that she would gain the Sight one day, that everything would be fine.

Then the door opened, before Lirael could say "Come in." That was enough to tell her that it wasn't a Nine Day Watcher concerned for her safety. It was Aunt Kirrith, Guardian of the Young. Or more the other way round, since she never treated Lirael any differently from the others, and particularly didn't show her the affection you might expect from an aunt.

"There you are!" boomed Kirrith unnecessarily in her

annoying, falsely jolly voice. "I looked for you at breakfast, but there was such a crush I just couldn't find you. Happy birthday, Lirael!"

Lirael stared at Kirrith and at the present she was holding out. A large, square package, wrapped in red and blue paper dusted with gold. Very pretty paper, too. Aunt Kirrith had never given her a present before. She explained this by saying that she never accepted presents either, but Lirael thought that this missed the point. It was all about giving, not receiving.

"Go on, open it," exclaimed Kirrith. "We haven't got much time till the Awakening. Fancy it being little Annisele!"

Lirael took the package. It was soft, but quite heavy. For a moment, all her thoughts of killing herself were gone, driven away by curiosity. What could the present be?

Then, as she felt the package again, a terrible presentiment struck her. Quickly, she tore a hole in the corner of the paper, and saw the telltale blue. "It's a tunic," said Lirael, the words seeming to come from someone else, and a long way away. "A child's tunic."

"Yes," said Kirrith, resplendent in her own white robe, the circlet of silver and moonstones secure on her white-blond head. "I noticed your old one was too short, not really seemly, with the way you've grown. . . ."

She kept on talking, but Lirael didn't hear a word. Nothing seemed real anymore. Not the new tunic in her hands. Not Aunt Kirrith talking away. Nothing.

"Come on then, get dressed!" Kirrith encouraged her, straightening the folds of her own robe. She was a large and tall woman, one of the tallest of the Clayr. Lirael felt very small in front of her, and somehow dirty compared to the great expanse of white that was Kirrith's robe. She stared at that whiteness and began to think again of ice and snow.

She was lost in her thoughts when Kirrith tapped her on
the shoulder.

"What?" Lirael asked, realizing that she'd missed most of
Kirrith's words.

"Get dressed!" repeated Aunt Kirrith. A slight frown folded
the skin on her forehead, making her circlet move down and
shadow her eyes. "It would be terribly rude to be late."

Mechanically, Lirael pulled off her old tunic and slipped on the
new one. It was heavy linen, stiff with newness, so she struggled
a little with it, till Aunt Kirrith pulled it down smartly. When
her arms were through and the tunic settled on her shoulders, it
reached just above her ankles.

"Plenty of room for growth," remarked Aunt Kirrith
with satisfaction. "Now we really must get on."

Lirael looked down at the sea of blue cloth that swathed her
entire body, and thought that there was more room than she
could ever possibly fill. Aunt Kirrith must expect her never to
wear the white of the Awakening, for this tunic would fit even
if she kept on growing till she was thirty-five.

"You go on—I'll catch up in a minute," she lied, thinking
of the Starmount Stair, the cliffs beyond, and the waiting ice. "I
have to go to the toilet."

"Very well," said Kirrith as she hurried back out into the
corridor. "But be quick, Lirael! Think of what your mother
would say!"

Lirael followed her, turning left towards the nearest water
closet. Kirrith turned right, clapping her hands to hasten on a
trio of eight-year-olds who were dressing as they walked, their
tunics half over their heads, smothering giggles.

Lirael had no idea what her mother would have said about
anything. She had been teased about Arielle often enough when
she was younger, before she became too much of an outsider

to be teased. It was quite normal for the Clayr to seek casual lovers from visitors to the Glacier, and not even that uncommon to find one outside. But it was unheard of not to record the parentage of children.

Her mother had compounded her strangeness by leaving the Glacier—and a five-year-old Lirael—called by some vision she had not shared with the other Clayr. Years later, Aunt Kirrith had told Lirael that Arielle was dead, though no details ever came. Lirael had heard various theories, including Arielle being poisoned by jealous rivals in the court of some barbarian lordling in the frozen wastes of the North or killed by beasts. Apparently she'd been serving as a seer, something that no Clayr would think was a suitable occupation for people of their Blood.

The pain of losing her mother was locked away in Lirael's heart, but not so deep it could not be uncovered. Aunt Kirrith was an expert at bringing it back.

Once Kirrith and the three suddenly chastened girls were gone, Lirael doubled back to her room and got her outdoor gear: a coat of heavy wool, greasy with lanolin; a cap of double felt with earflaps; oilskin overshoes; fur-lined gloves; and leather goggles with lenses of smoked green glass. Part of her said it was stupid to get these things, since she was going to her death anyway, but another small voice inside her said that she might as well be properly dressed.

Because all the inhabited parts of the Clayr's domain were heated by steam piped up from the deep springs, Lirael carried her outdoor gear, the smaller items wrapped in the coat. It was going to be hot enough climbing the Starmount Stair without wearing all that wool. As a last-minute gesture of defiance, she pulled off the new tunic and threw it on the floor. Instead, she chose to put on the neutral garments worn when the Clayr were on kitchen or scullery duty in the Lower Refectory, a long grey cotton shirt that came down to the knees, over thin blue woollen leggings. There was a canvas apron that went with this ensemble, but Lirael left that behind.

It was strange slinking down the Northway with no one in sight. Normally, there would be dozens of the Clayr going about their business on this busy thoroughfare, either heading to or from the Nine Day Watch or engaged in the myriad more mundane tasks of the community. The Clayr's Glacier was really a small town, albeit a very strange one, since its primary business was to look into the future. Or, as the Clayr had to constantly explain to visitors, the numerous possible futures.

At the point where the Northway met the Zigzag, Lirael made sure she was unobserved. Then she went a few steps along the first zig of the Zigzag, looking for a small, dark hole at waist height. When she found it, she took out the key she wore on a chain around her neck. All the Clayr had such keys, and they opened most of the common doors. The Starmount Door was not often used, but Lirael didn't think it needed a special key.

There was no sign of a door around the keyhole until Lirael put in the key and turned it twice. Then a faint silvery line spread from the floor and slowly traced a doorway in the yellowish stone.

Lirael pushed the door open. Cold air rushed in, so she went through quickly. If there were any other people about, they would notice a cold breeze more quickly than anything else. The Clayr might live in a mountain that was half smothered by a glacier, but they didn't revel in the cold.

The door swung shut behind Lirael, and the silver lines that marked its outline slowly faded. Ahead of her, the steps rose up in a straight line, the Charter marks above them providing light that was dimmer than that in the main halls. The risers were higher than usual, something Lirael hadn't remembered from a class excursion many years before, when all steps had seemed high. She grimaced as she started to climb, knowing that her calf muscles would soon protest the extra six-inch rise.

There was a bronze handrail for the first hundred or so steps, where the Stair went up in a dead straight line. Lirael gripped it as she climbed, the cool of the metal soothing under her hand. As was her habit, she started counting steps, the regular rhythm temporarily banishing the mental images of herself falling down an endless slope of ice.

She hardly noticed when the handrail stopped and the steps began to turn inwards, into the long spiral that would take her to the top of the mountain, Starmount. Its sister peak was Sunfall, and the two mountains held the glacier between them. The glacier had once had its own name, but it was long forgotten. So for thousands of years it had been called after the Clayr who lived above, beside, and sometimes beneath it. Over time that name had come to be extended to the Clayr's realm as well, so both the great mass of ice and the halls of stone were known as the Clayr's Glacier, as if they were all one.

Not that the Clayr chose rooms too close to the glacier as a rule. They had lived in the mountain for millennia, following the tunneling of the now almost extinct drill-grubs or carrying out their own magical or physical excavations. At the same time, the glacier had continued its inexorable march down the valley, and into the mountains that gripped its sides. Ice ground down and broke through stone, and the glacier was indifferent if that also meant crashing through the tunnels of the Clayr.

Of course, the Clayr could See where the glacier was going to have its unthinking way, but that hadn't stopped various ambitious builders of bygone days. Obviously they had felt their extensions would last as long as they did, and probably for at least three or four generations after them—time enough to make the work worthwhile.

Lirael thought of all those builders and wondered why the Stair had been made with such uncomfortably high steps.

But after a while, even mechanically counting steps couldn't keep her imagination under rein. She started to imagine how Annisele would be looking right at that instant. Perhaps she was standing at the children's end of the Great Hall, a single figure in white amidst a field of blue. She would be staring down the other end, no doubt, barely aware of the ranks and ranks of white-clad Clayr, sitting in the pews that lined both sides of the Hall for several hundred yards, twenty-one ranks deep. Pews made from ancient dark mahogany, with silk cushions that were replaced every fifty years, with considerable ceremony.

At the far end of the Hall, there would be the Voice of the Nine Day Watch, and perhaps some of the Watchers, too, their business permitting. They would be standing around the Charter Stone that rose up from the floor of the Hall, a single menhir swarming with all the glowing, changing marks of the Charter that described everything in the world, seen or unseen. And on the Charter Stone, higher than anyone could reach, save the Voice with her metal-tipped wand, there would be the circlet of the new Clayr, the silver and moonstones reflecting the Charter marks of the Stone.

Lirael forced her tired legs up another step. Annisele's walk wouldn't be tiring at all. Just a few hundred steps, with smiling faces on all sides. Then, when the circlet was placed on her head at last, the tumult as all the Clayr rose to their feet, followed by the great cheer that would echo through the Hall and beyond. The Awakening of Annisele, a true Clayr, a mistress of the Sight. Acclaimed by one and all.

Unlike Lirael, who was, as always, alone and unregarded. She felt like crying but brushed the tears away. Only another hundred steps to go, and she would be at the Starmount Gate. Once through the gate and across the wide terrace in front of it, Lirael would stand on the edge of the glacier, looking down into icy death.

Chapter Three

PAPERWINGS

A<small>T THE TOP</small> of the Starmount Stair, Lirael rested for a while, till the chill coming through the stone got too much to bear. Then she donned her outdoor gear, turning the world green as she slipped on her goggles. Last, she drew a silk scarf from the pocket of her coat, tied it across her nose and mouth, and folded down the earflaps of her cap.

Dressed like that, she might be one of the Clayr. No one could see her face, hair, or eyes. She looked exactly like any other Clayr. When they found her body, they wouldn't even know who it was till cap, scarf, and goggles were removed.

Lirael would look like one of the Clayr for the last time.

Even so, she hesitated before the door that led from the Stair to the Paperwing hangar and the Starmount Gate. It probably wasn't too late to go back, to say she'd eaten something that disagreed with her so she'd had to stay in her room. If she hurried, she'd almost certainly be back before everyone returned from the Awakening.

But nothing would have changed. There was nothing to look forward to down there, Lirael decided, so she might as well go and look at the cliffs. She could make her final decision there.

She took her key out again, clumsy in her gloves, and unlocked the door. A visible one, this time, but magically guarded as well. Lirael felt the Charter Magic inside it flow out through the key, through the fur of her gloves and into her hands. She tensed for a moment, then relaxed as it ebbed away again. Whatever it guarded against, the spell wasn't interested in her.

It was colder still past the door, though Lirael was still inside the mountain. This large chamber was the Paperwing hangar, where the Clayr kept their magical aircraft. Three of them slept nearby. They looked rather like slim canoes, with hawk-wings and tails. Lirael felt an urge to touch one of them, to see if it really did feel like paper, but she knew better than that. Physically, the Paperwings were made from thousands of sheets of laminated paper. But they were also made with considerable magic, and were partially sentient as a result. The painted eyes at the front of the closest green and silver craft might be dull now, but they would light up if she touched it. Lirael had no idea what it might do then. She knew the craft were controlled by whistled Charter marks, and she could whistle, but she didn't know the marks or any special technique that might be required.

So Lirael crept past the Paperwings, across to the Starmount Gate. It was huge—big enough for thirty people or two Paperwings to pass abreast—and easily four times as tall as Lirael. Fortunately, she didn't have to even try to open it, because there was a smaller sally port cut into the large Gate's left quarter. A moment's work with her key, the touch of the guarding spell, then the door was open, and Lirael stepped outside.

Cold and sunshine hit her at the same time, the former strong enough to feel even through her heavy clothes, and the latter fierce enough to make her half-close her eyes, even behind goggles.

It was a beautiful summer day. Lower down in the valley, below the glacier, it would be hot. Here it was cold, the chill mainly coming from the breeze that blew along the glacier and then up, over, and around the mountain.

Ahead of Lirael, a broad, unnaturally flat terrace was carved into the mountainside. It was about a hundred yards long and fifty yards wide, and snow and chunks of ice were piled up all around it in deep drifts. But the terrace itself had only a light dusting of snow. Lirael knew it was kept like that by Charter sendings—magically created servants who shoveled, raked, and repaired all the year round, oblivious to the weather. There were none to be seen now, but the Charter Magic that would send them into action lurked beneath the paving stones of the terrace.

On the far side of the terrace, the mountain fell away in a sheer precipice. Lirael looked across to it but saw nothing but blue sky and a few wisps of low cloud. She would have to cross the terrace and look down to see the main bulk of the glacier a thousand feet below. But she didn't cross. Instead, she pictured what might happen if she jumped. If she threw herself out far enough, she would fall free, down to the waiting ice and a speedy end. If she fell short, she would hit a spur of rock maybe only thirty or forty feet down, then slide and tumble the rest of the way, breaking a new bone with every momentary impact.

Lirael shivered and looked away. Now that she was actually here, only a few minutes' brisk walk from the precipice, she wasn't sure that making her own death was such a good idea. But every time she tried to think of a continuing future for herself, she felt weak and blocked, as if all the ways forward were closed off by walls too high to climb.

For now, she forced herself to move and take a few steps across the terrace, to at least look at the drop. But her legs seemed to have a life of their own, walking her along the length of the terrace instead, without getting any closer to the cliff-side.

Half an hour later, she headed back to the Starmount Gate, having walked the length of the terrace four times without once daring to go anywhere near the cliff on the far side. The closest she'd got was the sudden drop at the end of the terrace, where the Paperwings actually took off. But that was a fall of only a few hundred feet, down a much less steep face of the mountain, and not onto the glacier. Even then she hadn't gone within twenty feet of the edge.

Lirael wondered how the Paperwings would launch off that far end. She had never seen one take off or land, and she spent some time trying to imagine how it would look. Obviously, they would slip along the ice and then at some point leap into the sky, but where exactly? Did they need a long run-up like the blue pelicans she'd seen on the Ratterlin, or could they shoot straight up like falcons?

All these questions made Lirael curious about how the Paperwings actually worked. She was thinking of risking a closer look at one back in the hangar when she realized that the black speck she'd noticed high above wasn't a product of her imagination, or a tiny storm cloud. It was a real Paperwing, and it was obviously coming in to land.

At the same time she heard the deep rumble of the Starmount Gate as it started to swing open. She looked back at it, then at the Paperwing again, her head moving in frantic starts. What was she going to do?

She could run across the terrace and throw herself off, but she really didn't feel like doing that. The moment of her darkest despair had passed, at least for now.

She could just stand on one side of the terrace and watch the Paperwing land, but that would almost certainly lead to a serious scolding from Aunt Kirrith, not to mention several months' worth of extra kitchen duties. Or some even worse punishment she didn't know about.

Or she could hide and watch. After all, she had wanted to see a Paperwing land.

All these options raced through her mind, and it took only an instant for the last one to be chosen. Lirael ran to a snowdrift, sat down in it, and started to drag snow across herself. Soon she was almost completely hidden, save for the line of footprints that led across the snow to her hiding place.

Quickly, Lirael visualized the Charter, then reached into its eternal flow to pull out the three marks she needed. One by one they grew into brilliance inside her mind, filling it until she could think of nothing else. She drew them into her mouth, then puffed the marks out towards her tracks in the snow.

The spell left her as a whirling ball of frosted breath that grew until it was an arm's span wide. It drifted back across her path, sweeping her footsteps clean. Then, its work done, the ball let itself be taken by the wind, breath and Charter marks dissolving into nothing.

Lirael looked up, hoping whoever was in the Paperwing hadn't seen the strange little cloud. The aircraft was closer now, the shadow of its wings passing along the terrace as it circled once more, losing height with every pass.

Lirael squinted, her sight obscured by goggles and the snow that covered nearly all her face. She couldn't quite see who was in the Paperwing. It was a different color from the ones used by the Clayr. Red and gold, the colors of the Royal House. A messenger, perhaps? There was regular communication between the King in Belisaere and the Clayr, and Lirael had often seen messengers in the Lower Refectory. But they didn't normally arrive by Paperwing.

Some whistled notes, redolent with power, drifted down to Lirael, and for a nausea-inducing moment she felt as if she herself were flying and must turn into the wind. Then she saw the Paperwing come swooping down once more, turn into the wind, and come to a sliding, snow-spraying stop on the terrace—much too close to Lirael's hiding place for comfort.

Two people climbed wearily out of the cockpit and stretched their arms and legs. Both were so heavily wrapped in furs that Lirael couldn't see whether they were male or female. They weren't Clayr, though, she was certain, not in those clothes. One wore a coat of black and silver marten fur, the other a coat of some russet-red fur Lirael didn't recognize. And their goggles were blue lensed, not green.

The russet-furred one reached back into the cockpit and pulled out two swords. Lirael thought he—she was reasonably certain this one was a he—would hand one over, but he buckled both onto his broad leather belt, one on either side of his waist.

The other person—the one in black and silver—was a woman, Lirael decided. There was something about the way she took off her glove and rested her palm on the nose of the Paperwing, like a mother checking the temperature of a child's forehead.

Then the woman also reached into the cockpit, and she pulled out a leather bandolier. Lirael craned forward to see better, ignoring the snow that fell down inside her collar. Then she almost gasped and gave herself away, as she recognized what was in the pouches on the bandolier. Seven pouches, the smallest the size of a pillbox, the largest as long as Lirael's hand. Each pouch had a mahogany handle sticking out of it. The handles of bells, bells whose voices were stilled in the leather. Whoever this woman was, she carried the seven bells of a necromancer!

The woman put the bandolier on and reached for her own sword. Longer than the ones the Clayr used, and older, too.

Lirael could feel some sort of power in it, even from where she was hidden. Charter Magic, in the sword, and in both the people.

And in the bells, Lirael realized, which finally told her who this person must be. Necromancy was Free Magic, and forbidden in the Kingdom, as were the bells that necromancers used. Except for the bells of one woman. The woman who was charged with undoing the evil that necromancers wrought. The woman who put the Dead to rest. The woman who alone combined Free Magic with the Charter.

Lirael shivered, but not from cold, as she realized that she was only about twenty yards away from the Abhorsen. Years ago, the legendary Sabriel had rescued the petrified prince Touchstone and with him defeated the Greater Dead creature called Kerrigor, who had almost destroyed the Kingdom. And she had married the Prince when he became King, and together they had—

Lirael looked at the man again, noting the two swords and the way he stood close to Sabriel. He must be the King, she realized, feeling almost sick. King Touchstone and the Abhorsen Sabriel here! Close enough to go and talk to—if she was brave enough.

She wasn't. She settled further back into the snow, ignoring the damp and the cold, and waited to see what would happen. Lirael didn't know how you were supposed to bow or curtsy or whatever it was, or what you were supposed to call the King and the Abhorsen. Most of all, she didn't know how to explain what she was doing there.

Having equipped themselves, Sabriel and Touchstone drew close together and spoke quietly, their muffled faces almost touching. Lirael strained her ears but couldn't hear anything. The wind was blowing their words the wrong way. However, it was clear that they were waiting for something—or someone.

They didn't have to wait long. Lirael slowly turned her head towards the Starmount Gate, careful not to disturb the snow packed around her. A small gathering of the Clayr was issuing out of the Gate and hurrying across the terrace. They'd obviously come straight from the Awakening, because most of them had simply thrown cloaks or coats over their white robes, and nearly all of them still wore their circlets.

Lirael recognized the two in front—the twins Sanar and Ryelle—the flawless embodiment of the perfect Clayr. Their Sight was so strong they were nearly always in the Nine Day Watch, so Lirael hardly ever crossed paths with them. They were both tall and extremely beautiful, their long blond hair shining even more brightly than their silver circlets in the sun.

Behind them came five other Clayr. Lirael knew them all vaguely and, if pressed, could recall their names and their familial relationship to her. None was closer than a third cousin, but she recognized all of them as being particularly strong in the Sight. If they weren't part of the Nine Day Watch right now, they would be tomorrow, and probably had been last week.

In short, they were seven of the most important Clayr in all the Glacier. They all held significant ordinary posts in addition to their Sighted work. Small Jasell, for example, bringing up the rear, was First Bursar, in charge of the Clayr's internal finances and its trading bank.

They were also the very last people Lirael wanted to meet somewhere she wasn't supposed to be.

Chapter Four

A GLINT IN THE SNOW

A
s SANAR AND Ryelle led the others forward, Lirael thought she would see them do whatever it was you did when you met the King and his Queen, who had the added distinction of being the Abhorsen.

But Sabriel and Touchstone didn't wait for whatever that was. They met Sanar and Ryelle with hugs and, after pushing up their goggles and removing their scarves, with kisses on both cheeks. Once again, Lirael leaned forward to hear what was being said. The wind was still blowing the wrong way, but it had lessened, so she could catch the conversation.

"Well met, cousins," said Sabriel and the King together, both smiling. Now that she could see their faces, Lirael thought they both looked very tired.

"We Saw you last night," said Sanar—or Ryelle—Lirael wasn't sure. "But we had to guess the time from the sun. I trust you haven't been waiting long?"

"A few minutes," said Touchstone. "Just long enough to stretch."

"He still doesn't like flying much," said Sabriel, with a smile at her husband. "No confidence in the pilot."

Touchstone shrugged and laughed. "You get better all the time," he said.

Lirael sensed that he wasn't just talking about flying Paperwings. There seemed to be a semi-secret line of energy

and feeling that ran between Touchstone and Sabriel. They
shared something unseen, something that brought laughter and
the smile in Sabriel's eyes.

"We didn't See you staying," continued Sanar. "I take it
we got that right?"

"You did," replied Sabriel, and the smile was gone from her
eyes. "There is trouble in the West, and we cannot linger. Only
long enough to take counsel. If you have any to give."

"The West again?" asked Sanar, and she shared a troubled
look with Ryelle, as did the others of the Clayr behind her.
"We See nothing for too great a part of the West. Some power
exists there that blocks all but the briefest glimpses. Yet we
know that it is from the West that trouble will come to pass.
So many futures show snatches of it, but never enough to be
useful."

"Plenty of present trouble, too," said the King, sighing. "I
have raised six Charter Stones around Edge and the Red Lake
in the last ten years. Only two remain from year to year, and I
can no longer spare the time to keep repairing the others. We
go there now to quell whatever the current trouble is, and to
attempt to find the source, but I am not confident we will.
Particularly if it is strong enough to hide from the Clayr's
Sight."

"It is not always strength that can blind our Sight," said one
of the Clayr, the oldest there. "Nor even evil. There are subtle
powers that divert our Sight for reasons we can only guess, and
there is always simply the fact that we See too many futures,
too briefly. Perhaps whatever blinds us near the Red Lake is no
more than this."

"If it is, then it also breaks Charter Stones with the blood of
Charter Mages," said Touchstone. "And it draws the Dead and
Free Magic to it more than anywhere else. Of all the Kingdom,

it is the region around the Red Lake and the foothills of Mount Abed that most resists our rule. Fourteen years ago, Sabriel and I promised that the broken Charter Stones would be made anew, the villages re-established, the people once again free to go about their lives and business, without fear of the Dead and Free Magic. We have made it so from the Wall to the Northern Desert. But we cannot defeat whatever it is that opposes us in the West. Apart from Edge itself, that part of the West is still the wilderness that Kerrigor made it over two hundred years ago."

"You grow weary of your toils," said the old Clayr suddenly, and both Touchstone and Sabriel nodded. But their shoulders were straight, and while they admitted the weariness, they gave no sign that they refused the burden.

"We get no rest," said Touchstone. "There is always some new trouble, some danger that can be dealt with only by the King or the Abhorsen. Sabriel gets the worst of it, for there are still too many Dead abroad, and too many idiots who would open further doors to Death."

"Like the one who is currently causing havoc near Edge," said Sabriel. "Or so the messages say. A necromancer or Free Magic sorcerer, one who wears a bronze mask. She—for it is reported she is a woman—has a company of both the Dead and living men, and they have been raiding farms and steadings from Edge to the east, almost as far as Roble's Town. Yet we have heard nothing from you. Surely you must have Seen some of this?"

"We rarely See anything near the Red Lake," replied Ryelle with a troubled frown. "But we usually have no problem farther afield. In this case, I regret that we have given you no warning for what has happened, and can give you no guide as to what will."

"A company of the Guard is riding from Qyrre," said

Touchstone. "But they will not arrive for at least three days. We plan to be at Roble's Town ourselves by the morning."

"Hopefully a bright morning," added Sabriel. "If the reports are true, this necromancer has many Dead Hands under her control. Maybe even enough to attack a town at night, or under heavy cloud."

"I think we would definitely See an attack upon Roble's Town," said Ryelle. "And we have not."

"That's some relief," said Touchstone, but Lirael saw that he didn't entirely believe them. She was herself shocked, because she had never heard of the Sight being blocked, or of there being some place where the Clayr couldn't See. Except beyond the Wall to Ancelstierre, of course, but that was different. No magic worked in Ancelstierre, at least not once you got well south of the Wall. Or so the stories said. Lirael didn't know anyone who'd ever been to Ancelstierre, though the rumor was that Sabriel had grown up there.

The wind strengthened as Lirael mulled over what she'd heard, so she couldn't quite catch the next bit of conversation. But she saw the Clayr bow, and Sabriel and Touchstone motion for them to rise.

"Don't get formal on me!" exclaimed Touchstone. "You can't See everything, just as we can't do everything. Somehow we've managed so far, and we'll keep on managing."

"'Keeping on' being the watchword of this year and all the years behind it," said Sabriel, sighing. "Speaking of such, we'd best turn the Paperwing around and take flight again. I want to visit the House on the way to Roble's Town."

"To take counsel with—?" asked Ryelle, but the rest of her words were lost to Lirael, carried away by a gust of wind. She leaned forward a bit more, still trying not to dislodge the snow from her cap.

Sabriel said something in return, but Lirael couldn't make it out, save for the last part. ". . . still sleeps most of the year, under Ranna's . . ."

Then there was more lost talk, as they all clustered around the Paperwing and slid it around. Lirael craned forward as far as she dared, snow slipping from her face. It was infuriating to see them and hear the occasional word but not be able to understand. For a moment she even wildly thought of casting a spell to improve her hearing. She'd seen references to such a spell, but she didn't know all the marks. Besides, Sabriel and the others would almost certainly notice Charter Magic nearby.

Suddenly, the wind dropped, and Lirael could hear clearly again.

"They're still at school in Ancelstierre," Sabriel said, obviously in answer to a question asked by Sanar. "They'll be here for the holidays in three, no . . . four weeks. If all works out with this current emergency, we might just get to the Wall in time to meet them, and we had planned a few weeks together in Belisaere. But I expect some new trouble will arise that will take at least one of us away until they have to go back."

She sounded sad when she said that, Lirael thought. Touchstone must have thought so, too, because he took her hand, lending support.

"At least they're safe there," he said, and Sabriel nodded, her weariness showing through again.

"We have Seen them crossing the Wall, though it may be the next time, or the one after that," affirmed Ryelle. "Ellimere looks . . . will look . . . very like you, Sabriel."

"Fortunately," said Touchstone, laughing. "Though she takes after me in some other respects."

Lirael realized that they had been talking about their children. They had two, she knew. A Princess who was roughly her own age, and a Prince who was younger, she didn't know by how much. Sabriel and Touchstone obviously cared about them a great deal, and missed them. That made her think of her own mother and father, who must not have cared about her at all. Once again she remembered the touch of that soft, cool hand. But her mother had still left her, and who knew whether her father ever even knew of her birth?

"She will be Queen," said a strong voice, dragging Lirael's attention back to the present. "She will not be Queen. She may be Queen."

It was one of the other Clayr, an older woman, speaking in the voice of prophecy, her eyes Seeing something other than the lump of ice she was staring at. Then she gasped and stumbled forward, hands flung out to break her fall into the snow.

Touchstone lunged and caught her before she could hit the ground, setting her back on her feet. She swayed there, still unsteady, her eyes wild and dreaming.

"A far future," she said, the strange timbre of foreseeing gone from her voice. "One in which your daughter, Ellimere, was older than you are now, reigning as Queen. But I also Saw many other possible futures, side by side, where there is nothing but smoke and ashes, the whole world burnt and broken."

Lirael felt a shiver pass through her entire body as the old Clayr spoke. Her voice carried so much conviction, Lirael could almost see the desolate ruins herself. But how could the whole world be burnt and broken?

"Possible futures," interjected Sanar, trying to sound calm. "We often catch glimpses of futures that will never be. It is part of the burden of the Sight."

"Then I for one am glad I don't have it," replied Touchstone, as he let the still shaky Clayr go into the helping hands of Sanar and Ryelle. He looked up at the sun, and then across at Sabriel, who nodded. "I regret to say that we must be on our way."

He and Sabriel shared a smile at this unintentional rhyme, turning their heads so that only they and the hidden Lirael saw it. Touchstone took off his swords and stowed them in the cockpit, then took Sabriel's sword and put that away as well. Sabriel took off the bell bandolier and gently laid it down, careful to not jar the bells. Lirael wondered why they had bothered to get them out for such a short time. Then she realized that they lived so much in danger that it was second nature to keep weapons close at hand. Like the merchants' guards in the Refectory that morning. The realization that the Abhorsen and the King didn't trust the Clayr's protection made Lirael suddenly think of her own weaponless state. What would she do if she were attacked out here after everyone had gone? She wasn't sure if her key would open the sally port from the outside. She hadn't even thought about it on the way up.

Lirael stopped watching the Paperwing in order to panic, imagining a night out here and a monstrous claw dragging her out of the snow. The prospect of an unchosen death didn't appeal to her at all. Then a sudden movement caught her eye. Sabriel, now in the Paperwing, was pointing. Pointing straight at Lirael's hiding place in the snow!

"You might want to investigate that green glint," said Sabriel, her words all too clear for once. "I think whatever lies beneath it is harmless, but you never know. Farewell, cousins of the Clayr. I hope we can meet again soon, and tarry longer."

"As we hope that we can be of greater service," said Sanar, looking where Sabriel pointed. "And See more clearly, both in the West and under our own noses."

"Farewell," added Touchstone, waving from the rear of the Paperwing. Sabriel whistled, a pure sound infused with magic.

The whistle rose up into the wind, turned it, and brought it down to lift the Paperwing, sending it sliding along the terrace. Sabriel and Touchstone waved; then the red and gold craft shot off the end and dropped out of sight.

Lirael held her breath, then sucked air in with relief as the Paperwing suddenly soared back into sight. It circled higher, then turned to the south and shot away, faster and faster as Sabriel called the wind behind them.

Lirael watched it go for a second, then tried to burrow deeper into the snow. Perhaps they would think she was an ice otter. But even as she disappeared into the drift, she knew it was no use. All seven of the Clayr were advancing upon her hiding place, and they did not look pleased.

Chapter Five

AN UNEXPECTED OPPORTUNITY

L IRAEL WASN'T QUITE sure how they got back into the Paperwing hangar so quickly. She knew she was grabbed by more pairs of hands than seemed possible for seven people and hustled across the snow much more uncomfortably than she could have managed on her own. For a few seconds she thought they were very, very angry with her. Then she realized they were just cold, and wanted to get back inside.

Once all were inside, it was clear that while the Clayr were not exactly furious, they weren't too happy, either. Hands snatched off her cap, goggles, and scarf without regard for the hair that was caught up in them, and seven somewhat wind-chilled faces looked down at her.

"Arielle's daughter," said Sanar, as if she were identifying a flower or a plant, dredging it up from a list. "Lirael. Not on the roster of the Watch. Therefore, not yet with the Sight. Is that correct?"

"Y-yes," stammered Lirael. No one had ever peered at her so intently before, and she generally avoided talking to other people, particularly fully fledged Clayr. Important Clayr made her nervous even when she was behaving herself. Now there were seven of them giving her their undivided attention. She wished she could somehow sink through the floor and reappear in her own room.

"Why were you hiding out there?" asked the old Clayr,

who Lirael suddenly remembered was named Mirelle. "Why aren't you at the Awakening?"

There was no warmth in her voice at all, just cold author-ity. Belatedly, Lirael remembered that this grey-haired, leather-faced old woman was also the commander of the Clayr's Rangers, who hunted and patrolled across Starmount and Sunfall, the glacier, and the river valley. They dealt with everything from lost travelers to foolish bandits or marauding beasts, and were not to be trifled with.

Mirelle asked her question again, but Lirael couldn't answer. Tears came into her eyes, though she managed to hold them back. Then, when it seemed Mirelle was about to shake both answer and tears out of her, she said the first thing that came into her head.

"It's my birthday. I'm fourteen."

For some reason, this seemed to be the right thing to say. All the Clayr relaxed, and Mirelle let go of her shoulders. Lirael winced. The woman had gripped her hard enough to leave bruises.

"So you're fourteen," said Sanar, much more kindly than Mirelle. "And you're worried because the Sight hasn't woken in you?"

Lirael nodded, not trusting herself to speak.

"It comes late to some of us," continued Sanar, her eyes warm and understanding. "But often the later it is, the more strongly it wakes. The Sight did not come to me and Ryelle till we were sixteen. Has no one told you that?"

Lirael looked up, fully meeting the Clayr's gaze for the first time, her eyes wide with shock. Sixteen! That was impossible!

"No," she said, the surprise and relief clear in her voice. "Not sixteen!"

"Yes," said Ryelle, smiling, taking over where Sanar left off.

"Sixteen and a half, in fact. We thought it would never come. But it did. I suppose you couldn't bear another Awakening. Is that why you came up here?"

"Yes," said Lirael, a small smile beginning to creep across her own face. Sixteen! That meant there was hope for her yet. She felt like jumping forward and hugging everybody, even Mirelle, and running down the Starmount Stair yelling for joy. All of a sudden, her plan to kill herself seemed incredibly stupid, and the hatching of it long ago and far away.

"Part of our problem back then was having too much time to think about our lack of the Sight," said Sanar, who had not missed the signs of relief in Lirael's face and posture, "since we weren't part of the Watch and didn't have the Sight training. Of course, we didn't want to do extra shifts on the roster duties, either."

"No," agreed Lirael hurriedly. Who would want to clean toilets or wash dishes any more than she had to?

"It wasn't usual for us to be assigned a post before we turned eighteen," continued Ryelle. "But we asked, and the Watch agreed that we should be given proper work. So we joined the Paperwing Flight and learned to fly. That was in the time before the return of the King, when everything was much more dangerous and unsettled, so we flew far more patrols, and farther afield, than we do now.

"After only a year of flying, the Sight woke in us. It could have been an awful year, as was the one before it, waiting and hoping for the gift, but we were too busy to even think about it much. Do you think that proper work might help you, too?"

"Yes!" replied Lirael fervently. A post would free her from the child's tunic, let her wear the clothes of a working Clayr. It would also give her somewhere to go, away from the younger children and Aunt Kirrith. She might even be able to stay away from Awakenings, depending on what the work was.

"The question is, what work would suit you best?" mused Sanar. "I do not think we have ever Seen you, so that's no help. Is there any posting you would particularly like? The Rangers? Paperwing Flight? The Merchant Office? The Bank? Building and Construction? The Infirmary? The Steamworks?"

"I don't know," said Lirael, trying to think of all the many and various jobs the Clayr did, in addition to the rostered community duties.

"What are you good at?" asked Mirelle. She looked Lirael up and down, clearly measuring her up as a potential recruit for the Rangers. The slight lift of her nose showed that she didn't seem to think much of Lirael's potential. "How's your sword-craft, and archery?"

"Not very good," replied Lirael guiltily, thinking of all the practice sessions she'd missed lately, having chosen to mope in her room instead. "I'm best at Charter Magic, I think. And music."

"Perhaps the Paperwings, then," said Sanar. Then she frowned and looked at the others. "Though fourteen is perhaps a shade too young. They can be a bad influence."

Lirael glanced at the Paperwings and couldn't hold back a small shiver. She liked the idea of flying, but the Paperwings frightened her a bit. There was something creepy about their being alive and having their own personalities. What would happen if she had to talk to one of them all the time? She hated talking to people, let alone Paperwings.

"Please," said Lirael, pursuing that thought to the logical place where she could avoid people the most. "I think I would like to work in the Library."

"The Library," repeated Sanar, looking troubled. "That can be dangerous to a girl of fourteen. Or a woman of forty, for that matter."

"Only in parts," said Ryelle. "The Old Levels."

"You can't work in the Library without going into the Old Levels," said Mirelle somberly. "At least some of the time. I wouldn't be keen on going to some parts of the Library, myself."

Lirael listened, wondering what they were talking about. The Great Library of the Clayr was enormous, but she had never heard of the Old Levels.

She knew the general layout well. The Library was shaped like a nautilus shell, a continuous tunnel that wound down into the mountain in an ever-tightening spiral. This main spiral was an enormously long, twisting ramp that took you from the high reaches of the mountain down past the level of the valley floor, several thousand feet below.

Off the main spiral, there were countless other corridors, rooms, halls, and strange chambers. Many were full of the Clayr's written records, mainly documenting the prophesies and visions of many generations of seers. But they also contained books and papers from all over the Kingdom. Books of magic and mystery, knowledge both ancient and new. Scrolls, maps, spells, recipes, inventories, stories, true tales, and Charter knew what else.

In addition to all these written works, the Great Library also housed other things. There were old armories within it, containing weapons and armor that had not been used for centuries but still stayed bright and new. There were rooms full of odd paraphernalia that no one now knew how to use. There were chambers where dressmakers' dummies stood fully clothed, displaying the fashions of bygone Clayr or the wildly different costumes of the barbaric North. There were greenhouses tended by sendings, with Charter marks for light as bright as the sun. There were rooms of total darkness, swallowing up the light and anyone foolish enough to enter unprepared.

Lirael had seen some of the Library, on carefully escorted excursions with the rest of her year gathering. She had always hankered to enter the doors they passed, to step across the red rope barriers that marked corridors or tunnels where only authorized librarians might pass.

"Why do you want to work there?" asked Sanar.

"It—it's interesting," stammered Lirael, uncertain how she should reply. She didn't want to admit that the Library would be the best place to hide away from other Clayr. And in the back of her mind, she hadn't forgotten that in the Library she might find a spell to painlessly end her life. Not now, of course, now she knew that the Sight might come. But later, if she grew older and older without the Sight and the black despair welled up again inside her, as it had done earlier today.

"It is interesting," replied Sanar. "But there are dangerous things and dangerous knowledge in the Library, too. Does that bother you?"

"I don't know," said Lirael, honestly. "It would depend on what it was. But I really would like to work there." She paused and then said in a very low voice, "I do want to be busy, as you said, and forget about not having the Sight."

The Clayr turned away from Lirael then, and gathered together in a tight circle that excluded her, speaking in whispers. Lirael watched anxiously, aware that something momentous was going to happen to her life. The day had been horrible, but now she had hope again.

The Clayr stopped whispering. Lirael looked at them through the fall of her hair, glad that it hid her face. She didn't want them to see how badly she wanted them to let her work.

"Since it is your birthday," said Sanar, "and because we believe it will be best, we have decided that we will put you to work as you ask, in the Great Library. You should report there tomorrow morning, to Vancelle, the Chief Librarian. Unless she finds you unsuitable for some reason, you will become a Third Assistant Librarian."

"Thank you," cried Lirael. It came out as a croak, so she had to say it again. "Thank you."

"There is one more thing," said Sanar, and she came and stood so close that Lirael had to look up and meet her eyes. "You heard talk today that you should not have heard. Indeed, you have seen a visit that did not take place. The stability of a Kingdom is a fragile thing, Lirael, and easily upset. Sabriel and Touchstone would not speak so freely elsewhere, or to a different audience."

"I won't say anything to anyone," said Lirael. "I don't talk, really."

"You won't remember," said Ryelle, who had moved around behind her. She gently released the spell she'd held ready, cupped in her hand. Before Lirael could even think about countering it, a chain of bright Charter marks fell over her head, gripping her at the temples.

"At least not until you need to remember," continued Ryelle. "You will recall everything you have done today, save the visit of Sabriel and Touchstone. That memory will be gone, replaced by a walk on the terrace, and a chance meeting with us here. You seemed troubled, so we talked of work and the gaining of the Sight. That is how you gained your new post, Lirael. You will remember that, and no more."

"Yes," replied Lirael, words rolling off her lips so slowly that she seemed to be drunk or incredibly tired. "The Library. Tomorrow I report to Vancelle."

Chapter Six

THE CHIEF LIBRARIAN had a large oak-paneled office, with a very long desk that was covered in books, papers, and a large brass tray with that morning's breakfast still half-eaten upon it. There was also a long, silver-bladed sword on the desk, unsheathed, with its hilt close to the Librarian's hand.

Lirael stood in front of the desk, her head bowed, as Vancelle read the note the girl had brought from Sanar and Ryelle.

"So," said the Librarian, her deep, commanding voice making Lirael jump. "You want to be a librarian?"

"Y-yes," stammered Lirael.

"But are you suitable?" asked the Librarian. She touched the hilt of her sword, and for a moment Lirael thought Vancelle was going to pick it up and wave it around, to see if it frightened her.

Lirael was already frightened. The Librarian scared her, even without the sword. Her face gave away no feelings, and she moved with an economy of force, as if she might at any moment explode into violent action.

"Are you suitable?" asked the Librarian.

"Um, I don't . . . . I don't know," whispered Lirael.

The Librarian came out from behind her desk, so swiftly that Lirael wasn't sure if she'd blinked and missed the motion.

Vancelle was only slightly taller than Lirael, but she seemed to loom over the young girl. Her eyes were bright blue, and her hair was a soft, shining grey, like the finest ash left from a cooling fire. She wore many rings on her fingers, and on her left wrist there was a silver bracelet set with seven sparkling emeralds and nine rubies. It was impossible to guess her age.

Lirael trembled as the Librarian reached out and touched the Charter mark on her forehead. She felt it flare, warm on her skin, and saw the light reflected in the Librarian's bejeweled rings and bracelet.

Whatever the Librarian felt in Lirael's Charter mark, no sign of it showed upon her face. She withdrew her hand and walked back behind her desk. Once again, she touched the hilt of her sword.

"We have never taken on a librarian whom we haven't already Seen as being a librarian," she said, tilting her head, like someone puzzling over how to hang a painting. "But no one has ever Seen you at all, have they?"

Lirael felt her mouth dry up. Unable to speak, she nodded. She felt the sudden opportunity that had been granted her slipping away. The reprieve, the chance of work, of being someone—

"So you are a mystery," continued the Librarian. "But there is no better place for mystery than the Great Library of the Clayr—and it is better to be a librarian than part of the collection."

For a moment, Lirael didn't understand. Then hope blossomed in her again, and she found her voice. "You mean . . . you mean I am suitable?"

"Yes," said Vancelle, Chief Librarian of the Great Library of the Clayr. "You are suitable, and you may begin at once. Deputy Librarian Ness will tell you what to do."

Lirael left in a daze of happiness. She had survived the ordeal. She had been accepted. She was going to be a librarian!

Deputy Librarian Ness merely sniffed at Lirael and sent her to First Assistant Librarian Roslin, who kissed her absently on the cheek and sent her to Second Assistant Librarian Imshi, who was only twenty and not long promoted from the yellow silk waistcoat of a Third Assistant to the red of a Second.

Imshi took Lirael to the Robing Room, a huge room full of all the equipment, weapons, and miscellaneous items the librarians needed, from climbing ropes to boathooks. And dozens and dozens of the special Library waistcoats, all in different sizes and colors.

"Third Assistant's yellow, Second Assistant's red, First Assistant's blue, Deputy is white, and the Chief wears black," explained Imshi, as she helped Lirael put on a brand-new yellow waistcoat over her working clothes. "Heavier than it looks, isn't it? That's because it's actually canvas, covered in silk. Much tougher that way. Now, this whistle clips on the lapel loops here, so you can bend your head and blow into it, even if something's holding your arms. But you should whistle only if you really need help. If you hear a whistle, run towards the sound and do whatever you can to help."

Lirael took the whistle, which was a simple brass pipe, and put it through the special lapel loops as instructed. As Imshi had said, she could easily blow into it just by lowering her head. But what did Imshi mean? What might be holding her arms?

"Of course, the whistle's good only when someone can hear it," continued Imshi, handing Lirael something that at first glance looked like a silver ball. She indicated that it should be placed in the front left pocket of her new waistcoat. "That's why you have the mouse. It's part clockwork, so you have to remember to wind it once a month, and the spell has to be renewed every year at Midsummer."

Lirael looked at the small silver object. It was a mouse with little mechanical legs, two bright chips of ruby for eyes, and a small key in its back. She could feel the warmth of a Charter-spell lying dormant inside it. She supposed that this would activate the clockwork mechanism at the right time and send it wherever it was supposed to go.

"What's it do?" Lirael asked, surprising Imshi a little. The younger girl hadn't spoken since they'd been introduced, and had stood there with her hair hanging over her face the whole time. Imshi had already written her off as one of the Chief's eccentric recruitment decisions, but perhaps there was still hope. She sounded interested, anyway.

"It gets help," replied Imshi. "If you're in the Old Levels or somewhere you don't think anyone will hear the whistle, put the mouse on the ground and speak or draw the activating mark, which I'll show you in a moment. Once it's activated, it'll run to the Reading Room and sound the alarm."

Lirael nodded and flicked back her hair to study the mouse more closely, running her finger over its silver back. When Imshi started to thumb through an index of Charter marks, Lirael shook her head and put the mouse in its special pocket.

"I know the mark, thanks," she said quietly. "I felt it in the spell."

"Really?" asked Imshi, surprised again. "You must be good. I can hardly manage to light a candle, or warm my toes out on the glacier."

But you have the Sight, thought Lirael. You are a real Clayr.

"Anyway, you have the whistle and the mouse," said Imshi, getting back to her task. "Here's your belt and scabbard, and I'll just see which dagger is sharpest. Ow! That'll do, I think. Now we have to put the number in the book, and you have to sign for everything."

Lirael buckled on the broad leather belt and settled the scabbard against her hip and thigh. The dagger that went into it was as long as her forearm, with a thin, sharp blade. It was steel but had been washed in silver, and there were Charter marks on the blade. Lirael touched them lightly with her finger, to see what they were supposed to do. They warmed under her touch, and she recognized them as marks of breaking and unraveling, especially useful against Free Magic creatures. They had been put there some twenty years ago, replacing older marks that had worn out. These too would last only another ten years or so, as they had not been placed with any great power or skill. Lirael thought she could possibly do better herself, though she wasn't particularly adept at working magic on inanimate objects.

Lirael looked up from the dagger and saw Imshi waiting expectantly, a quill in her hand, hovering above the huge leather-bound ledger that was chained to the desk at the front of the Robing Room.

"The number," said Imshi. "On the blade."

"Oh," said Lirael. She angled the blade till the Charter marks faded out and she could see the bare metal, and the letter and number etched there by conventional means.

"L2713," Lirael called out; then she slid the dagger home into the scabbard. Imshi wrote the number down, re-inked the quill, and passed it to Lirael to sign.

There in the ledger, in between ruled lines of red ink, was Lirael's name, the date, her position as Third Assistant Librarian, and a list of all the things she'd been given, neatly written by Imshi. Lirael scanned the list, but didn't sign.

"It says a key, here," she said cautiously, tipping up the quill so an incipient blob of ink didn't fall on the paper.

"Oh, a key!" exclaimed Imshi. "I wrote it down and then I forgot!"

She went over to one of the cupboards on the wall, opened it, and rummaged around inside. Finally, she pulled out a broad silver bracelet set with emeralds, the match of the one on her own wrist. Unlocking it, she clasped it around Lirael's right wrist.

"You'll have to go back to the Chief to have the spell inside woken up," explained Imshi, showing Lirael how two of the seven emeralds on her own bracelet swarmed with bright Charter marks. "Depending on your work and post, it will then open all the appropriate doors."

"Thanks," said Lirael briefly. She could feel the spell in the silver, Charter marks hiding deep within the metal, waiting to flow into the emeralds. There were actually seven spells, she could tell, one for each emerald. But she didn't know how they could be brought to the surface and made to work. This particular magic was beyond her.

Nor was she much wiser ten minutes later, when Vancelle took her wrist and quickly cast a spell that neither was spoken nor had any other obvious marks, signed or drawn. Whatever it was, the spell lit up only one emerald, leaving the other six dark. That, said Vancelle, was enough to open the common doors, which was more than enough for a new Third Assistant Librarian.

It took Lirael three months to work out how to wake the next four spells in her bracelet, though the secret of the sixth and seventh remained beyond her. But she didn't wake the extra spells at once, taking another month to create an illusion of the bracelet as it was supposed to be, that would sit over her own and hide the glow of the additional emeralds.

It was mainly curiosity that set her to working out the key spells. Originally she didn't plan to wake them, and intended to treat her discovery purely as an intellectual exercise. But there were so many interesting doors, hatches, gates, grilles, and locks that she couldn't help but wonder what was behind them. Once the spells in the bracelet were active, she found it very difficult not to think of using them.

Her daily work also led her into temptation. While there were Charter sendings to do much of the manual labor, ferrying materials to and from the Main Reading Room and the individual studies of scholars, all the checking, recording, and indexing was done by people. Generally, the junior librarians. There were also very special or dangerous items that had to be fetched in person, or even by large parties of armed librarians. Not that Lirael got to go on any of these exciting expeditions to the Old Levels. Nor would she, till she attained the red waistcoat of a Second Assistant, which usually took at least three years.

But in the course of her regular duties, she often passed interesting-looking corridors sealed off with red rope, or doors that beckoned to her, almost saying, "How can you walk past me every day and not want to go in?"

Without exception, any vaguely interesting portal was locked, beyond the original key spell and the sole glowing emerald of Lirael's bracelet.

Aside from the inaccessibility of the interesting parts, the Great Library met most of Lirael's hopes. She was given a small study of her own. Barely wider than her outstretched arms, it contained nothing but a narrow desk, a chair, and several shelves. But it was a refuge, somewhere she would be left alone, secure from Aunt Kirrith's intrusions. It was meant for quiet study, in Lirael's case, of the set texts of the beginning librarian: *The Librarian's Rules*, *Basic Bibliography*, and *The Large Yellow Book: Simple Spells for Third Assistant Librarians*. It had taken her only a month to learn everything she needed to from those volumes.

So she quietly "borrowed" any book she could get her hands on, like *The Black Book of Bibliomancy*, carelessly left off a returning list by a Deputy Librarian. And she spent a great deal of time analyzing the spells in her bracelet, slowly finding her way through the complex chains of Charter marks to find the activating symbols.

Lirael had been driven by curiosity at first, and by the sense of satisfaction she gained from working out magic that was supposed to be beyond her. But somewhere along the way, Lirael realized that she enjoyed learning Charter Magic for its own sake. And when she was learning marks and putting them together into spells, she completely forgot about her troubles and forgot about not having the Sight.

Learning to be a real Charter Mage also gave her something to do, when all the other librarians or her fellows from the Hall of Youth were engaged in more social activities.

The other librarians, particularly the dozen or so Third Assistants, had tried to be friendly at first. But they were all older than Lirael, and they all had the Sight. Lirael felt she had nothing to talk about or share with them, so she stayed silent, hiding behind her hair. After a while, they stopped inviting her to sit with them at lunch, or to play a game of tabore in the afternoon, or to gossip about their elders over sweet wine in the evening.

So Lirael was once again alone among company. She told herself that she preferred it, but she couldn't deny the pang in her heart when she saw laughing groups of young Clayr, so effortlessly talking and enjoying one another's friendship.

It was even worse when whole groups were called to join

the Nine Day Watch, as happened more and more frequently during Lirael's first few months of work. Lirael would be stacking books in the Reading Room, or writing in one of the registers, when a Watch messenger would come in, bearing the ivory tokens that summoned the recipient to the Observatory. Sometimes dozens of the Clayr in the huge, domed Reading Room would each receive a token. They would smile, curse, grimace, or take it stoically; then there would be a flurry of activity as they all stopped work, drawing back their chairs, locking away books and papers in their desk drawers, or returning them to shelves or sorting tables before trooping out the doors en masse.

At first Lirael was surprised that so many were called, and she was even more surprised when some of them returned only hours or days later, instead of the usual nine days that gave the Watch its name. She initially thought it must be some peculiarity of the librarians, that so many were called at once and not for the full term. But she didn't feel like asking anyone about it, so it was some time before she got some sort of answer, when she overheard two Second Assistant Librarians in the Binding Room.

"It's all very well to have a Ninety-Eight. But to go on to a Hundred and Ninety-Six and on up to yesterday's Seven Hundred and Eighty-Four is quite ridiculous," said one of the Second Assistants. "I mean we did all fit in the Observatory. But now there's talk of a Fifteen Sixty-Eight! That'll be nearly everybody, I should think—and making the Watch bigger doesn't seem to make it work any better than the usual Forty-Nine. I couldn't tell the difference."

"I don't mind, myself," replied the other Second Assistant as she carefully applied glue to the binding of a broken-backed book. "It makes a change from here, and at least it's over quicker with a larger Watch. But it is tedious when we have to try to focus where we can't See anything. Why don't the high-ups just admit that no one can See anything around that stupid lake and leave it at that?"

"Because it's not so simple," interrupted a stern-voiced Deputy, bearing down on them like a huge white cat on two plump mice. "All the possible futures are connected. Not being able to See where futures begin is a significant problem. You should know that, and you also should know not to talk about the business of the Watch!"

The last sentence was said with a general glare about the room. But Lirael, even half-hidden behind a huge press, felt it was particularly aimed at her. After all, everybody else in the room was a full Clayr and eligible to be a member of the Nine Day Watch.

Her cheeks burnt with embarrassment and shame as she threw all her strength into turning the great bronze handles of the screw, tightening the press. Talk slowly resumed around her, but she ignored it, concentrating only on her task.

But that was the moment when she resolved to wake the dormant magic in her bracelet, and use the spell she'd made to hide the glow of the additional emeralds.

She might not be able to join the Watch in the Observatory, but she would explore the Library.

Chapter Seven

BEYOND THE DOORS OF SUN AND MOON

EVEN AFTER SHE woke the extra spells in her bracelet, Lirael found it hard to explore the areas formerly closed to her. There was always too much work, or there were too many other librarians around. After the first two heart-thumping moments of near-discovery in front of forbidden doors, Lirael decided to put off her exploration until there were fewer people around or she could more easily escape from work.

Her first real chance came almost five months after she had donned the yellow waistcoat of a Third Assistant. She was in the Reading Room, sorting books to be returned by the sendings, who gathered close around her, their ghostly, Charter-etched hands the only visible part of their shrouded forms. They were quite simple sendings, without any higher functions, but they loved their work. Lirael liked them, too, because they didn't require her to speak or ask her questions. She simply gave the appropriate books to the right sending, and it would take them away to its area and the proper shelf or store.

Lirael was particularly good at recognizing which sending was which, a valuable skill since the embroidered signs on their cowled robes were often obscured with dust or had become unpicked and indecipherable. They didn't have official names, only descriptions of their responsibilities. But most had nick-names, like Tad, who was in charge of Traveler's Tales, A–D, or Stoney, who looked after the geology collection.

Lirael was just giving Tad a particularly large and unwieldy volume bound in leather stamped with a three-humped camel motif when the Watch messenger arrived. Lirael didn't pay much attention to her at first, because she knew no ivory token would be given to her. Then she noticed that the messenger was stopping at every desk and speaking to every person, and a hum of whispered conversation was rising behind her. Lirael surreptitiously tucked her hair behind her ears and tried to listen. At first the murmur was indistinct, but as the messenger grew closer, Lirael caught the words "Fifteen Sixty-Eight" being repeated over and over again.

For a moment she was puzzled; then she realized that this must be what the Second Assistants had been talking about. The calling of one thousand five hundred sixty-eight Clayr to the Watch—an unprecedented concentration of the Sight.

It would also take nearly every librarian out of the Library, Lirael calculated, giving her the perfect chance for a secret excursion. For the first time ever, Lirael watched the messenger's distribution of tokens with excitement rather than with her usual depression and self-pity. Now she was wishing everyone else *would* get summoned to the Watch. Trying not to look too obvious, Lirael even wandered around the other side of the desk to see if anyone had been missed.

No one had. Lirael found it strangely hard to breathe as she waited to see if anyone would remember to tell her to do something—or not to. But none of the librarians with whom she usually worked were here. Imshi was not to be seen. Lirael guessed the messenger had met her on the way and had already given her a token.

She willed them all to go and started to sort her books with a concentrated ferocity, as if she didn't care what happened around her. The sendings approved, moving faster themselves as each one took its stack of books and another moved into place.

Finally, the last bright waistcoat gleamed in the doorway and was gone. More than fifty librarians, disposed of in less than five minutes. Lirael smiled and put the last book down with a definite snap, disappointing the sending who was waiting for a full load.

Ten minutes later, to allow for stragglers, she headed down the main spiral. There was a door about a half mile down, well into the Old Levels, a particular favorite that she wanted to investigate first. It had a bright sunburst emblem upon its otherwise unremarkable wooden surface, a golden disc with rays that spread from top to bottom. Of course, there was also a red rope across it, secured at either end with wax seals bearing the book and sword symbol of the Chief Librarian.

Lirael had long since worked out how to deal with this particular annoyance. She drew a short piece of wire with two wooden handles from her waistcoat pocket and held it near her mouth. Then she spoke three Charter marks, a simple charm to heat metal. With the wire momentarily red-hot, she quickly sliced the seals away and hid them and the rope in a nearby hole in the passage wall, away from the light.

Then came the real test. Would the door open to her brace-let, or would it need the last two spells she couldn't figure out?

Holding her wrist as she'd been taught, she waved her bracelet in front of the door. Emeralds flashed, breaking through the cloaking-spell she'd put upon them—and the door swung open without a sound.

Lirael stepped through, and the door slowly shut behind her. She found herself in a short corridor and was momentarily disoriented by the bright light at the other end. Surely this passage couldn't lead outside? She was in the heart of the mountain, thousands of feet underground. Blinking against the light, she walked forward, one hand on the hilt of her dagger, the other one on the clockwork emergency mouse.

The corridor didn't lead outside, but Lirael saw how she had been misled. It opened out into a vast chamber, bigger even than the Great Hall. Charter marks as bright as the sun shone in the distant ceiling, hundreds of feet above. A huge oak tree filled the center of the room, in full summer leaf, its spreading branches shading a serpentine pool. And everywhere, throughout the cavern, there were flowers. Red flowers. Lirael bent down and picked one, uncertain if it was some sort of illusion. But it was real enough. She felt no magic, just the crisp stalk under her fingers. A red daisy, in full bloom.

Lirael sniffed it, and sneezed as the pollen went up her nose. Only then did she realize how quiet it was. This huge cavern might mimic the outside world, but the air was too still. There was no breeze, and no sound. No birds, no bees happily at work amid the pollen. No small animals drinking at the pool. There was nothing living, save the flowers and the tree. And the lights above gave no warmth, unlike the sun. This place was the same temperature as the rest of the Clayr's inhabited realm, and had the same mild humidity, from the moist heat distributed via the huge network of pipes that brought superheated water from the geysers and steam plumes far, far below.

Lovely as it was, it was a bit disappointing. Lirael wondered if this was all there was to find on her first expedition. Then she saw that there was another door—a latticed gate, rather—on the far side of the cavern.

It took her ten minutes to walk across, longer than she would have thought. But she tried not to tread on too many flowers, and she gave the tree and the pool a very wide berth. Just in case.

The gate barred the way to another corridor, one that went into darkness rather than light. The gate, a simple metal grille, had the emblem of a silver moon upon it, rather than a sun. A crescent moon, with much sharper and longer points than could be considered usual or aesthetically pleasing.

Lirael looked through the gate to the passage beyond. For some reason it made her think about the whistle on her waist-coat, and things grabbing her arms. The whistle would be use-less here anyway—and the mouse, too, Lirael suddenly realized, since there was no one currently in the Reading Room to hear its squeaked alarm.

But aside from unknown dangers, there was no obvi-ous reason not to try the gate, at least. Lirael waved her arm, and once again the emeralds flashed, but the gate didn't open. She let her hand fall, tucked her hair back out of her eyes and frowned. Clearly, this was a gate that answered only to the higher spells.

Then she heard a click, and the right-hand leaf of the gate slowly swung open—barely wide enough for Lirael to squeeze through. To make it harder, the crescent moon protruded into the open space, the sharp points level with where Lirael's neck and groin would be.

She looked at the narrow way and thought about it. What if there were something horrible beyond? But then again, what did she have to lose? Fear and curiosity fought inside her for a moment. Curiosity won.

Acting on the latter impulse, Lirael took the mouse from her pocket and put it down amongst the flowers. If some-thing did go wrong beyond the gate, she could scream out the activating Charter mark and off it would go, taking its own devious mouseways to the Reading Room. Even if it was too late to save Lirael, it might be a useful warning to the others. According to her superiors and co-workers, it was not uncommon for librarians to lay down their lives for the benefit of the Clayr as a whole, either in dangerous research, simple overwork, or action against previously unknown dangers discovered in the Library's collection. Lirael believed this principle of self-sacrifice was particularly appropriate to herself, since the rest of the Clayr had the Sight and so needed to be alive much more than she did.

After placing the mouse, Lirael drew her dagger and slipped through the partly open gate. It was a very tight fit, and the moon's points were razor sharp, but she got through without damage to herself or her clothes. It did not occur to her that a grown man or woman would not be able to pass.

The corridor was very dark, so Lirael spoke a simple Charter-spell for light, letting it flow into her dagger. Then she held the blade up in front of her like a lantern, only not as bright. Either she'd muffed the spell a little or something was damping it.

Besides being dark, the corridor, evidently not connected to the Clayr's geothermal pipes, was also cold. Dust rose as Lirael walked, swirling around in strange patterns that Lirael thought might almost be Charter marks, ones she didn't know.

Beyond the corridor, there was a small rectangular room. Holding her dagger high, Lirael could see its shadowed corners, crawling with faint Charter marks that were so old, they'd almost lost their luminescence.

The whole room was afloat in magic—strange, ancient Charter Magic that she didn't understand and was almost afraid of. The marks were remnants of some incredibly old spell, now senile and broken. Whatever the spell had once been, now it was no more than hundreds of disconnected marks, fading into the dust.

Enough remained of the spell to make Lirael even more uneasy. There were marks of binding and imprisonment floating there, of warding and warning. Even in its broken form, the spell was trying to fulfill its purpose.

Worse than that, Lirael realized that though the marks were very old, the spell had not simply faded, as she first thought. It had been broken only recently, within weeks, or perhaps months.

In the middle of the room, there was a low table of black, glassy stone, a single slab, reminiscent of an altar. It, too, was covered in the remnants of some mighty charm or spell. Charter marks washed across its smooth surface, forever seeking connection to some master Charter mark that would draw them all together. But that mark was no longer there.

There were seven small plinths on the table, lined up in a row. They were carved of some sort of luminous white bone, and all were empty save one. The third from the left had a small model or statuette upon it.

Lirael hesitated. She couldn't quite make out what it was, but she didn't want to get any closer. Not without knowing more about the spells that had been broken here.

She stood there for some time, watching the marks and listening. But nothing changed, and the room was totally silent.

One more step forward, Lirael reasoned, wouldn't make a difference. She would see what was on the third plinth and then withdraw.

She stepped closer and raised her light.

As soon as her foot landed, she knew she'd made a mistake. The floor felt strange, unsteady under her. Then there was a terrible crack, and both feet suddenly went right through the panel of dark glass she had mistaken for more of the floor.

Lirael fell forward, only just keeping hold of her dagger. Her left hand fell on the table, instinctively grabbing the statuette. Her knees hit the lip where glass met stone, sending a jarring pain through to her head. Her feet were stinging, cut by the glass.

She looked down and saw something worse than broken glass and cut feet, something that had her moving again instantly, regardless of any further damage the shards might do.

For the glass had been the cover of a long, coffin-like trench, and there was something lying in it. Something that at first looked like a sleeping, naked woman. In the next horrified instant, Lirael saw that its forearms were as long as its legs, and bent backwards, with great claws on the ends, like those of a praying mantis. It opened its eyes, and they were silver fires, brighter and more terrible than anything Lirael had ever seen.

Even worse, there was the smell. The telltale metallic odor of Free Magic that left a sour taste in Lirael's mouth and throat and made her stomach roil and heave.

Both creature and Lirael moved at the same time. Lirael threw herself back towards the corridor as the thing struck out with its awful, elongated claws. They missed, and the monster let out a shriek of annoyance that was completely inhuman, making Lirael run faster than she had ever run before, cut feet or not.

Before the shriek had subsided, Lirael was squeezing through the gate, breathing in with such a panic that there were inches to spare. Beyond it, she turned and waved her bracelet, screaming out, "Shut! Shut!"

But the gate didn't close, and the creature was suddenly there, one leg and hideous arm thrust through. For a moment Lirael thought it wouldn't be able to pass the sharp points of the moon, but it suddenly thinned and grew taller, its body as malleable as soft clay. Its silver eyes sparkled, and it opened a mouth full of silver-spined teeth to lick its lips with a grey tongue that was striped yellow, like a leech.

Lirael didn't stay to watch it. She forgot the emergency mouse. She forgot about staying away from the pool and the tree. She just ran in an absolutely straight line, crashing through the flowers, daisy petals exploding in a cloud around her.

On and on she ran, thinking that at any moment a hooked claw would bring her down. She didn't slow at the outer corridor, and slid to a stop only just in time to avoid smashing into the door. There, she waved her bracelet and slipped through before it opened more than a crack, stripping all the buttons from her waistcoat.

On the other side, she waved her bracelet again, watching the open doorway with the wide-eyed, sick anticipation of a calf watching an approaching wolf.

The door stopped opening and slowly began to close again. Lirael sighed and fell to her knees, feeling as if she were going to vomit. She shut her eyes for a moment—and heard a snick that was not the shutting of the door.

Her eyes flashed open, and she saw a curving, insectile hook, as long as her hand, thrust through a finger-width gap. Then another followed it—and the door began to open.

Lirael's mouth went to her whistle, and its shrill cry echoed up and down the spiral. But there was no one to hear it, and when her hand went to the mouse pocket, it found a strange statuette of soft stone, not the familiar silver body of the mouse.

The door shuddered, and the gap increased, the creature clearly winning against the spell that tried to keep it shut. Lirael stared at it, unable to think of what to do next. She frantically glanced up and down the corridor, as if some unlooked-for help might come.

But none did come, and she could only think that whatever this thing was, it must not be let out into the main spiral. The words of the librarians telling her of self-sacrifice came back to her, as did her depressed climb up the Starmount Stairs only a few months before. Now that death seemed likely, she realized how much she wanted to stay alive.

Even so, Lirael knew what must be done. She drew herself up and reached into the Charter. There, in the endless flow, she drew out all the marks she knew for breaking and blasting, for fire and destruction, for blocking, barring, and locking. They came into her mind in a flood, brighter and more blinding than any light, so strong that she could barely weave them into a spell. But somehow she ordered them as she wished, and linked them together with a single master mark, one of great power, that she had never before dared to use.

With the spell ready, pent up inside her by will alone, Lirael did the bravest thing she had ever done. She touched the door with one hand, the creature's hook with the other, and spoke the master Charter mark to cast the spell.

Chapter Eight

DOWN THE FIFTH BACK STAIR

As SHE SPOKE, heat coursed through Lirael's throat. White fire exploded through her right hand into the creature, and a titanic force was unleashed from her left, slamming the door shut. She was hurled backwards, tumbling over and over till her head struck the stone floor with a terrible crack that sent her instantly into darkness.

When she came to, Lirael had no idea where she was. Her head felt as if a hot wire had pierced her skull. It was somehow wet as well, and her throat ached as if she were in the throes of a really bad flu. For a moment she thought she was sick in bed and would soon see Aunt Kirrith or one of the other girls bending over her with a spoonful of herbal restorative. Then she realized that there was cold stone under her, not a mattress, and she was fully clothed.

Hesitantly, she touched her head, and her fingers showed her what the wetness was. She looked at the bright blood, and a wave of cold and dizziness overcame her, shooting up from her toes and through her head. She tried to call for help, but her throat was too sore. Nothing came out, only a sort of breathy buzz.

Now she remembered what she'd been trying to do, and a bolt of pure panic banished the dizziness. She tried to raise her head, but that hurt too much, so she rolled on her side instead, to see the door.

It was shut, and there was no sign of the creature. Lirael stared at the door till the grain of the wood grew blurry, uncertain that it really was closed, the creature gone. When she was absolutely sure it was shut, she turned her head away and threw up, sour bile burning her already painful throat.

She lay still after that, trying to steady her breathing and her stammering heart. A further cautious examination of her head revealed the blood to be clotting already, so it probably wasn't too serious. Her throat seemed to be worse, damaged by speaking a master Charter mark that she didn't have the strength or the experience to use correctly. She tried to say a few words, but only a hoarse whisper came out.

Next, she investigated her feet, but they turned out to be more scratched than cut, though her shoes had so many holes that they had become like sandals. Compared to her head, her feet were fine, so she decided to try standing up.

That took her several minutes, even using the wall for support. Then it took another five minutes to bend down again, pick up her dagger, and ease it into the scabbard.

After that exercise, she stood for a while, till she felt steady enough to examine the door. It was shut properly, without a gap, and she could feel her own spell, as well as the door's magical lock, holding it closed. No one could get in or out now without breaking Lirael's spell. Even the Chief Librarian would have to get her to lift it, or break it.

Thinking of the Chief made Lirael pick up as many of her torn-off buttons as she could find, and replace the red rope and the seals across the door—though calling up a spell to warm the wax was almost beyond her. When she'd finished, she walked a few steps up the main spiral, but had to sit down, too weak to go on.

Slumping down, she lapsed into a semi-conscious daze,

unable to think about anything or to assess her situation. She sat for a long time, maybe even an hour. Then some natural resilience rose up in her, and Lirael realized where she was and the state she was in. Bloodied, bruised, her waistcoat buttonless and torn, her emergency mouse lost. All of which would need explanation.

The loss of the mouse reminded her of the statuette. Her hands were much clumsier than usual, frustratingly so, but she managed to get the small stone figure out of her pocket and set it on her lap.

It was a dog, she saw, carved from a soft grey-blue soap-stone that was pleasant to touch. It looked like a fairly hard-bitten sort of dog, with pointy ears and a sharp snout. But it also had a friendly grin, and the suggestion of a tongue in the corner of its mouth.

"Hello, dog," whispered Lirael, her voice so weak and scratchy, she could hardly hear it herself. She liked dogs, though there were none in the higher reaches of the Glacier. The Rangers had a kennel for their working dogs near the Great Gate, and visitors sometimes brought their dogs into the guest quarters and the Lower Refectory. Lirael always said hello to the visiting dogs, even when they were huge brindled wolfhounds with studded collars. The dogs were always friendly to her, often more so than their owners, who would get upset when Lirael spoke only to their dogs and not to them.

Lirael held the dog statuette and wondered what she was going to do. Should she tell Imshi or someone higher up about the thing that was loose in the flower-field chamber? And admit she had woken the extra key spells in her bracelet?

She sat there for ages, turning over ideas, scratching the stone head of the dog as if it were a miniature real animal. Telling the truth was probably the right thing to do, she concluded, but then she would almost certainly lose her job—and going back to the children's classes and the hated blue tunic would be unbearable. Once again, she toyed with the idea that death might provide an escape, but the reality of nearly being slain by the hooks of the creature made killing herself even less attractive than it had been before.

No, Lirael decided. She had got herself into trouble and she would get herself out of it. She'd find out what the creature was, learn how to defeat it, and then go and do it. It couldn't get out till then, or so she hoped. And no one else could get in, so it wouldn't be a danger to other librarians.

That left explaining her cut head, scratched feet, bruises, mislaid mouse, lost voice, and general disarray. All of which could probably be done with a single brilliant plan. Which Lirael didn't have.

"I might as well walk and think," she whispered to the dog statuette. It was oddly comforting to speak to the dog and hold it in her hand. She looked down at the way it sat, with its tail curled around its back legs, head up and forelegs straight, as if waiting for its mistress.

"I wish I had a real dog," Lirael added, groaning as she stood up and started slowly walking up the spiral corridor. Then she stopped and looked down at the statuette, a sudden wild thought blossoming in her mind. She could create a Charter sending of a dog, a complex one that could bark and every- thing. All she'd need was *On the Making of Sendings*, and perhaps *The Making and Mastery of Magical Beings*. Both were locked up, of course, but Lirael knew where they were. She could even make the sending look like the lovely dog statuette.

Lirael smiled at the thought of having a dog of her own. A true friend, someone she could talk to who wouldn't ask her questions or talk back. A loving and lovable companion.

She tucked the statuette back in her waistcoat pocket and limped on.

A hundred yards later she abruptly stopped thinking about how to create a sending and started to worry about how she would find out what the creature in the flower room was. There were bestiaries in the Library, she knew, but finding and getting access to them could be a problem.

She kept thinking about that for another hundred yards until she realized she had a far more pressing problem. She needed to work out an explanation for her injuries and the lost mouse, with a minimum of actual lying. Lirael felt that she owed the Library a lot, and didn't want to tell an outright lie. Besides, she didn't think she could lie, if it came to heavy-duty questioning from the Chief Librarian or someone like that.

The mouse was the tricky part. She stopped moving to try to think more clearly, and she was surprised by how much her body needed the rest. Normally she ran around the Library all day, up and down the spiral, up and down ladders, in and out of rooms. Now she could barely move without a major effort of will.

A fall would explain her head injury, Lirael thought, once again feeling the cut. It had stopped bleeding, but her hair was matted with blood, and she could feel a lump coming up.

A long fall, with a terrified scream, could also explain her sore throat. Buttons could be scraped off in that sort of fall, and a mouse easily lost from a pocket.

Steps, Lirael decided. A fall down a flight of steps would best explain everything. Particularly if someone found her at the bottom of the steps, so she wouldn't have to say anything much.

It took her only a little while to work out that the Fifth Back Stair between the main spiral and the Hall of Youth would be the most likely spot for her to have an accident. She could even pick up a glass of water from the Zally Memorial Fountain on the way. You weren't allowed to take the glasses away, of course, but that was probably a bonus. It would give everybody—particularly Aunt Kirrith—something to scold her for, and they wouldn't look for more serious crimes. And a broken glass would explain her scratched feet.

Now all she had to do was get there and not meet anyone on the way. If the past extra-large Watch gatherings were any indication, the Fifteen Sixty-Eight wouldn't last much longer. There was a definite correlation between the size of a particular Watch and how long it lasted. The normal Forty-Nine lasted nine days, giving the Watch its name. But when there were more people involved, the Clayr returned much sooner. The most recent Watch had taken the participating Clayr away for less than a day.

The closer she got to the Hall of Youth, the greater the danger of meeting youngsters or others not part of the Watch. Lirael decided that if she did meet anyone, she'd just fall down and pass out, hoping that whoever it was didn't get too inquisitive.

But she didn't meet anyone before she turned off the spiral, picked up her glass of water at the Zally Fountain, went through the permanently open stone doors of the Fifth Library Landing, and reached the Fifth Back Stair. It was a narrow, circular stair, not much used since it merely connected the Library with the western side of the Hall of Youth.

Wearily, Lirael climbed the first half dozen steps, to the point where it started to turn inwards. Then she threw the glass down, wincing as it broke. After that she had to work out where to lie so it looked as if she really had fallen down the steps. This made her dizzy, so she had to sit down. And once she

was sitting, it seemed quite natural to lay her head on an upper
step, cushioned by an outthrust arm.

She knew she should be artistically arranging herself on
the landing below, an obvious victim of a fall, but it all seemed
too hard. The strength that had sustained her to this point was
gone. She couldn't get up. It was so much easier to go to sleep.
Beautiful sleep, where no troubles could torment her . . .

Lirael awoke to a voice urgently calling her name, and two
fingers checking the pulse in her neck. This time, she came to
her senses fairly quickly, grimacing as the pain returned.

"Lirael! Can you talk?"

"Yes," whispered Lirael, her voice still very weak and
strangely husky. She was disoriented. Her last memory was of
lying on the steps, and now she was flat on the ground. She realized that she was on the landing, looking much more like the
victim of a fall than anything she could have arranged herself.
She must have slipped down the steps after passing out.

A blue-waistcoated First Assistant Librarian was bending
over her, peering closely at her face. Lirael blinked and wondered why this strange person was moving her hand backwards and forwards in front of Lirael's eyes. But it wasn't a
strange person after all. It was Amerane, whom she had worked
with for a few days last month.

"What happened?" asked Amerane, concern in her voice.
"Does anything feel broken?"

"I hit my head," whispered Lirael, and she felt tears spring-
ing up in her eyes. She hadn't cried before, but now she couldn't
stop, and her whole body started to shake as well, no matter
how hard she tried to stay still.

"Does anything feel broken?" Amerane repeated. "Does
it hurt anywhere else aside from your head?"

"N-no," sobbed Lirael. "Nothing's broken."

Amerane didn't seem to trust Lirael's opinion, because she lightly felt all the way up and down the girl's arms and legs, and gently pressed against her fingers and feet. Since Lirael didn't scream and there seemed to be no grating of bones or abnormal lumps or swellings, Amerane helped her get up.

"Come on," she said kindly. "I'll help you get to the Infirmary."

"Thanks," whispered Lirael, putting her arm around Amerane's shoulders and letting her take most of her weight. Her other hand went to her pocket, fingers wrapping around the little stone dog, its smooth surface a source of comfort, as Amerane carried her away.

Chapter Nine

CREATURES BY NAGY

A T FIRST, LIRAEL thought she would be out of the Infirmary within a day. But even three days after her "fall," she could barely speak, and she had lost all her energy, not even wanting to get up. While the pain in her head and throat lessened, fear grew everywhere else, sapping her strength. Fear of the silver-eyed, hook-handed monster that she could almost see waiting for her amidst the red daisies. Fear of her trespasses being found out, forcing the loss of her job. Fear of the fear itself, a vicious circle that exhausted her and filled what little sleep she got with nightmares.

On the morning of the fourth day, the Chief Healer clicked her teeth together and frowned at the patient's lack of progress. She called in another healer to look at Lirael, who bore this patiently. They both decided, in Lirael's hearing, that they would need to call Filris down from her dreaming room.

Lirael started nervously at this announcement. Among other things, Filris was the Infirmarian, and the oldest of the Clayr still living. For all of Lirael's life, Filris had spent most of her time in her dreaming room, and presumably working in the Infirmary as well, though Lirael had never seen her on either of the two occasions she had been hospitalized with childhood illnesses.

She had never seen any of the really old Clayr, the ones old enough to retire to dreaming rooms of their own. They needed such rooms because the Sight tended to grow progressively more difficult with age, sending more and more frequent visions, but in smaller splinters, which could not be controlled, even with the focusing powers of ice and the Nine Day Watch. It was not uncommon for some of the more ancient Clayr to perceive only these fragmented futures and not be able to interact with the present at all.

However, when Filris arrived an hour later, she came alone and clearly needed no help with the ordinary world. Lirael eyed her suspiciously, seeing a short, slight woman with hair as white as the snow atop Starmount and skin like aged parchment, the underlying veins a delicate tracery upon her face, counterpoint to the wrinkles of extreme age.

She inspected Lirael from head to foot, without speaking, her paper-dry hands gently prodding her to move in the directions she required. Finally, she looked down Lirael's throat, staring at it for some time, a small bauble of Charter-Magicked light floating an inch from Lirael's stiffening jaw. When Filris finally stopped looking, she sent the Healer from the ward and sat beside Lirael's bed. Silence crept over them, for the ward was empty now. The other seven beds were vacant.

Eventually, Lirael made a noise that was halfway between clearing her throat and a sob. She moved her hair away from her face and nervously looked at Filris—and was caught in the gaze of her pale blue eyes.

"So you are Lirael," said Filris. "And the healer tells me you fell down the stairs. But I do not think your throat was damaged by a scream. To be frank, I am surprised you are still alive. I know of no other Clayr your age—and few of any age—who could speak such a mark without being consumed by it."

"How?" croaked Lirael. "How can you tell?"

"Experience," replied Filris dryly. "I have worked in this Infirmary for over a hundred years. You are not the first Clayr

I have seen suffer from the effects of attempting overambitious magic. Also, I am curious as to how you came by these other injuries at the same time, particularly since the glass dug out of your feet is pure crystal, and certainly not the same as that of the glasses from the Zally Fountain."

Lirael swallowed, but didn't speak. The silence returned. Filris waited patiently.

"I'll lose my job," whispered Lirael at last. "I'll be sent back to the Hall."

"No," said Filris, taking her hand. "What passes between us here shall go no further."

"I've been stupid," said Lirael huskily. "I've let something out. Something dangerous—dangerous to everyone. All the Clayr."

"Hmph!" snorted Filris. "It can't be that bad if it hasn't done anything in the last four days. Besides, 'all the Clayr' can look after its collective self very well. It's you I'm concerned about. You are letting your fear come between you and getting better. Now start from the beginning, and tell me everything."

"You won't tell Kirrith? Or the Chief?" asked Lirael desperately. If Filris told anybody, they'd take her away from the Library, and then she'd have nothing. Nothing at all.

"If you mean Vancelle, no I won't," replied Filris. She patted Lirael's hand and said, "I won't tell anybody. Particularly since I am coming to the conclusion that I should have looked in on you long ago, Lirael. I had no notion you were more than a child . . . but tell me. What happened?"

Slowly, her voice so soft that Filris had to lean close, Lirael told her. About her birthday, about going up to the terrace, meeting Sanar and Ryelle, getting her job and how much it had helped her. She told Filris about waking the spells in the bracelet, about the sunburst and crescent-moon doors. Her voice grew softer still as she spoke of the horror in the glass-roofed coffin. The statuette of the dog. The struggle up the spiral and the plans she had made as her mind wandered. Her faked fall.

They spoke for more than an hour, Filris questioning, bringing out all Lirael's fears, hopes, and dreams. At the end of it, Lirael felt peaceful and no longer afraid, emptied of all the knotted pain and anguish that had filled her.

When Lirael finished talking, Filris asked to see the dog statuette. Lirael took the little stone dog from under her pillow and reluctantly handed it over. She had grown very attached to it, for it was the one thing that brought her some comfort, and she was afraid that Filris would take it away or tell her it must go back to the Library.

The old woman took the statuette in both hands, cupping it so only the snout was visible, thrusting out between her withered fingers. She looked at it for a long time, then gave a deep sigh and handed it back. Lirael took it, surprised by the warmth the stone had gained from the old woman's hands. Still, Filris didn't move or speak, till Lirael sat up straighter in bed, attracting her attention.

"I'm sorry, Lirael. I thank you for telling me the truth. And for showing me the dog statuette. It has been a long time coming, so long that I had thought I would be lost in the future, too mad to see it true."

"What do you mean?" asked Lirael uneasily.

"I saw your little dog long ago," explained Filris. "When the Sight still came clearly to me. It was the last vision that came to me whole and unbroken. I Saw an old, old woman, peering closely at a small stone dog clasped in her hands. It took me many years to realize that the old woman was myself."

"Did you See me, too?" asked Lirael.

"I Saw only myself," said Filris calmly. "What it means,

I'm afraid, is that we shall not meet again. I would have liked to help you defeat the creature you have released, by counsel if not by deed, for I fear that it must be dealt with as soon as you can. Things of that ilk do not wake without reason, or without help of some kind. I would also like to see your dog-sending. I regret that I will not. Most of all I regret that I have not lived enough in the present these last fifteen years. I should have met you sooner, Lirael. It is a failing of the Clayr that we tend to forget individuals sometimes, and we ignore their troubles, knowing that all such things will pass."

"What do you mean?" asked Lirael. For the first time in her life, she'd felt comfortable talking to someone about herself, about her life. Now it seemed that this was only a tantalizing taste of the intimacy other people enjoyed, as if she were fated to never have what other Clayr took for granted.

"Every Clayr is given the gift to See some portent of her death, though not the death itself, for no human could bear that weight. Almost twenty years ago I Saw myself and your little dog, and in time I realized that this was the vision that foretold my final days."

"But I need you," said Lirael, weeping, throwing her arms around the slight figure. "I need someone! I can't keep going on my own!"

"You can and you will," said Filris fiercely. "Make your dog your companion, to be the friend you need. You must learn about the creature you released and defeat it! Explore the Library. Remember that while the Clayr can See the future, others make it. I feel that you will be a maker, not a seer. You must promise me that it will be so. Promise me that you will not give in. Promise me that you will never give up hope. Make your future, Lirael!"

"I'll try," whispered Lirael, feeling the fierce energy of Filris flowing into her. "I'll try."

Filris gripped her hand, harder than Lirael would have thought possible with those thin, ancient fingers. Then she kissed Lirael on the forehead, sending a tingle of energy through her Charter mark, right through her body and out the soles of her feet.

"I was never close to Arielle, or her mother," Filris said quietly. "Too much a Clayr, I suppose, too much in the future. I am glad I was not too late to speak to you. Goodbye, my great-great-granddaughter. Remember your promise!"

With that, she walked out of the ward, straight-backed and proud, so that someone who didn't know her age would never guess that she had worked in these wards for more than a hundred years, and lived half as long again.

Lirael never saw Filris again. She wept with many others at the Farewell in the Hall, forgetting her distaste for the new blue tunic, hardly noticing that she stood a full head higher than all the other children and many of the white-clad Clayr who had newly Awoken to their gift.

She was unsure how much she cried for Filris and how much she cried for herself, left alone again. It seemed to be her fate that she would have no close friends. Only countless cousins, and one aunt.

But Lirael didn't forget Filris's words and was back at work the next day, though her voice was still weak, and she had a slight limp. Within a week, she managed to secretly obtain copies of *On the Making of Sendings* and *Superior Sendings in Seventy Days*, as *The Making and Mastery of Magical Beings* proved too difficult to spirit out of its locked case. The bestiaries proved troublesome, too, as all the ones she could find were chained to their shelves. She dipped into them when no one was around, but without immediate success. Clearly, it would take some time to find out exactly what the creature was.

Whenever she could, she passed the sunburst door and felt for her spell, checking that her magic still remained, binding door, hinges, and lock into the surrounding stone. The fear always rose in her then, and sometimes she thought she smelled the corrosive tang of Free Magic, as if the monster stood on the other side of the door, separated from her only by the thin barrier of wood and spells.

Then she would remember Filris's words, and hurry back to her study to work on her dog-sending; or to the latest bestiary she'd found, to see if it might describe a woman-like creature with eyes of silver fire and the claws of a praying mantis, a creature of Free Magic, malice, and awful hunger.

Sometimes she would wake in the night, a nightmare of the door opening fading as she struggled out of sleep. She would have checked the door more often, but following the day of the Watch of Fifteen Sixty-Eight, the Chief Librarian had ordered that all librarians must go into the Old Levels only in pairs, so it was harder to sneak there and back. The Watch had not Seen anything conclusive, Lirael heard, but the Clayr were obviously worried about something close to home. The Library was not the only department to take precautionary measures: extra Rangers patrolled the glacier and the bridges, the steampipe crews also now worked in pairs, and many internal doors and corridors were closed and locked for the first time since the Restoration.

Lirael checked the door to the flower-field room forty-two times over seventy-three days before she found a bestiary that told her what the creature was. In those ten weeks of worry, study, and preparation, she had searched through eleven bestiaries and done most of the preliminary work needed to create her dog-sending.

In fact, it was the dog-sending that was mostly on her mind when she finally did find a mention of the monster. She was thinking about when she could cast the next lot of spells even as her hands opened the small, red-bound book that was simply titled *Creatures by Nagy*. Flicking through the pages without expectation, her eye was caught by an engraving that showed exactly what she was looking for. The accompanying text made it clear that whoever Nagy was, or had been, he or she had encountered the same sort of monster Lirael had released from the glass-covered coffin.

It stands higher than a tall man, generally taking the shape of a comely woman, though its form is fluid. Often the Stilken will have great hooks or pincers in the place of forearms, which it uses with facility to seize its prey. Its mouth generally appears human till it opens, revealing double rows of teeth, as narrow and sharp as needles. These teeth may be of a bright silver, or black as night. The Stilken's eyes are also of silver, and burn with a strange fire.

Lirael shivered as she read this description, making the chain that held the book to the shelf rattle and clank. Quickly she looked around to see if anyone had heard and would come looking between the shelves. But there was no sound save her own breathing. This room was rarely used, housing a collection of obscure personal memoirs. Lirael had come here merely because *Creatures by Nagy* was cross-indexed in the Reading Room as a bestiary of sorts.

Stilling her hands, she read on, the words filling only part of her mind. The rest was struggling with the fact that, now that she had the knowledge she sought, she must face the Stilken and defeat it.

*The Stilken is an elemental of Free Magic, and so it cannot
be harmed by earthly materials, such as common steel. Nor
can human flesh touch it, for its substance is inimical to life.
A Stilken cannot be destroyed, except by Free Magic, at the
hands of a sorcerer more powerful than itself.*

Lirael stopped reading, nervously swallowed and read the
last line again. "Cannot be destroyed, except by Free Magic,"
she read, over and over again. But she couldn't do any Free
Magic. It wasn't allowed. Free Magic was too dangerous.

Unable to think of what she could do, Lirael read on—and
breathed a long sigh of relief as the book continued.

*However, while destruction is the province solely of Free
Magic, a Stilken may be bound by Charter Magic and
imprison'd within a vessel or structure, such as a bottle of
metal or wrought crystal (simple glass being too fragile for
surety) or down a dry well, covered by stone.*

*I have essayed this task myself, using the spells I list
below. But I warn that these bindings are of terrible force,
drawing as they do on no fewer than three of the master
Charter marks. Only a great adept—which I am not—
would dare use them without the assistance of an ensorceled
sword or a rowan wand, charged with the first circle of seven
marks for binding the elements, and in the case of fire and
air, the second circle too, and all of them linked with the
master mark—*

Lirael swallowed again, her throat suddenly sore. The
notation Nagy used was for the same master mark that had
burnt her. Worse than that, she didn't know the second circle
of marks for binding fire and air, and she had no idea how they

could all be put into a sword or a rowan wand. She didn't even know where she could find a rowan tree, for that matter.

Slowly, she shut the book and placed it back on the shelf, careful not to rattle the chain. Part of her was frustrated. Having finally found out what the creature was, she still had to find out more. Another part of her was relieved that she would not have to confront the Stilken. Not yet.

She would have time to create her dog-sending first. At least then she would have something . . . someone to talk to about all this. Even if it couldn't talk back, or help her.

Chapter Ten

DOG DAY

THE FINAL SPELL to create the dog-sending required four hours to cast, so Lirael had to wait for another opportunity when most of the librarians would be away. If she were interrupted during the casting, all her work of the previous months would be wasted, the delicately connected network of Charter-spells broken into their component marks, rather than brought together by the final spell.

The opportunity came sooner than Lirael had expected, for whatever the Clayr were trying to See obviously still eluded them. Lirael heard other librarians muttering about the demands of the Observatory, and it was clear that the Nine Day Watch was growing in size again, starting with a ninety-eight. This time, as each new, larger Watch was called, Lirael carefully observed the time of the summons and noted when the Clayr returned. When the full Fifteen Sixty-Eight was called—amidst considerable grumbling in the Reading Room—she estimated she had at least six hours. Time enough to finish her sending.

In her study, the dog statuette sat benignly, surveying Lirael's preparations from the top of her desk. Lirael spoke to it as she locked the door, with a spell since she wasn't senior enough to rate a key or bar.

"This is it, little dog," she said cheerfully, reaching over to stroke the dog's stone snout with one finger. The sound of her own voice surprised her, not because of the huskiness that still remained from her damaged throat, but because it sounded strange and unfamiliar. She realized then that she hadn't spoken for two days. The other librarians had long accepted her silence, and she had not recently been taxed with any conversation that required more than a nod, a shake of the head, or simply instant application to an ordered task.

The beginning of the dog-sending was under her desk, hidden by a draped cloth. Lirael reached in, removed the cloth, and gently slid out the framework she had built to start the spell. She ran her hands over it, feeling the warmth of the Charter marks that swam lazily up and down the twisted silver wires that formed the shape of a dog. It was a small dog, about a foot high, the size constrained by the amount of silver wire Lirael could easily obtain. Besides, she thought a small dog-sending would be more sensible than a big one. She wanted a comfortable friend, not a dog large enough to be a guard-sending.

Aside from the framework of silver wire, the dog shape had two eyes made from jet buttons and a nose of black felt, all of them already imbued with Charter marks. It also had a tail made from braided dog hair, clipped surreptitiously from several visiting dogs down in the Lower Refectory. That tail was already prepared with Charter marks, marks that defined something of what it was to be a dog.

The final part of the spell required Lirael to reach into the Charter and pluck forth several thousand Charter marks, letting them flow through her and into the silver-wire armature. Marks that fully described a dog, and marks that would give the semblance of life, though not the actuality.

When the spell was finished, the silver wire, jet buttons, and braided dog hair would be gone, replaced by a puppy-sized dog of spell-flesh. It would look like a dog till you got close enough to see the Charter marks that made it up, but she wouldn't be able to touch it. Touching most sendings was like touching water: the skin would yield and then re-form around whatever touched it. All the toucher would feel was the buzz and warmth of the Charter marks.

Lirael sat down cross-legged next to the silver-wire model and started to empty her mind, taking slow breaths, forcing them down so far that her stomach pushed outwards as the air reached the very bottoms of her lungs.

She was just about to reach into the Charter and begin when her eye caught sight of the small stone dog, up on the desk. It somehow looked lonely up there, as if it felt left out. Impulsively, Lirael got up and set it in her lap when she sat back down. The small carving tilted slightly but stayed upright, looking at the silver-wire copy of itself.

Lirael took a few more breaths and began again. She had written out the marks she required, in the safe shorthand all Mages used to record Charter marks. But those papers stayed by her side, still in a neat pile. She found that the first marks came easily, and those after them seemed to almost choose themselves. Mark after mark leapt out of the flow of the Charter and into her mind, then as quickly out, crossing to the silver-wire dog in an arc of golden lightning.

As more and more marks rushed through her, Lirael slipped further into a trance state, barely aware of anything except the Charter and the marks that filled her. The golden lightning became a solid bridge of light from her outstretched hands to the silver wires, growing brighter by the second. Lirael closed her eyes against the glare, and she felt herself slip towards the edge of dream, her conscious mind barely awake. Images moved restlessly between the marks in her mind. Images of dogs, many dogs, of all shapes, colors, and sizes. Dogs barking. Dogs running after thrown sticks. Dogs refusing to run. Puppies waddling on uncertain paws. Old dogs shivering themselves upright. Happy dogs. Sad dogs. Hungry dogs. Fat, sleepy dogs.

More and more images flashed through, till Lirael felt she had seen glimpses of every dog that had ever lived. But still the Charter marks roared through her mind. She had long lost track of where she was up to, or which marks were next—and the golden light was too bright for her to see how much of the sending was done.

Yet the marks flowed on. Lirael realized that not only did she not know which mark she was up to—she didn't even know the marks that were passing through her head! Strange, unknown marks were pouring out of her into the sending. Powerful marks that rocked her body as they left, forcing everything else out of her mind with the urgency of their passage.

Desperately, Lirael tried to open her eyes, to see what the marks were doing—but the glow was blinding now, and hot. She tried to stand up, to direct the flow of marks into the wall or ceiling. But her body seemed disconnected from her brain. She could feel everything, but her legs and arms wouldn't move, just as if she were trying to wake herself from the end of a dream.

Still the marks came, and then Lirael's nostrils caught the terrible, unmistakable reek of Free Magic, and she knew something had gone terribly, horribly wrong.

She tried to scream, but no sound came out, only Charter marks that leapt from her mouth towards the golden radiance. Charter marks continued to fly from her fingers, too, and swam in her eyes, spilling down inside her tears, which turned to steam as they fell.

More and more marks flew through Lirael, through her tears and her silent screaming. They swarmed through like an endless flight of bright butterflies forced through a garden gate. But even as the thousands and thousands of marks flung themselves into the brightness, the smell of Free Magic rose, and a crackling white light formed in the center of the golden glow, so bright it shone through Lirael's shut eyelids, piercing her brimming eyes.

Held motionless by the torrent of Charter Magic, Lirael could do nothing as the white light grew stronger, subduing the rich golden glow of the swirling marks. It was the end, she knew. Whatever she'd done now, it was much, much worse than freeing a Stilken; so much worse that she couldn't really comprehend it. All she knew was that the marks that passed through her now were more ancient and more powerful than anything she had ever seen. Even if the Free Magic that grew in front of her spared her life, the Charter marks would burn her to a husk.

Except, she realized, they didn't hurt. Either she was in shock and already dying, or the marks weren't harming her. Any one of them would have killed her if she'd tried to use them normally. But several hundred had already stormed through, and she was still breathing. Wasn't she?

Frightened by the thought that she might not be breathing, Lirael focused all her remaining energy on inhaling—just as the tremendous flow of marks suddenly stopped. She felt her connection to the Charter sever as the last mark jumped across to the boiling mass of gold and white light that had been her silver-wire dog. Her breath came with sudden force, and she overbalanced, falling backwards. At the last moment, she caught the edge of the bookshelf, almost pulling that on top of her. But the shelf didn't quite go over, and she pulled herself back up to a sitting position, ready to use her newly filled lungs to scream.

The scream stayed unborn. Where the Free Magic and Charter marks had fought in their sparking, swirling brilliance, there was now a globe of utter darkness that occupied the space where the wire dog and the desk had been. The awful tang of Free Magic was gone, too, replaced by a sort of damp animal odor that Lirael couldn't quite identify.

A tiny pinprick star appeared on the black surface of the globe, and then another, and another, till it was no longer dark but as star-filled as a clear night sky. Lirael stared at it, mesmerized by the multitude of stars. They grew brighter and brighter, till she was forced to blink.

In the instant of that blink, the globe disappeared, leaving behind a dog. Not a cute, cuddly Charter sending of a puppy, but a waist-high black and tan mongrel that seemed to be entirely real, including its impressive teeth. It had none of the characteristics of a sending. The only hint of its magical origin was a thick collar around its neck that swam with even more Charter marks that Lirael had never seen before.

The dog looked exactly like a life-size, breathing version of the stone statuette. Lirael stared at the real thing, then down at her lap.

The statuette was gone.

She looked back up. The dog was still there, scratching its ear with a back foot, eyes half-closed with concentration. It was soaking wet, as if it had just been for a swim.

Suddenly, the dog stopped scratching, stood up, and shook itself, spraying droplets of dirty water all over Lirael and all over the study. Then it ambled across and licked the petrified girl on the face with a tongue that most definitely was all real dog and not some Charter-made imitation.

When that got no response, it grinned and announced, "I am the Disreputable Dog. Or Disreputable Bitch, if you want to get technical. When are we going for a walk?"

Chapter Eleven

T HE WALK THAT Lirael and the Disreputable Dog took that day was the first of many, though Lirael never could remember exactly where they went, or what she said, or what the Dog answered. All she could recall was being in the same sort of daze she'd had when she'd hit her head— only this time she wasn't hurt.

Not that it mattered, because the Disreputable Dog never really answered her questions. Later, Lirael would repeat the same questions and get different, still-evasive answers. The most important questions—"What are you? Where did you come from?"—had a whole range of answers, starting with "I'm the Disreputable Dog" and "from elsewhere" and occasionally becoming as eloquent as "I'm your Dog" and "You tell me—it was your spell."

The Dog also refused, or was unable, to answer questions about her nature. She seemed in most respects to be exactly like a real dog, albeit a speaking one. At least at first.

For the first two weeks they were together, the Dog slept in Lirael's study, under the replacement desk that Lirael had been forced to purloin from an empty study nearby. She had no idea what had happened to her own, as not a bit of it remained after the Dog's sudden appearance.

The Dog ate the food Lirael stole for her from the Refectory or the kitchens. She went walking with Lirael four times a day in the most disused corridors and rooms Lirael could find, a nerve-wracking exercise, though somehow the Dog always managed to hide from approaching Clayr at the last second. She was discreet in other ways as well, always choosing dark and unused corners to use as a toilet—though she did like to alert Lirael to the fact that she had done so, even if her human friend declined to sniff at the result.

In fact, apart from her collar of Charter marks and the fact that she could talk, the Disreputable Dog really did seem to be just a rather large dog of uncertain parentage and curious origin.

But of course she wasn't. Lirael sneaked back to her study one evening after dinner, to find the Dog reading on the floor. The Dog was turning the pages of a large grey book that Lirael didn't recognize, with one paw—a paw that had grown longer and separated out into three extremely flexible fingers.

The Dog looked up from the book as her supposed mistress froze in the doorway. All Lirael could think of were the words in Nagy's book, about the Stilken's form being fluid—and the way the hook-handed creature had stretched and thinned to get through the gate guarded by the crescent moon.

"You *are* a Free Magic thing," she blurted out, reaching into her waistcoat pocket for the clockwork mouse, as her lips felt for the whistle on her lapel. This time she wouldn't make a mistake. She'd call for help right away.

"No, I'm not," protested the Dog, her ears stiffening in outrage as her paw shrank back to its normal proportions. "I'm definitely not a *thing*! I'm as much a part of the Charter as you are, albeit with special properties. Look at my collar! And I am definitely not a Stilken or any other of the several hundred variations thereof."

"What do you know about Stilken?" asked Lirael. She still

didn't enter the study, and the clockwork mouse was ready in her hand. "Why did you mention them in particular?"

"I read a lot," replied the Dog, yawning. Then she sniffed, and her eyes lit up with expectation. "Is that a ham bone you have there?"

Lirael didn't answer but moved the paper-wrapped object in her left hand behind her back. "How did you know I was thinking about a Stilken just then? And I still don't know you aren't one yourself, or something even worse."

"Feel my collar!" protested the Dog as she edged forward, licking her chops. Clearly the current conversation wasn't as interesting as the prospect of food.

"How did you know I was thinking about a Stilken?" repeated Lirael, giving each word a slow and considered emphasis. She held the ham bone over her head as she spoke, watching the Dog's head tilt back to follow the movement. Surely a Free Magic creature wouldn't be this interested in a ham bone.

"I guessed, because you seem to be thinking about Stilken quite a lot," replied the Dog, gesturing with a paw at the books on the desk. "You are studying everything required to bind a Stilken. Besides, you also wrote 'Stilken' fourteen times yesterday on that paper you burnt. I read it backwards on the blotter. And I've smelled your spell on the door down below, and the Stilken that waits beyond it."

"You've been out by yourself!" exclaimed Lirael. Forgetting that she had been afraid of whatever the Dog might be, she stormed in, slamming the door behind her. In the process, she dropped the clockwork mouse, but not the ham bone.

The mouse bounced twice and landed at the Dog's feet. Lirael held her breath, all too aware that the door was now shut at her back, which would greatly delay the mouse if she needed help. But the Dog didn't seem dangerous, and she was so much easier to talk to than people were . . . except for Filris, who was gone.

The Disreputable Dog sniffed at the mouse eagerly for an instant, then pushed it aside with her nose and transferred her attention back to the ham bone.

Lirael sighed, picked up the mouse, and put it back in her pocket. She unwrapped the bone and gave it to the Dog, who immediately snatched it up and deposited it in a far corner under the desk.

"That's your dinner," said Lirael, wrinkling her nose. "You'd better eat it before it starts to smell."

"I'll take it out and bury it later, in the ice," replied the Dog. She hesitated and hung her head a little before adding, "Besides, I don't actually need to eat. I just like to."

"What!" exclaimed Lirael, cross again. "You mean I've been stealing food for nothing! If I were caught I'd—"

"Not for nothing!" interrupted the Dog, sidling over to butt her head against Lirael's hip and look up at her with wide, beseeching eyes. "For me. And much appreciated, too. Now, you really should feel my collar. It will show you that I am not a Stilken, Margrue, or Hish. You can scratch my neck at the same time."

Lirael hesitated, but the Dog felt so like the friendly dogs she scratched when they visited the Refectory that her hand almost automatically went to the Dog's back. She felt warm dog skin and the silky, short hair, and she began to scratch along the Dog's spine, up towards the neck. The Dog shivered and muttered, "Up a bit. Across to the left. No, back. Aahhh!"

Then Lirael touched the collar, just with two fingers—and was momentarily thrown out of the world altogether. All she could see, hear, and feel were Charter marks, all around, as if she had somehow fallen into the Charter. There was no leather

collar under her hand, no Dog, no study. Nothing but the
Charter.

Then she was suddenly back in herself again, swaying and
dizzy. Both her hands were scratching the Dog under the chin,
without her knowing how they had got there.

"Your collar," Lirael said, when she got her balance back.
"Your collar is like a Charter Stone—a way into the Charter.
Yet I saw Free Magic in your making. It has to be there some-
where . . . doesn't it?"

She fell silent, but the Dog didn't answer, till Lirael stopped
scratching. Then she turned her head and jumped up, licking
Lirael across her open mouth.

"You needed a friend," said the Dog, as Lirael spluttered
and wiped her mouth with both sleeves, one after the other. "I
came. Isn't that enough to be going on with? You know my
collar is of the Charter, and whatever else I may be, it would
constrain my actions, even if I did mean you any harm. And
we do have a Stilken to deal with, do we not?"

"Yes," said Lirael. On an impulse, she bent down and
hugged the Dog around the neck, feeling both warm dog and
the soft buzz of the Charter marks in the Dog's collar through
the thin material of her shirt.

The Disreputable Dog bore this patiently for a minute, then
made a sort of wheezing sound and shuffled her paws. Lirael
understood this from her time with the visiting dogs, and let go.

"Now," pronounced the Dog. "The Stilken must be dealt
with as soon as possible, before it gets free and finds even
worse things to release, or let in from outside. I presume you
have obtained the necessary items to bind it?"

"No," said Lirael. "Not if you mean the stuff Nagy men-
tions: a rowan wand or a sword, infused with the Charter
marks—"

"Yes, yes," said the Dog hastily, before Lirael could recite the whole list. "I know. Why haven't you got one?"

"They don't just lie around," replied Lirael defensively. "I thought I could get an ordinary sword and put the—"

"Take too long. Months!" interrupted the Dog, who had started pacing to and fro in a serious manner. "That Stilken will be through your door spell in a few days, I would think."

"What!" screamed Lirael. Then she said more quietly, "What? You mean it's escaping?"

"It will soon," confirmed the Dog. "I thought you knew. Free Magic can corrode Charter marks as well as flesh. I suppose you could renew the spell."

Lirael shook her head. Her throat still hadn't recovered from the master mark she'd used last time. It would be too risky to chance speaking it again before she was completely better. Not without the added strength of a Charter-spelled sword— which brought her back to the original problem.

"You'll have to borrow a sword, then," declared the Dog, fixing Lirael with a serious eye. "I don't suppose anyone will have the right sort of wand. Not really a Clayr thing, rowan."

"I don't think swords redolent with binding spells are, either," protested Lirael, slumping into her chair. "Why couldn't I just be an ordinary Clayr? If I'd got the Sight, I wouldn't be wandering around the Library getting into trouble! If I ever do get the Sight, I swear by the Charter I am never going to go exploring, ever again!"

"Mmmm," said the Dog, with an expression Lirael couldn't fathom, though it seemed to be loaded with hidden meaning. "That's as may be. On the matter of swords, you are in error. There are a number of swords of power within these halls. The Captain of the Rangers has one, the Observatory Guard have three—well, one is an axe, but it holds the same spells within its steel. Closer to home, the Chief Librarian has one, too. A very old and famous sword, in fact, most appropriately named Binder. It will do nicely."

Lirael looked at the Dog with such a blank stare that the hound stopped pacing, cleared her throat, and said, "Pay attention, Lirael. I said that you were in error about—"

"I heard what you said," snapped Lirael. "You must be absolutely mad! I can't steal the Chief's sword! She always has it with her! She probably sleeps with it!"

"She does," replied the Dog smugly. "I checked."

"Dog!" wailed Lirael, trying to keep her breathing down to less than one breath a second. "Please, please do not go looking in the Chief Librarian's rooms! Or anywhere else! What would happen if someone saw you?"

"They didn't," replied the Dog happily. "Anyway, the Chief keeps the sword in her bedroom, but not actually in bed with her. She puts it on a stand next to her bed. So you can borrow it while she's asleep."

"No," replied Lirael, shaking her head. "I'm not creeping into the Chief's bedroom. I'd rather fight the Stilken without a sword."

"Then you'll die," said the Disreputable Dog, suddenly very serious. "The Stilken will drink your blood and grow stronger from it. Then it will creep out into the lower reaches of the Library, emerging every now and then to capture librarians, to take them one by one, feasting on their flesh in some dark corner where the bones will never be found. It will find allies, creatures bound even deeper in the Library, and will open doors for the evil that lurks outside. You must bind it, but you cannot succeed without the sword."

"What if you help me?" asked Lirael. There had to be some way of avoiding the Chief, some way that didn't involve swords at all. Trying to get Mirelle's sword, or the ones from the Observatory, would not be any easier than the Chief's. She didn't even know exactly where the Observatory was.

"I'd like to," replied the Dog. "But it is your Stilken. You let it out. You must deal with the consequences."

"So you won't help," said Lirael sadly. She had hoped, just for a moment, that the Disreputable Dog would step in and fix everything for her. She was a magical creature, after all, possibly of some power. But not enough to take on a Stilken, it seemed.

"I will advise," said the Dog. "As is only proper. But you will have to borrow the sword yourself, and perform the binding. Tonight is probably as good a time as any."

"Tonight?" asked Lirael, in a very small voice.

"Tonight," confirmed the Dog. "At the stroke of midnight, when all such adventures should begin, you will enter the Chief Librarian's room. The sword is on the left, past the wardrobe, which is strangely full of black waistcoats. If all goes well, you will be able to return it before the dawn."

"If all goes well," repeated Lirael somberly, remembering the silver fire in the Stilken's eyes, and those terrible hooks. "Do you . . . do you think I should leave a note, in case . . . in case all does not go well?"

"Yes," said the Dog, removing the last small shred of Lirael's self-confidence. "Yes. That would be a very good idea."

Chapter Twelve

INTO THE LAIR OF THE CHIEF LIBRARIAN

WHEN THE GREAT water-powered clock in the Middle Refectory showed fifteen minutes to midnight, Lirael left her hiding spot in the breakfast servery and climbed up through an air shaft to the Narrow Way, which would in turn take her to the Southscape and Chief Librarian Vancelle's rooms.

Lirael had dressed in her librarian's uniform in case she met anyone, and carried an envelope addressed to the Chief. A skeleton staff of librarians did work through the night, though they didn't usually employ Third Assistants like Lirael. If she was stopped, Lirael would claim she was taking an urgent message. In fact, the envelope contained her "just in case" note, alerting the Chief to the presence of the Stilken.

But she didn't meet anyone. No one came down the Narrow Way, which lived up to its name by being too narrow for two people to pass abreast. It was rarely used, because if you did meet someone going the other way, the more junior Clayr would have to backtrack—sometimes for its entire length, which was more than half a mile.

The Southscape was wider, and much more risky for Lirael because so many senior Clayr had rooms off its broad expanse. Fortunately, the marks that lit it so brightly during the day had faded to a glimmer at night, producing heavy shadows for her to hide in.

The door to the Chief's rooms, however, was brightly lit by a ring of Charter marks around the book-and-sword emblem that was carved into the stone next to the doorway.

Lirael looked at the lights balefully. Not for the first time, she wondered what she was doing. It probably would have been better to confess months ago when she initially got into trouble. Then someone else could deal with the Stilken—

A touch at her leg made her jump and almost scream. She stifled the scream as she recognized the Disreputable Dog.

"I thought you weren't going to help," she whispered, as the Dog jumped up and attempted to lick her face. "Get down, you idiot!"

"I'm not helping," said the Dog happily. "I've come to watch."

"Great," replied Lirael, trying to sound sarcastic. Secretly, she was pleased. Somehow, the lair of the Chief Librarian seemed less threatening with the Dog along.

"When is something going to happen?" the Dog asked a minute later, as Lirael still stood in the shadows, watching the door.

"Now," said Lirael, hoping that saying the word would give her the courage to begin. "Now!"

She crossed the corridor in ten long strides, gripped the bronze doorknob, and pushed. No Clayr needed to lock her door, so Lirael wasn't expecting any resistance. The door opened, and Lirael stepped in, the Dog whisking past her on the way.

She shut the door quietly behind her and turned to survey the room. It was mainly a living space, dominated by bookshelves on three walls, several comfortable chairs, and a tall, thin sculpture of a sort of squashed-in horse, carved out of translucent stone.

But it was the fourth wall that attracted Lirael's attention.

It was a single, vast window from floor to ceiling, made of the clearest, cleanest glass Lirael had ever seen.

Through the window, Lirael could see the entire Ratterlin valley stretching southward, the river a wide streak of silver far below, shining in the moonlight. It was snowing lightly outside, and snowflakes whirled about in wild dances as they fell down the mountainside. None stuck to the window, or left any mark upon it.

Lirael flinched and stepped back as a dark shape swooped past, straight through the falling snow. Then she realized it was only an owl, heading down the valley for a midnight snack.

"There's lots to do before dawn," whispered the Dog conversationally, as Lirael kept staring out the window, transfixed by that ribbon of silver winding off to the far horizon and by the strange moonlit vista that stretched as far as she could see. Beyond the horizon lay the Kingdom proper: the great city of Belisaere, with all its marvels, open to the sky and surrounded by the sea. All the world—the world that the other Clayr Saw in the ice of the Observatory—was out there, but all she knew of it was from books or from travelers' tales overheard in the Lower Refectory.

For the first time, Lirael wondered what the Clayr were trying to See out there with the greatly expanded Watches. Where was the place that resisted the Sight? What was the future that was beginning there, perhaps even as she looked out?

Something tickled at the back of her mind, a sense of déjà vu or a fleeting memory. But nothing came, and she remained entranced, staring at the outside world.

"A lot to do!" repeated the Dog, a little louder.

Reluctantly, Lirael tore herself away and concentrated on the task at hand. The Chief's bedroom had to be beyond this room. But where was the door? There were only the window, the door leading outside, and the bookshelves. . . .

Lirael smiled as she saw that the end of one shelf was occupied by a door-handle rather than tightly packed books. Trust the Chief to have a door that doubled as a bookshelf.

"The sword is on a stand just to the left," whispered the Dog, who suddenly seemed a bit anxious. "Don't open the door too much."

"Thanks," replied Lirael as she gingerly tested the door handle, to see if it had to be pulled, pushed, or turned. "But I thought you weren't helping."

The Dog didn't answer, because as soon as Lirael touched it, the whole bookcase swung open. Lirael only just managed to get a firm enough grasp on the handle to stop it from opening completely, and had to haul it back to leave a gap wide enough for herself to slide through.

The bedroom was dark, lit only by the moonlight in the outer chamber. Lirael poked her head in very slowly and let her eyes adjust, her ears trying to catch any sound of movement or sudden waking.

After a minute or so, she could see the faint dark mass of a bed, and the regular breathing of someone asleep—though she wasn't sure if she could really hear that or was just imagining it.

As the Dog had said, there was a stand near the door. A sort of cylindrical metal cage that was open only at the top. Even in the dim light, Lirael could see that Binder was there, in its scabbard. The pommel was only a few inches below the top of the stand, in easy reach. But she would have to be right next to the stand to lift the sword high enough to clear the cage.

She ducked back out and took a deep breath. The air seemed closer in the bedroom somehow. Darker, and cloying, as if it conspired against thieves like Lirael.

The Dog looked at her and winked encouragingly. Still, Lirael's heart started to beat faster and faster as she edged back through the door, and she suddenly felt strangely cold.

A few, small, careful steps took her next to the stand. She touched it with both hands, then gingerly moved to grab the sword by the grip, and the scabbard just below the hilt.

Lirael's fingers had barely touched the metal when the sword suddenly let out a low whistle, and Charter marks flared into brilliance across the hilt. Instantly, Lirael let go and hunched forward, trying to muffle both light and sound with her body. She didn't dare turn around. She didn't want to see the Chief awake and furious.

But there was no sudden shout of outrage, no stern voice demanding to know what she was doing. The red blur in front of her eyes faded as her night vision returned, and she cocked an ear to try and hear anything above the steady drumbeat of her own heart.

Both whistle and the light had lasted no more than a second, she realized. Even so, it was clear that Binder chose who would—or would not—wield it.

Lirael thought about this for a moment, then bent down and whispered, so low that she could hardly hear it herself.

"Binder, I would borrow you for this night, for I need your help to bind a Stilken, a creature of Free Magic. I promise that you will be returned before the dawn. I swear this by the Charter, whose mark I bear."

She touched the Charter mark on her forehead, wincing as its sudden flare of light lit up the stand. Then she touched the pommel of Binder with the same two fingers.

It didn't whistle, and the marks in its hilt merely glowed. Lirael almost sighed, but swallowed the sigh at the last moment, before it could give her away.

The sword came free of the stand without a sound, though Lirael had to lift it high over her own head for the point to clear, and it was heavy. She hadn't realized how heavy it would be, or how long. It felt as if it weighed double her little practice sword, and it was easily a third as long again. Too long to clip the scabbard to her belt, unless she wore the belt under her armpits, or let the point drag along the ground.

This sword was never made for a fourteen-year-old girl, Lirael concluded, as she edged back out and carefully shut the door. She resisted thinking any further than that.

There was no sign of the Disreputable Dog. Lirael looked around, but there was nothing big enough for the Dog to hide behind—unless she'd somehow shrunk herself and gone under one of the chairs.

"Dog! I've got it! Let's go!" hissed Lirael.

There was no answer. Lirael waited for at least a minute, though it seemed much longer. Then she went to the outer door and put her head against it, listening for footsteps in the corridor outside. Getting back to the Library with the sword would be the trickiest part of the venture. It would be impossible to explain to any Clayr she met.

She couldn't hear anything, so she slipped outside. As the door clicked shut behind her, Lirael saw a shadow suddenly stretch out of the dark edge on the other side, and a jolt of fear went through her. But once again, it was only the Disreputable Dog.

"You scared me!" whispered Lirael, as she hurried into the shadows herself, and along to the Second Back Stair that would take her directly down to the Library. "Why didn't you wait?"

"I don't like waiting," said the Dog, trotting along at her heels. "Besides, I wanted to take a look in Mirelle's rooms."

"No!" exclaimed Lirael, louder than she intended. She

dropped to one knee, put the sword into the crook of one arm, and gripped the Dog's lower jaw. "I told you not to go into people's rooms! What will we do if someone decides you're a menace?"

"I *am* a menace," mumbled the Dog. "When I want to be. Besides, I knew she wasn't there. I could smell she wasn't."

"Please, please, don't go looking anywhere people might see you," begged Lirael. "Promise me you won't."

The Dog tried to look away, but Lirael held her jaw. Eventually she muttered something that possibly contained the word "promise." Lirael decided that, given the circumstances, that would have to do.

A few minutes later, slinking down the Second Back Stair, Lirael remembered her own promise to Binder. She'd sworn she'd return it to Vancelle's bedroom before dawn. But what if she couldn't?

They left the Stair and headed down the main spiral until they were almost at the door to the flower-field room. When it came in sight, Lirael suddenly stopped. The Dog, who was several yards behind, loped up and looked at her enquiringly.

"Dog," Lirael said slowly. "I know you won't help me fight the Stilken. But if I can't bind it, I want you to get Binder and take it back to Vancelle's. Before the dawn."

"You will take it back yourself, Mistress," said the Dog confidently, her voice almost a growl. Then she hesitated, and said in a softer tone, "But I will do as you ask, if it proves necessary. You have my promise."

Lirael nodded her thanks, unable to speak. She walked the final thirty feet to the door. There, she checked that the clock-work mouse was in her right waistcoat pocket and the small silver bottle in her left. Then she unsheathed Binder and, for the first time, held it as a weapon, on guard. The Charter marks on the blade burst into brilliant fire as they sensed the foe, and

Lirael felt the latent strength of the sword's magic. Binder had defeated many strange creatures, she knew, and this filled her with hope—until she remembered that this was probably the first time it was being wielded by a girl who didn't really know what she was doing.

Before that thought could paralyze her, Lirael reached out and broke the locking-spell on the door. As the Dog had said, the spell had been corroded by Free Magic, a corrosion so fierce that the spell broke apart merely at her touch and a whispered command.

Then she waved her wrist. The emeralds of her bracelet flashed, and the door groaned open. Lirael braced herself for the sudden rush of the Stilken's attack—but there was nothing there.

Hesitantly, she stepped through the doorway, her nose twitching, seeking any scent of Free Magic, her eyes wide for the slightest hint of the creature's presence.

Unlike on her earlier visit, there was no bright light beyond the corridor—just an eerie glow, a Charter Magic imitation of moonlight that reduced all colors to shades of grey. Somewhere, in that half-darkness, the Stilken lurked. Lirael raised the sword higher and stepped out into the chamber, the flowers rustling under her feet.

The Disreputable Dog followed ten paces behind, every hair on her back stuck up in a ridge, a low growl rumbling in her chest. There were traces of the Stilken here, but no active scent. It was hiding somehow, waiting in ambush. For a moment the Dog almost spoke. Then she remembered: Lirael must defeat the Stilken alone. She hunkered down on her belly, watching as her mistress walked on through the flowers, towards the tree and the pool—where the Stilken's ambush must surely lie.

ONCE AGAIN, LIRAEL was struck by the silence in the vast chamber of flowers. Apart from the soft rustle of her passage through the daisies, there was no sound at all.

Slowly, circling every few steps to make sure nothing was creeping up on her, Lirael crossed the cavern, right up to the door with the crescent moon. It was still partly open, but she didn't venture inside, thinking that the Stilken might be able to lock her in somehow, if it was still hiding out in the field.

The tree was the most likely spot for the creature to be, Lirael thought, imagining it twined around a branch like a snake. Hidden by the thick green leaves, its silver eyes following her every movement . . .

In the strange light, the oak was only a blot of shadow. The Stilken could even be behind the trunk, slowly circling to keep the tree between it and Lirael. Lirael kept her eyes on the tree, opening them as wide as she could, as if they might capture extra light. Still nothing stirred, so she started to walk towards the tree, her steps getting shorter and shorter and her stomach tighter, twisting with dread.

She was so intent on the tree that her feet splashed into the edge of the pool before she realized it was there. Bright ripples, reflecting in the ersatz moonlight, spread for an instant, then once again the water was still and dark.

Lirael stepped back, shook her feet, and began to skirt around the pool. She could see some definition in the oak now, see separate clumps of leaves and individual branches. But there were also clots of shadow that could be anything. Every time her eyes shifted, she thought she saw movement in the darkness.

It was time for a light, she decided, even if that meant giving her own position away. She reached into the Charter, and the requisite marks began to swim into her mind—and were lost, as the Stilken erupted out of the pool beside her and attacked with its ferocious hooks.

Somehow, Binder met them in a spray of white sparks and steam, and a shock that nearly dislocated Lirael's shoulder. She stumbled back, screaming with sudden battle rage as much as panic, instinctively dropping into the guard position. Sparks flew again and water hissed as the Stilken attacked again, its hooks barely parried in time by Lirael and Binder.

Without conscious thought, Lirael gave ground, backing towards the oak. All her knowledge of the binding-spells had left her head, as had her sense of the Charter. Survival was all that mattered now, getting her sword in place to block the murderous assault of the monster.

It swung again, low, towards her legs. Lirael parried, and surprised herself as her incompletely trained muscles took over. She riposted directly at the thing's torso. Binder's point hit and skittered across its gut, sending up a blaze of sparks that peppered Lirael's waistcoat with tiny holes.

But the Stilken didn't seem hurt, only annoyed. It attacked again, every sweep of its hooks forcing Lirael back several paces. Desperately, she swung Binder, feeling the shock of every parry through to her bones. The weight of the sword was already wearing her out. She had never been much of a swordswoman and had never regretted it—till now.

She stepped back again, and her foot met slight resistance and then went back a lot more than it should have, into an unexpected hole. Lirael lost her balance, tumbling over backwards as a sharp hook sliced the air in front of her throat.

Time seemed frozen as she fell. She saw her parry going wide as her arms windmilled in her attempt to regain her balance. She saw the hooks of the Stilken scything forward, towards her, almost certain to meet around her waist.

Lirael hit the ground hard, but she didn't notice the pain. She was already rolling aside, dimly registering that it was a hollow between two roots that had tripped her, and tree roots were pummeling her body as she rolled over them.

Earth—flowers—the distant ceiling and its Charter lights like far-off stars—earth—flowers—the artificial sky—with every roll, Lirael expected to see the Stilken's silver gaze and feel the searing pain of its hooks. But she didn't see it, and no death blow came. On the sixth roll, she stopped and threw herself forward, stomach muscles stabbing in agony as she flipped back onto her feet.

Binder was still in her hand, and the Stilken was trying to extricate its left hook from where it was stuck, deep in one of the great taproots of the oak. Instantly, Lirael realized it must have missed her as she fell—and struck the root instead.

The Stilken looked at her, silver eyes blazing, and made an awful gobbling noise, deep in its throat. Its body started to shift, weight moving from the trapped left arm to the right side of its body. It grew squatter, and muscles moved under the seemingly human skin like slugs under a leaf, gathering in the caught arm. Before the process was finished, it heaved, straining to free itself and come after Lirael.

This was her chance, Lirael knew—these scant few seconds.

Charter marks flared on Binder's blade as she reached out to them, joining them to others drawn out of the Charter. Four master marks she needed, but to use them she had first to protect herself with lesser marks.

Binder helped her, and the marks slowly formed a chain in her mind, all too slowly, as the Stilken gobbled and strained, pulling its hook out inch by inch. The oak itself seemed to be trying to keep the creature trapped, Lirael realized, with that small part of her mind not totally focused on the Charter-spell. She could hear the tree rustling and creaking, as if it fought to keep the cut in its taproot closed, the hook with it.

The last mark came, flowing into Lirael with easy grace. She let the spell go, feeling its power rush through her blood and every bone, fortifying her against the four master marks she needed to call.

The first of these master marks blossomed in her mind as the Stilken finally pulled its hook free, with a great groan from the oak and a spray of white-green sap. Even with the protective spell upon her, Lirael didn't let the master mark linger in her mind. She cast it forth, sending it down Binder's blade, where it spread like shining oil, till it suddenly burst into fire, surrounding the blade with golden flames.

The Stilken, already leaping to attack, tried to twist away. But it was too late. Lirael stepped forward, and Binder leapt out in a perfect stop thrust, straight through the Stilken's neck. Golden fire raged, white sparks plumed up like a skyrocket's trail, and the creature froze a mere two paces from Lirael, its hooks almost touching her on either side.

Lirael called forth the second master mark, and it, too, ran down the blade. But when it reached the Stilken's neck, it disappeared. A moment later, the creature's skin began to crack and shrivel, blazing white light shining through when the shriv-

eled skin sloughed off onto the ground. Within a minute, the
Stilken had lost its semi-human appearance. Now it was just a
featureless column of fierce white light, transfixed by a sword.

The third master mark left Binder and went into the column.
Instantly, what was left of the Stilken began to shrink, dwindling
away until it was a blob of light an inch in diameter, with Binder
now resting point first upon it.

Lirael took the metal bottle out of her waistcoat pocket, put
it on the ground, and used the sword to roll the shining remnant
of the Stilken inside. Only then did she withdraw the blade,
drop it, and thrust in the cork. A moment later, she sealed it
with the fourth master mark, which wrapped itself around both
cork and bottle in a flash of light.

For a moment the bottle jumped and wriggled in her hand,
then it was still. Lirael put it back in her pocket, and sat down
next to Binder, gasping. It was really over. She had bound the
Stilken. All by herself.

She leaned back, wincing at the aches and pains that sprang
up along her back and arms. A brief flash of light caught her eye,
from somewhere over near the tree. Instantly, she was back on
the alert again, her hand going to Binder, all her pains forgotten. Picking up the sword, she went to investigate. Surely there
couldn't be another Stilken? Or could it have got out at the last
instant? She checked the bottle, which was definitely sealed.
Might there have been the briefest instant when she blinked,
just as the fourth mark came?

The light flashed again, soft and golden as Lirael approached,
and she sighed with relief. That had to be Charter Magic, so she
was safe after all. The glow came from the hole she had tripped
over.

Warily, Lirael poked at the hole with Binder, clearing the
soil away. She saw that the glow came from a book, bound

in what looked like fur or some sort of hairy hide. Using the sword as a lever, she flipped the book out. She'd seen the tree trying to hang on to the Stilken—she didn't want it getting a grip on her.

Once it was clear of the roots, she picked the book up. The Charter marks on its cover were familiar ones, a spell to keep the book clean and free of silverfish and moths. Lirael tucked the thick volume under her arm, suddenly conscious that she was drenched in sweat, caked in dirt and flower petals, and completely exhausted, not to mention bruised. But only her waistcoat had suffered permanent damage, drilled through by sparks in a hundred places, as if it had been attacked by incendiary moths.

The Dog rose up out of the flowers to meet her as she headed back to the exit. She had Binder's scabbard in her mouth and didn't let it go as Lirael slid the sword home.

"I did it," said Lirael. "I bound the Stilken."

"Mmmpph, mmpph, mmph," said the Dog, prancing on her back feet. Then she carefully laid the sword down and said, "Yes, Mistress. I knew you would. Reasonably certainly."

"Did you?" Lirael looked at her hands, which were starting to shake. Then her whole body was shaking, and she had to sit down till it stopped. She hardly noticed the Dog's warm bulk against her back, or the encouraging licks against her ear.

"I'll take the sword back," offered the Dog, when Lirael finally stopped shaking. "You rest here till I return. I won't be long. You will be safe."

Lirael nodded, unable to speak. She patted the Dog on the head and lay back on the flowers, letting their scent waft over her, the petals soft against her cheek. Her breathing slowed and became more regular, her eyes blinked slowly once, twice—and then they closed.

The Dog waited until she was sure Lirael was asleep. Then

she let out a single short bark. A Charter mark came with it, expelled out of the Dog's mouth to hover in the air over the sleeping girl. The Dog cocked her head and looked at it with an experienced eye. Satisfied, she picked up the sword in her powerful jaws and trotted off, out into the main spiral.

When Lirael awoke, it was morning, or at least the light was bright again in the cavern. For a second she had the impression that there was a Charter mark above her head, but clearly that was only a dream, for there was nothing there when she came fully awake and sat up.

She felt very stiff and sore, but no worse than she usually did after one of the annual sword-and-bow exams. The waistcoat was beyond repair, but she had spares, and there didn't seem to be any other physical signs of her combat with the Stilken. Nothing that would require a trip to the Infirmary. The Infirmary . . . Filris. For a moment Lirael was sad she couldn't tell her great-great-grandmother that she had defeated the Stilken after all.

Filris would have liked the Disreputable Dog, too, Lirael thought, glancing over to where the hound slept nearby. She was curled into a ball, her tail wrapped completely around her back legs, almost up to her snout. She was snoring slightly and twitching every now and then, as if she dreamed of chasing rabbits.

Lirael was about to wake up the Dog when she felt the book poking into her. In the light, she realized it wasn't bound in fur or hide, but had some sort of closely knitted cover over heavy boards, which was very peculiar indeed.

She picked it up and flicked it open to the title page, but even before she read the first word, she knew it was a book of power. Every part of it was saturated with Charter Magic. There were marks in the paper, marks in the ink, marks in the stitching of the spine.

The title page said merely *In the Skin of a Lyon*. Lirael turned it over, hoping to see a list of contents, but it went straight into the first chapter. She started to read beyond the words "Chapter One," but the type suddenly blurred and shimmered. She blinked, rubbed her eyes, but when she looked again the page had the heading "Preface," though she was sure it could not have turned. She turned back, and there was the title page again.

Lirael frowned and flipped forward. It still said "Preface." Before it could change, she started to read.

"The making of Charter-skins," she read,

> *allows the Mage to take on more than the mere semblance or seeming of a beast or plant. A correctly woven Charter-skin, worn in the prescribed fashion, gives the Mage the actual desired shape, with all the peculiarities, perceptions, limitations, and advantages of that shape.*
>
> *This book is a theoretical examination of the art of making Charter-skins; a practical primer for the beginning shapewearer; and a compendium of complete Charter-skins, including those for the lyon, the horse, the hopping toade, the grey dove, the silver ash, and divers other useful shapes.*
>
> *The course of study contained herein, if followed with fortitude and discipline, will equip the conscientious Mage with the knowledge needed to make a first Charter-skin within three or four years.*

"A useful book, that one," said the newly awake Dog, interrupting Lirael's reading by thrusting her snout across the pages, clearly demanding a morning scratch between the ears.

"Very," agreed Lirael, trying to keep reading around the Dog, without success. "Apparently if I follow the course of study in it, I'll be able to take on another shape in three or four years."

"Eighteen months," yawned the Dog sleepily. "Two years if you're lazy. Though you *wear* a Charter-skin—you don't change your own shape, as such. Make sure you start on a Charter-skin that'll be useful for exploring. You know, good at getting through small holes and so on."

"Why?" asked Lirael.

"Why?" repeated the Dog incredulously, pulling her head out from under Lirael's hand. "There's so much to see and smell here! Whole levels of the Library that no one has been into for a hundred, a thousand years! Locked rooms full of ancient secrets. Treasure! Knowledge! Fun! Do you want to be just a Third Assistant Librarian all your life?"

"Not exactly," replied Lirael stiffly. "I want to be a proper Clayr. I want to have the Sight."

"Well, maybe we'll find something that can wake it in you," declared the Dog. "I know you have to work, but there's so much other time that shouldn't go to waste. What could be better than walking where no others have walked for a thousand years?"

"I suppose I might as well," Lirael agreed, her imagination taking fire from the Dog's words. There were plenty of doors she wanted to open. There was that strange hole in the rock, for instance, down where the main spiral came to an abrupt end—

"Besides," the Dog added, interrupting her thoughts, "there are forces at work here that want you to use the book. Something freed the Stilken, and the creature's presence has woken other magics, too. That tree would not have given up the book if you weren't meant to have it."

"I suppose," said Lirael. She didn't like the idea that the Stilken had had help to break free from its prison. That implied that there was some greater force of evil down here in the Old Levels, or that some power could reach into the Clayr's Glacier from afar, despite all their wards and defenses.

If there was something like the Stilken—some Free Magic entity of great power—in the Library, Lirael felt it was her duty to find it. She felt that by defeating the Stilken, she had unconsciously taken the first step towards assuming the responsibility for destroying anything else like the creature that might be a threat to the Clayr.

Exploring would also fill up the time and distract her. Lirael realized she hadn't thought much at all about Awakenings, or the Sight, over these last few months. Creating the Dog and discovering how to defeat the Stilken had filled nearly all her waking thoughts.

"I will learn a useful Charter-skin," she declared. "And we will explore, Dog!"

"Good!" said the Dog, and she gave a celebratory bark that echoed around the cavern. "Now you'd better run and get washed and changed, before Imshi wonders where you are."

"What time is it?" asked Lirael, startled. Away from the peremptory whistle-blasts of Kirrith in the Hall of Youth, or the chiming clock in the Reading Room, she had no idea what time of day it was. She had thought it roughly dawn, for she felt she hadn't had much sleep.

"One half past the . . . sixth hour of the morning," replied the Dog, after cocking her ear, as if to some distant chime. "Give or take . . ."

Her voice trailed off, because Lirael had already left, breaking into a somewhat limping run. The Dog sighed and launched herself into a body-extending lope, easily catching up with Lirael before she shut the door.

PART TWO

ANCELSTIERRE
1928 A.W.
THE OLD KINGDOM

Eighteenth Year of the Restoration of
King Touchstone I

Chapter Fourteen

PRINCE SAMETH HITS A SIX

SEVEN HUNDRED MILES south of the Clayr's Glacier, twenty-two boys were playing cricket. In the Old Kingdom, beyond the Wall that lay thirty miles to the north, it was late autumn. Here in Ancelstierre, the last days of summer were proving warm and clear, perfect for the concluding match in the fiercely contested Senior Schoolboys' Shield series, the primary focus for the sporting sixth formers of eighteen schools.

It was the last over of the match, with only one ball left to bowl, and three runs needed to win the innings, the match, and the series.

The batsman who faced that last ball was a month short of his seventeenth birthday and half an inch over six feet tall. He had tightly curling dark brown hair and distinctive black eyebrows. He was not exactly handsome, but pleasing to the eye, a striking figure in his white cricket flannels. Not that they were as crisp and starched as they had been earlier, since they were now drenched with the sweat of making seventy-four runs in partnership, sixty of them his own.

A large crowd was watching in the stands of the Bain Cricket Ground—a much larger crowd than normal for a schoolboy match, even with one of the teams coming from the nearby Dormalan School. Most of the onlookers had come to see the tall young batsman, not because he was any more talented than others on the team, but because he was a Prince. More to the point, he was a Prince of the Old Kingdom. Bain was not only the closest town to the Wall that separated Ancelstierre from that land of magic and mystery, it had also suffered nineteen years before from an incursion of Dead creatures that had been defeated only with the aid of the batsman's parents, particularly his mother.

Prince Sameth was not unaware of the curiosity the towns-folk of Bain felt towards him, but he didn't let it distract him. All his attention was on the bowler at the other end of the pitch, a fierce, redheaded boy whose ferociously quick bowling had taken three wickets already. But he seemed to be tiring, and his last over had been quite erratic, letting Sam and his batting part-ner, Ted Hopkiss, slog the ball all over the field in the effort to get those vital last runs. If the bowler didn't recover his strength and former precision, Sameth thought, he had a chance. Mind you, the bowler was taking his time, slowly flexing his bowling arm and looking at the clouds that were rolling in.

The weather was a bit distracting, though only to Sameth. A wind had sprung up a few minutes before. Blowing in directly from the North, it carried magic with it, picked up from the Old Kingdom and the Wall. It made the Charter mark on Sameth's forehead tingle and heightened his awareness of Death. Not that this cold presence was very strong where he was. Few people had died on the cricket pitch, at least in recent times.

At last the bowler went into his run-up, and the bright red ball came howling down the pitch, bouncing up as Sameth stepped forward to meet it. Willow met leather with a mighty crack, and the ball soared off over Sameth's left shoulder. Higher and higher, it arced over the running fielders to the stands, where it was caught by a middle-aged man, leaping out of his seat to display some long-disused cricketing form.

A six! Sameth felt the smile spread across his face as applause erupted in the stands. Ted ran down to shake his hand, babbling something, and then he was shaking hands with the opposing team and then all sorts of people as he made his way back to the changing rooms in the pavilion. In between handshakes, he looked up to where the telegraph board was clicking over. He had made sixty-six not out, a personal best, and a fitting end to his school cricket career. Probably his entire cricket career, he thought, thinking of his return to the Old Kingdom, only two months away. Cricket was not played north of the Wall.

His friend Nicholas was the first to congratulate him in the changing rooms. Nick was a superb spin bowler, but a poor batsman and an even worse fielder. He often seemed to go off in a dream, studying an insect on the ground or some strange weather pattern in the sky.

"Well done, Sam!" declared Nick, vigorously shaking his hand. "Another trophy for good old Somersby."

"It *will* be good old Somersby soon," replied Sam, easing himself onto a bench and unstrapping his pads. "Odd, isn't it? Ten years of moaning about the place, but when it's time to leave . . ."

"I know, I know," said Nick. "That's why you should come up to Corvere with me, Sam. Pretty much more of the same, university. Put off that fear of the future—"

Whatever else he was going to say was lost as the rest of the team pushed through to shake Sameth's hand. Even Mr. Cochrane, the coach and Somersby's famously irascible Games Master, deigned to clap him on the shoulder and declare, "Excellent show, Sameth."

An hour later, they were all in the school's omnibus, all damp from the sudden shower that had come with the northern wind. Patches of sun and patches of rain were alternating, sometimes only for minutes. Unfortunately, the last rainy one had come when they crossed the road to the bus.

It was a three-hour drive, almost due south to Somersby, along the Bain High Road. So the passengers on the bus were surprised when the driver turned off the High Road just outside Bain, into a narrow, single-lane country road.

"Hold on, driver!" exclaimed Mr. Cochrane. "Where on earth are you going?"

"Detour," said the man succinctly, hardly moving his mouth. He was a replacement for Fred, the school's regular driver, who had broken his arm the day before in a fight over a disputed darts contest. "High Road's flooded at Beardsley. Heard it from a postman, back at the Cricketer's Arms."

"Very well," said Cochrane, his frown indicating the reluctance of his approval. "It is most odd. I wouldn't have thought there's been enough rain. Are you sure you know a way around, driver?"

"Yes, guv'nor," the man affirmed, something that was possibly meant to be a smile crossing his rather weasely face. "Beckton Bridge."

"Never heard of it," said Cochrane dismissively. "Still, I suppose you know best."

The boys paid little attention to this discussion, or to the road. They'd been up since four o'clock in order to get to Bain on time, and had played cricket all day. Most of them, including Nick, fell asleep. Sameth stayed awake, still buoyed up by the excitement of his winning six. He watched the rain on the windows and the countryside. They passed settled farms, the warm glow of electric light in their windows. The telegraph poles flashed by the side of the road, as did a red telephone booth as they whisked through a village.

He would be leaving all that behind soon. Modern technology like telephones and electricity simply didn't work on the other side of the Wall.

Ten minutes later, they passed another sight Sameth wouldn't see beyond the Wall. A large field full of hundreds of tents, with dripping laundry hung on every available guy rope, and a general air of disorder. The bus slowed as it passed, and Sameth saw that most of the tents had women and children clustered in their doorways, looking out mournfully into the rain. Nearly all of them had blue headscarves or hats, identifying them as Southerling refugees. More than ten thousand of them were being given temporary refuge in what the *Corvere Times* described as "the remote northern regions of the nation," which clearly meant close to the Wall.

This must be one of the refugee settlements that had sprung up in the last three years, Sameth realized, noting that the field was surrounded by a triple fence of concertina wire and that there were several policemen near the gate, the rain sluicing off their helmets and dark-blue slickers.

The Southerlings were fleeing a war among four states in the far South, across the Sunder Sea from Ancelstierre. The war had started three years previously, with a seemingly small rebellion in the Autarchy of Iskeria proving an unlikely success. That rebellion had grown to be a civil war that drew in the neighboring countries of Kalarime, Iznenia, and Korrovia, on different sides. There were at least six warring factions that Sameth knew about, ranging from the Iskerian Autarch's forces and the original Anarchist rebels to the Kalarime-backed Traditionalists and the Korrovian Imperialists.

Traditionally, Ancelstierre did not interfere with wars on the Southern Continent, trusting to its Navy and the Flying Corps to keep such trouble on the other side of the Sunder Sea. But with the war now spread across most of the continent, the only safe place for noncombatants was in Ancelstierre.

So Ancelstierre was the refugees' chosen destination. Many were turned back on the sea or at the major ports, but for every large ship returned, a smaller vessel would make landfall somewhere on the Ancelstierran coast and disgorge the two or three hundred refugees who had been packed aboard like sardines.

Many more drowned, or starved, but this did not discourage the others.

Eventually, they would be rounded up and put in temporary camps. Theoretically, they would then be eligible to become proper immigrants to the Commonwealth of Ancelstierre, but in practice, only those with money, connections, or useful skills ever gained citizenship. The others stayed in the refugee camps while the Ancelstierran government tried to work out how to send them back to their own countries. But with the war growing worse and getting more confused by the day, no one who had escaped it would willingly go back. Every time mass deportment had been attempted, it had ended in hunger strikes, riots, and every form of possible protest.

"Uncle Edward says that Corolini chap wants to send the Southerlings into your neck of the woods," said Nicholas sleepily, wakened by the bus's decrease in speed. "Across the Wall. No room for them here, he says, and lots of room in the Old Kingdom."

"Corolini is a populist rabble-rouser," replied Sameth, quoting an editorial from the *Times*. His mother—who conducted most of the Old Kingdom's diplomacy with Ancelstierre—had an even harsher opinion of this politician, who had risen to prominence since the beginning of the Southern War. She thought he was a dangerous egotist who would do anything to gain power. "He doesn't know what he's talking about. They would all die in the Borderlands. It's not safe."

"What's the problem with it?" asked Nick. He knew

his friend didn't like talking about the Old Kingdom. Sam always said that it was not at all like Ancelstierre and that Nick wouldn't understand. No one else knew anything much about it, and there was little information of consequence in any library Nick had seen. The Army kept the border closed, and that was it.

"There are dangerous . . . dangerous animals and . . . um . . . things," replied Sameth. "It's like I've told you before. Guns and electricity and so on don't work. It's not like—"

"Ancelstierre," interrupted Nicholas, smiling. "You know, I've a good mind to come and visit you during the vac and see for myself."

"I wish you would," Sameth said. "I'll need to see a friendly face after six months of Ellimere's company."

"How do you know it's not your sister I want to visit?" asked Nick, with an exaggerated leer. Sam never had a good word to say about his older sister. He was about to say more, but his words were cut short as he looked out the window. Sam looked, too.

The refugee camp was long past and had given way to a fairly dense forest. The distant, rain-blurred orb of the sun hung just above the trees. Only they were both looking out the left-hand side of the bus, and the sun should have been on the right. They were going north, and must have been for some time. North, towards the Wall.

"I'd better tell Cockers," said Sameth, who was in the aisle seat. He'd just got up, and started to make his way to the front of the bus, when the engine suddenly spluttered and the bus jerked, nearly throwing Sam to the floor. The driver cursed and crashed down several gears, but the engine kept spluttering. The driver cursed again, revving the engine so hard its whine woke up anyone left asleep. Then it suddenly stopped. Both the interior light and the headlights went out, and the bus rolled to a silent stop.

"Sir!" Sam called out to Mr. Cochrane, above the sudden hubbub of waking boys. "We've been going north! I think we're near the Wall."

Cochrane, who was peering through his own window, turned back as Sam spoke and stood in the aisle, his commanding bulk enough to silence the closer boys.

"Settle down!" he said. "Thank you, Sameth. Now everyone stay in your seats, and I'll soon sort—"

Whatever he was going to say was interrupted by the sound of the driver's door, as he slammed it shut behind him. All the boys rushed to the windows, despite Cochrane's roar, and saw the driver leap the roadside wall and run off through the trees as if pursued by some mortal enemy.

"What on earth?" exclaimed Cochrane, as he turned to look out the windscreen. Whatever had scared the driver clearly didn't seem so terrible to him, since he merely opened the passenger door and stepped out into the rain, unfurling his umbrella as he did so.

As soon as he left the bus, everyone rushed to the front. Sam, from his position in the aisle, was the first to get there. Looking out, he first saw a barrier across the road, and a large red sign next to it. He couldn't quite read it, because of the rain, but he knew what it said anyway. He'd seen identical signs every holiday, when he went home to the Old Kingdom. The red signs marked the beginning of the Perimeter, the military zone that the Ancelstierran Army had established to face the Wall. Beyond that sign, the woods on either side of the road would vanish, replaced by a half-mile-wide expanse of strong points, trenches, and the coils and coils of barbed wire that stretched from the east coast to the west.

Sam remembered exactly what the sign said. Pretending he had an amazing ability to see through fogged-up windscreens, he recited the familiar warning to the others. It was important for them to know.

PERIMETER COMMAND
NORTHERN ARMY GROUP
Unauthorized egress from the Perimeter Zone
is strictly forbidden.
Anyone attempting to cross the Perimeter Zone will
be shot without warning.
Authorized travelers must report to the
Perimeter Command H.Q.
REMEMBER—NO WARNING WILL BE MADE

A moment of silence met this recitation, as the seriousness of it sank in. Then a babble of questions broke out, but Sam didn't answer. He had thought the driver had run away because he was afraid of being so close to the Wall. But what if he had brought them there on purpose? And why had he run away from the two red-capped military policemen who were walking up from their sentry box?

Sameth's family had many enemies in the Old Kingdom. Some were human, and might be able to pass as harmless in Ancelstierre. Some were not, but they might be powerful enough to cross the Wall and get this little distance south. Especially on a day when the wind blew from the north.

Not bothering to get his raincoat, Sam jumped down from the bus and hurried over to where the two military policemen had just met Mr. Cochrane. Or rather, to where the MP sergeant had started to shout at Cochrane.

"Get everyone off that bus and get them moving back as

quick as you can," the sergeant shouted. "Run as far as you can, then walk. Got it?"

"Why?" asked Mr. Cochrane, bristling. Like most of the teachers and staff at Somersby, he wasn't from the North, and he had no idea about the Wall, the Perimeter, or the Old Kingdom. He had always treated Sameth as he treated the school's other Prince, who was an albino from far-off Karshmel—like an adopted child who wasn't quite a member of the family.

"Just do it!" ordered the sergeant. He seemed nervous, Sameth noted. His revolver holster was open, and he kept looking around at the trees. Like most soldiers on the Perimeter—but totally unlike any other units of the Ancelstierran Army—he also wore a long sword-bayonet on his left hip, and a mail coat over his khaki battledress, though he'd kept his MP's red cap, rather than wearing the usual neck- and nasal-barred helmet of the Perimeter garrison. Sam noted that neither of the two men had a Charter mark on his forehead.

"That's not good enough," Cochrane protested. "I insist on speaking to an officer. I can't have my boys running about in the rain!"

"We'd better do as the sergeant says," said Sam, coming up behind him. "There is something in the wood—and it's getting closer."

"Who are you?" demanded the sergeant, drawing his sword. The lance-corporal with him instantly followed suit, and started to sidle around behind. Both of them were looking at Sam's forehead, and the Charter mark that was just visible under his Cricket XI cap.

"Prince Sameth of the Old Kingdom," said Sam. "I suggest you call Major Dwyer of the Scouts, or General Tindall's headquarters, and tell them I'm here—and that there are at least three Dead Hands in the woods over there."

"That's torn it!" swore the sergeant. "We knew something was up with this wind. How did they get— Well, it doesn't matter. Harris, double back to the post and alert HQ. Tell them we've got Prince Sameth, a bunch of schoolkids, and at least three category-A intruders. Use a pigeon and the rocket. The phone'll be out for sure. Move!"

The lance-corporal was gone before the sergeant's mouth shut, and just as Cochrane began.

"Sameth! What are you going on about?"

"There's no time to explain," replied Sam urgently. He could sense Dead Hands—bodies infused with spirits called from Death—moving through the forest, parallel to the road. They didn't seem to have sensed the living yet, but once they did, they would be there within minutes. "We have to get everyone out of here—we have to get as far away from the Wall as we can."

"But . . . But . . ." blustered Cochrane, red-faced and astounded at the impertinence of one of his own boys ordering him around. He would have said more, if the sergeant hadn't drawn his revolver and calmly said, "Get them going now, sir, or I'll shoot you where you stand."

Chapter Fifteen

THE DEAD ARE MANY

FIVE MINUTES LATER, the entire team was out in the rain, on the road, jogging south. At Sameth's suggestion, they had armed themselves with cricket bats, metal-tipped cricket stumps, and cricket balls. The MP sergeant ran with them, his revolver continuing to silence Cochrane's protests.

The boys took it all as a bit of a joke at first, with much bravado and carrying-on. But as it got darker and the rain got heavier, they grew quieter. The jokes stopped altogether when four quick shots were heard behind them, and then a distant, anguished scream.

Sameth and the sergeant exchanged a look that combined fear and a dreadful knowledge. The shots and the scream must have come from Lance-Corporal Harris, who had gone back to the post.

"Is there a stream or other running water near here?" panted Sameth, mindful of the warning rhyme he'd known since childhood about the Dead. The sergeant shook his head but didn't answer. He kept glancing back over his shoulder, almost losing his balance as they ran. A little while after they heard the scream, he saw what he was looking for and pointed it out to Sameth: three red parachute flares drifting down from a few miles north.

"Harris must have got the pigeon off, at least," he puffed. "Or maybe the telephone worked, since his pistol did. They'll have the reserve company and a platoon of Scouts out here soon, sir."

"I hope so," replied Sameth. He could sense the Dead on the road behind them now, coming up quickly. There seemed to be no hope of safety anywhere ahead. No stout farmhouse or barn, or a stream, whose running water the Dead couldn't cross. In fact, the road went down to become a sunken lane, even darker and more closed in, a perfect site for an ambush.

As Sam thought of that, he felt his sense of Death suddenly alter. It disoriented him at first, till he realized what it was. A Dead spirit had just risen in front of them, somewhere in the darkness around the high-banked road. Worse than that, it was new, brought out of Death at that very moment. These were no self-willed Dead spirits that had infiltrated through the Perimeter. They were Dead Hands, raised by a necromancer on the Ancelstierran side of the Wall. Controlled by the necromancer's mind, they were much more dangerous than rogue spirits.

"Stop!" screamed Sam, his voice cutting through the beat of rain and footsteps on the asphalt. "They're ahead of us. We have to leave the road!"

"Who are ahead, boy?" shouted Cochrane, furious again. "This has gone quite far enough. . . ."

His voice faltered as a figure stumbled out of the shadows ahead, out into the middle of the road. It was human, or had once been human, but now its arms were hanging threads of flesh, and its head was mostly bare skull, all deep eye hollows and shining teeth. It was unquestionably dead, and the reek of decomposition rolled off it, over the soft smell of the rain. Clods of earth fell from it as it moved, showing that it had just dug itself out of the ground.

"Left!" shouted Sam, pointing. "Everyone go left!"

His shout broke the silent tableau into action, boys leaping over the stone wall that bordered the road. Cochrane was one of the first over, throwing his umbrella aside.

The Dead thing moved, too, breaking into a shambling run as it sensed the Life it craved. The sergeant propped himself against the wall and waited till it was ten feet away. Then he emptied his heavy .455 revolver into the creature's torso, five shots in quick succession, accompanied by a gasp of relief that the weapon actually worked.

The creature was knocked back and finally down, but the sergeant didn't wait. He'd been on the Perimeter long enough to know that it would get back up again. Bullets could stop Dead Hands, but only if the creatures were shredded to pieces. White phosphorus grenades worked better, burning them to ash—when they worked. Guns and grenades and all such standards of Ancelstierran military technology tended to fail the closer they got to the Wall and the Old Kingdom.

"Up the hill!" shouted Sam, pointing to a rise in the ground ahead, where the forest thinned out. If they could make it there, at least they could see what was coming and have the slight advantage of high ground.

A harsh, inhuman cry rose behind them as they ran, a sound like a broken bellows accidentally trodden on, more squeal than scream. Sam knew it came from the desiccated lungs of a Dead Hand. This one was farther to the right than the one the sergeant had shot. At the same time, he sensed others, moving around to the right and left, beginning to encircle the hill.

"There's a necromancer back there," he said as they ran. "And there must be a lot of dead bodies, not too far gone."

"A truck full of those Southerlings . . . ran off the road near here, six weeks ago," said the sergeant, speaking rapidly between breaths. "Nineteen killed. Bit of a . . . mystery where they was going . . . anyway . . . churchwarden at Archell wouldn't . . . have 'em . . . the Army crematorium neither . . . so they was buried next to the road."

"Stupid!" cried Sameth. "It's too close to the Wall! They should have been burnt!"

"Bloody paper-pushers," puffed the sergeant, nimbly ducking under a branch. "Regulations say no burying within the . . . Perimeter. But this is . . . outside, see?"

Sameth didn't answer. They were climbing the hill itself now, and he needed all his breath. He sensed there were at least twelve Dead Hands behind them now, and three or four on each side, going wide. And there was something, some presence that was probably the necromancer, back where the bodies were—or had been—buried.

The top of the hill was clear of trees, save for a few windblown saplings. Before they reached it, the sergeant called a halt, just short of the crest.

"Right! Get in close. Are we missing anyone? How many—"

"Sixteen, including Mr. Cochrane," said Nick, who was a lightning calculator. Cochrane glared at him but was silent, ducking his head back down as he tried to get his breath back. "Everyone's here."

"How long have we got, sir?" the sergeant asked Sam, as they both looked back down into the trees. It was hard to see anything. Visibility was reduced by both the increasingly heavy rain and the onset of night.

"The first two or three will be on us in a few minutes," said Sameth grimly. "The rain will slow them a little. We'll have to knock them down and run stumps through them, to try to keep them pinned. Nick, organize everyone into groups of three. Two batsmen and someone to hold the stumps ready.

No, Hood—go with Asmer. When they come, I'll distract them with a . . . I'll distract them. Then the batsman must hit as hard as they can straight off, in the legs, and then hammer a stump through each arm and leg."

Sameth paused as he saw one of the boys eyeing the two-and-a-half-foot-long wooden stump with its metal spike on the end. From the expression on the boy's face, it was clear he couldn't imagine hammering it through anything.

"These are not people!" Sam shouted. "They're already Dead. If you don't fight them, they will kill us. Think of them as wild animals, and remember, we're fighting for our lives!"

One of the boys started crying, without making a noise, the tears falling silently down his face. At first Sam thought it was the rain, till he noticed the despairing stare that signified complete and utter terror.

He was about to try some more encouraging words when Nick pointed downhill and shouted, "Here they come!"

Three Dead Hands were coming out from the treeline, shambling like drunks, their arms and legs clearly not fully under control. The bodies had been too broken up in the crash, Sam thought, gauging their strength. That was good. It would make them slower and more uncoordinated.

"Nick, your team can take the one on the left," he commanded, speaking quickly. "Ted, yours the middle, and Jack's the right. Go for their knees and hammer the stumps home as soon as you get them down. Don't let them get a grip on you—they're much stronger than they look. Everyone else—including you, please, Sergeant, and Mr. Cochrane—hold back and help any team that gets in trouble."

"Yes, sir!" replied the sergeant. Cochrane merely nodded dumbly, staring at the approaching Dead Hands. For the first time in Sam's memory, the man's face was not flushed red. It was white, almost as white as the sickeningly pallid flesh of the approaching Dead.

"Wait for my order," shouted Sam. At the same time, he reached into the Charter. It was impossible to reach in most of Ancelstierre, but this close to the Wall, it was merely difficult, rather like trying to swim down to the bottom of a deep river.

Sameth found the Charter and took a moment's comfort from the familiar touch of it, its permanence and its totality linking him to everything in existence. Then he summoned the marks he wanted, holding them in his mind while he formed their names in his throat. When he had everything ready, he punched out his right hand, three fingers splayed, each finger indicating one of the approaching Dead creatures.

"Anet! Calew! Ferhan!" he spat, and the marks flew from his fingers as shining silver blades, whistling through the air quicker than any eye could follow. Each one struck a Dead Hand, blowing a fist-sized hole straight through decaying flesh. All three staggered back, and one fell down, waving its arms and legs like a beetle thrown on its back.

"Bloody hell!" exclaimed one of the boys next to Sam.

"Now!" shouted Sam, and the schoolboys rushed forward with a roar, waving their makeshift weapons. Sam and the sergeant went with them, but Cochrane struck out on his own, running down the hill at a right angle to everyone else.

Then there was a blur of screaming, bats rising and falling, the dull thud of stumps being driven through Dead flesh and into the sodden ground.

Sam experienced it all in a strange frenzy, such a tangled mess of sound, images, and emotion that he was never really sure what happened. He seemed to come out of this concentrated fury to find himself helping Druitt Minor hammer a stump through the forearm of a writhing creature. Even with a stump through each limb, it still struggled, breaking one stump and almost getting free, before some of the boys in reserve cleverly rolled a boulder over the loose arm.

Everyone was cheering, Sam realized, as he stepped back and wiped the rain off his face. Everyone except him, because he could sense more Dead, coming up from the road and on the other side of the hill. A quick survey showed that there were only three stumps left, and two of the five bats were broken.

"Get back," he ordered, quelling the cheering. "There's more on the way."

As they moved back, Nick and the sergeant came up close to Sam. Nick spoke first, quietly asking, "What do we do now, Sam? Those things are still moving! They'll get free within half an hour."

"Troops from the Perimeter will be here before then," muttered Sam, glancing at the sergeant, who nodded in affirmation. "It's the new ones coming up I'm worried about. The only thing I can think of doing . . ."

"What?" asked Nick, as Sam stopped in mid-sentence.

"These are all Dead Hands, not free-willed Dead," replied Sam. "Newly made ones. The spirits in them are just whatever the necromancer could call quickly, so they're neither powerful nor smart. If I could get to the necromancer who's controlling them, they would probably attack each other, or wander in circles. Quite a few might even snap back into Death."

"Well, let's get this necromancer chap!" declared Nick stoutly. His voice was steady, but he couldn't help a nervous look back down the hill.

"It's not as easy as that," said Sam absently. Most of his attention was on the Dead Hands he could sense around them. There were ten down near the road, and six on the other side of the hill somewhere. Both groups were getting themselves into ragged lines. Obviously, the necromancer planned to have them all attack at once, from both sides.

"It's not so easy," Sam repeated. "The necromancer is down there somewhere, physically at least. But he's almost certainly in Death, leaving his body protected by a spell or some sort of bodyguard. To get at him, I'll have to go into Death myself—and I don't have a sword, or bells, or anything."

"Go into Death?" asked Nick, his voice rising half an octave. He was clearly about to say something else but he looked down at the staked-out Dead Hands and shut up.

"Not even time to cast a diamond of protection," Sam muttered to himself. He had never actually been into Death by himself before. He'd gone only with his mother, the Abhorsen. Now he wished desperately that she were here. But she wasn't, and he couldn't think of anything else to do. He could almost certainly get away himself, but he couldn't leave the others.

"Nick," he said, making up his mind. "I am going to go into Death. While I'm there, I won't be able to see or sense anything here. My body will seem to be frozen, so I'll need you—and you, sergeant—to guard me as best you can. I plan to be back before the Dead get here, but if I'm not, try to slow them down. Throw cricket balls, stones, and anything else you can find. If you can't stop them, grab my shoulder, but don't touch me otherwise."

"Right-oh," replied Nick. He was clearly puzzled, and afraid, but he put out his hand. Sam took it, and they shook hands, while the other boys looked at them curiously, or stared out into the rain. Only the sergeant moved, handing Sam his sword, hilt first.

"You'll need this more than I do, sir," he said. Then, echoing Sam's own thoughts, he added, "I wish your mum was here. Good luck, sir."

"Thanks," said Sam, but he handed the sword back. "I'm afraid only a spelled sword would help me. You keep it."

The sergeant nodded and took the sword. Sam dropped into a boxer's defensive stance and closed his eyes. He felt for the boundary between Life and Death and found it easily, for a moment experiencing the strange sensation of rain falling down the back of his neck while his face was hit by the terrible chill of Death, where it never rained.

Exerting all his willpower, Sam pushed towards the cold, making his spirit cross into Death. Then, without warning, he was there, and the cold was all around him, not just on his face. His eyes flashed open, and he saw the flat grey light of Death and felt the tug of the river's current at his legs. In the distance, he heard the roar of the First Gate, and shivered.

Back in Life, Nick and the sergeant saw Sam's entire body stiffen suddenly. A fog came from nowhere, twining up his legs like a vine. As they kept staring, frost formed on his face and hands—an icy coat that was not washed off by the rain.

"I'm not sure I can believe what I'm seeing," whispered Nick, as he looked away from Sam and down at the approaching Dead.

"You'd better believe it," said the sergeant grimly. "Because they'll kill you whether you believe in them or not."

Chapter Sixteen

INTO DEATH

APART FROM THE distant roar of the waterfall that marked the First Gate, it was completely silent in Death. Sam stood still, staying close to the border with Life, listening and looking. But he couldn't see very far in the peculiar grey light that seemed to flatten everything out and warp perspective. All he could see was the river around him, the water completely dark save where it rushed in white rapids around his knees.

Carefully, Sam began to walk along the very edge of Death, fighting the current that tried to suck him under and carry him off. He guessed that the necromancer would also be staying close to the border with Life, though there was no guarantee that Sam was going in the right direction to find him, or her. He wasn't skilled enough to know where he was in Death in relation to Life, except for the point where he would return to his own body.

He moved much more warily than he had when last in Death. That was a year past, with his mother, the Abhorsen, at his side. It felt very different now that he was alone and unarmed. It was true he could gain some control over the Dead by whistling or clapping his hands, but without the bells he could neither command nor banish them. And while he was a more than proficient Charter Mage, this necromancer could easily be a Free Magic adept, completely outclassing him.

His only real chance would be to creep up on the necromancer and catch him unawares, and that would be possible only
if the necromancer were totally focused on finding and binding
Dead spirits. Even worse, Sam realized, he was making a lot of
noise by wading at right angles to the current. No matter how
slowly he tried to wade, he couldn't help splashing. It was hard
work, too, physically and mentally, as the river tugged at him
and filled him with thoughts of weariness and defeat. It would
be easier to lie down and let the river take him; he could never
win. . . .

Sameth scowled and forced himself to keep wading, suppressing the morbid pressure on his mind. There was still no
sign of the necromancer, and Sam began to worry that his
enemy might not be in Death at all. Perhaps he was out there
in Life even now, directing the Dead to attack. Nick and the
sergeant would do their best to protect his body, Sam knew,
but they would be defenseless against the Free Magic of the
necromancer.

For a moment, Sam thought about going back—then a
slight sound returned all his attention to Death. He heard a
distant, pure note that seemed far away at first but was moving
rapidly towards him. Then he saw the ripples that accompanied
the sound, ripples that ran at a right angle to the flow of the
river—straight towards him!

Sam clapped his hands to his ears, grinding his palms into
his head. He knew that long, clear call. It came from Kibeth,
the third of the seven bells. Kibeth, the Walker.

The single note slid between Sam's fingers and into his
ears, filling his mind with its strength and purity. Then the note
changed and became a whole series of sounds that were almost
the same, but not. Together they formed a rhythm that shot
through Sam's limbs, tweaking a muscle here and a muscle

there, rocking him forward, whether he liked it or not.

Desperately, Sam tried to purse his lips, to whistle a counter-spell or even just a random noise that might disrupt the bell's call. But his cheeks wouldn't move, and his legs were already stumping through the water, carrying him quickly towards the source of the sound, towards the wielder of the bell.

Too quickly, for the river found its chance in Sam's sudden clumsiness. The current surged and wove itself between Sam's feet. Caught on one leg, he teetered for a moment, then went over like a bowling pin, crashing into the river. The cold stabbed into him like a thousand thin knives, all over his body.

Kibeth's call was cut off in that moment, but it still held him, as if he were a fish on a line. Kibeth tried to walk him back, even as the current tried to keep him in its grip. Sam himself fought only to get his head clear, to get a breath of air before he was forced to take a breath of water. But the effects of the bell and the current were too much, locking him in a struggle in which he could not control his body. And while he could no longer hear Kibeth, his whole body trembled, shot through with the tremendous power of the First Gate, the waterfall that was sucking him deeper and closer with every second.

Desperately, Sam thrust his face towards the surface, and for a moment he broke free to snatch a breath. But at that instant, he heard the roar of the Gate rise to a crescendo. He was too close, he knew, and at any moment he would be swept through the Gate. Without bells, he would be easy prey for any denizen of the Second Precinct. Even if he escaped them, he was prob-ably already too weak to resist the pull of the river. It would take him on, all the way through to the Ninth Gate and the ultimate death that lay beyond.

Then something grabbed his right wrist and he came to a sudden stop, the river raging and frothing impotently about him. Sam almost struggled against his rescuer, for fear of what it might be, but his fear of the river was greater and he needed to breathe so desperately that he could think of nothing else. So he simply fought to get a proper footing, and cough up at least some of the water that had managed to get into his throat and lungs.

Then he realized that steam was billowing from his sleeve, and his wrist was burning. He cried out. Fear of his captor rose in him again, and he was almost too afraid to look and see who—or what—it might be.

Slowly Sam raised his head. He was being held by the necromancer he'd hoped to surprise. A thin, balding man, who wore leather armor with red-enameled plates for reinforcement—and a bandolier of bells across his chest.

Here in Death, Free Magic magnified his stature, cloaking him with a great shadow of fire and darkness that moved as he moved, transforming his presence into something truly terrible and cruel. The touch of his hand blistered Sam's wrist, and flames burnt where the whites of his eyes should be.

In his left hand he held a sword level with Sam's neck, the sharp edge a few inches from his throat. Dark flames ran slowly down the blade like mercury and fell to the surface of the river, where they continued to burn as the current carried them away.

Sam coughed again, not because he needed to, but to cover an attempt to reach into the Charter. He had hardly begun when the sword swung even closer, the acrid fumes of the ensorceled blade making him cough for real.

"No," said the necromancer, his voice redolent with Free Magic, his breath carrying the reek of drying blood. Desperately, Sam tried to think of what he could do. He couldn't reach the Charter, and he couldn't fight barehanded against that sword.

He couldn't even move, for that matter, as his sword-arm was held impossibly still in the necromancer's burning grasp.

"You will return to Life and seek me out," ordered the necromancer, his voice low and hard, supremely confident. It wasn't just words either, Sam realized. He felt a compulsion to do exactly what the necromancer said. It was a Free Magic spell—but one that Sam knew would not be complete till it was sealed with the power of Saraneth, the sixth bell. And there was his chance, because the necromancer would have to let go of Sam or sheathe his sword in order to wield the bell.

Let me go, Sam wished fervently, trying not to tense his muscles too much and give his intentions away. Let me go.

But the necromancer chose to sheathe his sword instead, and draw the second-largest of the bells with his right hand. Saraneth, the Binder. With it he would bind Sam to his will, though it was strange that he wanted Sam to return to Life. Necromancers did not normally care for living servants.

His grip on Sam's wrist did not slacken. The pain there was intense, so bad that it had gone beyond bearing, and his mind had decided to shut it out. If he hadn't still been able to see his fingers he would have believed that his hand had been burnt off at the wrist.

The necromancer carefully opened the pouch that held Saraneth. But before he could transfer his grip to grasp the bell by its clapper and pull it out, Sam threw himself backwards and scissored his legs around the necromancer's waist.

Both of them plunged into the icy water, the necromancer sending up a huge plume of steam as he hit. Sam was underneath, the water instantly filling his mouth and nose, beating at the last breath in his lungs. He could feel the flesh of his thighs burning, even through the cold, but he did not let go. He felt the necromancer twisting and turning to get free, and through half-closed eyes he saw that under the river, the necromancer was a shape of fire and darkness, more monstrous and much less human than he had seemed before.

With his free hand, Sam desperately clawed at the necromancer's bandolier, trying to get one of the bells. But they felt strange, the ebony handles biting to his touch, quite unlike the smooth, Charter-spelled mahogany of his mother's bells. His fingers couldn't close on any handle, his legs were slowly being unlocked by the necromancer's inhuman strength, the grip on his wrist was unrelenting—and his breath was almost gone.

Then the current quickened, picking them both up and turning them into a dizzy spin, till Sam couldn't tell which way he could stretch to find a breath. Then they were hurtling down—down through the waterfall of the First Gate.

The waterfall spun them about viciously, and then they were in the Second Precinct, and Sam couldn't hold the necromancer anymore. The man got free of Sam's scissored legs and elbowed Sam savagely in the stomach, driving the last pathetic remnant of air from his lungs in one choked-off explosion of bubbles.

Sam tried to hit back, but he was already sucking in water instead of air, and his strength was almost gone. He felt the necromancer let go and slip away from him, moving through the water like a snake, and he lost all thought save the desperate urge for survival.

A second later, he broke the surface, coughing madly, getting as much water as air. At the same time, he fought to keep his balance against the current and locate his enemy. Hope sparked in him as he caught no sign of the necromancer. And he seemed to be close to the First Gate. It was hard to tell in the Second Precinct, where some quality of the light made it impossible to see farther than you could touch.

But Sam could see the froth of the waterfall, and when he stumbled forward, he touched the rushing water of the First Gate, and all he had to remember was the spell that would let him past. It was from *The Book of the Dead*, which he had begun to study last year. As he thought of it, pages appeared in his mind, the words of the Free Magic spell shining, ready for him to say.

He opened his mouth—and two burning hands came down on his shoulders, driving him face-first into the river. This time he had no chance of holding his breath, and his scream was nothing more than bubbles and froth, barely disturbing the flow of the river.

It was pain that brought him back to consciousness. Pain in his ankles, and a strange feeling in his head. It took him a moment to realize that he was still in Death—but back at the border with Life. And the necromancer was holding him upside down by the ankles, water still pouring from his ears and nose.

The necromancer was speaking again, speaking words of power that rose up around Sam like bands of steel. He could feel them pressing against him, making him their prisoner, and he knew that he should try to resist. But he couldn't. He could barely keep his eyes open, even that small thing taking all the willpower and energy he had left.

Still the necromancer kept on speaking, the words weaving around and around him, till Sam finally understood the single most important thing: the necromancer was sending him back into Life, and this binding was to make sure that he did what he was told.

But the binding didn't matter. Nothing mattered, save that he was going back to Life. He didn't care that back in Life, he would have to follow some terrible purpose of the sorcerer. He would be back in Life. . . .

The necromancer let go of one ankle, and Sam swung like a pendulum, his head just brushing the surface of the river. The necromancer seemed to have grown much taller, for he wasn't holding his arm very high. Or perhaps, Sam thought muzzily through the pain and shock, he was the one who had shrunk.

"You will come to me in Life, near where the road sinks and the graves lie broken," ordered the necromancer finally, when the spell had settled on Sam so tightly that he felt like a fly trussed up by a spider. But it had to be sealed by Saraneth. Sam tried to struggle as he saw the bell come out, but his body wouldn't respond. He tried to reach the Charter, but instead of the cool comfort of the endless flow of marks, he felt a great whirlpool of living fire, a maelstrom that threatened to maim his mind as much as his body had already been burnt.

Saraneth sounded, deep and low, and Sam screamed. Some instinct helped him hit the one note that would be most at discord with the bell. The scream cut through Saraneth's commanding tone, and the bell jarred in the necromancer's hand, becoming suddenly shrill and raucous. Instantly, he let go of Sam, his free hand stilling the clapper, for a bell gone awry could have disastrous consequences for its wielder.

When the bell was finally still, the necromancer turned his attention back to the boy. But there was no sign of him, and no chance the current could have taken him out of sight so soon.

Chapter Seventeen

NICHOLAS AND THE NECROMANCER

S AM RETURNED TO Life to hear the harsh tap-tap-tap of machine-gun fire and to see the landscape turned black and white by the stark brilliance of the parachute flares that were falling slowly through the rain.

Ice cracked as he moved, the frost on his clothes crazing into strange patterns. He took half a step forward and fell to his knees, sobbing with pain and shock as his fingers scrabbled at the muddy earth, seeking comfort from the feel of Life.

Slowly he became aware that there were arms around him, and people speaking. But he couldn't hear properly, because the necromancer's words kept repeating in his head, telling him what he must do. He tried to speak himself, through teeth that chattered with cold, unconsciously imitating the rhythm of the gunfire.

"Necromancer . . . sunken road . . . near graves," he said haltingly, not really knowing what he was saying or whom he was talking to. Someone touched his wrist and he screamed, the pain blinding him more than the flares that continued to blossom in the sky above. Then, after the brightness, there was sudden darkness. Sam had fainted.

"He's hurt," said Nick, staring at the blistered finger-marks on Sam's wrist. "Burnt somehow."

"What?" asked the sergeant. He was staring down the slope, watching red tracer rounds fly in low arcs from the neighboring hill down into and along the road. Every now and then one would be accompanied by the sudden bang, whoosh, and blinding sunburst of white phosphorus. Clearly the troops from the Perimeter were fighting their way towards where the sergeant and the boys were. What worried the sergeant was the way the machine-gunners were traversing their fire to the left and right of the road.

"Sam's burnt," replied Nick, unable to tear his eyes off the livid marks on his friend's wrist. "We have to do something."

"We sure do," said the sergeant, suddenly faceless again as the last flare fizzled out. "The boys down there are driving the Dead towards us—and they must think we're already done for, because they're not being real careful. We'll be taking rounds any minute now if we don't clear off."

As if to punctuate his remark, another flare arced up overhead, and a sudden flurry of tracer shot over their heads with a whip and a crack. Everybody ducked, and the sergeant shouted, "Down! Get down!"

In the light of the new flare, Nick saw dark shapes emerge from the trees and start up the hill, their telltale shambling gait showing what they were. At the same time, one of the boys farther around the hill screamed out, "They're coming up behind! Lots of—"

Whatever he was saying was drowned out by more machine-gun fire, long bursts of tracer that drew lines of red light right through the Dead, clearly hitting them many times. They twitched and staggered under the multiple impacts, but still they came on.

"Got 'em enfiladed from that hill," said the sergeant. "But they'll get here before the guns rip them apart. I've seen it before. And we'll get shot to pieces as well."

He spoke slowly, almost dumbly, and Nick realized that he

wasn't able to think—that his brain had become saturated with danger and could not deal with the situation.

"Can't we signal the soldiers somehow?" he shouted above yet another burst of fire. Both the dark silhouettes of the Dead and the momentarily bright shifting lines of tracer were advancing towards them at an inexorable rate, like something slow but unstoppable, a hypnotic instrument of fate.

One line of tracer suddenly swung farther up towards them, and bullets ricocheted off stone and earth, whistling past Nick's head. He pressed himself further into the mud, and pulled Sam closer, too, shielding his unconscious friend with his own body.

"Can't we signal?" Nick repeated frantically, his voice muffled, mouth tasting dirt.

The sergeant didn't answer. Nick looked across and saw that he was lying still. His red-banded cap had come off, and his head was in a pool of blood, black in the flare light. Nick couldn't tell if he was still breathing.

Hesitantly, he reached out towards the sergeant, pushing his arm through the mud, dreadful visions of bullets smashing through the bone making him keep it as low as possible. His fingers touched metal, the hilt of the man's sword. He would have flinched and drawn back, but at that moment someone screamed behind him, a scream of such terror that his fingers convulsively gripped the weapon.

Twisting around, he saw one of the boys silhouetted, grappling with a larger figure. It had him gripped around the neck and was shaking him around like a milk shake.

Without thinking of getting shot, Nick leapt up to help. Even as he did so, other boys jumped up, too, hacking at the Dead Hand with bats, stumps, and rocks.

Within seconds they had it down and stumped through, but

not quickly enough to save its victim. Harry Benlet's neck was broken, and he would never take three wickets in a single afternoon ever again, or hurdle every desk in the exam hall at Somersby just for the fun of it.

The fight with the Hand had taken them to the crest of the hill, and there Nick saw that there were Dead on both sides. Only the ones on the forward slope were being slowed by gun-fire. He could see where the soldiers were firing from, and could make out groups of them. There were several machine-guns on the neighboring hill, and at least a hundred soldiers were advancing through the trees on either side of the road.

As Nick watched, he saw one line of tracer suddenly swing up towards them. It got within thirty yards and suddenly stopped. It was too far to see clearly with the rain, but Nick realized that the gun had only stopped for reloading or to shift the tripod, as soldiers moved swiftly around it. Obviously they had seen a target of opportunity: figures silhouetted on the hilltop.

"Move!" he shouted, rushing down the side of the hill in a half-crouch. The others followed in a mad, sliding dash that ended only when several boys crashed into each other and fell over.

A moment later, tracer shot overhead and the hilltop exploded in a spray of water, mud, and ricocheting bullets.

Nick instinctively ducked, though he was well down the slope. In that second, he realized three terrible facts: he had left Sam behind, halfway around the hill; they absolutely had to signal the soldiers to avoid getting shot; and even if they kept moving, the Dead would catch them before the soldiers finished off the Dead.

But with those dreadful realizations came sudden energy, and a determination Nick had never known, a clarity of thought that he'd never experienced before.

"Ted, get out your matches," he ordered, knowing Ted's

affectation of smoking a pipe, though he was no good at it. "Everyone else, get out anything you've got that's dry and will burn. Paper, whatever!"

Everyone clustered around as he spoke, their fear-filled faces revealing their eagerness to be doing something. Letters were proffered, dog-eared playing cards, and after a moment's hesitation pages torn from a notebook that had up till then contained what its owner imagined was his deathless prose. Then came the prize of the lot, a hip flask of brandy from, of all people, the very rules-conscious Cooke Minor.

The first three matches fizzled out in the rain, increasing everyone's anxiety. Then Ted used his cap to shield the fourth. It lit nicely, as did the brandy-soaked paper. A bright fire sprang up, of orange flames tinged with brandy blue, suddenly bringing color back to the monochrome landscape, lit by the seemingly endless succession of parachute flares.

"Right," snapped Nick. "Ted, will you and Mike crawl around and drag Sam back here? Stay off the crest. And do be careful of his wrists—he's burnt."

"What are you going to do?" asked Ted, hesitating as more tracer rounds flew over the hill, and white phosphorus grenades exploded in the distance. Clearly he was afraid to go but didn't want to admit it.

"I'm going to try to find the necromancer, the man who controls the things out there," said Nick, brandishing the sword. "I suggest everyone else start singing, so the Army knows there are real people here, by the fire. You'll have to keep the creatures away, too, though I'm going to try to draw the closer ones after me."

"Sing?" asked Cooke Minor. He seemed quite calm, possibly because he'd drunk half the contents of his hip flask before handing it over. "Sing what?"

"The school song," replied Nick over his shoulder as he

headed down the hill. "It's probably the only thing everybody knows."

To keep out of the way of the machine-guns, Nick ran around the hill before he headed down, towards the Dead, who were now behind their original position. As he ran, he waved the sword above his head and shouted, meaningless words that were half-drowned by the constant chatter of the guns.

He was halfway to the closest Hands when the singing started, loud enough to be heard even above the gunfire, the boys singing with a volume greater than the Somersby choirmaster would have believed possible.

Snatches of the words followed Nick as he dummied a left turn in front of the Hands and then darted right, turning back towards the trees and the road.

"Choose the path that honor takes—"

He slowed to avoid a tree trunk. It was much darker among the trees, the flare light diminished by the foliage overhead. Nick risked a glimpse behind and was both pleased and terrified to see that at least some of the Dead had turned and were following him. Terror was the stronger emotion, making him run faster between the trees than common sense called for.

"Play the game for its own sakes—"

The words of the school song were suddenly cut off as Nick left the trees, smacked into a stone wall, tumbled over it, and fell down six or seven feet into the sunken road. The sword spun out of his hand, and his palms skidded across asphalt, which took off most of the skin.

He lay on the road for a moment, gathering his wits, then started to get up. He was on his hands and knees when he became aware that someone was standing right in front of him. Leather boots, with metal plates at the knee, clanked as whoever it was stepped forward.

"So, you have come as ordered, even without Saraneth to seal the pledge," said the man, his voice somehow turning off all the other sounds that had filled Nick's ears. Gunfire, grenade explosions, the singing—all of it was gone. All he could hear was that terrible voice, a voice that filled him with indescribable fear.

Nick had started to lift his head as the man spoke, but now he was afraid to look. Instinctively he knew that this was the necromancer he'd so foolishly sought. Now all he could do was hang his head, the peak of his cricket cap shielding his face from what he knew would be a terrible gaze.

"Lift up your hand," ordered the necromancer, the words as piercing as hot wires through Nick's brain. Slowly, the boy knelt as if in prayer, his head still bowed—and he held out his right hand, bloody from the fall.

The necromancer's hand slowly came to meet it, palm outwards. For a moment, Nick thought he was going to shake hands, and he suddenly thought of the pattern in the terrible burns on Sam's wrists. A pattern of finger-marks! But he couldn't move. His body was locked in place by the power of the necromancer's words.

The necromancer's hand stopped several inches away, and something quivered under the skin of his palm, like a parasite trying to get out. Then it was free, a sliver of silver metal that slowly oriented itself towards Nick's open hand. It hung suspended for another second, then it suddenly leapt across the gap.

Nick felt it strike his hand, felt it break through his skin and enter his bloodstream. He screamed, his body arched back in convulsions, and for the first time the necromancer saw his face.

"You are not the Prince!" shouted the necromancer, and his sword flashed through the air, straight at Nick's wrist. But it stopped suddenly, less than a finger's width away, as the convulsions stopped and the boy looked up at him calmly, cradling his hand to his chest.

Inside that hand, the sliver of arcane metal swam, negotiating the complex pathway of the boy's veins. It was weak here, on the wrong side of the Wall, but not too weak to reach its ultimate destination.

It hit Nicholas Sayre's heart a minute later, and lodged there. A minute later still, puffs of thick, white smoke began to issue from his mouth.

Hedge waited, watching the smoke. But the white smoke suddenly dissipated, and Hedge felt the wind swing around to the east, and his own power diminish. He heard the sound of many hob-nailed boots farther up the road, and the whoosh of a flare being fired directly overhead.

Hedge hesitated for a moment, then leapt up the embankment with inhuman dexterity, into the trees. Lurking there, he watched as soldiers cautiously approached the unconscious boy. Some of them had rifles with bayonets fixed, and there were two with Lewin light machine-guns. These were no threat to Hedge, but there were others there, those who wielded proper swords that bore glowing Charter marks, and shields that carried the symbol of the Perimeter Scouts. These men had the Charter mark on their foreheads, and were practiced Charter Mages, even if the Army denied that any such thing existed.

There were enough of them to hold him off, Hedge knew. His Dead Hands were almost all gone, too, either immobilized in some way he still didn't understand, or driven back into Death when their newly occupied bodies were too damaged to hold them.

Hedge blinked, holding his eyes shut for a full second—his only acknowledgment that his plan had gone awry. But he had been in Ancelstierre for four years, and his other plans were in full motion. He would come back for the boy.

As Hedge fled into the darkness, stretcher bearers picked up Nick; a young officer convinced the schoolboys on the hill that they really could stop singing; and Ted and Mike tried to tell the barely conscious Sam what had happened as an Army medic looked at the burns on his wrist and legs and prepared a surette of morphine.

Chapter Eighteen

A FATHER'S HEALING HAND

THE HOSPITAL IN Bain was relatively new, built six years before, when a flurry of hospital reform came sweeping up from the South. Even in only six years, many people had died there, and it was close enough to the Wall for Sam's sense of Death to remain active. Weakened by pain and by the morphine they were giving him for it, Sam was unable to drive away his sense of Death. Always it loomed close, filling his bones with its bitter chill, making him shiver constantly and the doctors increase his medication.

He dreamed of bodiless creatures that would come from Death and finish off what the necromancer had begun, and he could not wake himself from the dreams. When he did wake, he often saw that same necromancer stalking towards him, and would scream and scream until the nurse who it really was gave him another injection and started the cycle of nightmares again.

Sam suffered four days of this, drifting in and out of consciousness, without ever really waking up, and never losing his sense of Death and the fear that accompanied it. Sometimes he was lucid enough to realize that Nick was there, too, in the next bed, his hands bandaged. Sometimes they talked briefly, but it wasn't ever a real conversation, since Sam could neither answer questions nor continue whatever talk Nick began.

On the fifth day, everything changed. Sam was once again

in the grip of a nightmare, once again in Death, facing a necromancer who was many things all at once, simultaneously in,
under, and above the water. Sam was running, and falling and
drowning, as had actually happened, and then came the grip on
his wrist . . . but this time it wasn't on his wrist, it was on his
shoulder, and it was cool and comforting. A grip that somehow
led him out of the nightmare, lifting him up through a sky that
was all Charter marks and sunshine.

When Sam opened his eyes, he could see clearly for the
first time, his vision clear of the drug haze and vertigo. He felt
fingers resting lightly on his neck, on the pulse there, and knew
his father's hand before he even looked up. Touchstone was
right next to him, his eyes closed as he directed a healing-spell
into his son's body, the marks flashing under his fingers as they
left him and entered Sam.

Sam looked up at Touchstone, grateful that his father's eyes
were closed and he couldn't see the pathetic relief on his son's
face, or the tears that he hastened to brush away. The Charter
Magic was making him warm for the first time in days. Sam could
feel the marks driving the drugs out of his bloodstream, while
they took over quelling the pain from his burns. But it was
the mere presence of his father that had driven away the fear of
Death. He could still sense Death, but it was dim and far away,
and he was no longer afraid.

King Touchstone I finished the spell and opened his eyes.
They were grey, like his son's, but Touchstone's were the more
troubled now, and he was obviously tired. Slowly, he took his
hand away from Sam's neck.

They almost hugged until Sam saw that there were two doctors, four of Touchstone's guards, and two Ancelstierran Army
officers in the ward as well as a whole crowd of Ancelstierran
police, soldiers, and officials gathered out in the corridor, peering

in. So Sam and Touchstone gripped one another's forearms instead, Sam sitting up in the bed. Only the tightness of Sam's grip and his reluctance to let go indicated just how glad he was to see his father.

Both doctors were amazed that Sam was even conscious, and one checked the chart at the foot of the bed to affirm that the patient really had been receiving intravenous morphine for days.

"Really, this is impossible!" the doctor began, till a cold glance from one of Touchstone's guards convinced him that his conversation was currently not required. A slight further movement convinced him that his presence was not required either, and he backed away to the door. Like the King, the guards were all wearing three-piece suits of a sober charcoal grey, so as not to alarm delicate Ancelstierran sensibilities. This effect was only slightly spoiled by the fact that they also carried swords, badly disguised in rolled-up trenchcoats.

"The entourage," said Touchstone dryly, seeing Sam look out at all the people in the corridor. "I told them I was simply here as a private individual to see my son, but apparently even that requires an official escort. I hope you're feeling up to riding. If we stay here any longer, I'll be cornered by some sort of committee or politician for sure."

"Riding?" asked Sam. He had to say it twice, his throat initially too weak to get the word out. "I'm to leave school before the end of term?"

"Yes," said Touchstone, keeping his voice low. "I want you home. Ancelstierre is no longer a safe haven. The police here caught your bus driver. He was bribed, and bribed with Old Kingdom silver deniers. So one of our enemies has found a way to work on both sides of the Wall. Or has at least found out how to spend money in Ancelstierre."

"I think I'm well enough to ride," said Sam, wrinkling his brow. "I mean, I don't know whether I'm really hurt. My wrist is sore. . . ."

He paused and looked at the bandage on his wrist. Charter marks still moved around the edge of the bandage, oozing out of his pores like golden sweat. Healing him, Sam realized, for his wrist really was only sore, where it had been excruciatingly painful before, and the pain from the lesser burns on his thighs and ankles was completely gone.

"The bandage can come off now," said Touchstone, and he began to untie it. As he unwound it, he lowered his head still closer to Sam and whispered, "You have not been badly hurt in body, Sam. But I feel that you have suffered an injury of the spirit. That will take time to heal, for it is beyond my power to repair."

"What do you mean?" asked Sam anxiously. He felt very young all of a sudden, not at all like the nearly adult Prince he was supposed to be. "Can't Mother fix it up?"

"I don't think so," said Touchstone, resting his hand on Sam's shoulder, the small white scars from years of sword practice and actual fighting bright across his knuckles in the hospital light. "But then I cannot tell the nature of it, only that it has happened. I would guess that as a result of your going into Death unprepared and unprotected, some small fragment of your spirit has been leeched away. Not much, but enough to make you feel weaker, or slower . . . basically less than yourself. But it will come back, in time."

"I shouldn't have done it, should I?" whispered Sam, looking up into his father's face, searching for some sternness or sign of disapproval. "Is Mother furious with me?"

"Not at all," said Touchstone, surprised. "You did what you thought was necessary to save the others, which was both brave and in the best traditions of both sides of the family. Your mother is more worried about you than anything else."

"Then where is she?" asked Sam, before he could stop himself. It was a petulant question, and as soon as his mouth closed, he wished he hadn't said it.

"Apparently, there is a Mordaut riding the ferryman at Oldmond," explained Touchstone patiently, as he had explained so many of Sabriel's necessary absences over the course of Sam's childhood. "We received word of it as we reached the Wall. She took the Paperwing and flew off to deal with it. She'll meet us back at Belisaere."

"If she doesn't have to go somewhere else," said Sam, knowing he was being bitter and childish. But he could have died, and apparently that still wasn't enough for his mother to come and see him.

"Unless she has to go somewhere else," agreed Touchstone, as calmly as ever. His father worked hard at staying calm, Sam knew, for there was the old berserker blood in him, and Touchstone feared its rise. The only time Sam had ever seen that fury was when a false ambassador from one of the northern clans had tried to stab Sabriel with a serving fork at a formal dinner in the Palace. Touchstone, roaring like some sort of terrible beast, had picked up the six-foot barbarian and hurled him the length of the table, onto a roast swan. This had scared everyone much more than the assassination attempt, particularly when Touchstone then tried to pick up the double throne and throw that after the man. Fortunately, he'd failed and was eventually calmed by Sabriel stroking his brow as he blindly wrenched at the marble footing of the throne.

Sam remembered this as he saw his father's eyelids close just a fraction and a line appear on his forehead.

"Sorry," Sam mumbled. "I know she has to do it. Being the

Abhorsen and everything."

"Yes," said Touchstone, and Sam got a slight hint of his father's own deep feelings about the many and frequent absences required by Sabriel's battles with the Dead.

"I'd better get dressed, then," said Sam, and he swung his legs out of the bed. Only then did he notice that the opposite bed was empty and made up.

"Where's Nick?" he asked. "He was there, wasn't he? Or did I just dream that?"

"I don't know," said Touchstone, who had met his son's friend on previous visits to Ancelstierre. "He wasn't here when we arrived. Doctor! Was Nicholas Sayre in this bed?"

The doctor hurried forward. He didn't know who this strange but obviously important visitor was, or who the patient was either, since the Army had insisted on secrecy and the use of first names only. Now he wished that he hadn't heard the other patient's surname, since the name Sayre was not unknown to him. But the Chief Minister didn't have a son of that age, so the fellow could only have been a cousin or something, which was some relief.

"The patient Nicholas X," he said, emphasizing the "X," "was released to one of his parents' confidential servants yesterday. He only had minor shock and some abrasions."

"Did he leave me a message?" asked Sam, surprised that his friend wouldn't have tried to communicate in some way.

"I don't believe so——" the doctor started to say, when he was interrupted by a nurse who pushed her way through the massed ranks of blue, khaki, and grey in the corridor. She was quite young and pretty, with striking red hair not very well concealed under her starched cap.

"He left a letter, Your Highnesses," she said, with the characteristic accent of the North. Obviously a native of

Bain, she knew exactly who both Sam and Touchstone were, much to the doctor's annoyance. The doctor took the letter in her outstretched hand with a sniff and handed it to Sam, who immediately tore it open.

He didn't recognize the handwriting at first; then he realized that it was Nick's, only the individual letters were much larger and the flourishes less regular. It took a moment for him to work out that this must be a consequence of Nick's writing with heavily bandaged hands.

Dear Sam,

I hope you are soon well enough to read this. I seem to be quite recovered myself, though I admit that the events of our unusual evening are somewhat hazy. I guess you wouldn't know that I took it in my head to chase down that necromancer fellow you went after first, wherever it was you went. Unfortunately, what with the dark and the rain and perhaps a little too much zing in my step, all I managed to do was fall into the sunken road and knock myself out. I was lucky not to break any bones, the doctors say, though I have some interesting bruises. I don't expect that the debs back in Corvere will be as prepared to look at them as Nurse Moulin, though!

I understand that the Army got hold of your pater and he's coming down to take you home, so you won't be finishing the term. I daresay I won't bother either, since I already have my place at Sunbere. It won't be the same without you, or poor Harry Benlet. Or even Cochrane. They found him five miles away the next morning, apparently, gibbering and frothing, and I expect he's locked up in Smithwen Special Hospital by now. Should have been done years ago, of course.

*In fact, I was thinking that I might come and visit you
in your mysterious Old Kingdom before I have to go up to
college next spring. I admit that my scientific interest has
been piqued by those apparently animated corpses and your
own exhibition of whatever it was. I'm sure you think of it
as magic, but I expect it can all be explained by the proper
application of scientific method. I hope I can be the one to do
so, of course. Sayre's Theory of Surreality. Or Sayre's Law
of Magical Explication.*

*It's very boring in hospital, particularly if your wardmate
can't carry a conversation. So you'll have to excuse me
rambling on. Where was I? Oh yes, experiments in the
Old Kingdom. I expect the reason no one has done the
proper scientific work before is due to the Army. Would you
believe that no less than a colonel and two captains were here
yesterday, wanting me to sign the Official Secrets Act and a
declaration that I wouldn't ever speak or write of the recent
odd events near the Perimeter? They forgot sign language, so
I expect I shall inform a deaf journalist when I get back.*

*I won't, of course. At least not until I have something
better to tell the world—some truly great discovery.*

*The officers wanted you to sign as well, but since you
weren't in a signing mood, they just waited and got cross
with each other. Then I told them that you weren't even a
citizen of Ancelstierre, and they got thoughtful and had a big
discussion outside with the lieutenant in charge of the guards.
Something tells me the right hand knoweth not what the
left hand doeth, since they were from Corvere Legal Affairs
and the guards outside are from the Perimeter Scouts. I
was interested to note that the latter belong to your peculiar
religion, with the caste mark or whatever it is on their
foreheads. Not that sociology is really in my field of*

interest, I hasten to add.

I must go now. The aged parents have sent some sort of private undersecretary to the oversecretary chamberlain of the personal privy type of fellow to collect me and take me home to Amberne Court. Apparently Father is too busy with the Southerling refugee problem, questions in the House and all that sort of thing, and Uncle Edward needs his support blah blah blah as per usual. Mother probably had a charity dinner or something equally all-engrossing. I'll write soon so we can arrange my visit. I expect I'll have everything prepared in a couple of months, three at the outside.

Chin up!

Nick, the mysterious patient X

Sam folded the letter, smiling. At least Nick had come out of that awful night without any real harm, and with his sense of humor intact. It was typical of him that the Dead had only triggered his scientific interest, rather than a much more sensible fear.

"All well?" asked Touchstone, who had been waiting patiently. At least half the onlookers had lost interest, Sam saw, withdrawing farther down the corridor and out of sight, where they felt they could talk.

"Father," said Sam, "did you bring me some clothes? My school stuff must have been ruined."

"Damed, the bag, please," said Touchstone. "Everybody else, outside if you don't mind."

Like two flocks of sheep that have difficulty mixing, the people left in the ward tried to get out while the people in the corridor tried to help and actually made it more difficult. Eventually, they did all get out, except for Damed—Touchstone's principal bodyguard, a small thin man who moved alarmingly fast. Damed handed over a compact suitcase before he left, shutting the door.

There were Ancelstierran clothes in the bag, procured—like Touchstone's and the guards'—from the Bain consulate of the Old Kingdom.

"Wear these for now," said Touchstone. "We'll get changed at the Perimeter. Back into sensible clothes."

"Armored coat and helmet, boots and sword," said Sameth, pulling his hospital gown off over his head.

"Yes," said Touchstone. He hesitated, then said, "Does that bother you? I suppose you could go south instead. I must return to the Kingdom. But you might be safe in Corvere—"

"No!" Sam said. He wanted to stay with his father. He wanted the heavy weight of his armored coat and the pommel of a sword under his palm. But most of all, he wanted to be with his mother in Belisaere. Because only then would he really be safe from Death . . . and the necromancer who he was sure even now waited in that cold river, waiting for Sam to return.

Chapter Nineteen

ELLIMERE'S THOUGHTS ON
THE EDUCATION OF PRINCES

AFTER TWO WEEKS of hard riding, bad weather, indifferent food, and sore muscles that were slow to re-adapt to horseback, Sam arrived in the great city of Belisaere to find that his mother was not there. Sabriel had already been and gone, called away again to deal with a reported Free Magic sorcerer cum bandit chief, who was attacking travelers along the northern extremes of the Nailway.

Within a day, Touchstone was gone, too, riding to sit at a High Court in Estwael, where an ancient, simmering feud between two noble families had broken out into murders and kidnappings.

In Touchstone's absence, Sam's fourteen-month-older sister Ellimere was named co-regent, along with Jall Oren, the Chancellor. It was a formality really, since Touchstone would rarely be more than a few days away by message-hawk, but a formality that would greatly affect Sam. Ellimere took her responsibility seriously. And she thought that one of her duties as co-regent was to address the shortcomings of her younger brother.

Touchstone had been gone only an hour when Ellimere came looking for Sam. Since Touchstone had left at dawn, Sam was still asleep. He had recovered from his physical wounds, but he still did not feel quite himself. He grew tired more easily than before, and wanted to be alone more. Fourteen days of rising before dawn and riding till after dusk, accompanied by the hearty humor of the guards, had not helped him feel less tired or more gregarious.

Consequently, he was not amused when Ellimere chose to wake him on his first morning in his own bed by ripping back the curtains, flinging his window open, and ripping the blankets off. It was already several days into winter in the Old Kingdom, and decidedly cool. The sea breeze that came roaring in could even be accurately described as cold, and all the feeble sunshine did was hurt Sam's eyes.

"Wake up! Wake up! Wake up!" caroled Ellimere, who had a surprisingly deep singing voice for a woman.

"Go away!" growled Sam, as he attempted to snatch the blankets back. A brief tug-of-war ensued, which Sam gave up when one of the blankets got ripped in half.

"Now look what you've done," Sam said bitterly. Ellimere shrugged. She was supposed to be pretty—some even considered her beautiful—but Sam couldn't see it. As far as he was concerned, Ellimere was a dangerous pest. By making her co-regent, his parents had elevated her to the status of a monster.

"I've come to discuss your schedule," said Ellimere. She sat down on the end of the bed, her back very straight and her hands clasped regally in her lap. Sam noted that she wore a fine, bell-sleeved tabard of red and spun gold over her everyday linen dress, and a sort of demi-regal circlet kept her long and immaculately brushed black hair in place. Since her normal attire was old hunting leathers with her hair carelessly tied back out of the way, her dress did not bode well for Sam's own desire for informality.

"My what?" Sam asked.

"Your schedule," continued Ellimere. "I'm sure that you were planning to spend most of your time tinkering in that

smelly workshop of yours, but I'm afraid your duty to the Kingdom comes first."

"What?" asked Sam. He felt very tired, and certainly not
up to this conversation. Particularly since he had indeed planned
to spend most of his time in his tower workroom. For the last
few days, as they'd got closer and closer to Belisaere, he'd been
looking forward to the solitude and peace of sitting at his workbench, with all his tools carefully arranged on the wall, above
the chest of tiny drawers, each filled with some useful material,
like silver wire or moonstones. He had managed to survive the
last part of the trip by dreaming up new toys and gadgets he
would make in his little haven of calm and recuperation.

"The Kingdom must come first," reiterated Ellimere. "The
people's morale is very important, and each member of the
family must play a part in maintaining it. As the only Prince
we've got, you'll have to—"

"No!" exclaimed Sam, who suddenly realized where she
was heading. He jumped out of bed, his nightshirt billowing
around his legs, and scowled down at his sister, until she stood
up and looked down her nose at him. She not only was slightly
taller than he was, but also had the advantage of wearing shoes.

"Yes," said Ellimere sternly. "The Midsummer Festival.
You're needed to play the part of the Bird of Dawning. Rehearsals start tomorrow."

"But it's five months away!" protested Sam. "Besides, I
don't want to be the blasted Bird of Dawning. That suit must
weigh a ton, and I'd have to wear it for a week! Didn't Dad tell
you I'm sick?"

"He said you needed to be busy," said Ellimere. "And since
you've never danced the Bird, you'll need five months' practice.
Besides, there's the appearance at the end of the Midwinter
Festival, too—and that's only six weeks away."

"I haven't got the legs for it," muttered Sameth, thinking of the cross-gartered yellow stockings worn under the gold-feathered plumage of the Bird of Dawning. "Get someone with tree-trunk legs."

"Sameth! You are going to dance the Bird, like it or not," declared Ellimere. "It's about time you did something useful around here. I've also scheduled you to sit with Jall at the Petty Court every morning between ten and one, and you'll have sword practice twice a day with the Guard, of course, and you must come to dinner—no ordering meals to your grubby work-shop. And for Perspective, I've assigned you to work with the scullions every second Wednesday."

Sam groaned and sank back on the bed. Perspective was Sabriel's idea. For one day every two weeks, Ellimere and Sam would work somewhere in the palace, supposedly like the ordinary people there. Of course, even when they were washing dishes or mopping floors, the servants could rarely forget that Sam and Ellimere would be Prince and Princess again tomor-row. Most of the servants dealt with the situation by pretending Sam and Ellimere weren't there, with a few notable exceptions like Mistress Finney, the falconer, who shouted at them like everyone else. So Perspective was usually a day of drudgery performed in strange silence and isolation.

"What are *you* doing for Perspective?" Sam asked, suspi-cious that Ellimere would skip it now she was co-regent.

"Stables."

Sam grunted. The stables were hard work, particularly since it would probably be a day of mucking out. But Ellimere loved horses and all the work around them, so she probably didn't mind.

"Mother also said you were to study this." Ellimere drew a package out of her voluminous sleeve. It wasn't immediately recognizable, being wrapped in oilskin and tied with thick, hairy twine.

Sam reached for the package, but as his fingers touched the wrapping, he felt a terrible chill and the sudden presence of Death, despite the spells and charms that were supposed to prevent any traffic with that cold realm, woven into the very stone around them.

Sam snatched his hand back and retreated to the other end of the bed, his heart suddenly thumping wildly, sweat beading his face and hands.

He knew what was inside that seemingly innocuous package. It was *The Book of the Dead*. A small volume, bound in green leather, with tarnished silver clasps. Leather and silver laden with protective magic. Marks to bind and blind, to close and imprison. Only someone with an innate talent for Free Magic and necromancy could open the book, and only an uncorrupted Charter Mage could close it. It contained all the lore of necromancy and counter-necromancy that fifty-three Abhorsens had gathered over a thousand years—and more besides, for its contents never stayed the same, seemingly altering at the book's own whim. Sam had read a little of it, at his mother's side.

"What's wrong with you?" asked Ellimere curiously, as Sam went paler and paler and his teeth began to chatter. She put the package on the end of his bed and came over, touching the back of her hand to Sam's forehead.

"You're cold," she said, surprised. "Really cold!"

"Sick," muttered Sam. He could barely speak. Fear gripped his throat. Fear of somehow being thrown into Death by the book, of being plunged once again under the surface of the cold river, to go crashing through the First Gate . . .

"Get back into bed," ordered Ellimere, suddenly solicitous. "I'll get Dr. Shemblis."

"No!" cried Sam, thinking of the court doctor and his curious, inquiring ways. "It'll pass. Just leave me alone for a while."

"All right," replied Ellimere, as she closed the window and helped re-arrange what was left of the blankets. "But don't think this is going to get you off playing the Bird of Dawning. Not unless Dr. Shemblis says you're really, really sick."

"I'm not," said Sam. "I'll be all right in a few hours."

"What happened to you, anyway?" asked Ellimere. "Dad was a bit vague, and we didn't have time to talk. Something about you going into Death and getting into trouble."

"Something like that," whispered Sam.

"Sooner you than me."

Ellimere picked up the package and hefted it curiously, then threw it down next to Sam. "I'm glad I had no aptitude for it. Imagine if you were going to be the King, and me the Abhorsen! Still, I'm glad you've already started popping into Death, because Mother certainly needs the help at the moment, and you'll be a lot more use doing that than mucking about making toys. Mind you, I was going to ask if you could make me two tennis racquets, so I suppose I shouldn't complain. I can't get anyone else to understand what I want, and I haven't played a game since I left Wyverley. You could make some, couldn't you?"

"Yes," replied Sam. But he wasn't thinking about tennis. He was thinking about the book next to him, and the fact that he was the Abhorsen-in-Waiting. Everyone expected him to succeed Sabriel. He was going to have to study *The Book of the Dead*. He would have to walk in Death again, and confront the necromancer—or even worse things, if that were possible.

"Are you sure I shouldn't get Shemblis?" Ellimere asked. "You do look very pale. I'll have someone come up with some chamomile tea, and I suppose you don't have to start your proper schedule till tomorrow. You will be better tomorrow, won't you?"

"I think so," said Sam. He was frozen immobile by the proximity of the book.

Ellimere looked at him again, with a look that contained equal parts of concern, annoyance, and irritation. Then she swung around and swept out, banging the door behind her.

Sam lay in bed, trying to take regular, slow breaths. He could feel the book next to him, almost as if it were a living thing. A coiled snake that was waiting to strike when he moved.

He lay there for a long time, listening to the sounds of the Palace that came wafting up to his tower room, even with the window closed. The regular watch-cry of the guards on the wall; the sudden conversation of people in the courtyard below, as they met on their business; the clash of sword on sword from the practice field that lay beyond the inner wall. Behind it all there was the constant crash of the sea. Belisaere was almost an island, and the Palace was built upon one of its four hills, in the northeast quarter. Sam's bedchamber was in the Sea Cliff tower, about halfway up. During the wildest winter storms, it was not unusual for sea spray to splash upon his window, despite the tower's distance from the shore.

A servant brought chamomile tea, and they spoke briefly, though Sam had no idea what he had said. The tea cooled, and the sun rose higher, till it had passed beyond his window and the air grew colder again.

Finally, Sam moved. With shaking hands, he forced himself to pick up the package. He cut the string with the knife that lay sheathed upon his bedhead and quickly unwrapped the oilskin, knowing that if he stopped, he'd be unable to go on.

Sure enough, it was *The Book of the Dead*, the green leather shining as if it were coated with sweat. The silver clasps that held it closed were clouded, their brightness dimmed. They cleared as Sam watched, and then frosted again, though he had not breathed upon them.

There was a note, too, a single sheet of rough-edged paper that bore only a Charter mark and Sam's own name, written in Sabriel's firm, distinctive hand.

Sam picked up the note, then used the oilskin wrapper like a glove to slip the Book under his bed. He couldn't bear to look at it. Not yet.

Then he touched the Charter mark on the paper, and Sabriel's voice sounded inside his head. She spoke quickly, and from the other noises in the background, Sam guessed she had made this message immediately before flying out in her Paperwing. Flying out to combat the Dead.

Sam—

I hope you are well and can forgive me for not being there for you now. I know from your father's last message-hawk that you are fit enough to be riding home, but that your encounter in Death has left you sorely tried. I know what that can be like—and I am proud that you risked entering Death to save your friends. I don't know that I would be brave enough myself to go into Death without my bells. Be assured that any hurt to your spirit will pass in time. It is the nature of Death to take, but the nature of Life to give.

Your brave action has also shown me that you are ready to formally begin training as the Abhorsen-in-Waiting. This makes me both proud and a little sad, because it means that you have grown up. The burdens of an Abhorsen are many, and one of the worst is that we are doomed to miss so much of our children's lives—of your life, Sam.

*I have delayed teaching you to some degree because I
wanted you to stay the dear little boy I can so easily remember.
But of course you have not been a little boy for many years,
and now you are a young man and must be treated as such.
Part of that is acknowledging your heritage, and the essential
role you have in the future of our Kingdom.*

A great part of that heritage is contained within The
Book of the Dead, *which you now have. You have studied
a little of it with me, but now it is time for you to master
its contents, as much as this is possible for anyone to do.
Certainly, in these present days, I have need of your
assistance, for there is a strange resurgence of trouble from
both the Dead and those who follow Free Magic, and I
cannot find the source of either.*

*We will speak more of this on my return, but for now
I want you to know that I am proud of you, Sameth. Your
father is, too. Welcome home, my son.*

*With all my love,
Mother*

Sam let the paper fall from his grasp and fell back on the pillow.
The future, so bright when that cricket ball had arced over the
stands for a six, now seemed very dark indeed.

Chapter Twenty

A DOOR OF THREE SIGNS

TO CELEBRATE HER nineteenth birthday, Lirael and the Dog decided to explore somewhere special, to venture through the jagged hole in the pale green rock where the main spiral of the Great Library came to a sudden end.

The hole was too small for Lirael to enter, so she had made a Charter-skin for the expedition. In the years since finding *In the Skin of a Lyon*, she had learned to make three different Charter-skins. Each had been very carefully selected for its natural advantages. The ice otter was small and lithe, and enabled Lirael to move in narrow ways and across ice and snow with ease. The russet bear was larger, and much stronger, than her natural form, and its thick fur was protection against both cold and harm. The barking owl gave her flight and made darkness no burden, though she had yet to fly outside some of the great chambers of the Library, which were never truly dark.

But the Charter-skins had their disadvantages as well. The ice otter's vision was in shades of grey, its perspective was low to the ground, and it induced a fondness for fish that lasted for days after Lirael shucked the skin. The russet bear's sight was weak, and wearing it made Lirael bad-tempered and gluttonous, also for some time after it was taken off. The barking owl was of little use in full daylight, and after wearing it Lirael would find her eyes watering under the bright lights of the Reading Room. But all in all she was pleased with the Charter-skins and the choices she had made, and proud that she had learned three

Charter-skins in less time than *In the Skin of a Lyon* suggested would be possible.

Their major drawback was the time they took to prepare and put on. Typically, it would take Lirael five hours or more to prepare a Charter-skin, another hour to fold it properly so that it would last a day or two in a pouch or bag, and then at least half an hour to put on. Sometimes it took longer, particularly the ice-otter skin, because it was so much smaller than Lirael's normal form. It was like forcing a foot into a sock that was only big enough for a toe, with the sock stretching while the foot shrank. Balancing the process was quite difficult, and it always made Lirael dizzy and a bit nauseated, to feel herself both changing and shrinking.

But on her birthday, since the hole in the rock was less than two feet wide, only the ice-otter shape would do. Lirael began to put it on, as the Disreputable Dog scrabbled at the hole. Somehow the Dog made herself longer and thinner in the process, till she looked like one of the sausage dogs that the Rasseli shepherd-queens carried around their necks, as illustrated in Lirael's favorite travelogue.

After a few minutes of furious work with her back legs, the Dog disappeared. Lirael sighed, and kept forcing herself into the Charter-skin. The Dog had a well-known problem with waiting, but Lirael felt a bit aggrieved that the hound couldn't even wait on her birthday, or let her go first.

Not that she really expected it. Her birthday was Lirael's most hated time of the year, the day she was forced to remember all the bad things in her life.

This year, as on every past birthday, she had woken without the Sight. It was an old hurt now, scarred over and locked deep within her heart. Lirael had learnt not to show the pain it caused her, not even to the Disreputable Dog, who otherwise shared all her thoughts and dreams.

Nor did Lirael contemplate suicide, as she had done on her fourteenth birthday, and briefly on her seventeenth. She had managed to forge a life for herself that, if not ideal, was satisfying in many ways. She still lived in the Hall of Youth, and would till she was twenty-one and assigned her own chambers, but since she spent every waking hour in the Library, she was largely free of Kirrith's interference. Lirael had also long since stopped going to Awakenings or any other ceremonial functions that would require her to wear the blue tunic, that hated, obvious sign that she was not a proper Clayr.

She wore her Librarian's uniform instead, even at breakfast, and had taken to tying a white scarf around her head like some of the older Clayr. It hid her black hair, and in her uniform there was no doubting who she was, even amongst the visitors in the Lower Refectory.

The week before her birthday, these working clothes had been greatly enhanced by the transition from a yellow to a red waist-coat, proud symbol of Lirael's promotion to Second Assistant Librarian. The promotion was very welcome but not without trouble, as the formal letter announcing it came unexpectedly, late one afternoon. In the letter, Vancelle, the Chief Librarian, congratulated Lirael and noted that there would be a brief cer-emony the next morning—at which time an additional key spell would be woken in her bracelet and certain spells taught her as was "concomitant to the responsibilities and offices of a Second Assistant Librarian in the Great Library of the Clayr."

Consequently, Lirael had stayed up all night in her study trying to put the extra key-spells she'd already awoken in her bracelet back to sleep, so as not to reveal her unauthorized wanderings. But the sleeping proved harder than the waking. Hours and hours later, without success, her groans of despair at four in the morning had woken the Dog, who breathed on the bracelet, which returned the extra spells to their dormant state and sent Lirael into a sleep so heavy she almost missed the ceremony anyway.

The red waistcoat was an early birthday present, followed by others on the actual day. Imshi and the other young librarians who worked most closely with Lirael gave her a new pen, a slender rod of silver that was engraved with the faces of owls and had two slender claws where a variety of steel nibs could be screwed in. It came in a velvet-lined box of sweet-smelling sandalwood, with an ancient inkwell of cloudy green glass that had a golden rim etched with runes that no one could read.

Both pen and inkwell were an unspoken commentary on Lirael's now long-established habit of speaking as little as possible. She wrote notes whenever she could get away with it. In the last few years, she had rarely said more than ten words in a row, and often she would not speak to other humans for days at a time.

Of course, the other Clayr didn't know that Lirael's silence was more than made up for in her conversations with the Dog, with whom she would talk for hours. Sometimes, her superiors would ask her why she didn't like to talk, but Lirael couldn't answer. All she knew was that talking to the Clayr reminded her of all the things she couldn't talk about. The Clayr's conversations would always return to the Sight, the central focus of their lives. By not speaking, Lirael was simply protecting herself from pain, even if she wasn't conscious of the reason.

At her birthday tea in the Junior Librarians' Common Room, an informal chamber normally given to lots of talk and laughter, Lirael was able only to say "thank you," and smile, though it was a smile accompanied by teary eyes. They were very kind, her fellow librarians. But they were still Clayr first and librarians second.

Lirael's last present was from the Disreputable Dog, who

gave her a big kiss. As dog kisses seemed to consist of energetic licks to the face, Lirael was happy to curtail the well-wishing by handing over the leftover cake from her birthday tea.

"That's all I get, a dog kiss," muttered Lirael. She was more than halfway into the ice-otter skin, but it would still be ten minutes before she could pursue her friend.

Lirael did not know it, but there were a number of other people who would have liked to give her a birthday kiss. Quite a few of the young men among the guards and merchants who regularly visited the Clayr had looked on her with increasing interest over the years. But she made it clear that she wanted to keep herself to herself. They also noted that she did not speak, not even to the Clayr on kitchen duty. So the young men simply watched her, and the more romantic of them dreamed of the day when she would suddenly come over and invite them upstairs. Other Clayr occasionally did so, but not Lirael. She continued to eat alone, and the dreamers continued to dream.

Lirael herself rarely thought about the fact that at nineteen she had never been kissed. She knew all about sex in theory, from the compulsory lessons in the Hall of Youth and books in the library. But she was too shy to approach any of the visitors, even the ones she saw regularly in the Lower Refectory, and there were very few male Clayr.

She often overheard the other young librarians talking freely of men, sometimes even in detail. But these liaisons were clearly not as important to the Clayr as the Sight and their work in the Observatory, and Lirael judged by their standards. The Sight was the most important, and it came first. Once she had the Sight, she might think of doing as the other Clayr did, and bring a man up to the Upper Refectory for dinner and a walk in the Perfumed Garden, and perhaps then . . . to her bed.

In fact, Lirael couldn't even imagine that any man would

be interested in her, compared to a real Clayr. As in everything else, Lirael thought a real Clayr would always be more interesting and attractive than herself.

Even outside work, Lirael took a different path from the other young Clayr. When they all finished at the Library at four in the afternoon, most would go to the Hall of Youth or their own living quarters, or to one of the Refectories or the areas where Clayr gathered for recreation, like the Perfumed Garden or the Sun Steps.

Lirael always went the other way, down from the Reading Room to her study, to wake up the Disreputable Dog. She'd been given a new study with her promotion, and now had a larger room that had a tiny bathroom off it, complete with water closet, sink, and hot and cold water.

Once the Dog had been woken up and the various items that had been knocked over in their exuberant greeting had been replaced, Lirael and the Dog usually waited till the night-watch assembly, when all the librarians on duty gathered briefly in the Main Reading Room to be given their tasks. Thus safe from observation, Lirael and the Dog would creep down the main spiral, passing into the Old Levels, where the other librarians seldom came.

Over the years, Lirael had come to know the Old Levels and many of their secrets and dangers well. She had even secretly helped out other librarians, without their knowing. At least three of them would have died if Lirael and the Dog hadn't taken care of several unpleasant creatures that had somehow entered the Library.

"Come on!" said the Dog, sticking her head back out of the hole. Lirael was fully in the otter skin, but there was something strange about her stomach. It looked different, but she couldn't work out what it was. She turned around to stare at it and rolled across the floor.

"Proud of your new waistcoat, I see," said the Dog, sniffing.

"What?" asked Lirael. She sat up and bent her head down to look at her furry stomach. It was a different shade of grey than normal, but she didn't remember making any changes.

"Ice otters don't usually have red stomachs, Miss Second Assistant Librarian," said the Dog. "Come on!"

"Oh," said Lirael. She'd never changed the color of her fur before. Still, it did show at least an unconscious mastery in making a Charter-skin. She smiled, and bounded up behind the Dog. They'd always meant to find out what was down this passage, but something had always interrupted them before. Now they would discover what lay beyond the end of the main spiral.

"The tunnel has fallen in," said the Disreputable Dog, wagging her tail in a manner that diluted the apparent seriousness of the news.

"I can see that!" snapped Lirael. She was feeling irritable, mainly from having been in her ice-otter Charter-skin for the last two hours. It had started to get very uncomfortable, like extremely sweaty clothes that stick in all the wrong places. There was nothing to distract her from the discomfort, either, because the hole at the end of the main spiral had proved to be quite boring. It had widened out after a while, but otherwise simply zigzagged back and forth without coming to any interesting intersections, chambers, or doors. Now it had ended with a wall of tumbled ice that blocked their way.

"No need to get snarky, Mistress," replied the Dog. "Besides, there is a way across. The glacier has pushed through, all right, but sometime or other a drill-grub has cut through above. If we climb up we can probably use the bore to get across to the other side."

"Sorry," said Lirael, sighing, shrugging her otter shoulders in a movement that flowed right through the rest of her long white-furred body. "What are you waiting for, then?"

"It's almost dinnertime," the Dog said primly. "You'll be missed."

"You mean you'll miss whatever I can steal for you," grumbled Lirael. "No one will miss me. Besides, you don't need to eat."

"But I like to," protested the Dog, pacing backwards and forwards, nimbly avoiding the chunks of ice that had fallen from the spur of the glacier and were now blocking their further progress along the tunnel.

"Just find the way, please," instructed Lirael. "Use your famous nose."

"Aye, aye, Captain," said the Dog with resignation. She started climbing up the tumbled ice, claws leaving deep, melting cuts. "The drill-grub bore is right at the top."

Lirael bounded up after her, enjoying the almost liquid feel of being an ice otter in movement. Of course, when she stopped wearing the Charter-skin, that memory of liquid movement would make her stumble and jerk for a few minutes, till her mind realized it was connecting with different muscles.

The Disreputable Dog was already scrabbling into the drill-grub's hole—a perfectly cylindrical bore about three feet in diameter that cut straight through the ice barrier. That was only a medium-sized grub's bore. The big ones were more than ten feet across. The grubs were rare now, in all sizes. Lirael was probably one of the few inhabitants of the Clayr's Glacier who had ever seen one.

In fact, she had seen two, many years apart. Both times the Dog had smelt them first, so they had had time to get out of the way. The grubs weren't dangerous, at least intentionally, but they were slow to react, and their rotating, multiple jaws chewed up anything in their path: ice, rock, or slow-moving human.

The Dog slipped for a moment, but didn't slide back, as a real dog probably would have. Lirael noticed that her canine friend's claws had grown to twice their normal length to cope with the ice. Definitely not something a real dog could do, but Lirael had long since come to terms with the fact that she didn't really know what the Dog was. That she had been born of both Charter and Free Magic there was no doubt, but Lirael didn't care to dwell on that. Whatever the Dog was, she was Lirael's one true friend and had proved her loyalty a hundred times and more in the past four and a half years.

Despite her magical origins, the Dog's smell was all too like a real dog's, Lirael thought, particularly when she was wet. Like now, when Lirael's wrinkling otter-nose was pressed up against the Dog's hind legs and tail as she followed her through the bore. Fortunately, the tunnel wasn't long, and Lirael forgot the Dog's odor as she saw that there wasn't just more boring tunnel on the other side. She could see the glow of a Charter-Magicked ceiling, and some sort of tiled wall.

"It's old, this room," announced the Dog, as they slid out of the bore and onto the pale blue and yellow tiles of the chamber floor. Both shook off the ice with a wriggle, Lirael copying the Dog's expressive shiver from shoulder to tail.

"Yes," agreed Lirael, suppressing an urge to scratch herself vigorously around the neck. The Charter-skin was fraying already, and she would need it to go back through the bore and the tunnel. Forcing her clawed forepaws to be still, she tried to concentrate on the room, hampered by her otterish vision, with its different field of view and lack of color.

The room was lit by common Charter marks for light,

glowing in the ceiling, though Lirael immediately saw that they were faded, and much older than most such marks would last. A desk of some deep red wood took up one corner, but without a chair. Empty bookcases lined one wall, glass doors shut. Charter marks for repelling dust moved endlessly across them like the sheen of oil on water.

There was a door on the far wall, of that same reddish wood, studded with tiny golden stars, golden towers, and silver keys. The golden stars were the seven-pointed variety that were the emblem of the Clayr, and the golden tower was the blazon of the Kingdom itself. The silver key Lirael did not know, though it was not an uncommon sigil. Many cities and towns used silver keys in their blazons.

She could feel considerable magic in the door. Charter marks of locking and warding ran with the grain of the wood, and there were other marks, too, describing something Lirael couldn't quite grasp.

She started towards it to see what they were, all her itchiness forgotten, but the Dog put herself in the way, as if curbing an exuberant puppy.

"Don't!" she yelped. "It has a guard-sending on it, who would only see—and slay—an ice otter. You must approach in normal form and let it sense your blood untainted."

"Oh," said Lirael, slumping down, slim head resting on her forepaws, glittering dark eyes focused on the door. "But if I change back, it'll take me at least half the night to make a new Charter-skin. We'll miss dinner—and the midnight rounds."

"Some things," the Dog said portentously, "are worth missing dinner for."

"And the rounds?" asked Lirael. "It'll be the second time this week. Even if it *is* my birthday, it will be extra kitchen duty for me—"

"I like you having extra kitchen duty," replied the Dog, licking her lips, and then licking Lirael's face for good measure.

"Eeerrggh!" exclaimed Lirael. She still hesitated, thinking not only of the extra kitchen duty but also the lecture that would accompany it from Aunt Kirrith.

But just over there, the door of stars and towers and keys beckoned. . . .

Lirael shut her eyes and began to think of the sequence of Charter marks that would unravel the otter-skin, her mind dipping into the never-ending flow of the Charter, picking out a mark here, a symbol there, weaving them into a spell. In just a few minutes she would be plain Lirael again, with her long, unruly black hair so unlike that of her blond- and brown-haired cousins; her pointy chin so much sharper than their round faces; her pale skin that would never tan, not even in the harsh sunlight reflecting off the glacial ice; and her brown eyes, when all the Clayr had blue or green. . . .

The Disreputable Dog watched her change, the ice-otter skin glowing with crawling Charter marks that spun and wove till they became a tornado of light, shining brighter and brighter and spinning faster and faster till it vanished. A slight young woman stood there, frowning, eyes tightly shut. Before her eyes opened, her hands ran over her body, checking that the red waistcoat was there, with dagger, whistle, and clockwork emergency mouse. In some of Lirael's early Charter-skins, all her clothes had fallen off in pieces when she'd shucked the skin, every seam unpicked in an instant.

"Good," said the Disreputable Dog. "Now we can try the door."

Chapter Twenty-One

BEYOND THE DOORS OF WOOD AND STONE

LIRAEL TOOK TWO steps towards the red wood door, then stopped, as Charter Magic flared and swirled before her and a fierce yellow light shone from the door-frame, forcing her to duck her head and blink.

When she looked up, a Charter-sending stood in front of the door—a creature of spell-flesh and magic-bone, conjured for a specific purpose. Not one of the passive Library helpers, but a guard of human shape, though much taller and broader than any living man, clad in silver mail, a closed steel helm hiding whatever face the spell had wrought. Its sword was in its hand, outthrust, held steady as a statue, the point a few inches from Lirael's bare throat. Unlike their spell-flesh, the weapons or tools of sendings were always made to be completely tangible. Sometimes, as Lirael suspected was the case with this sword, they were even harder, sharper, and more dangerous than they would be if wrought of steel rather than magic.

The sending held the sword extended for a few seconds without a waver. Then, so quickly she didn't see it move, the point flicked against Lirael's throat—just enough to break the skin, capturing a single bead of blood on the very tip of the blade.

Lirael gulped down a startled cry but remained frozen, fearful that it would strike again if she flinched. She knew much of the lore of sendings, having continued her studies even after "creating" the Dog. But she could not gauge the true purpose of this one. For the first time since she had gone to confront the Stilken, she felt afraid, and the chill dread of Charter Magic gone wrong welled up inside her bones.

The sending lifted its sword again, and Lirael did flinch this time, unable to control the twitch of fright. But the guard was simply making that drop of blood run down the gutter of the blade in a slow, stately roll, like a bead of oil, not leaving a trace on the Charter-woven steel. After what seemed an age, the bead reached the hilt and sank into the crossguard like butter into toast.

Behind Lirael, the Dog let out a long, half-woofed sigh, even as the sending saluted with the sword—and broke apart, the Charter symbols that had made it momentarily real spinning out into the air before fading away into nothingness. In a few seconds, no sign of the sending remained.

Lirael realized she'd been holding her breath, and let it out with a relieved whoosh. She touched her neck, expecting to feel the unpleasant wetness of blood. But there was nothing, no cut, not even a slight unevenness in the skin.

The Dog's snout nudged her behind the knee. Then the hound slipped past and grinned back at her.

"Well, you passed that test," she said. "You can open the door now."

"I'm not sure I want to," replied Lirael thoughtfully, still fingering her neck. "Maybe we should go back."

"What!" exclaimed the Dog, her ears sticking up in disbelief. "Not look? Since when have you become Miss We Shouldn't Be Here?"

"It could have cut my throat," said Lirael, her voice trembling. "It nearly did."

The Disreputable Dog rolled her eyes and collapsed onto

her front paws in exasperation. "It was only testing you, to make sure you have the Blood. You're a Daughter of the Clayr— no Charter-made creature would harm you. Though as the greater world is full of danger, you'd better start getting used to the idea that you can't give up at the first thing that scares you!"

"Am I a Daughter of the Clayr?" whispered Lirael, tears starting in her eyes. She had held her sorrow in all year, but it was always worst on her birthday. Now it could not be repressed. She crouched down and hugged the Dog, ignoring the damp reek of dog-smell. "I'm nineteen and I still haven't got the Sight. I don't look like everyone else. When that sending put out its sword, I suddenly realized that it knew. It knew I'm not a Clayr, and it was going to kill me."

"But it didn't, because you are a Clayr, idiot," said the Dog, quite gently. "You've seen the hunting dogs, how every now and then one will be born with floppy ears or have a brown back instead of gold. They're still part of the pack. You're just a floppy-ear."

"But I can't See the future!" cried Lirael. "Would the pack accept a dog that couldn't smell?"

"You can smell," said the Dog, rather illogically. She licked Lirael's cheek. "Besides, you have other gifts. None of the others are half the Charter Mage you are, are they?"

"No," whispered Lirael. "But Charter Magic doesn't count. It's the Sight that makes the Clayr. Without it, I am nothing."

"Well, perhaps there are other things you can learn," encouraged the Dog. "You might find something else—"

"What? Like an interest in embroidery?" Lirael said in a depressed monotone, cradling her head in her tear-dampened forearms. "Or perhaps you think I should take up leather-work?"

"That," said the Dog, her voice losing all sympathy, "is self-pity, and there's only one way to deal with it."

"What?" asked Lirael sullenly.

"This," said the Dog, lunging forward and nipping her quite sharply on the leg.

"Ow!" Lirael shrieked, leaping up and stumbling against the door. "What did you do that for?"

"You were being pathetic," said the Dog, as Lirael rubbed the spot on her calf where visible tooth-marks indented her soft wool leggings. "Now you're just cross, which is an improvement."

Lirael eyed the Dog balefully but didn't answer, because she couldn't think of anything to say that wouldn't—quite accurately—be seen as sulky or bad-tempered. Besides, she remembered a particular dog bite from her seventeenth birthday and had no desire to add a nineteenth-birthday scar.

The Dog stared back, her head tilted to one side, ears cocked, waiting for some sort of reply. Lirael knew from experience that the Dog could sit like that for hours if necessary, and gave up the struggle to maintain her self-pity. Clearly, the Dog just didn't understand how important it was to have the Sight.

"So—how do I open this?" asked Lirael.

Without realizing it, she'd been leaning against the door, catching her balance there after the nip-assisted leap. She could feel the Charter Magic in it, warm and rhythmic under the palm of her hand, moving in slow counterpoint to the pulse in her wrist and neck.

"Give it a push," suggested the Dog, moving closer, sniffing at the crack where the door met the floor. "The sending probably unlocked it for you."

Lirael shrugged and placed both palms against the door. Curiously, the metal studs seemed to have moved while she wasn't looking. They had been all mixed up but were now sorted into three distinct patterns, though there was no obvious meaning to them. Lirael wasn't sure which particular symbols were under her palms, though she could feel them leaving an imprint on her skin.

Even the metal studs were impregnated with Charter symbols, Lirael felt. She didn't know precisely what they were, but it was clear the door was a major work of magic, the result of many months of superior spell-casting and equally masterful metalwork and carpentry.

She pushed once, and the door groaned. She pushed more forcefully, and it suddenly slid back like a concertina, separating into seven distinct panels. Lirael didn't notice that as this happened, one of the three symbols completely disappeared, leaving only two types of studs visible. She was overcome by a sudden surge of Charter Magic that flowed out of the door and somehow into Lirael herself. She felt it coursing through her, infusing her with a heady happiness she had not felt since the Disreputable Dog had first come to banish her loneliness. It swam in her blood, sparked in her breath—then it was gone, and she staggered against the door-frame. At the same time, the impression of the studs on her hands faded before she could see what they meant.

"Whew!" she said, shaking her head, one hand unconsciously feeling for the comforting bulk of the Dog at her side. "What was that?"

"The Door just said hello," replied the Dog. Slipping from Lirael's grasp, she was already questing ahead, paws clicking as she essayed the first steps of a flight that spun downwards into the mountain.

"What do you mean?" asked Lirael. The Dog's upthrust, wagging tail whisked down and around the curve of the spiral. "How can a door say hello? Wait! Wait for me!"

The Disreputable Dog wasn't known for listening to commands, requests, or even entreaties, but she was waiting about twenty steps lower down. There were fewer Charter marks providing light here, and the steps were covered in dark moss. Clearly no one had passed this way for a very long time.

She looked up as Lirael reached her, then immediately took off down the steps again, easily re-establishing her twenty-step lead, and was once again lost to sight, though Lirael could hear her paws steadily clicking down the steps.

Lirael sighed and followed more slowly, not trusting the moss-covered stair. There was something farther down that she didn't quite like, and she felt oppressed by some sense of unease, below the level of consciousness. A sort of vaguely unpleasant pressure that was increasing with every downwards step.

The Dog waited, at least momentarily, eight more times before they reached the bottom of the deep stairs. Lirael guessed they were now more than four hundred yards deeper under the mountain than she had ever been before. There were no ice intrusions here, either, adding to her feeling of strangeness. It wasn't like any other part of the Clayr's domain.

It kept getting darker, too, the lower they went, the old Charter marks for light fading till there were only a few flickering here and there. Whoever had built this stair had started from the bottom, Lirael realized, looking at the marks. The lower ones were much older and had not been replaced for centuries.

Normally, she didn't mind the darkness, but it was different here, deep in the mountain. Lirael called up a light herself, two bright Charter marks of illumination that she wove into her hair, to send a bobbing fall of light ahead of her as she descended.

At the bottom of the stairs, the Dog was scratching the back of her ear in front of another Charter-bound door. This one was of stone, and there were some letters carved into it, large, deep-cut letters using the Middle Alphabet, as well as the Charter symbols only a Charter Mage could see.

Lirael bent closer to read them, then recoiled, turned to the steps, and tried to run away. Somehow the Dog got between her legs, tripping her. Lirael fell and lost control of her light spell, and the bright marks went out, twisting back into the endless flow of the Charter.

For a moment of pure panic, she scrabbled in the darkness, heading for what she thought were the steps. Then her fingers met the soft, wet nose of the Dog, and she saw a faint, spectral glow outlining the shape of her canine companion.

"That was smart," said the Dog in the darkness, moving closer to woofle wetly in Lirael's ear. "I take it you didn't suddenly remember a pie in the oven?"

"The door," whispered Lirael, making no effort to get up. "It's a grave door. To a crypt."

"Is it?"

"It's got my name on it," muttered Lirael.

There was a long pause. Then the Dog said, "So you think someone went to all the trouble to make you a crypt a thousand years ago on the off chance you might turn up one day, walk in, and have a convenient heart attack?"

"No . . ."

There was another long pause, and then the Dog said, "Presuming that this actually is the door to a crypt, may I ask how rare the name Lirael is?"

"Well, I think there was a great-aunt I'm named after, and there was another one before her—"

"So if it is a crypt, it's probably that of some long-ago Lirael," the Dog suggested kindly. "But what makes you think it is a crypt door, anyway? I seem to recall there were two words on the door. And the second one didn't look like 'grave' or 'crypt.'"

"What did it say, then?" asked Lirael, wearily standing up, already mentally reaching for the Charter marks that would give her light, hands ready to sketch them in the air. She couldn't even remember reading the second word, but didn't want to admit to the Dog that she'd just had the overwhelming feeling that it was a crypt. That feeling, combined with seeing her own name, had created a moment of total panic, when her only thought was to get out, to get back to the safety of the Library.

"Something quite different," said the Dog with satisfaction, as light bloomed from Lirael's fingertips, falling cleanly on the door.

This time, Lirael looked long at the carved letters, her hands touching the deep-etched stone. Her forehead wrinkled as she read the words again and again, as if she couldn't quite put the letters together into a sensible word.

"I don't understand," she said finally. "The second word is 'path.' It says 'Lirael's Path'!"

"Guess you should go through, then," said the Dog, unperturbed by the sign. "Even if you're not the Lirael whose path it is, you are a Lirael, which in my book is a pretty good excuse—"

"Dog. Shut up," said Lirael, thinking. If this gate was the beginning of a path named for her, it had been made at least a thousand years ago. Which was not impossible, for the Clayr sometimes had visions of such far-distant futures. Or possible futures, as they called them, for the future was apparently like a many-branching stream, splitting, converging, and splitting again. Much of the Clayr's training, at least as far as Lirael knew, was in working out which possible future was the most likely—or the most desirable.

But there was a catch to the notion that the long-ago Clayr had Seen Lirael, because the Clayr of the present time couldn't See Lirael's future at all and had never been able to do so. Sanar and Ryelle had told her that even when the Nine Day Watch tried to See her, there was nothing. Lirael's future was impenetrable, as was her present. No Clayr had ever Seen her, not even in a chance-found minute showing her in the Library, or asleep in bed a month hence. Once again she was different, not able to See and also Unseen.

If even the Nine Day Watch couldn't See her, Lirael thought, how could the Clayr of a thousand years past know she would come this way? And why would they build not only this door but also the stairs? It was far more likely that this path was named for one of her ancestors, some other Lirael of long ago.

That made her feel better about opening the door. She leaned forward, pushing with both hands against the cold stone. Charter Magic flowed in this door, too, but it did not leap into her, instead just pulsing gently against her skin. It was like an old dog by the fire, content to be stroked, knowing it need not obviously show delight.

The door moved slowly inwards, resisting her push, with a long-drawn-out screech of stone on stone. Colder air flowed from the other side, ruffling Lirael's hair, making the Charter lights dance. There was a damp smell, too, and the strange, oppressive feeling Lirael had encountered on the stairs grew stronger, like the beginning buzz of a toothache that heralds future pain.

A vast chamber lay beyond the door, space stretching up and out, seemingly endless, beyond the pool of light around her. A cavern, measureless in the dark, perhaps going on forever.

Lirael stepped in and looked up, up into darkness, till her neck ached, and her eyes slowly grew accustomed to the gloom.

Strange luminescence, not from Charter Magic lights, shone in patches here and there, rising up so high that the farthest glow was like a distant swathe of stars in the night. Still looking up, Lirael realized that she stood at the bottom of a deep rift that stretched up almost to the very pinnacle of Starmount itself. She looked across and saw that she stood on a broad ledge, and the rift continued past it, down into still deeper darkness, perhaps even to the root of the world itself. With that sight came recognition, for she knew only one chasm so narrow and so deep. Much higher up, it was spanned by closed bridges. Lirael had crossed it almost unknowingly many times, but had never seen its terrifying depth.

"I know this place," said Lirael, her voice small and echoing. "We're in the bottom of the Rift, aren't we?"

She hesitated, then added, "The burial place of the Clayr."

The Disreputable Dog nodded but didn't say anything.

"You knew, didn't you?" continued Lirael, still looking up. She couldn't see them, but she knew the higher reaches of the Rift were pockmarked with small caves, each one holding the mortal remains of a past Clayr. Generations of dead, carefully tucked away in this vertical cemetery. In a weird way, she could feel the presence of the graves, or the dead inside them . . . or something.

Her mother was not there, for she had died alone in some foreign land, far from the Clayr, too far for the body to be returned. But Filris rested here, as did others whom Lirael had known.

"It *is* a crypt," she said, looking sternly at the Dog. "I knew it."

"Actually it's more of an ossuary," the Dog began. "I understand that when a Clayr Sees her death, she is lowered down by rope to a suitable ledge, where she digs her own—"

"They do not!" interrupted Lirael, shocked. "They only know when, to some degree. And Pallimor and the gardeners usually prepare the caves. Aunt Kirrith says it's very ill-bred to want to dig your own cave—"

She stopped suddenly and whispered, "Dog? Am I here because they've Seen me die and I have to dig my own cave because I'm ill-bred?"

"I'm going to have to bite you properly if you keep up that nonsense," growled the Dog. "Why this sudden preoccupation with dying, anyway?"

"Because I can feel it, feel it all around me," muttered Lirael. "Particularly here."

"That's because the doorways to Death are ajar where many people have died, or where many lie buried," said the Dog absently. "The Blood mixes a little, so there are always Clayr who are sensitive to Death. That's what you feel. You shouldn't be afraid of it."

"I'm not, really," replied Lirael, puzzled. "It's like an ache or an itch. It makes me want to do something. Scratch it. Make it go away."

"You don't know any necromancy, do you?"

"Of course not! That's Free Magic. It's forbidden."

"Not necessarily. Clayr have dabbled in Free Magic before, and some still do," said the Dog in a distracted manner. She'd caught the scent of something and was snuffling vigorously around Lirael's feet.

"Who dabbles in Free Magic?" asked Lirael. The Dog didn't answer but continued to sniff around Lirael's feet. "What can you smell?"

"Magic," said the Dog, looking up for a second before resuming her snuffle, roaming out in an ever-increasing circle. "Old, old magic. Hidden here, in the depths of the world.

How very, very . . . *yow!*"

Her last words ended in a yelp as a sudden sheet of flame sprang up across the rift, heat and light exploding everywhere. Lirael, totally unprepared, staggered back, falling across the open doorway. An instant later, the Dog collided with her, smelling distinctly singed.

Inside the fiery wall, forms began to take shape, humanoid figures that flexed arms and legs within the flame. Charter marks roared and swam in the yellow-blue-red inferno, flowing too fast for Lirael to see what they were.

Then the figures stepped out of the flames, warriors composed entirely of fire, their swords white-hot and brilliant.

"Do something!" barked the Dog.

But Lirael just kept staring at the advancing warriors, mesmerized by the flames that flickered through their bodies. They were all part of one great Charter-spell, she saw, one enormously powerful sending made up of many parts. A guardian-sending, like the one on the red wood door . . .

Lirael stood up, patted the Dog once on the head, and walked out, straight towards the ferocious heat and the guardians with their swords of flame.

"I am Lirael," she said, investing her speech with the Charter marks of truth and clarity. "A Daughter of the Clayr."

Her words hung in the air for a moment, cutting through the buzz and crackle of the fiery sendings. Then the guardians raised their swords as if in salute—and a wave of even more intense heat rolled forward, robbing Lirael's lungs of air. She choked, coughed, took one step back . . . and fainted.

When she came to, the Disreputable Dog's tongue was just about to lick her face. For about the tenth time, judging from the thick film of dog saliva on her cheek.

"What happened?" she asked, quickly looking around. There were no fires now, no burning guardians, but small Charter marks for light twinkled all around her like tiny stars.

"They burnt up your air when they saluted. I think that whoever created those sendings expected people to identify themselves from the door," said the Dog, attempting another lick, only to be fended off. "Or else they were particularly stupid sendings. Still, at least one of them had the good grace to throw out a handful of these little lights. Some of your hair has been burnt off, by the way."

"Curse it!" exclaimed Lirael, examining the singed ends of her hair, where they stuck out from under her scarf. "Aunt Kirrith will notice that for sure! I'll have to tell her I leant over a candle or something. Speaking of Kirrith, we'd better start back."

"Not yet!" protested the Dog. "Not after all this effort. Besides, the lights mark a path. Look! That must be it. Lirael's Path!"

Lirael sat up and looked where the Dog was pointing—in the classic pose, one foreleg up and snout eagerly forward. Sure enough, there was a path of tiny, twinkling Charter lights, leading farther along the ledge, to where the Rift narrowed into an even more ominous darkness.

"We really should go back," she said, half-heartedly. The path of lights was there, beckoning. The sendings had let her past. There must be something at the other end worth getting to. Maybe even something that would help her gain the gift of Sight, she thought, helpless against that longing, the tiny hope that still lived inside her heart. All her years of searching in the Library had not helped her. Perhaps it would be otherwise, here in the ancient heart of the Clayr's realm.

"Come on, then," she said, pushing herself up with a groan. Burnt hair and bruises—that was all she'd found so far. "What are you waiting for?"

"You go first," retorted the Dog. "My nose still hurts from your stupid relatives' blazing doormen."

The path of lights led farther along the ledge, and the Rift narrowed, the rock walls closing in, till Lirael could reach out and run her fingers along the cold, wet stone on either side of her. She stopped doing that when she discovered that the luminescence came from a damp fungus that made her fingertips glow and smell like rotten cabbage.

As the way grew narrower, it also descended farther into the mountain, and a chill dankness banished the last remnants of heat from Lirael's scorched face. There was also a sound, a deep rumbling that vibrated up through her feet, getting louder as they walked on. At first, Lirael thought she was imagining it, that perhaps it was part of what the Dog called her sense of Death. Then she realized what it was: the full-throated roar of rushing water.

"We must be near an underground river or something," she said, nervously raising her voice to counter the rising roar of the water. Like most of the Clayr, she could barely swim, and her experience of rivers was confined to the awesome ice-melt torrents that raged from the glacier every Spring.

"We are almost upon it," replied the Dog, who could see farther in the glow of the star-lined path. "As the poet had it:

> *"Swift river born in deepest night,*
> *Rushing forth to catch the light.*
> *Deep ice and dark its swaddling cloth,*
> *The Kingdom's foes will feel its wroth.*
> *Till mighty Ratterlin spends its strength,*
> *In the Delta at full length.*

"Hmmm . . . I may have forgotten a line there. Let's see, 'Swift river—' "

"The Ratterlin's source is here?" interrupted Lirael, pointing ahead. "I thought it was just meltwater. I didn't know it had a source."

"There is a spring," replied the Dog, after a pause. "A very old spring. In the heart of the mountain, in the deepest dark. Stop!"

Lirael obeyed, one hand instinctively clutching at the loose fold of skin on the Dog's neck, just behind her collar.

At first she didn't understand why the Dog had stopped her, till the hound led her on, a few more cautious steps. With those steps, the sound of the river suddenly became a thundering roar, and cold spray slapped her in the face.

They had come to the river. The path ahead was a slender, slippery bridge of wet stone that stretched out twenty paces or more, to end in yet another door. The bridge had no rails, and was less than two feet wide. Its narrowness, and the rushing water below, were a clear indication that it was designed to be a barrier to the Dead. Nothing of that kind could cross here.

Lirael looked at the bridge, the door, then down at the dark, rushing water, feeling both fear and a terrible fascination. The constant motion of the water and the incessant roar were mesmerizing, but finally she managed to tear her gaze away. She looked at the Dog, and though her words were half-drowned by the crash of the river, exclaimed, "I am not going to cross that!"

The Dog ignored her, and Lirael started to repeat herself. But the words stayed on her tongue as Lirael saw that the Dog's paws had grown twice as large as usual, and flattened out. She also looked quite smug.

"I bet you've even grown suckers," shouted Lirael, shuddering with distaste at the thought. "Like an octopus."

"Of course I have," the Dog shouted back, lifting one paw

with a squelching pop that Lirael could hear even over the river's roar. "This looks like a very treacherous bridge."

"Yes, it does," bawled Lirael, looking at the bridge again. Clearly the Dog intended to cross, and with her sucker-footed help, Lirael guessed, crossing would go from impossible to merely dangerous. Sighing, she bent down and took off her shoes, eyes blinking against the constant spray. After tying the laces of her soft leather ankle-boots through her belt, she wriggled her toes on the stone. It was very cold, but Lirael was relieved to feel faint cross-hatching that she hadn't seen in the dim light. That would give her some grip.

"I wonder what this bridge was designed to keep out," she said, carefully slipping her fingers under the Dog's collar, feeling the comforting buzz of the Charter Magic there and the even more comforting bulk of a well-balanced dog.

They had only taken the first step when Lirael voiced her second thought, her words inaudible with the river's bellow all around them.

"Or what it was designed to keep in."

Chapter Twenty-Two

POWER OF THREE

THE DOOR AT the far end of the bridge opened as soon as Lirael touched it. Once again, she felt Charter Magic flow into her, but it was not the friendly touch of the upper door, or the quiet recognition of the stone portal at the entrance to the Rift. This one was more like a wary examination, followed by immediate, but not necessarily friendly, recognition.

Under her hand, the Dog shivered as the door swung open. Lirael felt the tremor and wondered why, till she caught the distinctive, corrosive scent of Free Magic. It was coming from somewhere ahead, strangely overlaid with Charter Magic that bound and contained it.

"Free Magic," whispered Lirael, hesitating. But the Dog continued to move forward, dragging her along. Reluctantly, Lirael followed her through the doorway.

As soon as Lirael passed the threshold, the door slammed shut behind her. In an instant, the roar of the river was cut off. So was the light from the Charter-marked trail. It was dark, darker than any darkness Lirael had ever known, a true dark in which it was suddenly difficult to even imagine light. The darkness pressed upon Lirael, making her doubt her own senses. Only the Dog's warm skin under her hand told her that she was still standing, that the room had not changed, and the floor had not tilted.

"Don't move," whispered the Dog, and Lirael felt a canine snout briefly press against her leg, as if the spoken warning weren't enough.

The smell of Free Magic grew stronger. Lirael pinched her nose with one hand, trying not to breathe anything in, while her other hand went to the clockwork emergency mouse in her waistcoat pocket. Not that it was likely that even this clever device could find its way from here to the Library.

She could feel Charter Magic building, too, strong marks floating in the air like pollen, their usual internal light dampened. She could sense Charter and Free Magic working together, winding and twisting about her, weaving some spell she couldn't even begin to identify.

Fear began to knot in Lirael's stomach, slowly spreading to paralyze her lungs. She wanted to breathe, to force air slowly in and out, to calm herself with the steadiness of her own breath. But the air was heavy with strange magic, magic she could not—would not—breathe in.

Then lights began to sparkle in the air; tiny, fragile balls of light made up of hundreds of hair-thin spines, like luminous dandelion clocks, wafting about on some breeze Lirael couldn't feel. With the lights, the taint of Free Magic abated, the Charter Magic began to strengthen, and Lirael took a slight, cautious breath.

In the strangely mottled, constantly changing light, Lirael saw that she was in an octagonal chamber. A large room, but not of cold, carved stone as she'd expected, here in the heart of the mountain. The walls were tiled in a delicate pattern of golden stars, towers, and silver keys. The ceiling was plastered and painted with a night sky, full of black, rain-fat clouds advancing upon seven bright and shining stars. And there was carpet under her bare feet, Lirael realized. A deep blue carpet, soft and warm under her toes after the cold, wet stone of the bridge.

In the middle of the room, a redwood table stood in solitary splendor, its slender legs ending in silver, three-toed feet. On its rich, polished surface there were three items, arranged in a line: a small metal case about the size of Lirael's palm; a set of what looked like metal panpipes; and a book, bound in deep blue leather with silver clasps. The table, or the items on it, were clearly the focal point for the magic, for the dandelion lights swarmed thickest there, creating an effect like luminous fog.

"Off you go, then," said the Dog, sitting back on her haunches. "That looks like what we've come for."

"What do you mean?" asked Lirael suspiciously, drawing a series of deep and calming breaths. She felt reasonably safe now, but there was a lot of magic in the room that she didn't know, and she couldn't even begin to guess what it was for or where it came from. And she could still taste Free Magic at the back of her mouth and on her tongue, a cold iron tang that just wouldn't go away.

"The doors opened for you; the path lit up for you; the guardians here didn't destroy you," said the Dog, nuzzling Lirael's open hand with her cold, damp nose. She looked up at Lirael knowingly and added, "Whatever's on that table must be meant for you. Which equally means it's not meant for me. So I'm going to sit down here. Or lie down, actually. Wake me up when it's time to go."

With that, the Dog stretched luxuriously, yawned, and lowered herself to the carpet. Comfortably settled on her side, she swished her tail a few times and then, to all appearances, fell deeply asleep.

"Oh, Dog!" exclaimed Lirael. "You can't sleep now! What'll I do if something bad happens?"

The Dog opened one eye and said, with the least possible jaw movement, "Wake me up, of course."

Lirael looked down at the sleeping Dog, then over at the table. The Stilken was the worst thing she'd encountered in the Library. But she'd found other dangerous things over the past few years—fell creatures, old Charter-spells that had unraveled or become unpredictable, mechanical traps, even poisoned book bindings. All these were the regular hazards of a librarian's life, but nothing like what she faced now. Whatever these items were, they were guarded more heavily, and with stranger and more powerful magic, than anything Lirael had ever seen.

Whatever magic was concentrated here was very old, too, Lirael realized. The walls, the floor, the ceiling, the carpet, the table—even the air in the room—were saturated with layer upon layer of Charter marks, some of them at least a thousand years old. She could feel them moving everywhere, mixing and changing. When she closed her eyes for a moment, the room felt almost like a Charter Stone, a source of Charter Magic rather than just a place upon which many spells had been cast.

But that was impossible, at least as far as she knew. . . .

Suddenly made dizzy by the thought, Lirael opened her eyes again. Charter marks flowed against her skin, into her breath, swam in her blood. Free Magic floated between the marks. The dandelion lights spread out towards her like tendrils, wrapped gently around her waist, and slowly reeled her in towards the table.

The magic and the lights made her feel light-headed and dazed, as if she'd woken from the final moments of a dream. Lirael fought the feeling for a moment, but it was a pleasant feeling, not at all threatening. She let the sleeping Dog lie and walked forward slowly, swathed in light.

Then she was suddenly at the table, with no memory of

crossing the intervening space. Her hands were resting on the cool, polished surface of the table. As could be expected of a Second Assistant Librarian, she reached for the book first, her fingers touching the silver clasp that held it shut as she read the title embossed in silver type upon the spine: *The Book of Remembrance and Forgetting*.

Lirael undid the clasp, feeling Charter Magic there, too, noting the marks that chased each other across the silver surface and deep in the metal itself. Marks of binding and closing, burning and destruction.

But the clasp was open by the time she realized what the marks were, and she stood unharmed. Carefully, she turned back the cover and the title page, the crisp, leaf-thin paper turning easily. There were Charter marks inside the pages, put there at the time of the paper's making. And Free Magic, constrained and channeled into place. Magic of both kinds lay in the boards and leather of the cover, and even in the glue and stitching of the spine.

Most of all, there was magic and power in the type. In the past, Lirael had seen similar, if less powerful, books, like *In the Skin of a Lyon*. You could never truly finish reading such a book, for the contents changed at need, at the original maker's whim, or to suit the phases of the moon or the patterns of the weather. Some of the books had contents you couldn't even remember till certain events might come to pass. Invariably, this was an act of kindness from the creator of the book, for such contents invariably dealt with things that would be a burden to recall with every waking day.

The lights danced around Lirael's head as she began to read, making shadow patterns from her hair flicker across the page. She read the first page, then the next, then the one after. Soon Lirael had finished the first chapter, as her hand reached out every few minutes to turn the page. Behind her, the Dog's heavy, sleepy breath seemed to match the slow rhythm of the turning pages.

Hours later, or even days—for Lirael had lost all knowledge of time—she turned what seemed to be the last page and closed the book. It latched itself shut, the silver clasp snapping.

Lirael drew back at the snap but didn't leave the table. Instead, she picked up the panpipes, seven small tubes of silver, ranging in size from the length of her little finger to a little shorter than her hand. She held the pipes up to her lips, but didn't blow. They were much more than they appeared. The book had told her how the pipes were made, and how they should be used, and Lirael now knew that the Charter marks that moved in the silver were only a veneer on the Free Magic that lurked within.

She touched each of the pipes in turn, smallest to largest, and whispered their names to herself before putting the instrument back on the table. Then she picked up the last item, the small metal case. This was silver, too, etched with pleasing decorations as well as Charter marks. The latter were similar to those on the book, all threatening retribution if the box were opened by someone not of the True Blood. It didn't say which particular blood, but Lirael thought that if the book opened for her, the case would, too.

She lightly touched the catch, recoiling a little as she felt the heat of Free Magic blazing within. The case remained shut. Briefly, she thought that the book might be wrong, or she might have misread the marks, or not have the right blood. She shut her eyes and firmly pressed the catch.

Nothing terrible happened, but the case shivered in her hand. Lirael opened her eyes. The case had sprung open into two halves, hinged in the middle. Like a small mirror, to be balanced on a shelf or table.

Lirael opened it completely and placed it, vee-shaped, on

the table. One side of it was silver, but the other was something she couldn't describe. Where the bright reflective surface of a mirror would be, there was a nonreflective rectangle of . . . nothing. A piece of absolute darkness, a shape of something made from the total absence of light.

The Book of Remembrance and Forgetting called it a Dark Mirror, and Lirael had read, at least in part, how it might be used. But the Dark Mirror would not work in this room, or in any part of the world of Life. It could be used only in Death, and Lirael had no intention of going there, even if the book professed to show her how to come back. Death was the province of the Abhorsen, not the Clayr, even though the peculiar use of the Dark Mirror could possibly be related to the Clayr's gift of Sight.

Lirael snapped shut the Dark Mirror and laid it on the table. But her fingers still rested upon it. She stood there like that for a full minute, thinking. Then she picked it up and slipped it into her left waistcoat pocket, to join the company of a pen nib, a length of waxed string, and a seriously foreshortened pencil. After another moment of hesitation, she picked up the panpipes and put them in her right pocket with the clockwork mouse. Finally, she picked up the *Book of Remembrance and Forgetting* and tucked it into the front of her waistcoat.

She walked back to the Disreputable Dog. It was time for the two of them to have a very serious talk about what was going on. The Book, the Dark Mirror, and the panpipes had lain here for a thousand years or more, waiting in the dark for someone the Clayr of long ago had known would come.

Waiting in the dark for a woman named Lirael.

Waiting for *her*.

Chapter Twenty-Three

A TROUBLESOME SEASON

PRINCE SAMETH STOOD shivering on the narrow sentry walk of the Palace's second tallest tower. He was wearing his heaviest fur cloak, but the wind still cut through it, and he couldn't be bothered to cast a Charter-spell for warmth. He half wanted to catch a cold, because it would mean escaping from the training schedule Ellimere had forced upon him.

He was standing on the sentry walk for two reasons. The first reason was that he wanted to look out in the hope that he would see either his father or his mother returning. The second was that he wanted to avoid Ellimere and everyone else who wanted to organize his life.

Sam missed his parents, not just because they might free him from Ellimere's tyranny. But Sabriel was constantly in demand away from Belisaere, flying her red and gold Paperwing from one trouble spot to the next. It was a bad winter, people repeatedly said in Sam's hearing, with so much activity from the Dead and from Free Magic creatures. Sam always shivered inside as they said it, knowing their eyes were on him and that he should be studying *The Book of the Dead*, preparing himself to help his mother.

He should be studying now, he thought glumly, but he continued to stare out over the frosted roofs of the city and through the rising smoke of thousands of cozy fires.

He hadn't opened the book at all since Ellimere had given

it to him. The green and silver volume remained safely locked in a cupboard in his workroom. He thought about it every day, and looked at it, but couldn't bring himself to actually read it. In fact, he spent the hours he was supposed to be studying it trying to work out how he could tell his mother that he couldn't. He couldn't read the book, and he couldn't face going into Death again.

Ellimere allowed him two hours a day for study of the book, or "Abhorsen prep" as she called it, but Sam did no reading. He wrote instead. Speech after speech in which he tried to explain his feelings and his fears. Letters to Sabriel. Letters to Touchstone. Letters to both parents. All of them ended up in the fire.

"I'll just tell her," announced Sam to the wind. He didn't speak too loudly in case the sentry on the far side of the tower heard him. The guards already thought he was a miserable excuse for a Prince. He didn't want them thinking he was a mad Prince as well.

"No, I'll tell Dad, and then he can tell her," he added after a moment's thought. But Touchstone had barely returned from Estwael when he had had to ride south to the Guard Fort at Barhedrin Hill, just north of the Wall. There had been reports that the Ancelstierrans were allowing groups of Southerling refugees to cross the Wall and settle in the Old Kingdom—or in actuality, to be killed by the creatures or wild folk who roamed the Borderlands. Touchstone had gone to investigate these reports, to see what the Ancelstierrans were up to, and to save any of the Southerlings who might have survived.

"Stupid Ancelstierrans," muttered Sam, kicking the wall. Unfortunately, his other foot slipped on the icy stone, and he skidded into the wall, smacking his funny bone.

"Ow!" he exclaimed, clutching his elbow. "Blast it!"

"You all right, sir?" asked the guard, who came at a run, his hob-nailed boots providing much better purchase than Sam's rabbit-fur slippers. "You don't want to break a leg."

Sam scowled. He knew that the prospect of his dancing the Bird of Dawning provided no end of amusement for the guards. His sense of self-worth wasn't helped by their badly disguised snickering or the ease with which Ellimere practiced her own future role, acting as co-regent with grace and authority—at least to everyone except Sam.

Sam's stumbling rehearsals for the Bird of Dawning part in the Midwinter and Midsummer Festivals was only one of the many areas in which he displayed himself as poorer royal material than his sister. He couldn't pretend enthusiasm for the dances, he often fell asleep in Petty Court, and while he knew he was a very competent swordsman, he somehow didn't feel like stretching his ability at practice with the guards.

Nor did he show up well at Perspective. Ellimere always threw herself into the task at hand, working like fury. Sam did quite the reverse, staring into space and worrying about his clouded future, often becoming so engrossed that he stopped doing whatever he was supposed to be doing.

"Sir, are you all right?" the guard repeated.

Sam blinked. There, he was doing it again. Staring into space while he thought about staring into space.

"Yes, thank you," he said, flexing his gloved fingers. "Slipped. Hit my funny bone."

"See anything interesting out there?" asked the guard. His name was Brel, Sam remembered. Quite a friendly guard, not one who stifled a smile every time Sam walked past in his Bird of Dawning costume.

"No," replied Sam, shaking his head. He looked out again, down into the interior of the city. The Midwinter Festival was to start in a few days. Construction of the Frost Fair was in full swing. A great, bustling tent town on the frozen surface of Lake Loesare, the Frost Fair had pageant wagons and players, jesters and jugglers, musicians and magicians, exhibitions and expositions, and all sorts of games, not to mention food from every corner of the Old Kingdom and beyond. Lake Loesare covered ninety acres of Belisaere's central valley, but the Frost Fair overflowed it, extending into the public gardens that lined the lakeshore.

Sam had always liked the Frost Fair, but he looked down on it now without interest. All he could feel was a cold and black depression.

"All the fun of the fair," said Brel, clapping his hands together. "It looks like it'll be a good festival this year."

"Does it?" asked Sam bleakly. He would have to dance on the final day of the Festival, as the Bird of Dawning. It was his job to carry the green sprig of Spring at the tail end of the Winter procession, behind Snow, Hail, Sleet, Fog, Storm, and Frost. They were all professional dancers on stilts, so they not only loomed threateningly over the Bird but also showed up Sam's lack of expertise.

The Winter Dance was long and complicated, weaving through two miles of the Fair's winding ways. But it was much longer than that, because there was lots of doubling back as the Six Spirits of Winter ducked around the Bird and tried to prolong their season by stealing the sprig of Spring from under Sam's golden wing, or by tripping him up with their stilts.

There had been two full rehearsals so far. The Spirits of Winter were supposed to fail at tripping the Bird, but so far even the skill of the other dancers couldn't prevent the Bird from tripping himself. By the end of the first rehearsal, the Bird had fallen three times and bent its beak twice, and certainly had extremely ruffled feathers. The second rehearsal had been even worse, when the Bird crashed into Sleet and knocked her off her stilts. The new Sleet still wouldn't talk to him.

"They say a hard practice means an easy dance," said Brel.

Sam nodded and looked away from the guard. There was no sign of a Paperwing gliding in against the wind, or a troop of horsemen bearing the royal banner on the southern road. It was a waste of time looking for his parents.

Brel coughed into his glove. Sam glanced back as the guard inclined his head and resumed his slow march around the sentry walk, his trumpet bumping gently on its strap against his back.

Sam went downstairs. He was already late for the next rehearsal.

Brel was wrong about the bad rehearsals meaning a successful dance. Sam bumbled and stumbled all his way through it, and only the professionalism and energy of the Six Spirits saved the dance from disaster.

Traditionally, all the dancers from the Festival ate with the royal family at the Palace after the dance, but Sam chose to stay away. They'd done enough to him, and he'd done enough, with the bruises to show for it. He was sure Sleet had deliberately smacked him with her stilt near the end. She was the sister of the one he'd knocked off her stilts in rehearsal.

Instead of attending the dinner, Sam retired to his workshop, trying to forget his troubles in the construction of a particularly intricate and interesting magical-mechanical toy. Ellimere sent a page to get him but could do no more without embarrassing everyone, so he was left in peace—for that night at least.

But not the next day or the days following. Ellimere couldn't—or wouldn't—see that Sam's sullenness came from genuine trouble. So she simply made up more things for him to do. Even worse, she started foisting the younger sisters of her own friends on him, clearly thinking that a good woman could sort out whatever was wrong with him. Naturally, Sam took an instant dislike to anyone Ellimere so obviously seated next to him at dinner, or who "just happened" to drop by his work-room with a broken bracelet catch to be mended. His constant worry about the book and his mother's return left him little energy to pursue friendships, let alone romantic attachments. So he earned the reputation of being stiff and distant, not only among the young women introduced to him by Ellimere, but to everyone of his own age around the Palace. Even people who had been his friends in previous years, when he was home for the holidays, found that they no longer enjoyed his company. Sam, caught up in his own troubles and busy with his official duties, hardly noticed that people of his own age avoided him.

He did talk to Brel a bit, since they both tended to be up the second tallest tower around the same time. Fortunately, the guard was not naturally talkative and also didn't seem to mind Sam's silences or his tendency to stop and just stare out over the city and the sea.

"Your birthday today," said Brel, early one clear and very cold morning. The moon was still visible, and there was a ring around it, as only happened on the coldest nights of winter.

Sam nodded. Since it occurred two weeks after the Mid-winter Festival, his birthday was always somewhat eclipsed by the greater event. This year, it was made even less spectacular by the continued absence of Sabriel and Touchstone, who could only send messages and presents that, while obviously carefully chosen, did not cheer Sam. Particularly since one was a surcoat with the silver keys of the Abhorsen on a deep blue field, quartered with the royal line's golden castle on a red field, and the other was a book entitled *Merchane on the Binding of Free Magic Elementals*.

"Get any good presents?" asked Brel.

"Surcoat," said Sam. "And a book."

"Ah," said Brel. He clapped his hands together, to regain circulation. "Not a sword, then? Or a dog?"

Sam shook his head. He didn't want a sword or a dog, but either would have been more welcome than what he had been given.

"Expect Princess Ellimere will get you something good," Brel said after a long, thoughtful pause.

"I doubt it," said Sam. "She'll probably organize some sort of *lesson*."

Brel clapped his hands together again, stood still, and slowly scanned the horizon from south to north.

"Happy birthday," he said when his head had finished its slow movement. "What is it? Eighteen?"

"Seventeen," replied Sam.

"Ah," said Brel, and he walked around to the other side of the tower to repeat his scan of the horizon.

Sam went back downstairs.

Ellimere did organize a birthday feast in the Great Hall, but it was a lackluster affair, mainly due to Sam's depressing influence. He refused to dance, because it was the one day when he could refuse, and since it was his birthday, that meant no one else could dance, either. He refused to open his presents in front of everyone because he didn't feel like it, and he merely toyed with the grilled swordfish with lime and buttered smallwheat that had once been his favorite dish. In fact, he acted like a spoiled and sulky brat of seven, rather than like a young man of seventeen. Sam knew it but felt unable to stop. It was the first time in weeks that he'd been able to refuse Ellimere's orders or, as she called them, "strong suggestions."

The feast ended early, with everyone cross and short-tempered. Sam went straight to his workroom, ignoring the whispers and sidelong looks as he left the Hall. He didn't care what everyone thought, though he was uncomfortably aware of Jall Oren's hooded eyes watching his exit. Jall would certainly report on Sam's shortcomings when his parents returned, if he didn't decide before then to deliver one of his justly feared summations of exactly what was wrong with Sam's behavior.

But even one of Jall's lectures would pale to insignificance when his mother found out the truth about her son. Beyond that revelation, Sam daren't think. He couldn't imagine what would happen, or what his own future would be. The Kingdom had to have an Abhorsen-in-Waiting and a royal heir. Ellimere was demonstrably the perfect royal heir, so Sam had to be the Abhorsen-in-Waiting. Only he couldn't do it. Not wouldn't, as everyone was bound to think. Couldn't.

That night, as he had done scores of times before, Sam unlocked the cupboard to the left of his workbench and steeled himself to look at *The Book of the Dead*. It sat on a shelf, shining with its own ominous green light that overshadowed the soft glow of the Charter lights in the ceiling.

He reached out to it, like a hunter trying to pat a wolf in the vain hope that it might be only a friendly dog. His fingers touched the silver clasp and the Charter marks laid upon it, but before he could do more, a violent shaking overtook him, and his skin turned as cold as ice. Sam tried to still the shakes and ignore the cold, but he couldn't. He snatched back his hand and retreated to the front of the fireplace, where he crouched down in misery, hugging his knees.

A week after his birthday, Sam received a letter from Nick. Or rather, the remains of a letter, because it had been written on machine-made paper. Like most products of Ancelstierran technology, the paper had begun to fail upon crossing the Wall, and it was now crumbling into its component fibers. Sam had often told Nick in the past to use hand-made paper, but he never did.

Still, there was enough of it left for Sam to deduce that Nick was asking him for an Old Kingdom visa for himself and a servant. He intended to cross the Wall at Midwinter, and he would be grateful if Sam met him at the Crossing Point.

Sam brightened. Nick could always cheer him up. He immediately consulted his almanac to see what Midwinter in Ancelstierre would correspond with in the Old Kingdom. Generally, the Old Kingdom was a full season ahead of Ancelstierre, but there were some strange fluctuations that required double-checking in an almanac, particularly around the solstices and the turn of the seasons.

Old Kingdom/Ancelstierre almanacs like Sam's had been almost impossible to obtain once, but ten years ago Sabriel had lent hers to the royal printer, who had reset it to incorporate all the handwritten comments and marginalia of Sabriel and previous Abhorsens. That had been a long and laborious process. The end result was aesthetically very pleasing, with clear, slightly indented type on crisp linen paper, but was very expensive. Sabriel and Touchstone were careful about who was allowed to have these almanacs. Sameth had been very proud when he was entrusted with one on his twelfth birthday.

Fortunately, the almanac had an exact correspondence for Midwinter, rather than just an equation for Sam to work out, requiring moon sights and other observations. On that day in Ancelstierre, it would be the Day of Ships in the Old Kingdom, in the third week of spring. It was still many weeks off, but at least Sam had something positive to look forward to.

After the letter from Nick, Sam's mood improved a little,

and he got on better with everyone in the Palace except
Ellimere. The rest of winter passed without either of his parents coming home, and without any particularly terrible storms
or the intense, bone-numbing cold that sometimes rolled in
from the northeast, accompanied by pods of lost whales who
didn't otherwise enter the Sea of Saere.

Weather-wise it was a particularly mild winter, but in court
and city the people still spoke of it as a bad one. There had been
more trouble all over the Kingdom that season than in any of
the last ten winters, trouble such as hadn't been seen since the
early days of Touchstone's reign. Message-hawks flew constantly
to and from the Mews Tower, and Mistress Finney grew red-
eyed and even more irritable than normal, as her children, the
hawks, were hard-pressed to meet the demand for communication. Many of the messages the hawks carried were reports of the
Dead, and of Free Magic creatures. A large proportion turned out
to be false, but all too many were real, and all required Sabriel's
attention.

There was other news that troubled Sam. One letter from
his father reminded him too much of the terrible day on the
Perimeter, when the Dead Southerlings had attacked his cricket
team and he had faced the necromancer in Death.

Sam took the letter up the second-tallest tower to read over
and think, while Brel paced around him. One particular section
he read three times:

*The Ancelstierran Army, presumably under instructions
from the government, has allowed a group of Southerling
"volunteers" to enter the Old Kingdom at one of the old
Crossing Points on the Wall, in contravention of all past
agreements and common sense. Obviously, Corolini has
gained further support, and this is a test of his plan to send*

all the Southerlings into the Kingdom.

I have put a stop to further crossings as best I can, and reinforced the guards at Barhedrin. But there is no guarantee that the Ancelstierrans will not send more Southerlings across, though General Tindall has said he will delay acting on any such order and warn us if he can.

In any case, more than a thousand Southerlings have already crossed, and they are at least four days ahead of us. Apparently they were met by "local guides," but as no Perimeter Scouts were allowed to escort the refugees, I do not know whether these were even true men.

We will pursue, of course, but there is a smell about this I do not like. I am certain at least one Free Magic sorcerer is involved on our side of the Wall, and the Crossing Point the Southerlings used is the one closest to where you were ambushed, Sameth.

The necromancer, thought Sam as he folded the letter. He was glad the sun was out and that he was in the Palace, protected by wards and guards and running water.

"Bad news?" asked Brel.

"Just news," said Sam, but he was unable to suppress a shiver.

"Nothing the King and the Abhorsen can't deal with," said Brel, with total confidence.

"Wherever they are," whispered Sam. He put the letter inside his coat and went back downstairs. To his workshop, to lose himself in making things, in tiny details that required all his attention and the total dexterity of his hands.

With every step, he knew he should be going to open *The Book of the Dead.*

✿✤✿

Typically, Sam's parents returned on a beautiful spring evening, long after Sam had climbed down from the tower and Brel's watch had ended. The wind had turned to the east, the Sea of Saere was shifting color from winter black to summery turquoise, the sun was still warm even as it sank into the west, and the swallows that lived in the cliffs were stealing wool from Sam's torn blanket for their nests.

Sabriel arrived first, her Paperwing skimming low over the practice yard where Sam was sweating through forty-eight patterns of attack and defense with Cynel, one of the better guards. The shadow of the Paperwing startled them both and allowed Cynel to take the final point, since she recovered while Sam was momentarily paralyzed.

His day of doom had finally come, and all his prepared speeches and letters leaked out of his brain, as if his opponent had actually pierced his head rather than triumphantly clanging her wooden sword down on his heavily padded helmet.

He was hurrying inside to change out of his practice armor when the trumpets sounded above the South Gate. At first he thought they were for his mother, till he heard other trumpets farther away, up at the West Yard, where her Paperwing would have landed. So the trumpets at the South Gate had to be announcing the King. No one else got a fanfare.

It was indeed Touchstone. Sam met him twenty minutes later in the family's private solar—a large room, three stories above the Great Hall, with a single long window that looked down upon the city rather than the sea. Touchstone was looking out at his capital as Sam came in, watching the lights come on. Bright Charter lights and soft oil lights, flickering candles and fires. It was one of the best times to be in Belisaere, at lighting-up time on a warm spring evening.

As usual, Touchstone looked tired, though he'd managed

to wash and change out of armor and riding gear. He was wearing an Ancelstierran-style bathrobe, his curly hair still wet from a hasty bath. He smiled as he saw Sam, and they shook hands.

"You look better, Sam," said Touchstone, noting the flush in his son's face from the sword practice. "Though I had hoped you'd also develop as a letter writer this winter."

"Um," said Sam. He'd sent only two letters to his father all winter, and a few notes at the bottom of some of Ellimere's much more regular correspondence. Neither the letters nor the notes had contained anything very interesting and nothing at all personal. Sam had actually drafted some that did, but like the ones to his mother, they'd ended up in the fire.

"Dad, I . . ." Sam began hesitantly, and he felt a surge of relief as he finally began to broach the subject he'd stewed on all winter. "Dad, I can't—"

Before he could go on, the door swung open, and Ellimere breezed in. Sam's mouth snapped shut, and he glared at her, but she ignored him and rushed straight to Touchstone, hugging him with evident relief.

"Dad! I'm so glad you're home," she said. "And Mother, too!"

"One big happy family," muttered Sam under his breath.

"What was that?" asked Touchstone, a touch of sternness in his voice.

"Nothing," said Sam. "Where's Mother?"

"Down in the reservoir," replied Touchstone slowly. He kept one arm around Ellimere and drew Sam in with the other. "Now, I don't want you to get too worried, but she's had to go to the Great Stones, because she's been wounded—"

"Wounded!" exclaimed Ellimere and Sam together, turning in so that all three of them were in a tight circle.

"Not seriously," Touchstone said hastily. "A bite to the leg from some sort of Dead thing, but she couldn't attend to it at the time, and it went bad."

"Is she . . . is she going to . . ." Ellimere asked anxiously, staring down at her own leg in consternation. From the look on her face, it was plain that she found it hard to imagine Sabriel hurt and not completely in command of herself and everything around her.

"No, she is not going to lose her leg," Touchstone said firmly. "She's had to go down to the Great Charter Stones because both of us were simply too tired to cast the necessary healing spells. But we'll be able to down there. It is also the best place for all of us to have a private discussion. A family conference."

The reservoir where the six Great Charter Stones stood was in many ways the heart of the Old Kingdom. It was possible to access the Charter, the very wellspring of magic, anywhere in the Old Kingdom, but the presence of ordinary Charter Stones made it much easier, as if they were conduits to the Charter. However, the Great Charter Stones actually seemed to be *of* the Charter, not just connected to it. While the Charter contained and described all living things and all possibilities, and existed everywhere, it was particularly concentrated in the Great Stones, the Wall, and the bloodlines of the royal family, as well as the Abhorsens and the Clayr. Certainly, when two of the Great Stones were broken by Kerrigor, and the royal family apparently lost, the Charter itself had seemed to weaken, allowing greater freedom to Free Magic and the Dead.

"Wouldn't it be better to have the conference up here, after Mother's cast her spell?" asked Sam.

Despite its importance to the Kingdom, the reservoir had never been his favorite place, even before he had become so afraid of Death. The Stones themselves were comforting, even keeping the water around them warm, but the rest of the reservoir was cold and horrible. Touchstone's mother and sisters had been slain there by Kerrigor, and much later, Sabriel's father had died there, too. Sam didn't want to think about what it must have been like when there were two broken Stones, and Kerrigor lurked there in the darkness with his necromantic beasts and Dead servants.

"No," replied Touchstone, who had much more reason than his son to fear the place. But he had lost that fear years ago, in his long labor to repair the broken Stones with his own blood and fragments of barely remembered magic. "It's the only place where we will definitely not be overheard, and there are too many things you both must know, and no others should. Bring the wine, Sameth. We'll need it."

"Are you going like that?" asked Ellimere, as Touchstone strode over to the fireplace and into the left-hand side of the inglenook. He turned as she spoke, looked down on his robe and the twin swords belted across it, shrugged, and went on. Ellimere sighed and followed him, and both disappeared into the darkness behind the fire.

Sam scowled and picked up the earthenware jug of spiced wine that had been mulled and placed near the fire to keep hot. Then he followed, pressing his hand up against the rear of the inglenook, Charter marks flaring as the guard-spell let him push open the secret door. Beyond that, he could already hear his father and sister clattering down the one hundred fifty-six steps that led to the reservoir, the Great Charter Stones, and Sabriel.

Chapter Twenty-Four

COLD WATER, OLD STONE

THE RESERVOIR WAS a vast hall of silence, cold stone, and even colder water. The Great Stones stood in the darkness at its center, invisible from the landing where the Palace stairs met the water. Around the rim of the reservoir, shafts of sunlight came down from the grilled openings high above, casting cross-hatched ripples of light across the mirror-smooth surface of the water. Tall columns of white marble rose up like mute sentinels between the patches of light, supporting the ceiling sixty feet above.

The water was, as always, extremely clear. Sam dipped his hand in it as he helped his father untie the barge that was moored at the end of the Palace steps. As the water trickled between his fingers, he saw Charter marks sparkle briefly. All the water in the reservoir absorbed magic from the Great Charter Stones. Closer to the center, the water was almost more magic than anything else, and was no longer cold—or even wet.

The barge was not much more than a raft with gilded knobs on each corner. There were two of them in the reservoir, but Sabriel had obviously taken the other one. She would be on it, out there in the center, where no sunlight fell. The Great Stones glowed with all the millions of Charter marks that moved in and on them, but most of the time it was only a faint luminescence, no rival even to the filtered sunlight. They wouldn't see the glow until they were close, away from the light-dappled rim, past the third line of columns.

Touchstone undid the rope on his side, then placed his hand upon the planking and whispered a single word. Ripples moved across the still water as he spoke, and the barge began to edge away from the landing. There was no current in the reservoir, but the barge moved as if there were, or as if unseen hands pushed it through the water. Touchstone, Sam, and Ellimere stood close together in the middle, occasionally shifting balance as the barge swayed and rocked.

This was how Sam's long-dead aunts and his grandmother had traveled to their deaths, he thought. Standing on a barge—maybe even this same one, he thought, dredged up, repaired and re-gilded—all unsuspecting, till they were ambushed by Kerrigor. He had cut their throats, catching their blood in his golden cup. Royal blood. Blood for the breaking of the Great Charter Stones.

Blood for the breaking, blood for the making. The Stones had been broken by royal blood, and re-made with royal blood—his father's blood. Sam looked at Touchstone and wondered how he had done it. The weeks of laboring here alone, each morning taking a silver, Charter-spelled knife and deliberately re-opening the cuts in his palms from the day before. Cuts that had left white lines of scar tissue from his little finger to the ball of the thumb. Cutting his hands, and casting spells that he had not been sure of, spells that were terribly dangerous to the caster, even without the added risk and burden of the broken Stones.

But even more, Sam wondered about the use of blood, the same blood that ran in his veins. It felt strange to him that his pounding heart was in its way akin to the Great Stones ahead. How ignorant he was, particularly of the Charter's greater secrets. Why was royal, Abhorsen, and Clayr blood different from normal people's—even that of other Charter Mages, whose blood was sufficient to mend or mar only the lesser Stones? The three bloodlines were known as Great Charters, like the Great Stones ahead, and the Wall. But why? Why did their blood contain Charter Magic, magic that could not be duplicated by marks drawn from the generally accessible Charter?

Sam had always been fascinated by Charter Magic, particularly making things with it, but the more he used it, the more he realized how little he knew. So much knowledge had been lost in the two hundred years of the Interregnum. Touchstone had passed on as much as he knew to his son, but his own specialty was in battle magic, not in making, or any deeper mysteries. He had been a Royal Guard, a bastard Prince, not a mage, at the time of the Queen's death. After that, he had been imprisoned in the shape of a ship's figurehead for two hundred years, while the Kingdom sank slowly into disorder.

Touchstone had been able to mend the Great Stones, he had said, because the broken Stones wanted to be re-made. He had made many mistakes at first, and only survived by grace of the Stones' support and strength, nothing else. Even so, it had taken many months, and as many years off his life. There had been no silver in Touchstone's hair before the mending.

The barge passed between two columns, and Sam's eyes slowly adjusted to the strange twilight. He could see the six Great Stones ahead now, tall monoliths of dark grey, their irregular shapes quite different from the smooth masonry of the columns and only a third of their height. And there was the other barge, floating in the center of the ring of Stones. But where was Sabriel?

Fear suddenly gripped hard at his chest. He couldn't see his mother, and all he could think of was how the Dead Kerrigor

had taken on his former human shape and lured Sam's grandmother the Queen down to a dark and bloody death. Maybe
Touchstone wasn't really Touchstone, but something else that
had assumed his form. . . .

Something moved on the barge ahead. Sam, who had
unconsciously held his breath, gasped and choked, thinking
that all his fears were realized. Whatever it was had no human
shape, rising only as high as his waist, without arms or head
or discernible form. A lump of writhing darkness, where his
mother should be—

Then Touchstone slapped him on the back. He took a
sudden breath, and the thing on the barge cast a small Charter
light that sparkled in the air above like a tiny star—revealing
that it was Sabriel after all. She had been lying down, wrapped
in her dark blue cloak, and had just sat up. The light shone on
her face now, and her familiar smile met them. But it was not
the full, uncaring smile of complete happiness, and she looked
more tired and worn than Sam had ever seen her. Always pale,
her skin looked almost translucent in the Charter light, and it
was sheened with the sweat of pain and suffering. For the first
time, Sam saw white streaks in her hair, and he was struck with
the realization that she was not ageless but would one day grow
old. She was not wearing her bells, but the bandolier lay beside
her, the mahogany handles in easy reach, as did her sword and
pack.

Sam's barge drifted between two of the Stones and into the
ring. All three passengers started as it crossed, feeling a sudden
surge of energy and power from the Great Stones. Some weariness was stripped away from them, though not all. In Sam's case,
the fear and guilt that he had carried all winter were lessened.
He felt more confident, more like his old self. It was a feeling
he hadn't had since he'd walked out onto the pitch for that final

cricket match in the Schoolboys' Shield.

The two barges met. Sabriel didn't get up, but she held out her arms. A second later, she was hugging Ellimere and Sam, the barges rocking dangerously from their sudden rush and enthusiastic greetings.

"Ellimere! Sameth! I am so glad to see you, and so sorry I have been too long away," said Sabriel, after the initial very tight hug had given way to a looser one.

"That's all right, Mother," replied Ellimere, who sounded more as if she were the mother and Sabriel her daughter. "It's you we're worried about. Let's have a look at your leg."

She started to lift the cloak, but Sabriel stopped her just as Sam caught the faint, horrible smell of decaying flesh.

"It's still not pleasant," Sabriel said quickly. "A wound from the Dead rots quickly, I'm afraid. But I have cast healing-spells upon it, with the aid of the Great Stones, and fixed a poultice of feliac there, too. All will soon be well."

"This time," said Touchstone. He was standing outside the close group of Sabriel, Ellimere, and Sam, looking down at his wife.

"Your father is angry with me because he thinks I almost got myself killed," said Sabriel, with a slight grin. "I don't understand it myself, since I think he should be glad that I didn't."

Silence greeted this remark, till Sam hesitantly asked, "How badly were you hurt?"

"Badly," replied Sabriel, wincing as she moved her leg. Charter marks flared under the cloak, briefly visible even through the tightly woven wool. She hesitated, then quietly added, "If I hadn't met your father on the way back, I might not have made it here."

Sam and Ellimere exchanged horrified glances. All their

lives they had heard stories of Sabriel's battles and hard-won victories. She had been wounded before, but they had never heard her admit that she might have been killed, and had never really considered the possibility themselves. She was the Abhorsen, who entered Death only of her own accord!

"But I did make it, and I am going to be absolutely fine," Sabriel said firmly. "So there is no need for anyone to fuss."

"Meaning me, I suppose," said Touchstone. He sat down with a sigh, then stood up irritably to re-arrange his swords and bathrobe before sitting again.

"The reason I am fussing," he said, "is that I am concerned that all this winter someone, or something, has been deliberately and cleverly arranging situations to put you most at risk. Look at the places you've been called to, and how there are always more Dead than were reported, and more dangerous creatures—"

"Touchstone," interrupted Sabriel, reaching out to take his hand. "Calm down. I agree. You know I agree."

"Mmph," grumbled Touchstone, but he did not say any more.

"It's true," replied Sabriel, looking squarely at Sam and Ellimere. "There is a clear pattern, and not just in the Dead that have been raised solely to ambush me. I think that the increasing number of Free Magic elementals is also connected, as is the trouble that your father has been having with the Southerling refugees."

"It almost certainly is," said Touchstone, sighing. "General Tindall believes that Corolini and his Our Country Party are being funded with Old Kingdom gold, though he cannot definitely prove it. Since Corolini and his party now hold the balance of power in the Ancelstierre Moot, they've been able to get the Southerlings moved farther and farther north. They have also made it clear that their ultimate aim is to get all the Southerling refugees moved across the Wall, into our Kingdom."

"Why?" asked Sam. "I mean, what for? It's not as if northern Ancelstierre is over-populated."

"I'm not sure," replied Touchstone. "The reasons they make public in Ancelstierre are populist rubbish, pandering to the fears of the countryfolk. But there has to be a reason why someone here is supplying them with gold—enough gold to buy the twelve seats they've picked up in the Moot. I fear that reason may have something to do with the fact that we have not been able to find more than a score of the thousand people who were sent across a month ago, and none of that score alive. The rest have simply vanished—"

"How could that many people disappear? Surely they would leave some trace," interrupted Ellimere. "Perhaps I should go—"

"No." Touchstone smiled, amused by his daughter's obvious belief that she could do a better job than he could when it came to looking for something. The smile faded as he went on. "This is not as simple as it appears, Ellimere. Sorcery is involved. Your mother thinks that we will find them when we least want to, and that they will not be living when we do."

"This is the heart of the matter," said Sabriel gravely. "Before we discuss it further, I think we should take further precautions against being overheard. Touchstone?"

Touchstone nodded and stood up. Drawing one of his swords, he concentrated for a moment. The Charter marks on his sword began to glow and move, till the whole blade was wreathed in golden light. Touchstone flicked the sword up, and the Charter marks leapt across to the nearest Great Stone, splashing on it like liquid fire.

For a moment nothing happened. Then other marks caught

the light, and the golden flames spread to cover the whole Stone, roaring up like a crown-caught wildfire. More marks leapt to the next Stone till it kindled, too, and then to the next, until all six Great Stones were ablaze, and streams of bright Charter marks flew up and across to weave a tracery of light like a dome above the two barges.

Looking over the side, Sam saw that the golden fire had spread underwater, too, forming a crazy maze of marks that covered the reservoir floor. The four were now completely enclosed by a magical barrier, one that relied upon the power of the Great Stones. He wanted to ask how it was cast, and enquire about the nature of the spell, but his mother was already speaking.

"We can talk now without fear of being overheard, by natural ears or other means," said Sabriel. She took Sam's hand, and Ellimere's, holding them tight, so they felt the calluses on her fingers and palms, the result of so many years of wielding sword and bells.

"Your father and I are certain that the Southerlings were brought across the Wall to be killed—slain by a necromancer who has used the bodies to house Dead spirits who owe him allegiance. Only Free Magic sorcery can explain how the bodies and all other traces have disappeared, unseen by our patrols or the Clayr's Sight."

"But I thought the Clayr could See everything," said Ellimere. "I mean, they often get the time wrong, but they still See. Don't they?"

"Over the past four or five years the Clayr have become aware that their Sight is clouded, and possibly has always been clouded, in the region around the eastern shores of the Red Lake and Mount Abed," said Touchstone grimly. "A large area, which not coincidentally is also where our royal writ does not hold true. There is some power there that opposes both the Clayr and our authority, blocking their Sight and breaking the Charter Stones I have set there."

"Well, shouldn't we call out the Trained Bands and take them and the Guard and go down there and sort it out once and for all?" protested Ellimere, in the same tone that Sam imagined she had used when she led the Wyverley College hockey team back in Ancelstierre.

"We don't know where—or what—it is," said Sabriel. "Every time we undertake to really search the area for the source of the trouble, something happens somewhere else. We did think we might have found the root of it five years ago, at the Battle of Roble's Town—"

"The necromancer woman," interrupted Sam, who remembered the story well. He had thought a lot about necromancers over the past months. "The one with the bronze mask."

"Yes. Chlorr of the Mask," replied Sabriel, staring out at the golden barrier, obviously recalling unpleasant memories. "She was very old, and powerful, so I had presumed she was the architect of our difficulties there. But now I am not sure. It is clear someone else is still working to befuddle the Clayr and incite trouble across the Kingdom. There is also someone behind Corolini in Ancelstierre and perhaps even the Southerling wars as well. One possibility is the man you encountered in Death, Sam."

"The . . . the necromancer?" asked Sam. His voice came out as a pathetic squeak, and he unconsciously rubbed his wrists, his sleeves briefly riding up to show the skin still scarred from the burns.

"He must have great power to raise so many Dead Hands on the other side of the Wall," replied Sabriel. "And with that power, I should have heard of him, but I have not. How has he

kept himself hidden all these years? How did Chlorr hide when
we scoured the Kingdom after Kerrigor's fall, and why did she
reveal herself to attack Roble's Town? Now I am wondering
if perhaps I underestimated Chlorr. She may even have evaded
me at the last. I made her walk beyond the Sixth Gate, but I was
sorely tired, and I did not follow her all the way to the Ninth. I
should have. There was something strange about her, something
more than the usual taint of Free Magic or necromancy. . . ."

She paused, and her eyes stared out at nothing, unfocused.
Then she blinked and continued. "Chlorr was old, old enough
for other Abhorsens to have encountered her in the past, and I
suspect that this other necromancer is also ancient. But I have
found no record of either at the House. Too much knowledge was destroyed when the Palace burnt, and more has been
lost besides, simply by the march of time. And the Clayr, while
they keep everything in that Great Library of theirs, rarely find
anything useful in it. Their minds are too much bent upon the
future. I should like to look there myself, but that is a task
that would take months, if not years. I think Chlorr and this
other necromancer were in league, and may be still, if Chlorr
has survived. But who leads and who follows is unclear. I also
fear that we will find they are not alone. But whoever or whatever moves against us, we must make sure their plans come to
naught."

The light seemed to darken as Sabriel spoke, and the water
rippled as if an unwanted breeze had somehow passed the protection of the golden light around the Stones.

"What plans?" asked Ellimere. "What are they . . . it . . .
whatever . . . going to do?"

Sabriel looked at Touchstone, and a brief flash of uncer-
tainty passed between them before she continued.

"We think that they plan to bring all two hundred thousand

Southerling refugées into the Old Kingdom—and kill them,"
whispered Sabriel, as if they might be overheard after all. "Two
hundred thousand deaths in a single poisoned minute, to make
an avenue out of Death for every spirit that has lingered there
from the First Precinct to the very precipice of the Ninth Gate.
To summon a host of the Dead greater than any that has ever
walked in Life. A host that we could not possibly defeat, even if
all the Abhorsens who have ever lived were somehow to stand
against them."

Chapter Twenty-Five

A FAMILY CONFERENCE

SILENCE GREETED SABRIEL'S words, a silence that went on and on, as they all imagined a host of the Dead two hundred thousand strong, and Sam struggled not to. A horde of the Dead, a great sea of stumbling, Life-starved corpses that stretched from horizon to horizon, inexorably marching towards him—

"That will not happen, of course," said Touchstone, breaking into Sam's terrible imaginings. "We will make sure that it doesn't, that the refugees never even cross the Wall. However, we can't stop them on our side. The Wall is too long, with too many broken gates and too many old Crossing Points on the other side. So we must ensure that the Ancelstierrans don't send them across in the first place. Consequently your mother and I have decided to go to Ancelstierre ourselves—secretly, so as not to arouse alarm or suspicion. We will go to Corvere and negotiate with their government, which will undoubtedly take several months. That means we will be relying on you two to look after the Kingdom."

More silence greeted this revelation. Ellimere looked deeply thoughtful but otherwise calm. Sam swallowed several times, then said, "What, ah, what exactly do you mean?"

"As far as both our friends and enemies need know, I will be on a diplomatic mission to the barbarian chiefs at their Southern Stop, and Sabriel will be going about her business as mysteriously as she always does," replied Touchstone. "In our absence, Ellimere will continue as co-regent with Jall Oren—everyone seems to have become accustomed to that. Sameth, you will assist her. But most important, you will continue in your studies of *The Book of the Dead*."

"Speaking of such things, I have something for you," added Sabriel, before Sam could interject. She pushed her pack across with obvious effort. "Look in the top."

Slowly, Sam undid the straps. He suddenly felt very sick, knowing that he must tell them now or he would not be able to. Ever.

There was an oilskin-wrapped package in the pack. Sameth slid it out slowly, his fingers gone cold and clumsy. His eyes seemed to be strangely blurry, too, and Sabriel sounded as if she were talking from another room.

"I found these at the House—or rather, the sendings had set them out. I don't know where they found them, or why they've got them out now. They are very, very old. So old that I have no record of who bore them first. I would have asked Mogget, but he still sleeps—"

"Except for when I caught that salmon last year," interjected Touchstone crossly. Mogget, the Abhorsen's cat-shaped famil-iar, was bound by Ranna, the Sleepbringer, first of the seven bells. He had woken only five or six times in nearly twenty years, on three of those occasions to steal and eat fish caught by Touchstone.

"Mogget would not wake," continued Sabriel. "But as I have my own, these are clearly meant for the Abhorsen-in-Waiting. Congratulations, Sam."

Sam nodded dumbly, the remaining package unopened in his lap. He didn't need to look to know that wrapped inside the crinkled oilskin were the seven Charter-spelled bells of an Abhorsen.

"Aren't you going to open it?" asked Ellimere.

"Later," croaked Sam. He tried to smile but only made his mouth twitch. He knew Sabriel was looking at him, but he couldn't meet her eyes.

"I'm glad the bells have come," said Sabriel. "Most Abhorsens before me worked with their successors, sometimes for many years, as I hope we will work together. According to Mogget, my father trained with his aunt for nearly a decade. I have often wished I had had the same opportunity."

She hesitated again and then said quickly, "To tell the truth, I will need your help, Sam."

Sam nodded, unable to speak, as the words of his confession dried up in his mouth. He had the birthright, he had the book, he had the bells. Obviously, he just had to try harder to read the book, he told himself, trying to overcome the panic that twisted knots in his stomach. He *would* become the proper Abhorsen-in-Waiting everyone expected and needed. He had to.

"I'll do my best," he said, finally looking Sabriel in the eyes. She smiled, with a smile that made her whole face bright, and hugged him.

"I have to go to Ancelstierre, for I still know their ways much better than your father does," she said. "And quite a few of my old school friends have become influential, or have married so. But I didn't want to leave without knowing there was an Abhorsen here to protect the people from the Dead. Thank you, Sam."

"But I'm not . . ." Sam cried out before he could stop himself. "I'm not ready. I haven't finished the book, I mean, and—"

"I'm sure you know more than you think," Sabriel said. "In any case, there should be little trouble now that spring is in full bloom. Every stream and river is flowing with snow-melt and spring rain. The days are getting longer. There never are any major threats from the Dead this late in spring, or through the summer. The most you'll have to deal with is a rogue Hand or perhaps a Mordaut. I have every confidence you can manage that."

"What about the missing Southerlings?" asked Ellimere, with a look that spoke volumes about her confidence in Sam. "Nine hundred Dead are a major threat."

"They must have disappeared into the area around the Red Lake, or the Clayr would have Seen them," said Sabriel. "So they should be confined there by the spring floods. I would go and deal with them first, but the greater danger lies with the many more Southerlings in Ancelstierre. We will have to trust in the flooded rivers, and in you, Sam."

"But—" Sam began.

"Mind you, the necromancer or necromancers who oppose us are not to be trifled with," continued Sabriel. "If they dare to confront you, you must fight them in Life. Do not fight one of them in Death again, Sam. You were brave to do so before, but also lucky. You must also be very careful with the bells. As you know, they can force you into Death, or trick you into it. Use them only when you are confident you have learned the lessons in the book. Do you promise?"

"Yes," said Sam. Somehow or other he barely had breath for that single word. But there was relief in it, for he'd been given a reprieve of sorts. He could probably sort out most of the Lesser Dead with Charter Magic alone. His resolution to be a proper Abhorsen had not banished the fear that still lurked in his heart, and his fingers were cold where they touched the wrapped-up bells.

"Now," said Touchstone, "I wonder if you have any insights into dealing with the Ancelstierrans, you two, from your schooling there. This Corolini, for instance, the leader of the Our Country Party. Could he be from the Old Kingdom himself, do you think?"

"After my time," said Ellimere, who had been a whole year out of school and seemed to consider her Ancelstierran days as ancient history.

"I don't know," replied Sam. "He was in the newspapers a lot before I left, but they never mentioned where he came from. My friend Nicholas might know, and he would be able to help, I think. His uncle is the Chief Minister, Edward Sayre, you know. Nick is coming to visit me next month, but you should be able to catch him before he leaves."

"He's coming here?" asked Touchstone. "I'm surprised they'll let him. I don't think the Army has issued a permit in years, apart from that lot of refugees—and that was a political show. The Army didn't have a choice."

"Nick can be very persuasive," said Sam, thinking of various scrapes Nick had talked him into at school—and less often, out of the blame afterwards. "I asked Ellimere to seal a visa for him, for our side."

"I sent it ages ago," said Ellimere, with a snide glance at Sam. "Some of us are efficient, you know."

"Good," said Touchstone. "It will be a useful connection, and important for one of Ancelstierre's ruling families to see that we do not invent the stories they hear about the Kingdom. I'll also make sure the Barhedrin Guard Post provides an escort from the Wall. It wouldn't help negotiations if we lose the Chief Minister's nephew."

"What are we negotiating with?" asked Ellimere. "I mean, down in Corvere they like to pretend we don't even exist. I was always having to convince stuck-up city girls that I wasn't making the Kingdom up."

"Two things," replied Sabriel. "Gold and fear. We have

only a modest amount of gold, but it might be enough to tip the balance if it goes into the right pockets. And there are many Northerners who remember when Kerrigor crossed the Wall. We shall try to convince them that this will happen again if they send the Southerling refugees north."

"It couldn't be Kerrigor, could it?" asked Sam. "I mean, whoever is behind all the trouble."

"No," said Sabriel and Touchstone together. They exchanged a look, obviously remembering the terrible past and what Kerrigor had tried to do, both here in the Old Kingdom and in Ancelstierre.

"No," repeated Sabriel. "I looked in on Kerrigor when I visited the House. He sleeps still and forever under Ranna's spell, locked in the deepest cellar, bound with every Mark of ward and guard your father and I have ever known. It is not Kerrigor."

"Whoever, or whatever, it is, they shall be dealt with," said Touchstone, his voice powerful and regal. "We four shall see to that. But for now, I suggest we all drink some mulled wine and talk of better things. How was the Midwinter Festival? Did I tell you that I danced the Bird of Dawning when I was your age, Sam? How did you do?"

"I forgot the cups," said Sam, handing over the still-warm jug.

"We can drink from the jug," said Sabriel, after a moment when no one chose to answer Touchstone's question. She took the jug and expertly poured a stream of wine into her mouth. "Ah, that's good. Now tell me, how was your birthday, Sam? A good day?"

Sam answered mechanically, hardly noticing Ellimere's rather more pointed interjections. Clearly, his parents hadn't spoken to Jall yet, or they would be asking different questions.

He was relieved when they started questioning Ellimere, gently teasing her about her tennis and all the young men who were trying to learn this new sport. Obviously, gossip about his sister had traveled faster than news of Sam's shortcomings. He was brought briefly back into the conversation when Ellimere accused him of refusing to make any more racquets, which was a shame because no one else could make them quite so well, but a quick promise to produce a dozen dropped him out again.

The others continued to talk for a while, but the dark future weighed heavily on them all. Sameth, for his part, couldn't stop thinking about the book and the bells. What would he do if he were actually called upon to repel an incursion by the Dead? What would he do if it turned out to be the necromancer who'd tortured him in Death? Or even worse, what if there were some still more powerful enemy, as Sabriel feared?

Suddenly he blurted out, "What if it . . . this Enemy . . . isn't behind Corolini? What if he's going to do something else while you're both gone?"

The others, who were in the middle of a conversation about Heria, who'd tripped over her own dress and catapulted into Jall Oren at an afternoon party in honor of the Mayor of Sindle, looked up, startled.

"If that is so, we will be just a week away, ten days at the most," said Sabriel. "A message-hawk to Barhedrin, a rider to the Perimeter, a telegraph from there or Bain to Corvere, train back to Bain—maybe even less than a week. But we think that whatever this Enemy—as you have dubbed it so well—plans, it must involve a great number of the Dead. The Clayr have Seen many possible futures in which our entire Kingdom is nothing more than a desert, inhabited only by the Dead. What else could bring this about but the sort of massing of the Dead that we suspect? And that could be brought about only by killing all those poor, unprotected refugees. Our people are too well guarded. In any case, apart from Belisaere, there are not two hundred thousand people in one place in all the Kingdom. And certainly not two hundred thousand without a single Charter mark amongst them."

"I don't know what else it could be," said Sam heavily. "I just wish you weren't going."

"Being the Abhorsen is a weighty responsibility," Sabriel said quietly. "One that I understand you are wary of shouldering, even when it is shared with me. But it is your destiny, Sam. Does the walker choose the path, or the path the walker? I am sure you will do very well, and we will soon all be together again, speaking of happier things."

"When do you go?" asked Sam, unable to hide the hope of delay from his voice. Maybe he would be able to talk to Sabriel tomorrow, to get her help with *The Book of the Dead*, to overcome his paralyzing fear.

"Tomorrow, at dawn," replied Sabriel reluctantly. "Provided my leg is healed enough. Your father will ride with the real embassy to the Northern Barbarians, and I will fly west. But I will double back to pick him up tomorrow night, and we will then fly south to the House, to try to consult again with Mogget, then on to Barhedrin and the Wall. Hopefully this will confuse any spies who may be watching."

"We would stay longer," said Touchstone sadly, looking at his small family, so rarely all together in one place. "But as always, duty calls—and we must answer."

Chapter Twenty-Six

S AM LEFT THE reservoir that night with an empty wine jug, a bandolier of bells, a heavy heart, and much to think upon. Ellimere went with him, but Sabriel stayed behind, needing to spend the night within the circle of Great Charter Stones to speed her healing. Touchstone stayed with her, and it was obvious to the two children that their parents wished to be alone. Probably to discuss the shortcomings of their son, Sam thought as he wearily climbed the stairs, the package of bells in his hand.

Ellimere wished him an almost friendly good night at the door to her chambers, but Sam didn't go to bed. Instead he climbed another twisting stair to his tower workroom and spoke the word that brought the Charter lights to life. Then he put the bells in a different cupboard from the book, locking them out of sight if not out of mind. After that, he half-heartedly tried to resume work on a clockwork and Charter Magic cricketer, a batsman six inches high. He had some ideas of making two teams and setting them to play, but neither the clockwork nor the magic yet worked to his satisfaction.

Someone knocked on the door. Sam ignored it. If it was a servant, he'd call or go away. If it was Ellimere, she'd just barge in.

The knock was repeated, there was some sort of muffled call, and Sam heard something slide under the door, followed by footsteps going back down the stairs. A silver tray was on the floor, with a very ragged-looking letter upon it. Judging from the state it was in, it had to be from Ancelstierre, and that meant it was from Nicholas.

Sam sighed, put on his white cotton gloves, and picked up a pair of tweezers. Receiving one of Nick's letters was always more of a forensic exercise than a matter of reading. He picked up the tray and carried it over to his bench, where the Charter marks were brightest, and began to peel the paper apart and piece the rotten bits together.

Half an hour later, as the clock in the Grey Tower clanged out a dozen strokes for midnight, the letter was laid out clearly enough to read. Sam bent over it, his frown deepening the further he read.

Dear Sam,

Thanks for organizing the Old Kingdom visa for me. I don't know why your Consul at Bain was so reluctant to give me one. Lucky you're a Prince, I guess, and can get things done. I didn't have any trouble at this end. Father called Uncle Edward, who pulled the appropriate strings. Practically no one in Corvere even knew you could get a permit to cross the Perimeter. Anyway, I suppose it shows that Ancelstierre and the Old Kingdom aren't that different. It all comes down to who you know.

In any case, I intend to leave Awengate tomorrow, and if all the train connections go smoothly, I will be in Bain by Saturday and across the Wall by the 15th. I know this is earlier than we agreed, so you won't be able to meet me, but I'm not just rushing in on my own. I've hired a guide—a former Crossing Point Scout I ran into in Bain. Quite literally, in fact. He was crossing the road to avoid a

demonstration by these One Country fellows, stumbled and
nearly knocked me over. But it was a fortuitous meeting,
as he knows the Old Kingdom well. He also confirmed
something I've read about a curious phenomenon called the
Lightning Trap. He has seen it, and it certainly sounds
worth studying.

So I think we will go and take a look at this Lightning
Trap en route to your undoubtedly charming capital of
Belisaere. My guide didn't seem at all surprised that I knew
you, by the way. Perhaps he is as unimpressed by royalty as
some of our former schoolfellows!

In any case, the Lightning Trap is apparently near a
town called Edge, which I understand is not too far out of
the direct route north to you. If only you people believed in
normal maps and not quasi-mystical memorization aided by
blank pieces of paper!

I look forward to seeing you in your native habitat—
almost as much as I look forward to investigating the curious
anomalies of your Old Kingdom. There is surprisingly little
written about it. The College library has only a few old and
highly superstitious texts and the Radford little more. It
never gets mentioned in the papers, either, except obliquely
when Corolini is raving on in the Moot about sending
"undesirables and Southerlings" to what he calls "the
extreme North." I expect that I will be an advance guard
of one "undesirable" in his terms!

Everything about the Old Kingdom seems to fall under
a conspiracy of silence, so I am sure there will be many
things for an ambitious young scientist to discover and reveal
to the world.

I hope you are quite recovered, by the way. I have
been ill myself, on and off, with chest pains that seem to be

some sort of bronchitis. Strangely enough, they get worse the
farther south I go, and were terrible in Corvere, probably
because the air is absolutely filthy. I've spent the last month
in Bain, and have barely been troubled. I expect I will be
even better in your Old Kingdom, where the air should be
positively pristine.

In any case, I look forward to seeing you soon, and
remain your loyal friend,

Nicholas Sayre

P.S. I don't believe Ellimere is really six foot six and
weighs twenty stone. You would have mentioned it before.

Sameth put the letter down, careful not to break what was
left of it.

After he'd finished, he read the letter again, hoping that the
words had somehow changed. Surely Nick wouldn't cross into the
Old Kingdom with only a single—and possibly untrustworthy—
guide? Didn't he realize how dangerous the Borderlands near
the Wall were? Particularly to an Ancelstierran, lacking a
Charter mark and any sense of magic. Nick wouldn't even be
able to test whether his guide was a real man, a tainted Charter
bearer, or even a Free Magic construct, powerful enough to
cross the Perimeter without detection.

Sam bit his lip at the thought, teeth tapping at the skin in
unconscious concern, and consulted his almanac. According
to that, the fifteenth was three days ago, so Nick must have
already crossed the Wall. So it was too late to get there, even by
Paperwing, or to find one of the Palace message-hawks and send
it with orders to the guards. Nick had a visa for himself and a
servant, so the Barhedrin Post wouldn't detain him. He would
be in the Borderlands now, heading towards Edge.

Edge! Sam bit his lip harder. That was far too close to the Red Lake, and the region where the necromancer Chlorr had destroyed the Stones and even now the Enemy hid and hatched its plans against the Kingdom. It was the worst possible place for Nick to go!

A knock at the door interrupted his thoughts and made him bite his lip even harder, so he tasted blood. Irritated, he called out, "Yes! Who is it!"

"Me!" said Ellimere, breezing in. "I hope I'm not disturbing the act of creation or anything?"

"No," Sameth replied warily. He indicated his workbench with a half wave and a shrug, implying that his work wasn't going well.

Ellimere looked around with interest, since Sam usually pushed her out whenever she tried to come in. The small tower room had been given to Sameth on his sixteenth birthday and had had much use since then. Currently, the two workbenches were covered in the paraphernalia of a jeweler and many tools and devices that were obscure to her. There were also some small figurines of cricketers, thin bars of gold and silver, reels of bronze wire, a scattering of sapphires, and a small but still-smoking forge built into the room's former fireplace.

And there was Charter Magic everywhere. The faded afterimages of Charter marks shone in the air, crawled lazily across the walls and ceiling, and clustered by the chimney. Clearly Sameth was not just creating costume jewelry or the promised extra tennis racquets.

"What are you making?" Ellimere asked curiously. Some of the Charter symbols, or rather the fading reflections of them, were extremely powerful. They were marks she would be reluctant to use herself.

"Things," said Sameth. "Nothing you'd be interested in."

"How do you know?" asked Ellimere. The familiar tide of resentment was rising between them.

"Toys," snapped Sam, holding up his little batsman, which suddenly swung its tiny bat before freezing back into immobility. "I'm making toys. I know it's not a fit occupation for a Prince, and I should be asleep getting ready for a fun new day of dance classes and Petty Court, but I . . . can't sleep," he concluded wearily.

"Neither can I," said Ellimere in a conciliatory tone. She sat down in the one other chair, and added, "I'm worried. About Mother."

"She said she'd be fine. The Great Stones will heal her."

"This time. She needs help with her work, Sam, and you're the only person who can do it."

"I know," said Sam. He looked away, down at Nick's letter. "I know."

"Well," Ellimere continued uncomfortably, "I just wanted to say that studying to be the Abhorsen is the most important thing, Sam. If you need more time, you just have to say, and I'll reorganize your schedule."

Sam looked at her, surprised. "You mean take time away from the Bird of Dawning, or those afternoon parties with your friends' stupid sisters?"

"They're not—" Ellimere started to say; then she took a deep breath and said, "Yes. Things are different now. Now we know what's going on. I shall be spending more time with the Guard myself. Getting ready."

"Ready?" asked Sam nervously. "So soon?"

"Yes," said Ellimere. "Even if Mother and Dad are successful in Ancelstierre, there's going to be trouble. Whatever is behind it all isn't going to lie still while we stop its plans. Something will happen, and we need to be ready. *You* need to be ready, Sam. That's all I wanted to say."

She got up and left. Sam stared into space. There was nowhere to turn. He had to become a proper Abhorsen-in-Waiting. He had to help fight whatever the Enemy was. The people expected it. Everyone depended on him.

And so, he suddenly realized, did Nicholas. He had to go and find Nicholas, to save his friend before he got in trouble, because no one else would.

Suddenly Sam was filled with purpose, a feeling of decision that he didn't examine too closely. His friend was in danger, and he must go to save him. He would be away from *The Book of the Dead* and his Princely chores for only a few weeks. He would probably be able to find Nick quite quickly and bring him to safety, particularly if he could take half a dozen of the Royal Guard. As Sabriel had said, there was little chance of the Dead doing anything, what with the spring floods.

Somewhere deep down a small voice was telling him that what he was really doing was running away. But he smothered the voice with other more important thoughts, and didn't even look at the cupboards that held the book and the bells.

Once the decision was made, Sam thought about how it could be done. Ellimere would never let him go, he knew. So he must ask his father, and that meant rising before dawn in order to catch Touchstone in his wardrobe.

Chapter Twenty-Seven

SAM MAKES UP HIS MIND

D ESPITE HIS GOOD intentions, Sam overslept and missed Touchstone's departure from the Palace. Thinking that he might catch him at the South Gate, he ran down Palace Hill and then along the broad, tree-lined Avenue of Stars, named after the tiny metal suns embedded in its paving stones. Two guards ran with him, easily keeping pace despite the weight of their mail hauberks, helmets, and boots.

Sam had just sighted the rear ranks of his father's escort when he heard the cheers of the crowd and the sudden blare of trumpets. He jumped up on a cart that was stopped in the traffic and looked over the heads of the crowd. He was just in time to see his father ride out through the high gate of Belisaere, red and gold cloak streaming behind him over the horse's hindquarters, the early sun just catching his crown-circled helmet before he passed into the shadow of the gate.

Royal guards rode in front of and behind the King, twoscore tall men and women, bright mail flashing from the vertical cuts in their red and gold surcoats. The guards would continue north tomorrow, Sam knew, with someone dressed as Touchstone. The King would actually be flying south to Ancelstierre with Sabriel, to try to forestall the death of two hundred thousand innocents.

Sameth kept watching even after the last guard passed the gate and the normal traffic resumed; people, horses, wagons, donkeys, pushcarts, pullcarts, beggars . . . all flowed past him, but he didn't notice.

He had missed Touchstone, and now he would have to make up his mind all on his own.

Even when he crossed to the center of the road and turned against the tide flowing out of the city, his gaze was absent. Only the vacuum created around him by two burly guards prevented several pedestrian accidents.

Since Sam had started to think about going to find Nicholas, he found that he couldn't stop. He was sure that the letter was real. Sam was the only one who knew Nick well enough to track him down, the only one with a friendship bond that finding magic could flow through.

The only one who could save him from whatever trouble was brewing for everyone around the Red Lake.

But that meant Sam would have to leave Belisaere, abandoning his duties. He knew that Ellimere would never give him permission.

These thoughts, and multiple variations of them, swirled through his mind as he and his guards passed under one of the huge aqueducts that fed the city with pure, snow-melt water. The aqueducts had proved their worth in other ways, too. Their fast-flowing waters were a defense against the Dead, particularly during the two centuries of the Interregnum.

Sameth thought of that, too, as he heard the deep bellow of the aqueduct above his head. For a moment his conscience twinged. He was supposed to be a defense against the Dead himself.

He left the cool shadow of the aqueduct and began heading along the Avenue of Stars before the wearying climb up the switchbacked King's Road that led to Palace Hill. Ellimere was probably already waiting for him back at the Palace, since both of them were to sit in Petty Court this morning. She would be cool and composed in her judicial robes of black and white, holding the wand of ivory and the wand of jet that were used in the truth-testing spell. She would be cross that he was sweaty, dirty, inappropriately dressed, and unequipped—his wands had disappeared, though he had the vague notion that they might have rolled under his bed.

Petty Court. Belisaere Festival duties. Tennis racquets. *The Book of the Dead*. All of it surged up like a great dark wave that threatened to engulf him.

"No," he whispered, stopping so suddenly that both his guards nearly ran into him. "I'll go. I'll go tonight."

"What was that, sir?" asked Tonin, the younger of the two guards. She was the same age as Ellimere, and they had been friends since they had played together as children. She was nearly always one of his guards on his rare excursions into the city, and Sameth felt sure she reported his every movement to the Princess.

"Um, nothing, Tonin," replied Sameth, shaking his head. "I was just thinking aloud. Guess I'm not used to getting up before dawn."

Tonin and the other guard exchanged semi-tolerant glances behind his back as they moved on. They got up every day before dawn.

Sameth didn't know what his guards were thinking, as they finished the climb up the hill and entered the cool, fountain-centered court that led to the west wing of the Palace. But he'd seen the looks they'd exchanged, and he had a general idea that they did not consider him the perfect pattern of a Prince. He suspected most of the city folk shared their opinion. It was galling to someone who had been one of the leading lights of his school in Ancelstierre. There he had excelled at everything that was important. Cricket in the summer and Rugby in the winter. And he'd been first in chemistry class and in the top classes for everything else. Here, he couldn't seem to do anything right.

The guards left him outside his room, but Sam didn't immediately change into his judge's robes or make any motion to use the basin and ewer of water that stood in the tiled alcove that served him as a bathroom. The Palace, rebuilt with economy following its destruction by fire, did not have the steampipes and hot-water systems of Abhorsen's House or the Clayr's Glacier. Sam had plans for such a system, and indeed some of the original works remained deep below Palace Hill, but he had not had time to investigate the magic and engineering required to make it happen.

"I will go," he declared again, to the painting on the wall that showed a pleasant harvest scene. The reapers did not react, nor did the pitchfork crew, as he added, "The only question is—how?"

He paced around the room. It was not large, so he had made twenty circuits before he made a decision, at the same time he arrived in front of the silver mirror that hung on the wall to the right of his simple iron-framed bed.

"I'll be someone else," he said. "Prince Sameth can stay behind. I'll be Sam, a Traveler going to rejoin his band after seeking treatment for a sickness in Belisaere."

He smiled at that, looking at himself in the mirror. Prince Sameth looked back at him, resplendent in red and gold jerkin, somewhat sweaty white linen shirt, tan doeskin breeches, and gilt-heeled knee boots. And above the court finery a pleasant face, with the potential to be striking one day, although Sam didn't see that. Too youthful and open, he decided. His face lacked the definition of experience. He needed a scar or a broken nose or something like that.

As he looked, he was also reaching into the endless swim of the Charter, picking out a mark here, a symbol there, linking them into a chain in his mind. Holding them there, he drew the final Charter mark in front of his eyes with his forefinger, and all the marks rushed out, to hang in the air, a glowing constellation of magic symbols.

Sameth looked at them carefully, checking the spell before he stepped right into the glowing pattern. The marks brightened as they touched his skin, sparking against the Charter mark on his forehead, flowing in streaks of golden fire across his face.

He shut his eyes as the fire reached them, ignoring the tingle under his eyelids and a sudden urge to sneeze. He stood that way for several minutes, till the tingle vanished. He sneezed explosively, inhaled with equal force—and opened his eyes.

In the mirror, there were still the same clothes, with the same build of man inside them. But the face had changed. Sam the Traveler stared back, a man reminiscent of Prince Sameth but clearly several years older, with a carefully shaven mustache and goatee. His hair was a different color, too, lighter and straighter, and much longer at the back.

Better. Much better. Sameth—no, Sam—winked at the reflection and started to undress. His old hunting leathers would be best, and some plain shirts and underdrawers. He could buy a cloak in the city. And a horse. And a sword, since he couldn't take the Charter-Magicked blade his mother had given him on his sixteenth birthday. It wouldn't take a glamour and was too recognizable.

But he could take some of the things he'd made himself, he realized as he kicked off his boots and dug out some well-worn but durable thigh boots of black calfskin.

Thinking of his tower workshop inevitably led him to *The Book of the Dead*. Well, he certainly wouldn't take *that*. Just a quick run up the stairs, pick up a few things, including his little store of gold nobles and silver deniers, and then he'd be off!

Except that he couldn't go up to his workshop looking as he did now. And he also had to do something that would allay Ellimere's suspicions—otherwise he'd be chased down and brought back. Forcibly, he imagined, since the guards would have no problem taking Ellimere's orders over his own.

He sighed and sat down on the bed, boots in hand. Obviously this escape—or rather rescue expedition—was going to take more preparation than he thought. He'd have to make a temporary Charter sending that was a reasonable duplicate of himself and set up some situation so Ellimere couldn't get too close a look.

He could probably say that he had to do something from *The Book of the Dead* that required staying in his workroom for three days or so, to give himself a head start on any search. It wasn't as if he were completely giving up studying to be the Abhorsen. He just needed a break, he told himself, and three weeks of rescuing Nicholas had to be more important than three weeks of study that he could easily make up on his return.

Even if Ellimere asked the Clayr to find out where he was, a three-day start should be enough. Presuming she worked out what had happened after the third day and sent a message-hawk to the Clayr, it would be at least two days before they replied. Five days, in all.

He'd be halfway to Edge by then. Or a quarter of the way, he thought, trying to remember exactly how far away the little town on the Red Lake actually was. He'd have to get a map and look up the latest *Very Useful Guide* to see where to stop on the way.

Really, there were more than a dozen things to do before he could escape, Sam thought, dropping the boots to stand in front of the mirror again. The glamour would have to go for a start, if he didn't want to be arrested by his own guards.

Who would have thought that starting an adventure was so difficult?

Glumly, he began the process of dissolving the Charter-spell that disguised him, letting the component marks twist away and fall back into the Charter. As soon as that was done, he would go up to the tower room and begin to get organized. Provided, of course, that Ellimere didn't intercept him and take him off to Petty Court.

Chapter Twenty-Eight

SAM THE TRAVELER

ELLIMERE DID INTERCEPT Sam, so the rest of his day was lost to Petty Court: the sentencing of a thief who tried to lie despite the truth-spell turning his face bright yellow with every falsehood; the arbitration of a property dispute that defied any hard and fast truths as all the original parties were dead; the rapid processing of a series of petty criminals who confessed immediately, hoping that not having to bespell them would improve the court's outlook; and a long and boring speech from an advocate, which turned out to be irrelevant, as it relied on a point of law overturned by Touchstone's reforms more than a decade ago.

The night, however, was not taken up by official duties, though Ellimere once again produced a younger sister of one of her thousands of friends to sit next to Sam at dinner. To her surprise, Sam was quite talkative and friendly, and for days afterwards she defended him when other girls told tales of his distance.

After dinner, Sam told Ellimere that he would be studying for the next three days, and had to immerse himself in a spell that required total concentration. He would get food and water from the kitchens and then would be in his bedchamber and must not be disturbed. Ellimere took the news surprisingly well, which made Sam feel bad. But even that could not curb his growing excitement, and the long hours creating a very basic sending of himself did not diminish his sense of expectation. When he finished it at a little past midnight, the sending looked quite like him from the door, though it had no depth from other angles. And if it was spoken to, it could shout "Go away!" and "I'm very busy" in a fair imitation of his voice.

With the sending done, Sam went to his workroom and picked up his ready money and some of the things he had made, which might prove useful for the journey. He did not look at the cupboards, which stood like disapproving guardians in the corners of the room.

But he dreamed of them when he finally got to bed. He dreamed that he climbed the stairs again, and opened the cupboards, and put on the bandolier of bells and opened the book, and read words that burst into fire, and the words picked him up and swept him into Death, plunging him into the cold river, and he couldn't breathe—

He woke, thrashing in his bed, the sheets tangled around his neck, cutting off his air. He fought them in a panic, till he realized where he was and his heart began to slow from its frenzied pumping. Off in the distance, a clock struck the hour, followed by the shouts of the Watch, announcing all was well. It was four o'clock. He'd had only three hours' sleep, but he knew he could sleep no more. It was time to cast the glamour upon himself. Time for Sam the Traveler to take his leave.

It was still dark when Sam slipped out of the Palace, in the cool morning just before the dawn. Cloaked in Charter-spells of quiet and unseeing, he slipped down the stairs, past the guard post in the Southwest Courtyard, and along the steeply sloping corridor down to the gardens. He avoided the guards who tramped between the roses in the lowest terrace, and went out through a sally port that was locked by steel and spell. Fortunately, he had stolen the key for the lock, and the door knew him by his Charter mark.

Out in the lane that ran into the King's Road, he slung his surprisingly heavy saddlebags over his shoulder and wondered whether he should have gone through them again and taken things out, because they were bursting at the seams. But he couldn't think of anything to leave behind, and he was taking just the bare essentials: a cloak; spare shirts, trousers, and underclothes; a sewing kit; a bag of soaps and toiletries with a razor he hardly needed to use; a copy of *The Very Useful Guide*; some friction matches; slippers; two gold bars; an oilskin square that could be used as a makeshift tent; a bottle of brandy, a piece of salted beef, a loaf of bread, three ginger cakes; and a few devices of his own making. Besides what was in the saddlebags, he had only a broad-brimmed hat, a belt purse, and a fairly nondescript dagger. His first stop would be the central market to buy a sword, and then he would go to the Horse Fair at Anstyr's Field for a mount.

As he left the lane and stepped out into the King's Road to join the already rapidly building bustle of men, women, children, dogs, horses, mules, carts, beggars, and who-knew-what on the street, Sam felt a tremendous lift to his spirits, a feeling he hadn't had for years. It was the same sense of joy and expectation he'd felt as a child being given an unexpected holiday. Freed of responsibility, suddenly given license to have fun, to run, to scream, to laugh.

Sam did laugh, trying a deeper chuckle to fit his new personality. It came out rather strained, almost a gurgle, but he didn't mind. Twirling his new, Charter-Magicked mustache, he quickened his pace. Off to adventure—and, of course, to rescue Nicholas.

Three hours later, most of his pre-dawn exuberance was gone. His guise as a Traveler was very good for not being recognized, but it didn't help him get attention from merchants and horse-traders. Travelers were not known as great customers, for they rarely had any coins, preferring to barter services or goods.

It was also unseasonably warm, even for so late in spring, making the sword buying in the crowded market sweaty and unpleasant, with every second seeming to last an hour.

The horse-trading was even worse, with great swarms of flies settling on the eyes and mouths of man and beast alike. It was no wonder, Sameth thought, King Anstyr had ordered the Horse Fair set up three miles from the city all those centuries ago. The Fair had ceased during the years of the Interregnum, but had begun to grow again in Touchstone's reign. Now the permanent stables, corrals, and bidding rings covered a good square mile, and there were always more strings of horses in the pastures that surrounded the Horse Fair proper. Of course, finding a horse that you wanted to buy among the multitude took considerable time, and there was always competition for the better horses. People from all over the Kingdom, and even barbarians from the North, came to buy at the Fair, particularly at this time of year.

Despite the crowds, the flies, and the competition, Sameth came out of his two purchasing ordeals quite happily. A plain but serviceable longsword hung at his hip, its sharkskin hilt rough under his tapping finger. A somewhat nervous bay mare followed behind, constrained by a leading rein from giving in to her neuroses. Still, she seemed sound enough and was neither too noticeable nor expensive. Sam was toying with calling her Tonin after his least favorite guard, but he decided that this was both childish and vindictive. Her previous owner had—somewhat enigmatically—called her Sprout, and that would do.

Once out of the stink and crowding of the Horse Fair,

Sam mounted up, weaving Sprout through the steady stream of traffic, finding his way past carts and peddlers, donkeys with empty panniers going away from the city and those with full ones going in, gangs of workmen relaying the stone pavers of the road, and all the nondescript journeyers in between. Not far out of the city he was overtaken by a King's Messenger on a black thoroughbred that would have set the buyers bidding furiously at the Fair, and then later by a quartet of guards, setting a pace that could be maintained only in the knowledge that fresh horses awaited them at every posting house on the road. Both times Sam slouched in the saddle and pulled his hat down to shadow his face, even though the glamour still held.

With the help of *The Very Useful Guide*, Sam had already decided on his first stop. He would take the Narrow Way along the isthmus that joined Belisaere to the mainland because there was no other way to go. Then he would take the high road south to Orchyre. He had considered going west to Sindle and then to the Ratterlin, where he could take a boat as far as Qyrre. But *The Very Useful Guide* mentioned a particularly good inn at Orchyre that served a famous jellied eel. Sam was partial to jellied eel and saw no reason why he shouldn't take the most comfortable way to Edge.

Not that he was entirely sure what the most comfortable way would be after Orchyre. The Great South Road followed the east coast most of the way down, but Edge was all the way across on the west coast. So he would have to cut west sooner or later. Perhaps he could even leave the royal roads, as they were called, and cut cross-country from Orchyre, trusting that he would be able to find country roads that would take him in the right direction. The danger in that lay in the spring floods. The royal roads mostly had decent bridges, but the country roads did not, and their usual fords might be impassable now.

In any case, that was all in the future and not to be worried about till after Orchyre. The town was two days' steady riding away, and he could think about his next stage en route, or that evening when he planned to put up at some inn.

But planning the next stage of his journey was the last thing on Sameth's mind when he finally reached a village and a staging inn that could be considered far enough away from Belisaere to stop. He'd ridden only seven leagues, but the sun was already setting, and he was exhausted. He'd had too little sleep the night before, and his backside and thighs were reminding him that he'd hardly ridden all winter.

By the time he saw the swinging sign that declared the inn's name to be The Laughing Dog, he could do little more than tip the ostler to look after Sprout and collapse on a bed in the best room in the house.

He woke several times in the night, the first to kick off his boots and the second to relieve himself in the bedpan (with a broken lid) thoughtfully provided by the inn. The third time he woke, it was to insistent knocking on the door and the first rays of sunlight slipping through the shuttered windows.

"Who is it?" groaned Sameth, sliding out of the bed and into his boots. His joints were stiff, and he felt awful, particularly in his slept-in clothes, which smelled dreadfully of horse. "Is it breakfast?"

There was no answer save more knocking. Grumbling, Sameth went to the door, expecting some zany or village fool to grin up at him from behind a breakfast tray. Instead, he was greeted by two wide-shouldered men wearing the red and gold sashes of the Rural Constabulary over their leather cuirasses.

One, clearly the senior, carried some authority in his stern face and silver, short-buzzed hair. He also had a Charter mark on his forehead, which his younger assistant did not.

"Sergeant Kuke and Constable Tep," announced the silver-haired man, thrusting past Sameth quite roughly. His companion also pushed in, quickly closing the door after him and letting the bar fall back in place.

"What do you want?" asked Sam, yawning. He didn't intend to be rude, but he had no idea that they had an interest in him and had knocked on his door by choice rather than chance. His only previous experience with the Rural Constabulary was seeing them on parade, or inspecting some post of theirs with his father.

"We want a word," said Sergeant Kuke, standing close enough that Sam could smell the garlic on his breath and see the marks where he'd scraped the stubble off his chin not long before. "Let's be beginning with your name and station."

"I am called Sam. I'm a Traveler," replied Sameth, his eye following the constable, who had moved to the corner of the room and was examining his sword, propped against the saddle-bags. For the first time, he felt a twinge of apprehension. These constables might not be the clodpolls he thought. They might even discover who he was.

"Unusual for a Traveler to stay at a posting inn, let alone the best room in the house," said the constable, turning back from Sam's sword and saddlebags. "Unusual to tip the ostler a silver denier, too."

"Unusual for a Traveler's horse not to have a brand, or clan tokens in its mane," replied the sergeant, talking as if Sam wasn't there. "It'd be pretty strange to see a Traveler without a clan tattoo. I wonder if we'd see one on this laddie, if we looked. But maybe we should start looking in those bags, Tep. See if we can find something to tell us who we've got here."

"You can't do that!" exclaimed Sam, outraged. He took a

step towards the constable, but stopped abruptly as sharp steel pricked through his linen shirt, just above his belly. Looking down, he saw a poniard held steadily in Sergeant Kuke's hand.

"You could tell us who you really are and what you're up to," said the sergeant.

"It's none of your business!" exclaimed Sam, throwing his head back in disdain. As he did so, his tousled hair flew back, revealing the Charter mark on his forehead.

Instantly Kuke called out a warning, and the poniard was at Sam's neck, and his right arm pinioned behind him. Of all things the constables might fear, the bearer of a false or corrupted Charter mark was one of the worst, for he could only be a Free Magic sorcerer, a necromancer, or some thing that had taken human shape.

Almost at the same time, Tep opened a saddlebag and lifted out a dark leather bandolier, a bandolier of seven tubular pouches that ranged in size from a pillbox to a large jar. Wooden handles of dark mahogany thrust out of the pouches, making it quite clear what the bandolier held. The bells that Sabriel had sent to Sameth. The bells that he had locked away in his workroom and definitely hadn't packed.

"Bells!" exclaimed Tep, dropping them in fright and leaping back, almost as if he'd drawn out a nest of writhing serpents. He didn't notice the Charter marks that thronged upon both bandolier and handles.

"A necromancer," whispered Kuke, and Sam heard the sudden fear in his voice and felt the hold on him slackening, the poniard drifting away from his throat, the hand that held it beset by sudden shivering.

In that instant, Sameth pictured two Charter marks in his mind, drawing them from the endless flow like a skilled fisherman selecting his catch from a glittering shoal. He let the marks infuse into his held breath—then he blew them out, at the same time throwing himself to the ground.

One mark flew true, striking Tep with sudden blindness. But Kuke must have been some small Charter Mage himself, for he countered the spell with a general warding, the air sparking and flashing as the two Charter marks met.

Then, before Sam could even get up, Kuke's poniard stabbed out, sinking deep into his leg, just above the knee.

Sam screamed, the noise adding to Tep's shouts of blind despair as he groped around the room and Kuke's even louder shouts of "Necromancer!" and "A rescue!" That would bring every constable for miles and any guards who might be on the road. Even concerned citizens might come, but it would be brave ones since the word "necromancer" had been heard.

After the first split-second shock of pain, when his whole mind seemed to crack open, Sam instinctively did what he'd been taught to save his life in the event of an assassination attempt. Drawing several Charter marks in his mind, he let them grow in his throat and roared out a Death-spell to strike everyone unprotected in the room.

The marks left him like an incandescent spark, leaping to the two constables with terrible force. In a second, it was quiet, as Kuke and Tep tumbled to the floor like broken-stringed puppets.

Sam pushed himself to his feet, the realization of what he'd done rising through the pain. He'd killed two of his father's men . . . his own men. They'd simply been doing their job. The job that he was afraid to do. Protecting people from necromancers and Free Magic and whatever else . . .

He didn't stop to think any further. The pain was coming back, and he knew he had to get away. In a panic, he picked up his bags, thrust the cursed bells back in, buckled the sword around his waist, and left.

He didn't know how he managed the stairs, but a moment later he was in the common room, with people staring at him as they backed against the walls. He stared back, wide-eyed and wild, and limped through, leaving bloody footprints on the floor.

Then he was in the stables, saddling Sprout, the horse blowing wide-nostriled, eyes white with fear at the scent of human blood. Mechanically, he soothed her, hands moving without conscious thought.

A year later, or in no time at all, or somewhere in between, Sam was in the saddle, kicking Sprout into a trot and then a canter, all the while feeling his blood washing down his leg like warm water, filling up his boot till it overflowed the rolled-back top. Some part of his mind screamed at him to stop and tend to the wound, but the greater part shouted it down, wanting only to flee, flee the scene of his crime.

Instinctively, he headed west, putting the rising sun at his back. He zigzagged for a while, to lay a false trail, then took a straight track through the fields, towards a dark expanse of forest, not too far ahead. He had only to reach it and he could hide, hide and tend his hurt.

Finally, Sam reached the comforting shadow of the trees. He went in as far as he could and fell off his horse. Pain climbed up his leg, spiking all the way. The green world of the forest spun and lurched sickeningly, refusing to hold still. The morning light had gone from yellow to grey, like an overcooked egg. He couldn't focus on the healing spell. The Charter marks eluded him, slipping from his mind. They simply wouldn't line up as they should.

It was all too hard. Easier to let go. To fall asleep, to drift into Death.

Except that he knew Death, knew its chill. He was already falling into the cold current of the river. If he could have been sure of being taken under by that current, rushed through the cascade of the First Gate and then onwards, he might have given in. But he knew the necromancer who'd burnt him was waiting for him in Death, waiting for an Abhorsen-in-Waiting too incompetent to manage the manner of his own passing. The necromancer would catch him, take his spirit, and bind it to his will, use him against his family, his Kingdom. . . .

Fear grew in Sam, sharper than the pain. He reached for the Charter marks of healing once more—and found them. Golden warmth grew in his weakly gesturing hands and flowed into his leg, through the black and sodden trouser. He felt its heat rushing through, all the way to the bone, felt the skin and blood vessels knit together, the magic bringing everything back to the way it was supposed to be.

But he'd lost too much blood too quickly for the spell to render him completely whole. He tried to get up but couldn't. His head fell back, the leaf litter making him a pillow. He tried to force his eyes wide open but couldn't. The forest spun again, faster and faster, and then everything went black.

Chapter Twenty-Nine

THE OBSERVATORY OF THE CLAYR

THE DISREPUTABLE DOG woke with great reluctance, spending a number of minutes in stiff-legged stretching, yawning, and eye rolling. Finally, she shook herself and headed for the door. Lirael stood where she was, her arms crossed sternly across her chest.

"Dog! I need to talk to you!"

The Dog acted surprised, putting her ears back with a sudden jerk. "Shouldn't we be hurrying home? It's after midnight, you know. Third hour of the morning, in fact."

"No!" exclaimed Lirael, all thoughts of talks forgotten. "It can't be! We'd better hurry!"

"Still, if you want to have a talk," said the Dog, sitting back on her haunches and cocking her head in a prime listening attitude, "there's no time like the present, I always say."

Lirael didn't answer. She rushed to the door, pulling on the Dog's collar as she passed, yanking her upright.

"Ow!" yelped the Dog. "I was only joking! I'll hurry!"

"Come on, come on!" snapped Lirael, pushing her hands against the door and then trying to pull at it, which was difficult because it didn't have a handle or a knob. "Oh, how does this open?"

"Ask it," replied the Dog, calmly. "There's no point pushing."

Lirael let out a huff of frustration, took a deep breath, and then forced herself to say, "Please open, door."

The door seemed to think about it for a moment, then slowly swung inwards, giving Lirael enough time to back away. The roar of the river rose through the doorway, and a cool breeze came with it, lifting Lirael's sadly singed hair. The wind also brought something else, something that attracted the Dog's attention, though Lirael couldn't tell what it was.

"Hmmm," said the Dog, turning one ear towards the door and the Charter-lit bridge beyond it. "People. Clayr. Possibly even an aunt."

"Aunt Kirrith!" exclaimed Lirael, jumping nervously. She looked around wildly, seeking another way out. But there was nowhere to go except back across the slippery, river-washed bridge. And now she could see bright Charter lights out in the Rift, lights made fuzzy by the mist and spray from the river.

"What'll we do?" she asked, but her question echoed in the room, taking up the space where there should have been an answer. Quickly, Lirael looked back, but there was no sign of the Disreputable Dog. She had simply disappeared.

"Dog?" whispered Lirael, eyes scanning the room as tears started to blur her vision. "Dog? Don't leave me now."

The Dog had left before when people might have seen her, and every time she did, Lirael harbored the secret fear that her one and only friend would never come back. She felt that familiar fear uncoil in her stomach, adding to the fear she felt from what she'd learned. Fear of the secret knowledge she felt seething and broiling in the book she held under her arm. It was knowledge that she didn't want to have, for it was not of the Clayr.

A single tear ran down her cheek, but she quickly wiped it away. Aunt Kirrith wouldn't have the satisfaction of seeing her cry, she decided, tilting her head back to keep further tears at bay. Aunt Kirrith always seemed to expect the worst of Lirael, seemed to think that she would commit terrible crimes and never amount to anything. Lirael felt that it was all because she wasn't a proper Clayr, though some part of her mind had to acknowledge that this was the way Aunt Kirrith treated anybody who departed from her stupid standards.

Lirael kept her head proudly tilted back until she took her first step on the bridge, when she had to look down, down into the roiling mist and the fast-rushing water. Without the Dog's solid, sucker-footed body at her side, she found the bridge much, much scarier. Lirael took one step, faltered, then started to sway. For a moment, she felt she would fall, and in a panic she crouched down on all fours. *The Book of Remembrance and Forgetting* shifted as she moved, and it almost fell out of her shirt as well. But Lirael shoved it back in and started to crawl across the narrow bridge.

Even crawling took all her concentration, so she didn't look up until she was almost across. She was now also acutely aware that her hair was burnt and her clothes totally soaked by the spray that kept washing over the bridge. And she was barefoot.

When she finally did look up, she let out a stifled scream and made a reflexive hop like a frightened rabbit. Only the quick hands of the two closest Clayr saved her from a potentially fatal fall into the swift, cold waters of the Ratterlin.

They were also the people who had given her the shock, the last two people Lirael would expect to see looking for her: Sanar and Ryelle. As always, they looked calm, beautiful, and sophisticated. They were in the uniform of the Nine Day Watch, their long blond hair elegantly contained in jeweled nets and their long white dresses sprinkled with tiny golden stars. They also held wands of steel and ivory, proclaiming that they were the joint Voice of the Watch. Neither of them looked a day older than when Lirael had first met them properly, out on the Terrace on her fourteenth birthday. They were still everything Lirael thought the Clayr should be.

Everything she wasn't.

There were a whole lot of the Clayr behind them, as well. More of the highest, including Vancelle, the Chief Librarian, and what looked like more of the Nine Day Watch. Quickly counting, Lirael realized that it probably was *all* of the current Nine Day Watch. Forty-seven of them, lined up behind Sanar and Ryelle, white shapes in the darkness of the Rift.

But the total absence of Aunt Kirrith was the worst sign. That meant that whatever she'd done was punishable by something far worse than extra kitchen duties. Lirael couldn't even imagine what sort of punishment required the presence of the entire Watch. She'd never even heard of them leaving the Observatory, not all together.

"Stand up, Lirael," said one of the twins. Lirael realized that she was crouching, still supported by the two Clayr. Gingerly, she stood up, trying to avoid meeting their gaze, not to mention all the other blue and green eyes that she was sure were noting just how brown and muddy her own eyes were.

Words rose up in her mind, but her throat closed when they tried to pass. She coughed, and stuttered, then finally managed to whisper, "I . . . I didn't mean to come here. It just : . . . happened. And I know I missed dinner . . . and the midnight rounds. I'll make it up somehow. . . ."

She stopped as Sanar and Ryelle glanced at each other and laughed. But it was kind, surprised laughter, not the scorn she feared.

"We seem to have established a tradition of meeting you in strange places on your birthday," said Ryelle—or perhaps it was Sanar—looking down at the book poking out of Lirael's shirt and the silver panpipes glinting from her waistcoat pocket. "You need not worry about the rounds or a missed dinner. You seem to have claimed a birthright of sorts tonight, one that has waited long for your coming. Everything else is of little consequence."

"What do you mean by a birthright?" asked Lirael. The Sight was the Clayr's birthright, not a trio of strange magical devices.

"You know that alone amongst the Clayr you have never been Seen in the visions," the other twin began. "Never a glimpse, at least till now. But an hour ago, we—that is, the Nine Day Watch—Saw that you would be here, and in another place also. None of us even suspected that this bridge existed, nor the room beyond. But it is clear that while the Clayr of today have not Seen you in their visions, the Clayr of long ago Saw enough to prepare this place and the things you hold. To prepare you, in fact."

"Prepare me for what?" asked Lirael, panicked by the sudden attention. "I don't want anything! All I want is to be . . . to be normal. To have the Sight."

Sanar—for it was Sanar who had spoken last—looked down at the young woman, seeing the pain in her. Since their first meeting five years before, she and her sister had kept a cautious eye on Lirael, and they knew more about her life than their young cousin suspected.

She chose her words carefully.

"Lirael, the Sight may yet come to you in time, and be the stronger for the waiting. But for now you have been given other gifts, gifts that I am sure will be sorely needed by the Kingdom. And as all of us of the Blood are given gifts, we are also laden with the responsibility to use them wisely and well. You have the potential for great power, Lirael, but I fear that you will also face great tests."

She paused, staring into the billowing cloud of mist behind Lirael, and her eyes seemed to cloud, too, as her voice grew deeper and became less friendly, more impersonal and strange.

"You will meet many trials on a path that lies unseen, but you will never forget that you are a Daughter of the Clayr. You may not See, but you will Remember. And in the Remembering, you will see the hidden past that holds the secrets of the future."

Lirael shivered at the words, for Sanar had spoken with the truth of prophecy, and her eyes were sparkling with a strange, icy light.

"What do you mean by great tests?" Lirael asked, when the last faint echo of Sanar's words were lost, drowned in the roar of the river.

Sanar shook her head and smiled, the moment of the vision lost. Unable to speak, she looked at her sister, who continued.

"When we Saw you here this evening, we also Saw you somewhere else, somewhere we have labored for many years to See, without success," said Ryelle. "On the Red Lake, in a boat of woven reeds. The sun was high and bright, so we know it will be in summer. You looked much as you do now, so we know it is in the summer coming that you will be there."

"There will be a young man with you," continued Sanar. "A sick or wounded man, one we were asked to seek for the King. We do not know exactly where he is now, or how or when he will come to the Red Lake. He is surrounded by powers that cloak our vision, and his future is dark. But we do know that he lies at the center of some great and terrible danger. A danger not just to him but to all of us, to the Kingdom. And he will be there with you, in the reed boat, at the height of summer."

"I don't understand," whispered Lirael. "What's that to

do with me? I mean, the Red Lake, this man, and everything? I'm just a Second Assistant Librarian! What have I got to do with it?"

"We don't know," answered Sanar. "The visions are fragmented, and a dark cloud spreads like spilt ink across the pages of possible futures. All we know is that this man is important, for both good and ill, and we have Seen you with him. We think that you must leave the Glacier. You must go south and find the reed boat on the Red Lake, and find him."

Lirael looked at Sanar's lips, still moving, but she could hear no sound save the cry of the river. The sound of the water rushing to be free of the mountain, flowing away, away to some distant and unknown land.

I'm being thrown out, she thought. I don't have the Sight, I've grown too old, and they're throwing me out—

"We have also had another vision of the man," Sanar was saying as Lirael's hearing came back. "Come, we will show you, so you will know him at the proper time, and know something of the danger he is in. But not here—we must go up to the Observatory."

"The Observatory!" exclaimed Lirael. "But I'm not . . . I haven't Awoken—"

"I know," said Ryelle, taking her hand to lead her. "It is difficult for you to gaze upon your heart's desire when you may not possess it. If the danger were any less, or someone else could shoulder the burden, we would not press you so. If the vision were not of this place that resists us, we could probably show you elsewhere, too. But now we need the power of the Observatory, and the full strength of the Watch."

They walked back along the Rift, with Sanar and Ryelle on either side of an unprotesting Lirael. Lirael briefly felt what the Dog had called her sense of the Dead, a sort of pressure from all the dead Clayr buried throughout the Rift, but she paid it no heed. It was like someone far away calling someone else's name. All she could think of was that they were making her leave. She would be alone again, because the Disreputable Dog might not come. The Dog might not even be able to exist outside the Clayr's Glacier, like a sending that couldn't leave its bounds.

Halfway back along the Rift towards the door where she'd come in, Lirael was surprised to see that a long bridge of ice had spanned the depths. The Clayr were walking back across it and then into a deep cave-mouth on the other side of the Rift. Ryelle saw her look and explained, "There are many ways to and from the Observatory, when we have need. This bridge will melt when we have all crossed."

Lirael nodded dumbly. She'd always wondered where the Observatory actually was, and had tried to find it on more than one occasion. She'd had many daydreams of finding her way there, and finding her Sight within. But all those daydreams were destroyed now.

Across the bridge, the cave-mouth led into a rudely dug tunnel that sloped up quite steeply. It was hard going, and Lirael was hot and out of breath when the tunnel finally flattened out. Ryelle and Sanar stopped then, and Lirael wiped the sweat from her eyes before she looked around. They had left stone behind. Now there was nothing but ice all around, blue ice that reflected the Charter lights the Clayr carried. They had come to the heart of the Glacier.

A gate was carved in the ice, flanked by two guards in full mail, holding shields that bore the golden star of the Clayr. Their faces were stern under their open helms. One carried an axe that gleamed with Charter marks, the other a sword that shone brighter than the lights, casting a thousand tiny reflections in the ice. Lirael stared at the guards, for they were clearly Clayr, but no one she knew, which she had thought impossible. There were less than three thousand Clayr in the Glacier, and she had lived here all her life.

"I See you, Voice of the Nine Day Watch," said the woman with the axe, speaking in a strange, formal tone. "You may pass. But the other with you has not Awoken. By the ancient laws, she must not be allowed to See the secret ways."

"Don't be silly, Erimael," said Sanar. "What ancient laws? It's Lirael, Arielle's daughter."

"Erimael?" whispered Lirael, peering at the severe face, sharply defined by the edges of her helm. Erimael had joined the Rangers six years ago and hadn't been seen since. Lirael had thought Erimael must have been killed in an accident and that she'd missed her Farewell, as she had missed so many other events that required her to don the blue tunic.

"The laws are clear," said Erimael, still in the same stern voice, though Lirael saw her gulp nervously. "I am the Axe-Guard. She must be blindfolded if you wish her to pass."

Sanar snorted and turned to the other woman. "And what says the Sword-Guard? Don't tell me you agree?"

"Yes, unfortunately," said the other woman, who Lirael realized was much older. "The letter of the law is strict. Guests must be blindfolded. Anyone who is not an Awoken Clayr is a guest."

Sanar sighed and turned to Lirael. But Lirael had already hung her head, to hide her humiliation. Slowly, she undid her head scarf, folded it into a narrow band, and bound it around her head, covering her eyes. Behind the soft darkness of the cloth, she wept silently, the blindfold soaking up her tears.

Sanar and Ryelle took her hands again, and Lirael felt the sympathy in their touch. But it did not matter. This was even worse than when she was fourteen, standing alone in her blue tunic, suffering the public shame of not being a Clayr. Now she was irrevocably marked as an outsider. Not a Clayr at all, of any kind. Only a guest.

She asked only two questions as Ryelle and Sanar led her through what felt like a complicated, maze-like passage.

"When will I have to go?"

"Today," replied Ryelle, as she stopped Lirael and prepared her for another sharp turn by gently pushing her elbow till she was facing the right way. "That is to say, as soon as possible. A boat is being prepared for you. It will be spelled to take you down the Ratterlin to Qyrre. From there you should be able to get some constables or even some of the Guard to escort you to Edge, on the Red Lake itself. It should be a fast and uneventful journey, though we wish we could See some of it beforehand."

"Am I to go alone?"

Lirael couldn't see, but she sensed Sanar and Ryelle exchanging glances, silently working out who would speak. At last Sanar said, "That is how you have been Seen, so I'm afraid that is how you will have to go. I wish it were otherwise. We would fly you down by Paperwing, but all the Paperwings have been Seen elsewhere, so the river it must be."

Alone. Without even her one friend, the Disreputable Dog. It didn't really matter what happened to her now.

"There are some steps down here," said Ryelle, stopping Lirael again. "About thirty, I think. Then we will be in the Observatory, and you can take the blindfold off."

Lirael mechanically went with the twins down the steps. It was unsettling, not being able to see where her feet were going, and some of the steps seemed lower than the others. To make it worse, there was a weird rustling noise all around, and occasionally the hint of whispers or smothered conversations.

Finally, they arrived on level ground and took a half dozen steps forward. Sanar helped untie her blindfold.

Light was the first thing Lirael noticed, and space, and then the massed ranks of the Clayr, silently standing in their white, rustling robes. She stood in the center of a huge chamber carved entirely out of ice, a vast cave easily as large as the Great Hall she knew and hated so much. Charter Magic lights shone everywhere, reflecting from the many facets of the ice, so that there was not a hint of darkness anywhere.

Lirael instinctively looked down when she saw all the other Clayr, so she couldn't meet anyone's eyes. But as she cautiously peered out from behind her protective fall of singed hair, she saw that they were not looking at her. They were all looking up. She followed their gaze and saw that the angled ceiling was perfectly smooth and flat, one single enormous sheet of clear ice, almost like an enormous, opaque window.

"Yes," said Sanar, noting Lirael's stare. "That is where we focus our Sight, so all the fragments of the vision can become one, and everyone can See."

"I think we may begin," announced Ryelle, looking around at the massed, silent ranks of the Clayr. Nearly every Awoken Clayr was there, to join a Watch of Fifteen Sixty-Eight. They stood in a series of ever-wider circles around the small central area where Lirael, Sanar, and Ryelle stood, like some strange concentric orchard of white trees that bore silver and moonstone fruit.

"Let us begin!" cried Sanar and Ryelle, and they lifted their wands and clashed them together like swords. Lirael jumped as all the gathered Clayr shouted back, a great bellow that she felt through her bones.

"Let us begin!"

𝗣 ⚜ ⬦

As one, the Clayr in the closest circle joined hands, snapping together as in a military drill. Then the next circle joined hands, and the next, a wave of movement rippling from the center to the farthest circle in the Observatory, till all was still again.

"Let us See!" cried Sanar and Ryelle, clashing their wands again. This time, Lirael was prepared for the shout that came back, but not for the magic that followed. Charter marks seemed to well up out of the icy floor, flowing up through the Clayr of the first circle, till there were so many, they brimmed over and flowed into the next circle, and then the one after that. Charter marks that flowed like thick golden fog up the Clayr's bodies and along their arms.

Lirael watched the magic grow as it passed each circle, saw it wrap itself around the bodies of her cousins. She could see the Charter marks, feel the magic in her pounding heart, hunger for it. But it remained alien, somehow beyond her, as no other Charter Magic had ever been.

Then the outermost circle of the Clayr broke their hand-clasps and held their arms up towards the distant, icy ceiling. Marks flowed from them into the air, falling upwards like golden dust caught in shafts of sunlight. When it hit the ice, it splashed there, as if it were glorious paint and the ice a blank canvas waiting to come alive.

Each circle followed in turn, till all the magic they'd summoned had risen to fill the whole huge ice ceiling with swirling Charter marks. They stared at it, entranced, and Lirael saw their eyes move as if they all watched something there. But she saw nothing, nothing save the swirl of magic that she couldn't understand.

"Look," said Ryelle softly, and the wand she held suddenly became a bottle of bright green glass.

"Learn," said Sanar, and she waved her wand in a pattern

directly above Lirael's head.

Then Ryelle threw the contents of the bottle, seemingly at Lirael. But as the liquid flew over her head, Sanar's wand transformed it into ice. A pane of pure, translucent ice that hung horizontally in the air directly above Lirael's head.

Sanar tapped this pane with her wand, and it began to glow a deep, comfortable blue. She tapped it again, and the blue fled to the edges. Lirael stared at it, and then through it, and as she stared, she realized that this strange, suspended pane was helping her See what the Clayr Saw. The meaningless patterns on the ice ceiling above were starting to become clear. Hundreds, maybe even thousands of tiny pictures were joining together to make up a larger picture, like the puzzle pictures she'd played with as a child.

It was a picture of a man standing with his foot on a rock, Lirael saw now. He was looking at something below him.

Curious, Lirael craned her head back for a better view. That made her dizzy for an instant, and then it seemed as if she were falling upwards, through the blue pane and all the way up into the ceiling, falling into the vision. There was a flash of blue and a touch of something that made her shiver—and she was there!

She was standing next to the man. She could hear his rasping, unhealthy-sounding breath, smell the faintest hint of sweat, feel the heat and humidity of a summer day.

And she could taste the awful taint of Free Magic, stronger and more vile than she could ever have imagined, stronger even than her memory of the Stilken. So strong that the bile rose in her throat and she had to force it back, and dots danced before her eyes.

Chapter Thirty

NICHOLAS AND THE PIT

HE WAS YOUNG, Lirael saw, about her own age. Nineteen or twenty. And obviously ill. He was tall, but stooped over, as if a nagging pain bit his middle. His blond, unkempt hair was clean, but hung together like damp string. His skin was too pink in the cheeks and grey around his lips and eyes. Those eyes were blue, but dulled. He held a pair of dark spectacles loosely in one hand, the arms repaired with twine and one green lens cracked and starred.

He was standing on some sort of artificial hill of rough, loose earth, peering shortsightedly down towards a deep pit, a gaping hole in the ground. The pit—or whatever was in it—was the source of the Free Magic that was making Lirael nauseated, even through the vision. She could feel waves of it pulsating out of the scarred earth, cold and terrible, eating into her bones, biting away deep inside her teeth.

The pit had obviously been freshly dug. It was at least as wide across as the Lower Refectory, which could hold four hundred people. A spiral path wound around its edges, disappearing down into the dark depths. Lirael couldn't see how deep it was, but there were people carrying baskets of dirt and rock up and empty baskets back down. Slow, tired people, who seemed quite strange to Lirael. Their clothes were dirty and torn, but even so, Lirael could see that their cut and color were quite unlike anything she'd ever seen. And nearly all of them wore blue hats or the knotted remnants of blue headscarves.

Lirael wondered how on earth they could work with the corrosive taint of Free Magic all around, and looked at them more closely. Then she gasped and tried to move back, but the vision held her.

They weren't people. They were Dead. She could feel them now, feel the chill of Death close by. These workers were Dead Hands, enslaved by some necromancer's will. The blue hats shaded sightless eye sockets, the blue scarves held together rotting heads.

Lirael suppressed her instinctive desire to vomit and quickly looked at the young man next to her, fearful that he might be the necromancer and could somehow see her. But he had no Charter mark on his brow, either whole or perverted to Free Magic. His forehead was clear, save for dirty beads of sweat that had caught the dust from the air, and there was no sign of any bells.

He was looking up now, looking at the sky, and shaking some metal object on his wrist. Perhaps in ritual, Lirael thought. She suddenly felt sorry for him, and had a strange urge to touch the curve of his neck where it joined his ear, just with the very tip of her fingers. She even started to reach out, and was only reminded of where—and what—she was when he spoke.

"Damn it!" he muttered. "Why does nothing work?"

He lowered his arm but kept looking up. Lirael looked, too, seeing the dark thunderclouds that roiled there, low and close. Lightning flickered, but there was no cool breeze, no scent of rain. Just the heat and the lightning.

Then, without warning, a blinding bolt of lightning struck down into the pit, lighting the black depths in a bright flash of incandescence. In that moment, Lirael saw hundreds of Dead Hands digging, digging with tools if they had them and with their own rotting hands if not. They paid no attention to the lightning, which burnt and blackened several of their number, nor the deafening crash of thunder that came at almost the same time.

Within a few seconds, another bolt followed the first, seemingly hitting exactly the same place. Then another and another, thunder booming on and on, shaking the ground at Lirael's feet.

"Four in approximately fifty seconds," remarked the man to himself. "It's getting more frequent. Hedge!"

Lirael didn't understand this last call till a man strode out of the pit below and waved. A thin, balding man, clad in leather armor with gold-etched red enamel steel plates at his throat, elbows, and knees. He had a sword at his side—and a bandolier of bells across his chest, black ebony handles poking out of red leather pouches. Perversions of Charter marks moved across both wood and leather, leaving after-images of fire.

Even from so far away, he smelt of blood and hot metal. He must be the necromancer the Dead Hands served—or one of the necromancers, for there were many Dead. But this one was not the source of the Free Magic that burnt at Lirael's lips and tongue. Something far worse than he lay hidden in the depths of the pit.

"Yes, Master Nicholas?" called the man. Lirael noted that he waved the two Dead Hands that followed him back down into the shadows, as if he didn't want them too clearly seen.

"The lightning comes more quickly," said the young man, so identifying himself to Lirael as Nicholas. But what manner of man—a man without a Charter mark—would a necromancer call Master?

"We must be close," he added, his voice going hoarse. "Ask the men if they will work an extra shift tonight."

"Oh, they'll work!" shouted the necromancer, laughing at

some private jest. "Do you want to come down?"

Nicholas shook his head. He had to clear his throat several times before he could shout back, "I feel . . . I feel unwell again, Hedge. I'm going to lie down in my tent. I will look later. But you must call me if you find anything. It will be metal, I think. Yes, shining metal," he continued, eyes staring as if he saw it in front of him. "Two shining metal hemispheres, each taller than a man. We must find them quickly. Quickly!"

Hedge half bowed, but he didn't answer. He climbed out of the pit, leaving it to walk up to the hill of tailings where Nicholas stood.

"Who is that with you?" shouted Hedge, pointing.

Nicholas looked to where he pointed but saw nothing save the afterglow of the lightning and the image of the shining hemispheres—the image he saw in all his waking moments, as if it were imprinted on his brain.

"Nothing," he muttered, looking straight at Lirael. "No one. I am so tired. But it will be a great discovery—"

"Spy! You'll burn at the feet of my Master!"

Flames leapt from the necromancer's hands and spilled on the ground, red flames cloaked in black, choking smoke. They raced up the hill like wildfire, straight towards Lirael.

At the same time, she saw Nicholas's eyes suddenly focus on her. He reached out one hand in greeting, saying, "Hello! But I expect you're only another hallucination."

Then hands gripped her shoulders and she was pulled back into the Observatory as the red fire struck where she'd been and boiled up into a narrow column of fiery destruction and blackest smoke.

Ice shattered, and Lirael blinked. When she opened her eyes, she was standing between Ryelle and Sanar again, in a pool of broken shards, with pieces of blue ice sprinkled across her head and shoulders.

"You Saw," said Ryelle. It wasn't a question.

"Yes," replied Lirael, sorely troubled, as much by the experience of the vision as by what she'd Seen. "Is that what it is like to have the Sight?"

"Not exactly," replied Sanar. "We mostly See in short flashes, brief fragments from many different parts of the future, all mixed up. Only together, in the Watch, here in the Observatory, can we unify the vision. Even then, only the person who stands where you have stood will See it all."

Lirael thought about that and craned her head back again, ice dribbling down her neck under her shirt. The distant ceiling was only a patch of ice again. She looked back down and saw that all the Clayr were leaving without a word or a backwards glance. The outer ring had gone before she even noticed, and now the next was uncurling into a single file, leaving by a different door. There seemed to be many exits from the Observatory, Lirael thought. Soon she would take one herself, never to return again.

"What," Lirael began, forcing herself to think about the vision,"what am I supposed to do?"

"We don't know," said Ryelle. "We have been trying to See around the Red Lake for several years, without success. Then all of a sudden we Saw you in the room below, the vision we have shown you, and then a glimpse of you and the man in a boat upon the lake. All are obviously linked in some way, but we have not been able to See more."

"The man Nicholas is the key," said Sanar. "Once you find him, we think, you will know what to do."

"But he's with a necromancer!" exclaimed Lirael. "They're digging up something terrible! Shouldn't we tell the Abhorsen?"

"We have sent messages, but the Abhorsen and the King are in Ancelstierre, where they hope to avert a trouble that is also probably connected with whatever is in the pit that you Saw. We have also alerted Ellimere and her co-regent, and it is possible they will also act, perhaps with Prince Sameth, the Abhorsen-in-Waiting. But whatever they do, we know that it is you who must find Nicholas. It seems a little thing, I know, a meeting between two people on a lake. But it is the only future we can See now, with all else hidden from us, and it offers our only hope to avert disaster."

Lirael nodded, white-faced. Too many things were happening, and she was too tired and emotionally exhausted to cope. But it did seem that she was not just being thrown out. She really did have something important to do, not just for the Clayr, but for the whole Kingdom.

"Now, we must prepare you for the journey," added Sanar, obviously noting Lirael's weariness. "Is there anything personal you wish to take, or something special we can provide?"

Lirael shook her head. She wanted the Disreputable Dog, but that didn't seem possible, if the Clayr hadn't Seen her. Perhaps her friend was gone forever now, the spell that had brought her meeting some condition that triggered its end.

"My outdoor things, I suppose," she whispered finally. "And a few books. I suppose I should take the things I found, too."

"You should," said Sanar, obviously curious as to what exactly they were. But she didn't ask, and Lirael didn't feel like talking about them. They were just more complications. Why had they been left for her? What use would they be out in the wide world?

"We must also outfit you with a bow and sword," said Ryelle. "As befits a Daughter of the Clayr gone a-voyaging."

"I'm not very good with a sword," Lirael said in a small voice, choking a little at being called a Daughter of the Clayr. Those words, so long sought, sounded empty to her now. "I'm all right with a bow."

She didn't explain that she was competent with the laminated short bow used by the Clayr only because she shot rats in the Library, using blunted arrows so as not to puncture books. The Dog liked to retrieve the arrows but wasn't interested in eating the rats, unless Lirael cooked them with herbs and sauce, which she naturally refused to do.

"I hope you will need neither weapon," said Sanar. Her words seemed loud, echoing out into the huge cavern of ice. Lirael shivered. That hope seemed likely to be false. Suddenly it was cold. Nearly all the Clayr had gone, all fifteen hundred of them, in a matter of minutes, as if they had never been there. Only two armored guards remained, watching from the end of the Observatory. One had a spear and the other a bow. Lirael didn't need to get closer to know that these were also weapons of power, imbued with Charter Magic.

They had stayed, she knew, to make sure she was blindfolded. She looked away and took her scarf off, folding it with slow, deliberate movements. Then she tied it across her eyes and stood stiffly, waiting for Sanar and Ryelle to take her arms.

"I am sorry," said Sanar and Ryelle, at the same time, their voices blending into one. They sounded to her as if they were apologizing not just for the blindfold, but for Lirael's whole life.

By the time they reached her small chamber off the Hall of Youth, Lirael had not slept or eaten for more than eighteen hours. She was staggering with fatigue, so Sanar and Ryelle continued to support her. She was so tired that she didn't even realize Aunt Kirrith was present until she was taken into a sudden, unwelcome, extremely tight embrace.

"Lirael! What have you done now!" Aunt Kirrith exclaimed, her voice booming from somewhere above Lirael's head, which was kept firmly pressed into her aunt's neck. "You're too young to go off into the world!"

"Aunt!" protested Lirael, trying to free herself, embarrassed to be treated like a little girl in front of Ryelle and Sanar. It was typical of Aunt Kirrith to try to hug her when she didn't want her to, and to not hug her when she did want to be hugged.

"It'll be just like your mother all over again," Kirrith was saying, seemingly as much to the twins as to Lirael. "Going off who knows where and getting involved in who knows what with who knows whom. Why, you might even come back—"

"Kirrith! Enough!" snapped Sanar, surprising Lirael. She had never heard anyone speak to Kirrith like that. It was clearly a shock to Kirrith, too, because she let go of Lirael and took a deep, dignified breath.

"You can't talk to me like that, San . . . Ry . . . whichever one you are," Aunt Kirrith finally said after several deep breaths. "I'm Guardian of the Young, and I am in authority here!"

"And we, for the moment, are the Voice of the Clayr," replied Sanar and Ryelle in unison, lifting the wands they still held. "We have been invested with the powers of the Nine Day Watch. Do you challenge our right, Kirrith?"

Kirrith looked at them, tried to take an even deeper breath, and failed, her breath wheezing out of her like that of a toad that has been stepped on. It was clearly a recognition of their authority, if not a very dignified one.

"Fetch the things you want to take, Lirael," said Sanar, touching her on the shoulder. "We must soon go down to the boat. Kirrith, perhaps if we could speak outside?"

Lirael nodded wearily and went to the chest that held her clothes, while the others went out and shut the door. Without looking, she reached in. Her hand hit something hard, and her fingers were around it before she looked and gave a little gasp of recognition. It was the old soapstone carving of the hard-bitten dog, the one she'd found in the Stilken's chamber, the one that had vanished when the Disreputable Dog had appeared.

Lirael hugged it close to her chest for a moment, a faint hope breaking through her weariness. It was not the Dog, but it was a hint that the Dog could be summoned again. Smiling, she put the statuette in the pocket of a clean waistcoat, making sure its soapstone snout could not be seen poking out. She put the Dark Mirror in the same pocket and the panpipes in the other one, and transferred *The Book of Remembrance and Forgetting* to a small shoulder bag that seemed exactly made for it. The clockwork emergency mouse she put in a corner of the chest, followed by the whistle. Neither of them could help her where she was going now.

As she undressed and quickly washed, thankful for the larger room and simple bathroom she'd moved to on her eighteenth birthday, Lirael considered changing her clothes completely, to wear something that did not identify her as a Clayr. But when it came time to dress, she once again donned the working clothes of a Second Assistant Librarian. That was what she was, she told herself. She had earned the right to the red waistcoat. No one could take that away, even if she wasn't a proper Clayr.

She had just rolled some spare clothes into her cloak, and was thinking about her heavy wool coat and its likely usefulness in late spring and summer, when there was a knock on the door, followed immediately by Kirrith.

"I didn't mean any nastiness about your mother," Kirrith said from the doorway, sounding subdued. "Arielle was my little sister, and I loved her well. But she was outlandish, if you know what I mean, and prone to trouble. Always getting into scrapes and . . . well . . . it's not been easy, what with being Guardian and having to keep everyone in line. Perhaps I haven't shown you . . . well, it's hard when you can't See how others feel or will feel about you. What I mean to say is that I loved your mother—and I love you, too."

"I know, Auntie," replied Lirael, not looking back as she threw her coat back in the chest. Even a year ago she would have given anything to hear those words, to feel that she belonged. Now it was too late. She was leaving the Glacier, leaving it as her mother had done years before, when she had abandoned her daughter seemingly without a care.

But that was all history, Lirael thought. I can leave it behind, start my story afresh. I don't need to know why my mother left, or who my father was. I don't need to know, she repeated to herself.

I don't need to know.

But while she mumbled those words under her breath, her mind kept turning to *The Book of Remembrance and Forgetting* in the bag at her side, and the pipes and Dark Mirror in her waistcoat pockets.

She didn't need to know what had happened in the past. But while she had always been alone among the Clayr for her blindness to the future, now she was alone in another way as well. In a perverse reversal of all her hopes and dreams, she had been granted the exact opposite of her heart's desire.

For with the Dark Mirror, and her new-found knowledge, she could See into the past.

Chapter Thirty-One

A VOICE IN THE TREES

HIDDEN A MERE hundred yards into the fringe of the forest, Prince Sameth lay like a dead man, sprawled where he'd fallen from his horse. One leg was caked with drying blood, and black-red blotches marked the green leaves of the bushes that shivered around him in the breeze. Only a close inspection would have shown that he was still breathing.

Sprout, proving less neurotic than expected, grazed quietly nearby. Occasionally her ears twitched and her head went up, but all through the long day nothing disturbed her contented munching.

In the late afternoon, when the shadows began their slow crawl out from the trees to stretch and join together, the breeze picked up and relieved the heat of the late-spring day. It blew over Sam, partly covering him with leaves, twigs, wind-caught spiderwebs, beetle carcasses, and feathery grasses.

One thin blade of grass caught up against his nose and was trapped there, tickling his nostril. It rustled this way, then that, but didn't shift. Sameth's nose twitched in response, twitched again, then finally burst out in a sneeze.

Sam woke up. At first he thought he was drunk, hungover, and suffering. His mouth was dry, and he could taste the stench of his own breath. His head ached with a fierce pain, and his legs hurt even more. He must have passed out in someone's garden, which was incredibly embarrassing. He had been this drunk only once before, and hadn't wished to repeat the experience.

He started to call out, but even as the dry, pathetic croak left his lips, he remembered what had happened.

He'd killed two constables. Men who were trying to do their duty. Men who had wives, family. Parents, brothers, sisters, children. They would have left their homes in the morning with no expectation of sudden death. Perhaps their wives were even now waiting for them to come home for the evening meal.

No, thought Sameth, levering himself up to look bleakly at the red light of the setting sun filtering through the trees. They had fought early in the morning. The wives would know by now that their husbands were never coming home.

Slowly, he pushed himself further upright, brushing the forest debris from his clothes. He had to push the guilt down, too, at least for the moment. Survival required it.

First of all, he had best cut away his trouser leg and look at the wound. He dimly remembered casting the spell that had undoubtedly saved his life, but the wound would still be fragile, liable to reopen. He had to bind it up, for he was far too weak to cast another healing spell.

After that, he would somehow stand up. Stand up, catch the faithful Sprout, and ride deeper into the forest. He was somewhat surprised that he hadn't already been discovered by the local constabulary. Unless he had laid a more confusing trail than he'd thought, or they were waiting for reinforcements to arrive before they started looking for what they assumed to be a murderous necromancer.

If the constables—or even worse, the Guard—found him now, he'd have to tell them who he was, Sam decided. And that would mean a shameful return to Belisaere, there to be tried by

Ellimere and Jall Oren. Public disgrace and infamy would be sure to follow. The only other alternative would be a dishonorable covering up of his awful deed.

Either situation would be intolerable. The disappointment he could already imagine on his parents' faces would be too much to bear. No doubt his inability to be the Abhorsen-in-Waiting would also come out, and they would despair of him completely.

Better that he disappear. Go into the forest and hide out while he recovered, then continue to Edge with a newly conjured visage, for he was sure Nick still needed help. At least he would be able to do that. Not even Nick could get into more trouble than Sam had managed to get into himself.

Making the decisions proved easier than putting them into practice. Sprout backed away from him, her nostrils flaring, as he tried to grab her reins. She didn't like the smell of blood, or the occasional grunts of pain Sam let out as he accidentally put weight on his wounded leg.

Finally, he managed to push her into a sort of natural cul-de-sac, where three trees prevented any further retreat. Mounting proved to be another challenge. Pain flared as he swung his leg over, gasping at the hurt.

Now Sam was faced with another problem. It was rapidly getting dark, and he had no idea where to go. Civilization and all it offered lay east, north, and south, but he dared not go until he was strong enough to cast another spell to change his and Sprout's looks. Westward, there were many forest paths of doubtful use and direction. There might be some settlements or lone houses somewhere within the forest, but he couldn't visit them with any safety, either.

Worse, he had only a single canteen of yesterday's water, a hunk of very stale bread, and a lump of salted beef, his emergency provision in case he needed a snack between inns. The ginger cakes were long gone, eaten on the road.

It began to rain, the wind having brought clouds over from the sea—only a light spring shower, but it was enough to make Sam curse and wrestle with his saddlebags, trying to pull out his cloak. If he caught a cold on top of his existing hurts, there was no knowing how he'd end up. In a forest grave, most likely, he thought bitterly, not dug by human hands. Just a mound of wind-borne bits and pieces, linked by the grass growing up around his pathetic remains.

He was just thinking about this dismal future when his fingers, pulling at the cloak, felt leather and cold metal instead of wool. Instantly, he snatched his hand away, the tips of his fingers cold and already turning blue. The knowledge of what he'd just touched made him bend over his saddle horn and let out a great sob of despair and fright.

The Book of the Dead. He'd left it behind in his workroom, but it had refused to be left. Just like the bells. He would never be rid of them, even wounded and alone in this dark forest. They would follow him forever, even into Death itself.

He was just about to let himself break down when a voice came from the darkness between the trees.

"A little lost princeling, weeping in the forest? I would have thought you had more steel in your spine, Prince Sameth. Still, I am often wrong."

The voice had an electric effect on Sameth and Sprout. The Prince shot bolt upright in the saddle, gasped at the pain, and tried to draw his sword. Sprout, equally surprised, leapt forward into an instant canter, weaving amid the trees without a thought for her rider and low-slung branches.

Horse and rider raced along in a cacophony of breaking branches, shouts, and whinnies. They continued in this fashion

for at least fifty yards before Sameth got Sprout under control
and managed to turn her back in the direction the voice had
come from.

He also managed to draw his sword. It was half-dark now,
the tree-trunks pale ashen streaks in the gathering gloom, supporting branches where leaves hung like heavy clots of darkness.
Whoever . . . whatever . . . had spoken could easily creep up
on him now, but it was better to face it than be knocked off by
a branch in panicked flight.

The voice had been unnatural. He'd tasted Free Magic in
it, and something else. It wasn't a Dead creature—no, not that.
But it could be a Stilken or Margrue, Free Magic elementals that
occasionally hungered for the taste of Life. He wished now that
he had read the book that he'd been given for his birthday, the
one on binding, by Merchane.

Something rustled in the leaves of the closest tree, and Sam
started again, lifting his sword to the guard position. Sprout
fidgeted, kept in check only by the pressure of Sam's knees. The
effort sent bolts of pain up Sam's side, but he did not ease off.

There was something moving all right, moving up the
trunk—there—no, there. It was jumping from branch to
branch, moving behind him. Maybe more than one. . . .

Desperately, Sam tried to reach the Charter to draw out
the marks needed for a magical attack. But he was too weak,
the pain in his leg too strong, too fresh. He couldn't keep the
marks in his mind. He couldn't remember the spell he wanted
to form.

Perhaps the bells, he thought in desperation, as whatever it
was moved again. But he didn't know how to use the bells
against the Dead, let alone Free Magic beings. His hand
shook at the thought of using the bells, and he was reminded
of Death. At the same time a fierce determination rose in him.

Whatever ill luck had dogged him, he would not just lie down and die. He might be afraid, but he was a royal Prince, the son of Touchstone and Sabriel, and he would sell his life as dear as his strength could make it.

"Who calls Prince Sameth?" he shouted, words harsh in the darkling forest. "Show yourself, before I wreak a spell on you of great destruction!"

"Save the theatrics for those who respond to them," replied the voice, this time accompanied by the flash of two piercing green eyes, reflecting the last of the sun on a branch high above Sam's head. "And count yourself lucky that it's only me. You've left blood enough around to call a brace of hormagants."

With that speech, a small white cat leapt from the tree, catapulted off a lower branch, and landed a cautious distance from Sprout's forefeet.

"Mogget!" exclaimed Sam, peering down at him with dizzy incredulity. "What are you doing here?"

"Looking for you," said the cat. "As should be startlingly obvious to even the most dull-witted Prince. Loyal servant of the Abhorsen, that's me. Ready to baby-sit at a moment's notice. Anywhere. No trouble at all. Now get off that horse and make a fire, just in case there actually are some hormagants about. I don't suppose you've been sensible enough to bring anything to eat?"

Sameth shook his head, feeling something not exactly as positive as relief pass through him. Mogget *was* a servant of the Abhorsen, but he was also a Free Magic being of ancient power. The red collar he wore, engrained with Charter marks, and the miniature bell that hung from it, were the visible signs of the power that bound him. Once it had been Saraneth, the Binder, that rang on that collar. Since the defeat of Kerrigor, the bell that bound Mogget was a tiny Ranna. Ranna the

Sleepbringer, the first of the seven bells.

Sameth had hardly ever spoken to Mogget, for the strange cat-being had been awake only once when Sam was at Abhorsen's House, and that had been ten years before. As on the more recent occasion, he'd woken just long enough to steal Touchstone's fresh-caught salmon, and had addressed few words to the boy of seven who had stared incredulously as the "always sleeping" cat removed a fish as large as itself from a silver platter.

"I really don't understand," mumbled Sameth as he gingerly lowered himself off Sprout's back. "Did Mother send you to look for me? How did she wake you up?"

"The Abhorsen," replied Mogget, between bouts of licking his paw in a rather stately fashion, "had nothing directly to do with it. Having been associated with the family for so long, I am simply aware of when my services are required. For example, when a new set of bells appears, suggesting that an Abhorsen-in-Waiting is ready to come into his inheritance. Having woken, I simply followed the bells.

"But the return of Cassiel's bells did not waken me," continued Mogget, switching to his other paw. "I was already awake. Something is happening in the Kingdom. Things long dormant are stirring, or being woken, and the ripples of their waking have spread to Abhorsen's House, for whatever wakes threatens the Abhorsen—"

"Do you know what it is exactly?" Sam interrupted anxiously. "Mother said she feared some ancient evil was planning terrible things. I had thought it might be Kerrigor."

"Your uncle Rogir?" replied Mogget, as if answering a question about some slightly eccentric relative rather than the fearful Greater Dead Adept that Kerrigor had ultimately become. "Ranna holds him tighter than she does me. He sleeps in the deepest cellar of Abhorsen's House. And there he will sleep till the end of time."

"Ah," sighed Sam, relieved.

"Unless whatever is stirring wakes him up as well," Mogget added thoughtfully. "Now tell me why my leisurely journey to Belisaere and its justly famous fish markets has been suddenly interrupted by a side trip to a forest. Where do you think you're going, and why are you going there?"

"I'm going to find my friend Nicholas," explained Sam, though he felt Mogget's green eyes boring into him, seeking out the deeper reasons that he continued to hide from himself. Avoiding that gaze, he pushed together a small pyramid of twigs and dried leaves, and lit it with a friction match struck against his boot.

"And who is Nicholas?" asked Mogget.

"He's an Ancelstierran, a friend of mine from school. I'm worried because he has no idea what it's really like over here. He doesn't even believe in Charter Magic—or any other magic, for that matter," said Sam, as he added some larger sticks to the fire. "He thinks everything can be explained scientifically, the same way Ancelstierran things work. Even after the Dead attacked us near the Perimeter, he still wouldn't accept that there isn't some explanation other than magic. He's *very* stubborn. Once he decides something is just so, he won't change his mind unless you can prove it with mathematics or something he accepts. And he's important in Ancelstierre, because he's the Chief Minister's nephew. I mean, you probably know that Mother and Dad are going to negotiate—"

"Where is this Nicholas?" interrupted Mogget, hooding his eyes. Sameth could see the flames reflected in them for a moment before the lids closed, and he shivered. In the eyes of some Dead creatures, those flames would not be a reflection.

"He was supposed to wait for me to meet him at the Wall, but he's already crossed. At least that's what he said in his letter. He hired a guide, and he's going to look for some old legend called the Lightning Trap on the way to Belisaere," continued Sameth, feeding a larger branch into the fire. "I don't know what that is, or how he heard about it, but apparently it's somewhere near Edge. And of course that's where Mother and Dad think the Enemy is."

His voice trailed off as he realized that Mogget didn't seem to be listening.

"The Lightning Trap, near the Red Lake," muttered Mogget, his eyes closing to narrow slits of darkness. "The King and the Abhorsen in Ancelstierre, trying to stop a great multitude going to their deaths. A friend of the Abhorsen-in-Waiting, a Prince of sorts himself on the other side of the Wall. The Clayr Sightless, save for visions of total ruin . . . This does not bode well, and the connections cannot be purely coincidence. The Lightning Trap. I have not heard that name precisely, but something stirs. . . . Sleep grips and dulls my memory. . . ."

Mogget's voice had grown softer as he spoke, drifting into something like a growl. Sam waited for the cat to say something more, then realized that the growl had become a snore. Mogget was asleep.

Shivering—but not with cold—Sam put another branch in the fire and was comforted by the flare of friendly light. It had stopped raining, or never got properly started. Just a bit of spitting and a slight drop in temperature. But this was not good news to Sam, who would have preferred to be enduring heavy rain. The last few days had been unseasonably warm for the time of year, with summer heat in late spring, and teasing rain that had never quite developed into a real storm. That meant the spring floods would be sinking early. And the Dead would roam further afield, not confined by running water.

He looked at Mogget again and was startled to see one bright eye watching him, sparkling in the firelight, while the other eye was firmly closed.

"How were you wounded?" purred the cat, voice low, words matching the crackle of the fire. He sounded as if he already knew the answer, but wanted to confirm something.

Sam blushed and hung his head, hands unconsciously linking in an attitude of prayer.

"I got in a fight with two constables. They thought I was a necromancer. The bells . . ." His voice trailed off, and he gulped. Mogget kept staring at him with that one sardonic eye, obviously waiting to hear more.

"I killed them," whispered Sam. "A Death-spell."

There was a long silence. Mogget opened his other eye and yawned, pink mouth revealing sharp, ever-so-white teeth.

"Idiot. Worse than your father. Guilt, guilt, guilt," he said, mid yawn. "You didn't kill them."

"What!" exclaimed Sam.

"You can't have killed them," replied Mogget, turning around several times to knead the leaves into a more comfortable bed. "They're royal servants, sworn to the King. They carry his protection, even from one of his wayward children. Mind you, any other innocents about would have been slain. Very clumsy of you, to use that spell."

"I didn't think," replied Sam woodenly. He was enormously relieved that he wasn't a murderer. Now he could feel angry at Mogget for making him feel like a foolish schoolboy.

"Obviously," agreed Mogget. "And you haven't started thinking, either. If they'd died, you would have felt it. You're the Abhorsen-in-Waiting, Charter help us."

Sam bit back an angry reply as he realized that the cat was

correct. He *hadn't* felt the constables die. Mogget kept watching him, his eyes still slitted, apparently viewing Sam with deep suspicion.

"Coils within coils," murmured the cat. "Fleas upon fleas, idiots begetting idiots—"

"What?"

"Mmm, just thinking," whispered Mogget. "You should try it sometimes. Wake me in the morning. It may be quite difficult."

"Yes, Sire," said Sam, mustering as much sarcasm as possible. It had no effect upon Mogget, who now seemed to be really asleep.

"I always wondered why Dad said you were too big for your boots," Sam added, straightening his leg out in front of him and checking the bandage. He didn't add that when he had been seven years old and newly at school in Ancelstierre, he had pointed to an illustration from "Puss in Boots" and loudly repeated something his father had once said to Sabriel: "That bloody cat of yours is too big for his boots."

It had also been the first time he'd worn the dunce cap and stood in the corner. "Bloody" was not in the accepted vocabulary for the young gentlemen of Thorne Preparatory School.

Mogget didn't reply. Sam poked his tongue out at him, then dragged a half-rotted stump onto the fire, hopping on his good leg. The stump would burn till dawn, but just in case, he broke up some deadfall branches and laid them close by.

Then he lay down himself, with his sword under his hand and Sprout's saddle under his head. It was a warm night, so he didn't need his cloak or Sprout's odorous saddle blanket. Sprout herself dozed nearby, hobbled to prevent her starting off on her own nervous adventures. Mogget slept at Sam's side, more like a hunting dog than a cat.

For a few moments Sam thought about staying awake to

keep watch, but he didn't have the strength to keep his eyes open. Besides, they were in the heartland of the Kingdom, close to Belisaere. It had been safe here for the last decade at least. What could possibly trouble them?

Many things, Sam thought, as sleep battled with his awareness of all the subtle sounds of the night forest. He was deeply troubled by Mogget's enigmatic words, and was still cataloguing potential horrors and matching them to sounds when exhaustion overcame him and he fell asleep.

He awoke to the touch of sunlight on his face, filtered through the canopy of trees. The fire continued to smolder, smoke meandering about till he sat up, when it changed direction and blew across his face.

Mogget was still sleeping, now curled up into a tight white ball, almost buried in the leaves.

Sam yawned and tried to stand up. He'd forgotten about his leg, which had stiffened so much that he promptly fell over, letting out a shriek of pain. That startled Sprout, who jumped as far as her hobbles allowed her and rolled her eyes. Sam muttered soothing words at her while he used a hefty sapling to haul himself upright.

Mogget didn't wake then or later, sleeping on while Sam finished re-dressing his wound and cast a small Charter-spell to dull the pain and keep infection at bay. The cat stayed asleep even when Sam got out some bread and beef for a not very satisfactory breakfast.

After he'd eaten, Sam brushed Sprout and then saddled up. With nothing left to do but cover the remnants of the fire, he decided it was time to endure more of Mogget's insults.

"Mogget! Wake up!"

The cat didn't stir. Sam leaned down closer and shouted, "Wake up!" again, but Mogget didn't even twitch an ear.

Finally, he reached out and shook the little cat gently behind the collar. Aside from his feeling the buzz and interplay of Free and Charter Magic, nothing happened. Mogget slept on.

"What am I supposed to do with you?" asked Sam, looking down at him. This whole adventure/rescue business was getting out of hand. It was only his third day out of Belisaere, and he was already off the high road, wounded, and in the company of a strange and potentially extremely dangerous Free Magic construct. His question dredged up another one he'd been trying to avoid: What was he going to do now himself?

He didn't expect an answer to either question, but after a moment, a muffled reply came from the apparently still sleeping cat.

"Put me in a saddlebag. Wake me up when you find some decent food. Preferably fish."

"All right," replied Sam with a shrug. Picking up the cat without moving his wounded leg proved difficult, but eventually he managed it. Cradling Mogget in one forearm, he delicately transferred him to the left saddlebag, after checking that it wasn't the one with the bells and *The Book of the Dead*. He didn't like the idea of all three being put together, though he knew no reason why they shouldn't be.

Eventually Mogget was safely installed, with just his head poking out of the bag.

"I'm going to ride west through this small forest, then across the open country to the Sindlewood," explained Sam as he turned the stirrup and put his boot through, ready to mount. "We'll go through the Sindlewood to the Ratterlin, then follow it south till we can get a boat to take us to Qyrre. From there it shouldn't take long to get to Edge, and hopefully we'll find Nick straightaway. Does that sound like a good plan?"

Mogget didn't answer.

"So a day or so in this forest," continued Sam as he mustered his strength to swing up and over. He liked talking about his plans out loud—it made them seem more real and sensible. Particularly when Mogget was asleep and couldn't criticize them. "When we come out, we're bound to find a village, or a charcoal burner's camp or something. They'll sell us whatever we need before we cross the Sindlewood. There're probably woodcutters or people like that there, too."

He stopped talking as he mounted up, suppressing a cry of pain. His injured leg was feeling better than the day before, but not by much. And he felt a bit dizzy now, almost lightheaded. He'd have to be careful.

"By the way," he said, clicking Sprout into a walk, "last night you seemed to know something about this Lightning Trap Nick has gone to look for. You didn't like the sound of it, but you fell asleep before saying anything else. I was wondering if it had anything to do with the necromancer—"

"Necromancer?" came the immediate, yowled reply. Mogget erupted out of the saddlebag and crouched in front of Sam, looking in every direction, his fur standing on end.

"Um, not here. I was just saying that you started to talk about the Lightning Trap, and I wondered if it had to do with Chlorr of the Mask, or the other necromancer, the one . . . the one I fought."

"Humph," snorted Mogget darkly, subsiding back into the saddlebag.

"Well, tell me something!" demanded Sam. "You can't just sleep all day!"

"Can't I?" asked Mogget. "I could sleep all year. Particularly since I have no fish, which I note you have failed to procure."

"So what is the Lightning Trap?" prompted Sam, pulling lightly on the reins to direct Sprout towards a more westerly and well-traveled path.

"I don't know," Mogget said softly. "But I mislike the sound of it. A Lightning Trap. A gatherer of lightning? Surely it cannot be—"

"What?" asked Sam.

"It is probably only a coincidence," replied Mogget heavily, his eyes closing once more. "Perhaps your friend does only go to see a place where lightning strikes more commonly than it should. But there are powers working here, powers that hate everything of the Charter, Blood, and Stone. I smell plots and long-laid plans, Sameth. I do not like it at all."

"So what should we do?" Sam asked anxiously.

"We must find your friend Nick," whispered Mogget as he drifted back into sleep. "Before he finds . . . whatever it is that he seeks."

Chapter Thirty-Two

"WHEN THE DEAD DO WALK, SEEK WATER'S RUN"

GOADED ON BY Mogget's alarming presentiment, Sam pressed himself and Sprout hard—so they left the small, unnamed forest earlier than expected, on the evening of the first day, and began to cross the rolling green hills of the farmland beyond. This was part of the Middle Lands of the Old Kingdom, a wide belt of small villages, farm stead-ings, and sheep, stretching west across the country almost as far as Estwael and Olmond. Apart from Sindle to the north, there were no towns until Yanyl, twenty leagues past the western shore of the Ratterlin. Largely depopulated during the Interregnum, the area had recovered quickly during Touchstone's reign, but there were still far fewer people than in the heyday of the Kingdom.

Since his former disguise was now a liability, Sam removed the Charter-spell that disguised him as a Traveler and resumed his normal appearance. Sprout was already disguised by the mud on her legs and her very ordinary looks. In his sweaty, dirt-stained clothes, it was hard to tell what Sam looked like, anyway. He had a story ready, should he be asked. He would say he was the younger son of a Belisaere merchant's guard captain, traveling from the north to a cousin near Chasel, who would employ him as a retainer.

He also re-bound his wound and managed to slip on his spare trousers, so as not to show an obviously wounded, blood-stained leg. His limp he could not disguise, unlike his hat, which suffered the indignity of having its brim cut in half, rendering it both less shady and less distinctive.

Soon after leaving the forest, they entered a village, or a hamlet, really, since it boasted only seven houses. There was a Charter Stone nearby, though. Sam could feel it, somewhere behind the houses. He was tempted to find it and use it to help him cast another, stronger healing spell, but the villagers would surely notice him then.

The place lacked an inn. Though a comfortable bed was beyond hope, he did manage to buy some almost-fresh bread, a freshly cooked rabbit, and several small, sweet apples from a woman who was taking a cartload of fair-day purchases home to her farm.

Mogget slept through this transaction, hidden under the loosely tied flap of the saddlebag, which was just as well. Sam didn't know how he would even begin to explain why a white cat rode with him. It was better not to tempt interest.

Sam kept on riding till it was too dark to see and Sprout wandered into the mud on either side of what was supposed to be a road. He conjured a small Charter light, and they found an open-sided hayrick in which to take shelter. Mogget slept on, oblivious to the removal of the saddlebags and the scraping of at least some of the mud from man and horse.

Sam tried to wake him, to learn more about the Lightning Trap. But the bell that bound Mogget worked too well, its sleepy chime sounding whenever the cat moved as if to wake up. The miniature Ranna made even Sam weary when he leaned too close, so he fell asleep next to the cat in a most uncomfortable position.

The next day was much the same as the first. Not surprisingly, considering his thin bed of leftover straw, Sam found it easy to rise before dawn, and once again he pushed Sprout to a pace beyond her liking.

He met few people on the road—which was not much more than a track—and spoke little but pleasantries to them, for fear of discovery. Just enough to seem normal, when he bought some food, or asked about the best way through Sindlewood to the Ratterlin.

He had a fright in one village, when he stopped to buy some grain for Sprout and a bag of onions and parsnips for himself. Two constables rode straight towards him, but they didn't slow, merely nodding as they passed, riding back eastwards. Apparently, the word had not spread either about a dangerous necromancer-at-large or a missing Prince, or else he didn't look as if he could be either one. Whatever the cause, Sam was grateful.

In the main, it was an uneventful if tiring journey. Sam spent much of the time thinking about Nick, his parents, and his own shortcomings. These thoughts always led back to the Enemy. The more he thought about it, the more Sam was convinced that the necromancer who had burnt him must be the architect of all the current troubles. That necromancer had the power, and he had shown his hand by trying to capture and dominate Sam.

Mostly Sam agonized over what he should do and what might happen. He constructed many quite horrifying scenarios in his head, and he generally failed to work out what the best course of action would be if they turned out to be true. Each passing day made him envision more horrible possibilities. Every day Sam was more acutely aware that Nicholas might have already found something inimical in the Lightning Trap. Perhaps his doom.

Four days after his encounter with the constables, Sam found himself looking down from a pastured hill into the shadowy green borders of the ancient forest known as Sindlewood. It looked much larger, darker, and more overgrown than the small wood where he'd met Mogget. The trees were taller, too, at least the ones he could see on the fringe, and there was no obvious path.

Even as Sam looked at the forest, his thoughts were far away. Nick's situation weighed heavily on him, as did the presence of *The Book of the Dead* and the bells. All these things were closely entwined now, for it seemed that Sam's best hope of rescuing Nick—if he was in trouble—lay in mastering the skills of an Abhorsen. If Nick was held by the Enemy, he would probably be used to blackmail the Chief Minister in Ancelstierre and stop Sabriel and Touchstone's plan to prevent the Southerlings' being massacred, which in turn would mean an invasion by the Dead and the end of the Old Kingdom, and . . .

Sam sighed and looked back at the saddlebags. His imagination was getting out of control. But whatever was really happening, he would have to make a supreme effort to read the book, in order to become a rescuer and not just an idiot riding into disaster, getting himself killed or enslaved for nothing.

Of course, there was always the possibility that Mogget was lying. Sam was somewhat suspicious of Mogget, having the dim recollection that the cat never left Abhorsen's House without the Abhorsen. True, Sabriel couldn't have taken him into Ancelstierre on a diplomatic mission, and it was possible that she had granted him freedom to leave the House. But Sabriel also had the ring that could control the Free Magic being that would result if Mogget were unbound. If the creature within Mogget should be freed, it would kill any Abhorsen it could. Which, in this case, meant Sam. Surely Sabriel wouldn't have let the cat out without making sure it also brought Sam the ring.

Maybe it was her very absence in Ancelstierre, on the other side of the Wall, that had allowed Mogget to do what he liked.

Or perhaps Mogget had even been suborned by the Enemy and was actually guiding Sameth to his doom. . . .

Busy thinking unpleasant thoughts and trying to direct Sprout the best way down the hill, Sam was totally unprepared for the cold shiver that suddenly touched his spine. In that same instant, he realized he was being watched. Watched by something Dead.

The old rhyme, drilled into him since childhood, leapt into his head:

When the Dead do walk, seek water's run,
For this the Dead will always shun.
Swift river's best or broadest lake
To ward the Dead and haven make.
If water fails thee, fire's thy friend;
If neither guards, it will be thy end.

Even as the words were running through his head, Sam looked at the sun. There was little more than an hour of daylight left. Simultaneously he looked for running water—a stream or river—and saw a reflection, silver in the shadows, near the edge of the forest. Farther away than he would have liked.

He directed Sprout towards it, feeling the fear rise in him, coursing through his muscles. He couldn't see the Dead creature, but it was close. He felt its spirit like a clammy touch upon his skin. It must be strong, too, or it would not risk even the waning sun.

Sam's knees twitched, the reflex of an overwhelming urge to kick Sprout into a gallop. But they were still going down the hill, on broken ground. If Sprout fell on him, he would be trapped, easy prey for the Dead. . . .

No. Best not to think of that. He looked around again, squinting against the yellow-red sun, low in the sky. The creature was somewhere behind him . . . and no . . . to the right.

His fear grew as Sam realized there were two creatures, perhaps more. They must be Shadow Hands, slinking from the shade of rock to rock, almost impossible to see till they reared up to attack.

Fumbling, he reached back and opened the saddlebag. If he couldn't reach running water in time, the bells would be his only defense against Shadow Hands. A fairly pathetic defense, since he didn't know how to use them properly and they might easily work against him.

He felt one of the Dead move again, and his heart stammered at the awful swiftness of the thing. It was right next to him and he still couldn't see it, even in bright sunlight!

Then he looked up. A black speck hovered above him, just beyond arrow-shot. And another, behind the first and farther up.

Not Shadow Hands at all. Gore Crows. And where there were two, there would be many more. Gore Crows were always created in flocks, made from ordinary crows killed with ritual and ceremony, then infused with the splintered fragments of just one Dead spirit. Guided by this shattered but single intelligence, these decaying lumps of rotten flesh and feathers flew by force of Free Magic—and killed by force of numbers.

But as Sam scanned the horizon, he could see no more than two. Surely no necromancer would waste his power on just a pair of Gore Crows. They were too easy to kill in anything less than a flock. A sword-stroke could smash a single crow, but even a mighty warrior could be defeated by a hundred Gore

Crows attacking at once, sharp beaks striking at the eyes and neck.

It was also unusual for them to be out under the sun. The spell that drove them was quickly eroded by heat and light, even as their physical forms were shredded by the wind.

Unless, Sam suddenly thought, there really were only two Gore Crows, sharing the Dead vitality that would normally be spent on hundreds of crow bodies. If this was the case, they would last much longer and would be stronger under the sun. They could also be used in other ways than to merely attack.

Like watching, he thought grimly, as neither Dead bird sought to come any closer. They were keeping station above him, circling slowly, probably marking him for the assault of other Dead come nightfall.

As if to confirm his thoughts, one of the Gore Crows—the one farther away—let out a mocking, scratchy caw and turned away to the south, dropping rotten feathers as it flew, propelled more by magic than by the occasional beats of its wings.

It looked all too much like a messenger, with its partner the shadower, staying high to follow wherever Sam might go.

For a moment he contemplated casting a spell of destruction upon it, but it was too far away and obviously well instructed in caution. Besides, he was still weak from his wounded leg. He knew he must save his powers for the night.

Keeping a wary eye on the black speck above him, Sam urged Sprout on. The stream didn't look like much from here, but it would offer some protection. After a moment's hesitation, he also drew out the bell-bandolier and put it on. The weight of the bells and their power lay heavily upon his chest, and shortened and shallowed his breath. But if worst came to worst, he would try to use the lesser bells, drawing on the lessons he'd had from his mother. They were supposed to be merely a prelude for the study he'd abandoned. Ranna, at least, he could probably wield without fear of being forced unwillingly into Death.

A nagging voice at the back of his mind said that even now it was not too late to pick up *The Book of the Dead*, to learn more of the birthright that could save him. But even his fear of an attack by the Dead was not enough to conquer Sam's fear of the book. Reading it, he might find himself taken into Death. Better to fight the Dead in Life, with what little knowledge he had, than to confront them in Death itself.

Behind him, Sam thought he heard a chuckle, a muffled laugh that didn't sound like Mogget. He turned, hand instinctively going to his sword, but there was nothing and no one there. Just the sleeping cat in one saddlebag, and *The Book of the Dead* in the other. Sam let go of the hilt, already sweaty from his trembling fingers, and looked down at the stream again. If the bed was smooth, he would ride along it as far as he could. If he was lucky, it might even take him as far west as the Ratterlin, a mighty river even one of the Greater Dead couldn't cross.

And from there, a secret and cowardly voice said in his mind, he could take a boat to Abhorsen's House. He would be safe there. Safe from the Dead, safe from everything. But what, another voice asked, would happen to Nick, to his parents, to the Kingdom? Then both voices were lost as Sam concentrated on guiding Sprout down the hillside, towards the promised safety of the stream.

Sam lost sight of the Gore Crow when the last of the daylight was eaten up by the shadows of the trees and the falling darkness. But he could still feel the Dead spirit above him. It was lower now, braver with the cloaking night about it.

But not brave enough to descend too close to the running

water that burbled on either side of Sam's temporary camp. The
stream had proved to be a bit of a disappointment, and a clear
indication that the spring floods were already receding. It was
only thirty feet wide, and shallow enough to wade in. But it
would help, and Sam had found an islet, no more than a narrow
strip of sand, where the water ran swiftly on either side.

He had a fire going already, since there was no point trying
to hide with the Gore Crow circling above. All he had to do
to make his camp as secure as possible was to cast a diamond of
protection large enough for himself, the horse, and the fire.

If he had the strength to do it, Sam thought, as he made
Sprout stand still. As an afterthought, he also took off the
bandolier of bells, which had grown no easier to bear. Then
he limped to take up a spell-casting stance in front of Sprout,
unsheathed his sword, and held it outstretched. Keeping this
pose, he took four slow, deliberate breaths, drawing as much
oxygen into his tired body as he could.

He reached out for the four cardinal Charter marks that
would create the points of the diamond of protection. Symbols
formed in his mind, plucked out of the flow of the never-
ending Charter.

He held them in his mind, breath ragged at the effort, and
drew the outline of the first mark—the Eastmark—in the sand
in front of him. As he finished, the Eastmark in his head ran
down into the blade like golden fire. It filled the outline he'd
made in the sand with light.

Sam limped behind Sprout, past the fire, and drew the
Southmark. As this one flared into life, a line of yellow fire ran
to it from the Eastmark, forming a barrier impenetrable to both
the Dead and physical danger. Intent on moving on, Sam didn't
look. If he faltered now, the diamond would be incomplete.

Sam had cast many diamonds of protection before, but
never when he was wounded and so weary. When the last

mark, the Northmark, finally flared up, he dropped his sword and collapsed, wheezing onto the damp sand.

Sprout, curious, turned her head back to look at him, but she didn't move. Sam had thought he would have to spell her into immobility to keep her from accidentally moving out of the diamond, but she didn't stir. Perhaps she could smell the Gore Crow.

"I take it we're in danger," said a yawning voice close to Sam's ear. He sat up and saw Mogget extricating himself from the saddlebag, which lay next to the fire and a probably insufficient pile of rather damp wood.

Sam nodded, temporarily unable to speak. He pointed up at the sky, which was now beginning to show single stars and the great white swathe of the Mare's Tail. There were black clouds too, high to the south, crackling with distant lightning, but no sign of rain.

The Gore Crow was invisible, but Mogget seemed to know what Sam was pointing at. The cat rose up on his hind legs and sniffed, one paw absently batting down an oversized mosquito that had probably just dined on Sam.

"A Gore Crow," he said. "Only one. Strange."

"It's been following us," said Sam, slapping several mosquitoes that were coming in to land on his forehead. "There were two, but the other one flew away. South. Probably to get orders. Curse these bugs!"

"There is a necromancer at work here," agreed Mogget, sniffing the air again. "I wonder if he . . . or she . . . has been searching for you specifically. Or is it just bad luck for a wayward traveler?"

"It could be the one who caught me before, couldn't it?" asked Sam. "I mean, he knew where I was with the cricket team. . . ."

"Perhaps," replied Mogget, still staring up at the night sky.

"It is unlikely that there would be Gore Crows here, or that any lesser necromancer would dare to move against you, unless there is a guiding force behind them. Certainly these Crows are more daring than they have any right to be. Have you caught me a fish?"

"No," replied Sam, surprised by the sudden change of subject.

"How inconsiderate of you," said Mogget, sniffing. "I suppose I'll have to catch one myself."

"No!" exclaimed Sam, levering himself up. "You'll break the diamond! I haven't got the strength to cast it again. Ow! Charter curse these mosquitoes!"

"I won't break it," said Mogget, walking over to the Westmark and carefully poking out his tongue. The mark flashed white, dazzling Sam. When his vision cleared, Mogget was standing upright on the other side, intent on the water, one paw raised, like a fishing bear.

"Show-off," muttered Sam. He wondered how the cat had done it. The diamond was unbroken, the lines of magical fire streaming without pause between the brightness of the cardinal marks.

If only the diamond kept the mosquitoes out as well, he thought, slapping several more into bloody oblivion against his neck. Clearly their bites did not come into the spell's definition of physical harm. Suddenly he smiled, remembering something he'd packed.

He was getting this object out of the saddlebag when the Westmark flashed again, reacting to Mogget's return. The cat had two small trout in his mouth, their scales reflecting rainbows in the mix of firelight and Charter glow.

"You can have this one to cook," said Mogget, dropping the smaller one next to the fire. "What is that?"

"It's a present for my mother," replied Sam proudly, setting down a bejeweled clockwork frog that had the interesting anatomical addition of wings made of feathery bronze. "A flying frog."

Mogget watched with interest as Sam lightly touched the frog's back and it began to glow with Charter Magic as the sending inside the mechanical body waked from sleep. It opened one turquoise eye, then the other, lids of paper-thin gold sliding back. Then it flapped its wings, brazen feathers clashing.

"Very pretty," said Mogget. "Does it *do* anything?"

The flying frog answered the question itself, suddenly leaping into the air, a long and vibrantly red tongue flashing out to grab several startled mosquitoes. Wings beating furiously, it spiraled after several more, ate them, and then dived back down to land contentedly near Sam's feet.

"It catches bugs," stated Sam with considerable satisfaction. "I thought it would be handy for Mother, since she spends so much time in swamps hunting the Dead."

"You made it," said Mogget, watching the flying frog leap again to twirl and twist after its quarry. "Completely your invention?"

"Yes," replied Sam shortly, expecting some criticism of his handiwork. But Mogget was silent, just watching the frog's aerobatics, his green eyes following its every move. Then the cat shifted his gaze to Sam, making him nervous. He tried to meet that green stare, but he had to look away—and he suddenly realized that there were Dead nearby. Lots of Dead, drawing closer with every second.

Mogget obviously felt them, too, for he leapt up and hissed, the hair on his back rising to a ridge. Sprout smelt them, and shivered. The Flying Frog flew to the saddlebags and climbed in.

Sam looked out into the darkness, shielding his eyes from the firelight. The moon was occluded by cloud, but starlight reflected from the water. He could feel the Dead, out there in the forest, but the darkness lay too heavy under the branches of the old tangled trees. He couldn't see anything.

But he could hear twigs cracking, and branches snapping back, and even the occasional heavy footfall, all against the constant burble of the stream. Whatever was coming, some of them at least had physical forms. There could be Shadow Hands out there as well. Or Ghlims or Mordaut or any of the many kinds of Lesser Dead. He could feel nothing more powerful, at least for now.

Whatever they were, there were at least a dozen of them, on both sides of the stream. Forgetting his tiredness and his limp, Sam moved around the diamond, checking the marks. The running water was neither deep nor fast enough to do more than discourage the Dead. The diamond would be their true protection.

"You may have to renew the marks before dawn," said Mogget, watching Sam's inspection. "It hasn't been cast very well. You should get some sleep before you try again."

"How can I sleep?" whispered Sam, instinctively keeping his voice down, as if it mattered whether the Dead could hear him. They already knew where he was. He could even smell them now—the disgusting odor of decaying flesh and gravemold.

"They're only Hands," said Mogget, looking out. "They probably won't attack as long as the diamond lasts."

"How do you know that?" asked Sam, wiping the sweat from his forehead, along with several crushed mosquitoes. He thought he could see the Dead now—tall shapes between the darker trunks of the trees. Horrible, broken corpses forced back into Life to do a necromancer's bidding. Their intelligence and humanity ripped from them, leaving only inhuman strength and an insatiable desire for the life they could no longer have.

His life.

"You could walk out there and send them all back to Death," suggested Mogget. He was starting to eat the second fish, beginning with the tail. Sam hadn't seen him eat the first one.

"Your mother would," Mogget added slyly, when Sam didn't speak.

"I'm not my mother," replied Sam, dry-mouthed. He made no move to pick up the bells, though he could feel them there on the sand, calling out to him. They wanted to be used against the Dead. But they could be dangerous to the wielder, most of them, or tricksome at least. He would have to use Kibeth to make the Dead walk back into Death, and Kibeth could easily send him walking instead.

"Does the walker choose the path, or the path the walker?" Mogget asked suddenly, his eyes once again intent on Sam's sweating face.

"What?" asked the Prince, distracted. He'd heard his mother say that before, but it didn't mean anything to him then or now. "What does that mean?"

"It means that you've never finished *The Book of the Dead*," said Mogget in a strange tone.

"Well, no, not yet," said Sam wretchedly. "I'm going to, it's just that I—"

"It also means that we really are in trouble," interrupted Mogget, switching his gaze to the outer darkness. "I thought you would at least know enough to protect yourself by now!"

"What do you see?" asked Sam. He could hear movement

upstream, the sudden splintering of trees and the crash of rocks into the water.

"Shadow Hands have come," replied Mogget bleakly. "Two of them, well back in the trees. They are directing the Hands to dam the stream. I expect they will attack when the water no longer flows."

"I wish . . . I wish I were a proper Abhorsen," whispered Sam.

"Well you should be, at your age!" said Mogget. "But I suppose we will have to make do with whatever you do know. By the way, where is your own sword? An unspelled blade will not cut the stuff of Shadow Hands."

"I left it in Belisaere," Sam said, after a moment. "I didn't think . . . I didn't understand what I was doing. I thought Nick was probably in trouble, but not this much."

"That's the problem with growing up as a Prince," growled Mogget. "You always think that everything will get worked out for you. Or you turn out like your sister and think nothing gets done unless you do it. It's a wonder any of you are ever any use at all."

"What can I do now?" asked Sam humbly.

"We will have a little time before the water slows," replied Mogget. "You should try to place some magic in your blade. If you can make that Frog, I'm sure that will not be beyond you."

"Yes," said Sam dully. "I do know how to do that."

Concentrating on the blade, he delved once more into the Charter, reaching for marks of sharpness and unraveling, magic that would wreak havoc upon Dead flesh or spirit-stuff.

With an effort, he forced the marks into the blade, watching them slowly move like oil upon the metal, soaking into the steel.

"You are skilled," remarked the cat. "Surprisingly so. Almost you remind me of—"

Whatever he was about to say was lost as a terrible scream split the night, accompanied by frenzied splashing.

"What was that?" exclaimed Sam, going to the Northmark, his newly spelled sword held at guard.

"A Hand," replied Mogget, chuckling. "It fell in. Whoever controls these Dead is far away, my Prince. Even the Shadow Hands are weak and stupid."

"So we may have a chance," whispered Sam. The stream seemed little affected by the dam building upstream, and the diamond still shone brightly. Perhaps nothing would happen before the dawn.

"We have a good chance," said Mogget. "For tonight. But there will be another night tomorrow, and perhaps another after that, before we can reach the Ratterlin. What of them?"

Sam was still trying to think of an answer when the first of the Dead Hands came screaming across the water—and ran full tilt into the diamond, silver sparks exploding everywhere into the night.

Chapter Thirty-Three

FLIGHT TO THE RIVER

DAWN CAME SLOWLY to the outer fringes of the Sindlewood, light trickling over the treetops long before it penetrated the darker depths. When it did finally reach the lower regions, it was no longer a burning heat, but a greenish, diluted light that simply pushed the shadows back rather than extinguished them.

The sunlight reached Sameth's magic-girded islet much later than he would have liked. The fire had long since burnt itself out, and as Mogget had predicted, Sam had had to renew the diamond of protection long before the first hint of dawn, drawing on reserves of energy he hadn't known he possessed.

With the light came the full evidence of the night's work. The streambed was almost dry, the Dead-made dam upstream still holding. Six Charter-blasted corpses lay piled all around the islet: husks vacated by the Dead when the protective magic of the diamond burnt through too many nerves and sinews, rendering the bodies useless.

Sam looked at them warily, through red-rimmed puffy eyes, watching the sunlight crawl across the stinking remnants. He'd felt the Dead spirits shucking the bodies as snakes shed their skins, but in the confusion of their suicidal attacks, he wasn't sure whether all of them had gone. One might be lurking still, husbanding its strength, enduring the sun, hoping Sam would be overconfident and step out of the diamond.

He could still feel Dead nearby, but that was probably the Shadow Hands, taking up daytime refuges in rabbit holes or otter holts, slipping down into the dark earth under the rocks, where they belonged.

At last full sunshine lit the whole streambed, and Sam's sense of the Dead faded, save for the ever-present Gore Crow, circling high overhead. He sighed with relief, and stretched, trying to relieve the cramp in his sword-arm and the pain in his wounded leg. He was exhausted, but he was alive. For another day, at least.

"We'd better start moving," said Mogget, who had slept most of the night, ignoring the slam and sizzle of the Dead Hands' attempts to break through the diamond. He looked ready to slip back into that sleep at a moment's notice.

"If the Gore Crow's stupid enough to get close, kill it," he added, yawning. "That will give us a chance to escape."

"What will I kill it with?" asked Sam wearily. Even if the Gore Crow came closer, he was too tired to cast a Charter-spell, and he didn't have a bow.

There was no answer from Mogget. He was already asleep again, curled up in the saddlebag, ready to be put on Sprout. Sam sighed and forced himself to get on with the job of saddling up. But his mind, tired as it was, still grappled with the problem of the Gore Crow. As Mogget said, as long as it tracked them, other Dead would be able to find them easily. Perhaps it would be one of the Greater Dead next, or a Mordicant, or even just larger numbers of Lesser Dead. Sam would have to spend at least the next two nights in the forest, and he would be weaker and more tired with every passing hour. He might not even be able to cast a diamond of protection. . . .

But, he thought, looking down at the dry streambed and the hundreds of beautifully round pebbles there, I do have the strength to put a mark of accuracy on a stone, and make a sling from my spare shirt. He even knew how to use one. Jall Oren had been keen on tutoring the royal children in all manner of weapons.

For the first time in days, a smile crept upon Sam's face, banishing the weariness. He looked up. Sure enough, the Gore Crow was circling lower than yesterday, overconfident from Sam's lack of a bow and obvious inability to do anything. It would be a long shot, but a Charter-spelled stone should go the distance.

Still grinning, Sam knelt down, surreptitiously picked up several likely stones, and ripped the sleeves from his spare shirt. He'd let the Gore Crow follow them for a while, he decided, and grow even more confident. Then it would pay the price for spying on a scion of the Old Kingdom.

Sam led Sprout westwards along the streambed, till it joined another, larger watercourse, and he had a choice of directions. Upstream to the northeast or downstream to the southwest.

At the junction, he hesitated, using Sprout's bulk to shield himself from view as he cast a mark upon the stone and settled it into the makeshift sling. The Gore Crow, seeing his hesitation, circled lower to make sure it could see which way he chose. It was obviously put off by the running water of the larger stream and perhaps hoped he'd turn back.

Sam waited till its spiral turned it closest to him. Then he stepped away from Sprout, the sling whirring above his head. At just the right moment, he yelled "Hah!" and let the stone fly.

The Gore Crow had only an instant to react, and being stupid, sunstruck, and Dead, it simply flew straight into the rocketing stone, meeting it in an explosion of feathers, dry bones, and putrid gobbets of meat.

With great satisfaction and then outright joy, Sam watched

the disgusting creature fall. The crushed ball of feathers landed with a splash in the stream, and the fragment of Dead spirit inside it was instantly banished back to whence it came. Better still, it would drag all the other fragments of that same spirit back into Death. So any Gore Crows that shared it would be dropping inexplicably, wherever they might be.

With the fall of the Gore Crow, he could sense no Dead nearby. The Shadow Hands would be long hidden now, as would any Dead Hands that remained. The intelligence that commanded them from afar might guess that Sam would take the southwest stream towards the Ratterlin, but whoever or whatever it was would not know for sure, and might split its forces, increasing his chance of evasion and escape.

"We have a chance, faithful horse," announced Sam cheerfully, leading Sprout towards an animal track that ran parallel to the stream. "We have a definite chance."

But hope seemed to slip from Sam's grasp as the day progressed and the going became slower and more difficult, so he couldn't ride Sprout. The stream had grown considerably deeper and faster, but also much narrower, barely three or four strides across, so it was impossible to stand in it or make a camp that would be protected on both sides.

The track had grown narrower, too, and overgrown. Sam had to hack through low branches, high shrubs, and barbed coils of blackberries. His hands became heavily scratched, attracting hordes of flies to the lines of drying blood. That would attract the Dead later, too. They could smell blood a long way away, though fresh would bring them faster.

By late afternoon, Sam had begun to despair. He was really exhausted now. There would be no question of casting a diamond of protection this coming night. He would pass out just trying to visualize the marks—and the Dead would find his defenseless body stretched out upon the ground.

His weariness was closing down his senses, too, narrowing his sight to a blinkered view and his hearing to little more than a muffled awareness of Sprout's hooves, dull upon the soft, forgiving forest floor.

In that state, it took him several seconds to realize that Sprout's hooves were suddenly making a sharper sound, and the cool green light of the forest had given way to something much sharper and more bright. He looked up, blinking, and saw that they had come to a wide clearing. The clearing was easily a hundred paces wide, cutting through the forest from the southeast to the northwest, continuing in both directions as far as he could see. Saplings had grown up on its borders, but the middle was stark and bare—and there was a paved road in the middle of it.

Sam stared at the road and then at the sun, which he'd barely been able to see under the forest's shady roof.

"About two, maybe three hours to dusk," he mumbled to Sprout, as he fiddled with the stirrup and mounted up. "You've had a good meal of grain today, haven't you, Sprout? Not to mention an easy walk, without carrying me. Now you can pay me back, because we are going to ride."

He chuckled then, thinking of an expression from the moving pictures he'd often seen in the Somersby Orpheum in Ancelstierre.

"We're going to ride, Sprout!" he repeated. "Ride like the wind!"

An hour and a half later, Sprout was no longer running like the wind, but back at a walk, legs trembling, sweat drenching her flanks, and froth forming at her mouth. Sam wasn't in much better shape, walking again himself, to give Sprout a chance to recover. He wasn't sure now what hurt more—his leg or his backside.

Even so, they had covered six or seven leagues, thanks to

the road. It was no royal road now, but it had been built and drained properly long ago, and so was more than serviceable.

They were currently climbing up a slight ridge, the road attacking it directly rather than winding around. Sam lifted his head as they approached the top, hoping for a glimpse of the Ratterlin before the day came to an end. By his reckoning, the ride—and the road—had saved more than a day of foot travel through the forest, so they should be close to the river. They *must* be close to the river. . . .

He stood on his toes for a moment but still couldn't see. It was an annoying ridge, this one, full of false heights and annoying dips along the way. But surely in a moment he would see the Ratterlin!

Clip! Clop! Sprout's hooves sounded loud on the road, as loud as Sam's own beating heart, but much, much slower. His heart was racing, racing with a combination of hope and fear.

There was the real crest ahead. Sam pushed forward, trying to see, but the sun was setting directly in front of him, a huge red disc sinking into the west, blinding him.

He screwed his eyes almost shut and shielded them with a hand, looking again—and there, under the sun, was a thick ribbon of blue, reflecting orange-red streaks back into the sky.

"The Ratterlin! Ow!" exclaimed Sam, stubbing his toe as he stumbled over the rise. But he ignored the momentary pain. There was the swift river whose waters would bar any Dead. The river that would save him!

Except, he thought, with sudden dread, it was still half a league away, and the night had almost come. And with it, he realized, so had the Dead. There were Dead creatures not too far away—perhaps even ahead of him. This road—and the point where it joined the Ratterlin towpath—would be an obvious point to be watched.

Worse than that, he thought, looking down at the river, he

hadn't actually planned what he'd do once he reached it. What if there was no boat or raft to be found?

"Hurry," said Mogget from the saddlebag behind him, making Sam jump in surprise and start leading Sprout on again. "We must head for the mill and take shelter there."

"I can't see a mill," said Sam doubtfully, shielding his eyes once more. He couldn't see any detail near the river at all. His eyes were blurry from lack of sleep, and he felt as stupid as a Dead Hand.

"Of course there's a mill," snapped Mogget, leaping down from the saddlebag onto Sam's shoulder, making him start again. "The wheel does not turn—so we can hope it is abandoned."

"Why?" asked Sam blearily. "Wouldn't it be better if there's people? We can get food, drink—"

"Would you bring the Dead upon a miller and his family?" interrupted Mogget. "It will not be long before they find us—if they haven't already."

Sam didn't reply, merely encouraging Sprout with a gentle slap to the neck. Perhaps he wouldn't weary her too much if he hung on the stirrup, he thought. He hoped she'd make the distance, because he didn't think he could walk that far unaided.

As usual, Mogget was right. Sam could feel the Dead closer now and, looking up, saw two black specks spiraling down out of the night that swept in from the east. Clearly the particular necromancer who drove them had no shortage of Gore Crows. And where the Crows flew, there would soon be others, brought out of Death to seek their prey.

Mogget saw the Gore Crows, too, and whispered in Sam's ear.

"There can be little doubt, now. This is the work of a necromancer who bears you particular ill will, Prince Sameth. His servants will seek you wherever you flee, and he will use all the creatures of Death to drive you to your doom."

Sam swallowed. The dire pronouncement echoed in his ears, imbued with the faint hint of the Free Magic power that was contained within the cat form on his shoulder. He slapped Sprout on the rump to get her going; then he said the first thing that came into his head.

"Mogget. Shut up."

Sprout fell a hundred yards from the mill, worn out by her earlier gallop and the dead weight of Sam hanging on a stirrup. He let go just in time to avoid being trapped under her. Mogget leapt off his shoulder to get even farther out of the way.

"Foundered," said Mogget briskly, without looking at her, his green eyes peering sharply back into the night. "They're getting closer."

"I know!" said Sam, urgently pulling the saddlebags free and slinging them over his shoulder. He bent down to stroke Sprout's head, but she didn't respond. Her eyes showed white and rolled almost completely back. He took the reins and tried to pull her up, but she made no move to help, and he was too weak to force her.

"Hurry!" urged Mogget, pacing around him. "You know what to do."

Sam nodded and glanced back at the Dead. There were a score or more of them, dim, lumbering shapes in the gathering darkness. Their masters had clearly driven them hard from some distant cemetery or boneyard, walking them even under the sun. Consequently, they were slow, but implacable. If he lingered even for a minute longer, they would fall upon him like rats on a worn-out dog.

He drew his dagger and felt Sprout's neck. The pulse of her main artery was weak and erratic under his fingers. He rested the dagger there but didn't push it in.

"I can't," he whispered. "She might recover."

"The Dead will drink her blood and feast upon her flesh!" exclaimed Mogget. "You owe her better than that. Strike!"

"I can't take a life. Even that of a horse, in mercy," said Sam, standing up unsteadily. "I realized that after . . . after the constables. We'll wait together."

Mogget hissed, then jumped across Sprout's neck, one paw tracing a line of white fire across the horse's neck. For an instant, nothing happened. Then blood burst out in a terrible fountain, splashing Sam's boots and throwing hot drops across his face. Sprout gave a single, convulsive shudder—and died.

Sam felt her die and turned his head away, unable to look at the dark pool that stained the ground beneath her.

Something nudged at his shins. Mogget, urging him into motion. Blindly, he turned away and began to trudge towards the mill. Sprout was dead, and he knew Mogget had done the only possible thing. But it just didn't seem right.

"Quickly!" urged the cat again, dancing around his feet, a white blur in the darkness. Sam could hear the Dead behind him now, hear the clicking of their bones, the screech of dry knees bent at angles impossible in Life. Fear fought the tiredness in him, made him move, but the mill seemed so far away.

He stumbled and almost fell, but somehow recovered. The pain in his leg jabbed at his head again, clearing it a little. His horse might be dead, but there was no reason why he should join her in Death. Only his weariness had made that seem attractive—for a moment.

There was the mill ahead, built out into the mighty Ratterlin, with the mill race, sluice gate, and wheel cut into the shore. He need only reach the race and open the sluice gate, and the mill would be defended by swift water, diverted from the river.

He risked a look over his shoulder and stumbled again, surprised by the dark and the nearness and number of the Dead. There were far more than a score of them now, moving in lines from all directions, the closest little more than forty yards away. Their corpse-white faces looked like flocks of bobbing moths, stark in the starlight.

Many of the Dead wore the remnants of blue scarves and blue hats. Sam stared at them. They were dead Southerlings! Probably some of the ones his father had tried to find.

"Run, you idiot!" shouted Mogget, streaking ahead himself, as the Dead behind seemed to finally realize that their quarry might escape them. Dead muscles squealed, suddenly forced into speed, and Dead throats cried strange, desiccated battle cries.

Sam didn't look again. He could hear their heavy footfalls, the squelch of rotten meat pushed beyond even its magically supported limits. He pushed himself, breaking into a run, his breath burning in his throat and lungs, muscles sending streaks of pain through the length of his body.

He made the mill race—a deep, narrow channel—barely ahead of the Dead. Four steps and he was over the planks of the simple bridge, kicking it down into the race. But the channel was dry, so the first Dead Hands simply hurled themselves down and began to claw up the other side. Behind them came more Hands, line after line of them, a tide of Dead that could not be turned back.

Desperately, Sam rushed to the sluice gate and the wheel that would lift it, to send the roaring waters of the Ratterlin into the race and across the climbing Dead.

But the wheel was rusted tight, the sluice gate stuck in place. Sam put all his weight on the iron wheel, but it simply broke, leaving him clutching a piece of the rusted rim.

Then the first Dead Hand pulled itself out of the mill race and turned towards him. It was dark, true dark now, but Sam could just make it out. It had been human once, but the magic that had brought it back to Life had twisted the body as if following a mad artist's whim. Its arms trailed below its knees, its head no longer sat upon a neck but sank into its shoulders, and the mouth had split upwards, usurping the place that had once held a nose. There were more behind it, other twisted shapes, using the blades of the water-wheel like steps to climb out of the mill race.

"Through here!" commanded Mogget, his tail flicking as he leapt through a doorway into the mill itself. Sam tried to follow, but the Dead Hand barred his way, skeletal mouth grinning with too many teeth, its long hands outstretched with grasping, bare-boned fingers.

Sam drew his sword and hacked at it, all in one swift motion. The Charter marks on the blade blazed, silver sparks spewing into the night as spelled metal ate into Dead flesh.

The Hand reeled back, broken but not beaten, one arm hanging from a single strip of sinew. Sam punched it farther away with the pommel of his sword, back into two more that sought to close in. Then he swung around to strike at one leaping up behind him, and backed into the mill.

"The door!" spat Mogget from somewhere at his feet, and Sam reached out and felt wood. Desperately he gripped the door's edge and slammed it in the grinning faces of the Dead. Mogget jumped up, fur brushing Sam's hand, and a heavy thump told him the cat had just pushed down the bar. The door, at least for the moment, was closed.

He couldn't see a thing. It was completely, suffocatingly dark. He couldn't even see the bright white coat of Mogget.

"Mogget!" he yelped, panic in his voice. The single word

was suddenly drowned in a violent crash as the Dead Hands threw themselves against the door. They were too stupid to find some timber to use as a ram.

"Here," said the cat, calm as ever. "Reach down."

Sam reached, more urgently than he would have liked to admit, fingers grasping Mogget by his Charter-spelled collar. For an awful moment, he thought he'd inadvertently pulled the collar off. Then the cat moved, the miniature Ranna tinkled, and he knew the collar had stayed on. Ranna's sound sent a wave of drowsiness against him, but that was nothing compared to the relief of feeling the collar still tight against that feline neck. With the Dead so close and the door already splintering under their attack, it would take more than a miniature Ranna to send him into sleep.

"This way," said Mogget, a disembodied voice in the darkness. Sam felt him move again and quickly hurried after, every sense alert to the door behind.

Then Mogget suddenly turned, but Sam kept going for a step, his sword hitting something solid and rebounding, almost hitting him in the face. Sam sheathed his sword, nearly stabbing himself, and reached out to touch whatever it was.

His hand traced another door—a door that must lead to the river itself. He could hear the water rushing by, just audible under the crash of the Dead Hands hurling themselves against the other door. The noise reverberated up into the higher reaches of the mill. Despite the noise, they hadn't got in, and Sam offered up silent thanks to the miller who had built so well.

His trembling hands found the bar and lifted it, then the ring that turned the lock. He twisted it, met resistance, then twisted again, fear shooting through him. Surely this door couldn't be locked from the outside?

Behind him, he heard screaming hinges finally give way,

and the other door exploded inwards. Dead Hands came
bounding through, croaking cries that were inhuman echoes
of the triumphant yells of the Living.

Sam turned the ring the other way, and the door suddenly
swung open. He went with it, sprawling outside and down
some steps that led to a narrow landing stage. He landed there
with a thud that sent a blinding pain through his wounded leg,
but he didn't care. At last he had reached the Ratterlin!

He could see again, at least somewhat, by the stars above
and their reflections in the water. There was the river, rushing
past, little more than an arm's length away. There was a tin
bathtub, too, a big one, of the kind used to bathe several children at once, big enough for a grown person to lounge in. Sam
saw it and, in the same instant, picked it up and pushed it into
the river, holding it against the current with one hand while he
dropped his sword and the saddlebags in.

"I take it back," said Mogget, jumping in. "You're not as
stupid as you look."

Sam tried to answer, but his face and mouth seemed unable
to move. He climbed into the bathtub, clutching at the last step
of the landing stage. The tub sank alarmingly, but even when he
was fully in, it still had several inches of freeboard.

He pushed off as the Dead poured out of the door. The
first one recoiled at the proximity of so much running water.
But the others pushed behind it, and the Hand fell—straight at
Sam's makeshift boat.

The Dead creature screamed as it bounced on the steps,
sounding almost alive for a brief second. Its hands scrabbled as
it fell, trying to hold on to something, but it succeeded only in
changing the direction of its fall. A second later, it entered the
Ratterlin, and its scream was lost in a fountain of silver sparks
and golden fire.

It had missed the boat by only a few feet. The wave from its impact almost swamped the bathtub. Sam watched the creature's last moments, as did the Dead halted in the doorway above, and felt enormous relief well up inside him.

"Amazing," said Mogget. "We actually got away. What are you doing?"

Sam stopped squirming and silently held out the cake of dried, sun-shriveled soap he'd just sat on. Then he put his head back and draped his hands over the sides to rest in the sweet river that had rescued them.

"In fact," said Mogget, "I think I can even say 'Well done.'"

Sam didn't answer, because he'd just passed out.

PART THREE

THE OLD KINGDOM

Eighteenth Year of the Restoration of
King Touchstone I

Chapter Thirty-Four

FINDER

THE BOAT WAS tied up at a subterranean dock that Lirael knew about but had visited only once, years before. It was built all along one end of a vast cavern, with sunlight pouring in at the other end where it opened out onto the world, the Ratterlin welling up with frothing vigor below the dock. A line of icicles across the cavern-mouth testified to the presence of the glacier above, as did the occasional fall of ice and snow.

There were several boats tied up, but Lirael instinctively knew that the slim, curving vessel with the single mast was hers. She had a carved fantail at her stern and an arching figurehead at the bow—a woman with wide-awake eyes. Those eyes seemed to be looking straight at Lirael, as if the boat knew who her next passenger would be. For a moment Lirael thought the figurehead might even have winked at her.

Sanar pointed and said, "That is *Finder*. She will take you safely down to Qyrre. It is a journey she has made a thousand times or more, there and back, with or against the current. She knows the river well."

"I don't know how to sail," said Lirael nervously, noting the Charter marks that moved quietly over the hull, mast, and rigging of the boat. She felt very small and stupid. The sight of the outside world beyond the cavern-mouth combined with her weariness and made her want to hide somewhere and go to sleep. "What will I have to do?"

"There is little you need attend to," replied Sanar. "*Finder* will do most of it herself. But you will have to raise and lower the sail, and steer a little. I will show you how."

"Thank you," said Lirael. She followed Sanar into the boat, grabbing at the gunwale as *Finder* rocked beneath her. Ryelle passed Lirael's pack, bow, and sword across, and Sanar showed her where to stow the pack in the oilskin-lined box at the vessel's forepeak. The sword and bow went into special waterproof cases on either side of the mast, to be more accessible.

Then Sanar showed Lirael how to raise and lower *Finder's* single triangular mainsail, and how the boom would move. *Finder* would trim the sail herself, Sanar explained, and would guide Lirael's hand on the tiller. Lirael could even let the boat steer herself in an emergency, but the vessel preferred to feel a human touch.

"We hope that there will be no danger on the way," said Ryelle, when they had finished showing Lirael over the boat. "Normally the river-road is quite safe to Qyrre. But we cannot now be sure of anything. We do not know the nature of whatever lies in the pit you Saw, or its powers. Just in case, it would be best to anchor in the river at night, rather than going ashore— or to tie up at an island. There are many of those downstream. At Qyrre and onwards, you should seek whatever help you can get from the Royal Constables. Here is a letter from us as the Voice of the Watch, for that purpose. If we are lucky, there will also be guards present, and the Abhorsen may have returned from Ancelstierre. Whatever you do, you must make sure that you travel with a large and well-armed party from Qyrre to Edge. From there, I fear, we cannot advise you. The future is clouded, and we can See you only on the Red Lake, with nothing before or beyond that."

"All summed up, that means 'Be very careful,'" said Sanar. She smiled, but there was the hint of a frown in her forehead and at the corners of her eyes. "Remember that this is only one possible future we See."

"I will be careful," promised Lirael. Now that she was actually in the boat and about to depart, she felt very nervous. For the first time, she would be going out into a world that was not bounded by stone or ice, and she would have to see and speak to many strangers. More than that, she was going into danger, against a foe she knew nothing about and was ill prepared to face. Even her mission was vague. To find a young man, somewhere on a lake, sometime this summer. What if she did find this Nicholas and somehow survived all the looming dangers? Would the Clayr let her back into the Glacier? What if she was never allowed to return?

But at the same time Lirael also felt a blooming sense of excitement, even of escape, from a life that she couldn't admit was stifling her. There was *Finder*, and the sunshine beyond, and the Ratterlin streaming away to lands she knew only from the pages of books. She had the dog statuette, and the hope her canine companion would return. And she was going on official business, doing something important. Almost like a real Daughter of the Clayr.

"You may need this, too," said Ryelle, handing over a leather purse, bulging with coins. "The Bursar would have you get receipts, but I think you will have enough to worry about without that."

"Now, let us see you raise the sail yourself, and we will bid you farewell," continued Sanar. Her blue eyes seemed to see into Lirael, perceiving the fears that she had not voiced. "The Sight does not tell me so, but I am sure we will meet again. And you must remember that, Sighted or not, you *are* a Daughter of the Clayr. Remember! May fortune favor you, Lirael."

Lirael nodded, unable to speak, and hauled on the halyard to raise the sail. It hung slackly, the cavern dock being too sheltered for any wind.

Ryelle and Sanar bowed to her, then cast off the ropes that held *Finder* fast. The Ratterlin's swift current gripped the boat, and the tiller moved under Lirael's hand, nudging her to direct the eager vessel out towards the sunlit world of the open river.

Lirael looked back once as they passed from the shade of the cavern to the sun, with the icicles tinkling far above her head. Sanar and Ryelle were still standing on the dock. They waved as the wind came to fill *Finder*'s sail and ruffle Lirael's hair.

I have left, thought Lirael. There could be no turning back now, not against the current. The current of the river held the boat, and the current of her destiny held her. Both were taking her to places that she did not know.

The river was already wide where the underground source came to join it, fed by the lakes of snow-melt higher up, and the hundred small streams that wound their way like capillaries through and around the Clayr's Glacier. But here, only the central channel—perhaps fifty yards across—was deep enough to be navigable. To either side of the channel, the Ratterlin shallowed, content to sheet thinly across millions of clean-washed pebbles.

Lirael breathed in the warm, river-scented air and smiled at the heat of the sun on her skin. As promised, *Finder* was moving herself into the swiftest race of the river, while the mainsheet imperceptibly slackened till they were running before the wind from the north. Lirael's nervousness about sailing lessened as she realized that *Finder* really did look after herself. It was even fun, speeding along with the breeze behind them, the bow sending up a fine spray as it sliced through the small waves caused by wind and current. All Lirael needed to make the moment perfect was the presence of her best friend, the Disreputable Dog.

She reached into her waistcoat pocket for the soapstone statuette. It would be a comfort just to hold it, even if it would not be practicable to try the summoning spell until she got to Qyrre and could get the silver wire and other materials.

But instead of cool, smooth stone, she felt warm dog skin—and what she pulled out was a very recognizable pointy ear, followed by an arc of round skull and then another ear. That was immediately followed by the Disreputable Dog's entire head, which was much too big by itself to fit in the pocket—let alone the rest of her.

"Ouch! Tight fit!" growled the Dog, pushing out a foreleg and wiggling madly. Another foreleg impossibly followed, and then the whole dog leapt out, shook hair all over Lirael's leggings, and turned to give her an enthusiastic lick.

"So we're off at last!" she barked happily, mouth open to catch the breeze, tongue lolling. "About time, too. Where are we going?"

Lirael didn't answer at first. She just hugged the Dog very tightly and took several quick, jarring breaths to stop herself crying. The Dog waited patiently, not even licking Lirael's ear, which was a handy target. When Lirael's breathing seemed to get back to normal, the Dog repeated her question.

"More like *why* are we going," said Lirael, checking her waistcoat pocket to make sure the Dog's exit hadn't taken the Dark Mirror with it. Strangely enough, the pocket wasn't even stretched.

"Does it matter?" asked the Dog. "New smells, new sounds, new places to piss on . . . begging your pardon, Captain."

"Dog! Stop being so excited," ordered Lirael. The Dog partly obeyed, sitting down at her feet, but her tail kept wagging, and every few seconds she snapped at the air.

"We're not just going on one of our normal expeditions, like in the Glacier," Lirael explained. "I have to find a man—"

"Good!" interrupted the Dog, leaping up to lick her exuberantly. "Time you were bred."

"Dog!" Lirael, protested, forcing her back down. "It's not about that! This man is from Ancelstierre and he's trying to . . . dig up, I think . . . some ancient thing. Near the Red Lake. A Free Magic thing, so powerful it made me sick even when Ryelle and Sanar only showed it to me through a vision. And there was a necromancer who saw me, and lightning kept hitting the hole in the ground—"

"I don't like the sound of that," said the Dog, suddenly serious. Her tail stopped waving, and she looked straight at Lirael, no longer snuffling the air. "You'd better tell me more. Start at the beginning, from when the Clayr came to find you down below."

Lirael nodded and went over everything that the twins had said, and described the vision that they'd shared with her.

By the time she'd finished, the Ratterlin had widened into the mighty river that most of the Kingdom knew. It was over half a mile wide, and very deep. Here in the middle, the water was dark and clear and blue, and many fish could be seen, silver in the depths.

The Dog lay with her head upon her forelegs and thought deeply. Lirael watched her, looking at the brown eyes that seemed to focus on far distant things.

"I don't like it," the Dog said finally. "You're being sent into danger, and no one really knows what's going on. The

Clayr unable to See clearly, the King and the Abhorsen not even in the Kingdom. This hole in the ground that eats up lightning reminds me of something very bad indeed . . . and then there's this necromancer, as well."

"Well, I suppose we could go somewhere else," Lirael said doubtfully, upset by the strength of the Dog's reaction.

The Dog looked at her in surprise. "No, we can't! You have a duty. I don't like it, but we've got it. I never said anything about giving up."

"No," agreed Lirael. She was about to say that she hadn't suggested it, either. She was just stating a possibility. But it would clearly be better to let the point lie.

The Dog was silent for a while. Then she said, "Those things that were left for you in the room. Do you know how to use them?"

"They might not even be meant for me," Lirael said. "I just happened to find them. I don't want them, anyway."

"Choosers will be beggars if the begging's not their choosing," said the Dog.

"What does that mean?"

"I have no idea," said the Dog. "Now, do you know how to use the things that were left for you?"

"Well, I have read *The Book of Remembrance and Forgetting*," Lirael replied half-heartedly. "So I guess I know the theory—"

"You should practice," declared the Dog. "You may need actual expertise later on."

"But I'll have to go into Death," Lirael protested. "I've never done that before. I'm not even sure I should. I'm a Clayr. I should be Seeing the future, not the past."

"You should use the gifts you have been given," said the Dog. "Imagine how you'd feel if you gave me a bone and I didn't eat it."

"Surprised," replied Lirael. "But you do bury bones some-times. In the ice."

"I always eat them eventually," said the Dog. "At the right time."

"How do you know this is the right time for me?" asked Lirael suspiciously. "I mean, how do you even know what my gifts are for? I haven't told you, have I?"

"I read a lot. It comes from living in a library," said the Dog, answering the second question first. "And there's lots of islands ahead. An island would be a perfect place to stop. You can use the Dark Mirror on one of them. If anything follows you back from Death, we can get on the boat and just sail away."

"You mean if something Dead attacks me," said Lirael. That was the real danger. She actually did want to look into the past. But she didn't want to go into Death to do it. *The Book of Remembrance and Forgetting* told her how, and assured her she could come back. But what if it was wrong?

And the panpipes were all very well, in their way, as a weapon and protection against the Dead. Seven pipes, named after the seven bells used by a necromancer. Only they weren't as powerful as the bells, and one part of the book said that "though generally the instrument of a Remembrancer, the pipes are not infrequently used by Abhorsens-in-Waiting, till they succeed to their bells." Which didn't make the pipes sound all that fantastic.

But even if the pipes were not as strong as the bells, the book seemed to think they were powerful enough to assure her safety. Provided she could use them properly, of course, having only book-learning to go on. Still, there was some-thing she particularly wanted to see. . . . "We do need to get to Edge as soon as possible," she said with deliberation. "But

I suppose we could take a few hours off. Only I need to nap for a while first. When I wake up, we'll stop at an island, if there's one near. Then . . . then I will go into Death, and look into the past."

"Good," said the Dog. "I could do with a walk."

Chapter Thirty-Five

REMEMBRANCER

LIRAEL STOOD WITH the Dog in the center of a small island, surrounded by stunted trees and bushes that couldn't grow higher in the rocky ground. *Finder*'s mast towered behind them, no more than thirty paces away, showing where safety lay if they had to flee from something coming out of Death.

In preparation for entering that cold realm, Lirael buckled on the sword the Clayr had given her. The weight felt strange on her hip. The broad leather belt was tight against her lower stomach, and the sword, while longer and heavier than her practice sword, somehow felt familiar, though she had never seen it before. She would have remembered its distinctive silver-wired hilt and pommel with a single green stone set in bronze.

Lirael held the panpipes in her left hand, watching the Charter marks move across the silver tubes, weaving in with the Free Magic that lurked there. She looked at each pipe, remembering what the book had said about them. Her life could well depend on knowing which pipe to use. She said the names aloud, under her breath, to secure them in her mind and to delay actually going into Death.

"First, and least, is Ranna," recited Lirael, the relevant page from *The Book of Remembrance and Forgetting* clear in her head. "Ranna, the Sleepbringer, will take all those who hear it into slumber.

"Second is Mosrael, the Waker. One of the most dangerous bells, and still so in any form. Its sound is a seesaw that will
throw the piper further into Death, even as it brings the listener
into Life.

"Third is Kibeth, the Walker. Kibeth gives freedom of
movement to the Dead, or forces the Dead to walk at the piper's
will. But Kibeth is contrary and can make the piper walk where
she would not choose to go.

"Fourth is Dyrim, the Speaker, of melodious tone. Dyrim
may grant speech to the dumb, tongue-lost Dead, or give forgotten words their meaning. Dyrim may also still a tongue that
moves too freely.

"Fifth is Belgaer, the Thinker, which can restore independent thought, and memory, and all the patterns of what
was once in Life. Or, in a careless hand, erase them. Belgaer is
troublesome, too, always seeking to sound of its own accord.

"Sixth comes Saraneth, also known as the Binder. Saraneth
speaks with the deep voice of power, shackling the Dead to the
wielder's will."

Lirael paused before she recited the name of the seventh and
last pipe, the longest, its silver surface forever cold and frightening under her touch.

"Astarael, the Sorrowful," whispered Lirael. "Properly
sounded, Astarael will cast all who hear it deep into Death.
Including the piper. Do not call upon Astarael unless all else
is lost."

"Sleeper, Waker, Walker, Speaker, Thinker, Binder, and
Weeper," said the Dog, taking a break from a heavy-duty
scratching of her ear. "Bells would be better, though. Those
pipes are really only for children to practice with."

"Ssshhh," said Lirael. "I'm concentrating."

She knew better than to ask the Dog how she knew the names

of the pipes. The impossible hound had probably read *The Book of Remembrance and Forgetting* herself, while Lirael slept.

Having mentally prepared herself to use the panpipes—or to use only some of them—Lirael drew her sword, noting the play of Charter marks along its silvered blade. There was an inscription, too, she saw. She held the blade to the light and read it aloud.

"The Clayr Saw me, the Wallmakers made me, my enemies Remember me."

"A sister sword to Binder," remarked the Dog, nosing it with interest. "I didn't know they had that one. What's it called?"

Lirael twisted the blade to see if there was something written on the other side, but as she did so, the first inscription changed, the letters shimmering into a new arrangement.

" 'Nehima,' " read Lirael. "What does that mean?"

"It's a name," said the Dog blandly. Seeing Lirael's expression, she cocked her head to one side and continued, "I suppose you could say it means 'forget-me-not.' Though the irony is that Nehima herself is long forgotten. Still, better a sword than a block of stone, I suppose. It's certainly an heirloom of the house, if ever I saw one," the Dog added. "I'm surprised they gave it to you."

Lirael nodded, unable to speak, her thoughts once again turning back to the Glacier and the Clayr. Ryelle and Sanar had just casually handed the sword to her. Made by the Wallmakers themselves, it must be one of the greatest treasures the Clayr possessed.

A nudge at her leg reminded her of the business at hand, so she blinked away an incipient tear and focused all her thought, as *The Book of Remembrance and Forgetting* had told her to. Apparently she should feel Death and then sort of reach out to it. It was easier in places where lots of people had died, or were buried, but theoretically it was possible anywhere.

Lirael closed her eyes to concentrate harder, furrows forming across her forehead. She could feel Death now, like a cold pressure against her face. She pushed against it, feeling its chill sink into her cheekbones and lips, soaking into her outstretched hands. It was strange with the sun still hot against her bare neck.

It grew colder still, and colder, as the chill moved up her feet and legs. She felt a tug against her knees, a tug that wasn't one of the Dog's gentle reminders. It was like being gripped by a current, a strong current that wanted to take her away and force her under.

She opened her eyes. A river flowed against her legs, but it was not the Ratterlin. It was black and opaque, and there was no sign of the island, the blue sky, or the sun. The light was grey, grey and dull as far as she could see, out to a totally flat horizon.

Lirael shuddered, not just from the cold, for she had successfully entered Death. She could hear a waterfall somewhere in the distance. The First Gate, she supposed, from the description in the book.

The river tugged at her again, and without thinking, she went with it for a few steps. It tugged again, even harder, the cold spreading into her very bones. It would be easy to let that chill spread through her entire body, to lie down and let the current take her where it willed—

"No!" she snapped, forcing herself back a step. This was what the book had warned her about. The river's strength wasn't just in the current. She had also to resist its compulsion to walk farther into Death, or to lie down and let it carry her away.

Fortunately, the book was also right about something more favorable. She could feel the way back to Life, and instinctively knew exactly where to go and how to get back there, which was a relief.

Apart from the distant roar of the First Gate, Lirael could hear nothing else moving in the river. Lirael listened carefully, nerves drawn tight, muscles ready for immediate flight. Still there was nothing, not even a ripple.

Then her Death sense twitched, and she quickly scanned the river to either side of her again. For a moment, she thought she saw something move on the surface, a thin line of darkness under the water, moving farther back into Death. But then it was gone, and she could neither see nor sense anything. After a minute, she wasn't even sure if there had been anything there in the first place.

Sighing, she carefully sheathed her sword, put the panpipes back in her waistcoat pocket, and drew out the Dark Mirror. Here, in the First Precinct of Death, she could look just a little way into the past. To look further back, she would have to travel deeper in, past the First Gate or even far beyond it. But today she only planned to look back a matter of twenty years or so.

The click that accompanied the opening of the Mirror seemed far too loud, echoing across the dark waters. Lirael flinched at the sound—then screamed as it was followed by a loud splash directly behind her!

Reflexively, she jumped—farther into Death— swapped the Mirror into her left hand, and drew her sword, all before she even knew what was happening.

"It's only me," said the Dog, her tail slapping the water as it wagged. "I got bored waiting."

"How did you get here?" whispered Lirael, sheathing her

sword with a shaking hand. "You scared me to death!"

"I followed you," said the Dog. "It's just a different sort of walk."

Not for the first time, Lirael wondered what the Dog really was, and the extent of her powers. But there was no time for speculation now. *The Book of Remembrance and Forgetting* had warned her not to stay too long in any one place in Death, because things would come looking. Things she didn't want to meet.

"Who's going to guard my body if you're here?" she asked reproachfully. If anything happened to her body back in Life, she would have no choice but to follow the river onwards, or to become some sort of Dead spirit herself, eternally trying to get back into Life, by stealing someone else's body. Or to become a shadow, drinking blood and Life to keep itself out of Death.

"I'll know if anyone comes close," said the Dog, sniffing the river. "Can we go farther in?"

"No!" snapped Lirael. "I'm going to use the Dark Mirror here. But you're going back straight away! This is Death, Dog, not the Glacier!"

"True," mumbled the Dog. She looked up pleadingly at Lirael and added, "But it's only the very edge of Death—"

"Back! Now!" commanded Lirael, pointing. The Dog stopped her pleading look, showed the whites of her eyes in disapproval, and slunk away with her tail down. A second later, she vanished—back into Life.

Lirael ignored her and opened the Mirror, holding it close to her right eye. "Focus on the Mirror with one eye," the book had said, "and look into Death with the other, lest harm befall you there."

Good advice, but hardly practical, Lirael thought, as she struggled to focus on two different things at once. But after a

minute, the Mirror's opaque surface began to clear, its darkness lifting. Instead of looking at her reflection, Lirael found
that she was somehow looking through the mirror, and it was
not the cold river of Death she saw beyond. She saw swirling
lights, lights that she soon realized were actually the passage of
the sun across the sky, so fast it was a blur. The sun was going
backwards.

Excitement grew in her as she realized this was the beginning of the magic. Now she had to think of what she wanted
to see. She began to form an image of her mother in her mind,
borrowing more from the charcoal drawing Aunt Kirrith had
given her years ago than from her own recollection, which was
the mixed-up memory of a child, all feelings and soft-edged
images.

Holding the picture of her mother in her head, she spoke
aloud, infusing her voice with the Charter marks she'd learned
from the book, symbols of power and command that would
make the Dark Mirror show her what she wanted to see.

"My mother I knew, a little," Lirael said, her words loud
against the murmur of the river. "My father I knew not, and
would see through the veil of time. So let it be."

The swift passage of backwards suns began to slow as she
spoke, and Lirael felt herself drawn closer to the image in the
Mirror, till a single sun filled all her vision, blinding her with its
light. Then it was gone, and there was darkness.

Slowly, the darkness ebbed, and Lirael saw a room, strangely
superimposed upon the river of Death she saw through her other
eye. Both images were blurry, as if her eyes were full of tears,
but they were not. Lirael blinked several times, but the vision
grew no clearer.

She saw a large room—a hall, in fact—dominated at one end
by a large window, which was a blur of different colors rather

than clear glass. Lirael sensed there was some sort of magic in the window, for the colors and patterns changed, though she couldn't see it clearly enough to make it out.

A long, brilliantly polished table of some light and lustrous wood stretched the full length of the hall. It was loaded with silver of many kinds: candelabra with beeswax candles burning clean yellow flames, salt cellars and pepper grinders, sauce boats and tureens, and many ornaments Lirael had never seen. A roast goose, half-carved, sat on a platter, encircled by plates of lesser foods.

There were only two people at the table, sitting at the other end, so Lirael had to squint to try to see them more clearly. One, a man, sat at the head of the table in a high-backed chair, almost a throne. Despite his simple white shirt and lack of jewelry, he had the bearing of a man of rank and power. Lirael frowned and shifted the Dark Mirror a little, to see if she could make the vision sharper. Rainbows briefly rippled through the room, but nothing else seemed to change.

There were spells to use to refine the vision, but Lirael didn't want to try them just yet, in case they made the vision go away completely. Instead she concentrated on the other person. She could see her more clearly than the man.

It was her mother. Arielle, Kirrith's little sister. She looked beautiful in the soft candlelight, her long blond hair hanging in a brilliant waterfall down the back of her dress, an elegant creation of ice-blue adorned with golden stars. It was cut low across the neck and back, and she wore a necklace of sapphires and diamonds.

As Lirael concentrated, the vision of the past grew sharper around the two people, but even muddier everywhere else, as if all the color and light were gathering around the point of her focus. At the same time, her view of the river of Death clouded.

Sounds began to come to her, as if she were listening to two people conversing as they walked towards her. They were speaking in the courtly fashion, which was rarely used in the Glacier. Obviously they didn't know each other very well.

"I have heard many strange things under this roof, Mistress," the man was saying as he poured himself more wine, waving back a sending servant that had begun to attend to him. "But none so strange as this."

"It is not something I sought," replied the woman, her voice strangely familiar to Lirael's ears. Surely she didn't remember it? She had been only five when Arielle had abandoned her. Then she realized that it was Kirrith's voice it reminded her of. Though it was sweeter than Kirrith's had ever been.

"And none of your Vision-Sisters have Seen what you wish of me?" asked the man. "None of the Nine Day Watch?"

"None," said Arielle, bending her head, a blush spreading across her neck. Lirael watched in amazement. Her own mother embarrassed! But then the Arielle she saw here wasn't much older than herself. She seemed very young.

The man seemed to be thinking along similar lines, because he said, "My wife has been dead these eighteen years, but I have a daughter grown who would be near your age. I am not unfamiliar with the . . . the . . ."

"Imaginings of young women? Or the infatuations of youth?" interrupted Arielle, looking back up at him, her face angry now. "I am five and twenty, sir, and no girlish virgin dreaming of her mate. I am a Daughter of the Clayr, and nothing but my Sight would have brought me here to lie with a man I have never met who is old enough to be my father!"

The man put his cup down and smiled ruefully, but his eyes were tired and untouched by the smile.

"I beg your pardon, Mistress. In truth, I heard the sound of prophecy when you first spoke to me today, but I put it from my mind. I must leave here tomorrow, to face many perils. I have no time for thoughts of love, and I have been proven a less than perfect parent. Even if I were not away tomorrow, and could linger here with you, any child you bear would likely see little of its father."

"This is not a matter of love," said Arielle quietly, meeting his gaze. "And a single night may beget a child as well as a year of striving. As it will, for I have Seen her. As to the lack of a father, I fear she will have neither parent for very long."

"You speak of a certainty," said the man. "Yet the Clayr often See many threads, which the future may weave this way or that."

"I See only a single thread in this, sir," said Arielle, reaching across to take the man's pale hand in her own brown fingers. "I am here, called by the visions granted by my Blood, as you are governed by yours. It is meant to be, cousin. But perhaps we can at least enjoy our single night, forgetting higher reasons. Let us to bed."

The man hesitated, his fingers open. Then he laughed, and raised Arielle's hand to his lips for a gentle kiss.

"We shall have our night," he said, rising from the chair. "I know not what it means, or what future we will here secure. But for once I am tired of responsibility and care! As you say, my dear cousin, let us to bed!"

The two embraced, and Lirael shut her right eye, stricken with embarrassment and a slight, uneasy feeling of shame. If she kept watching, she might even see the moment of her own conception, and that was too embarrassing to even contemplate. But even with her eye shut, the vision lingered, till Lirael blinked it away, this time with an actual tear.

She had secretly expected more from the vision, some

indication of her parents' having a forbidden love or some great bond that would be revealed to their daughter. But it seemed she was the result of a single evening's coupling, which was either predestined or the result of her mother's mad imagination. Lirael didn't know which would be worse. And she still had no clear idea who her father was, though some of the things she had seen and heard were certainly suggestive and would require further thought.

Snapping the mirror shut, she put it back into her belt pouch. Only then did she realize that the sound of the First Gate had stopped. Something was coming through the waterfall— something from the deeper reaches of Death.

Chapter Thirty-Six

A DENIZEN OF DEATH

A FEW SECONDS after Lirael noticed the silence of the First Gate, the sound of the crashing water resumed. Whatever had stilled it had passed through, and was now in the First Precinct of Death. With Lirael.

Lirael peered into the distance, unable to see anything moving. The grey light and flatness of the river made it hard to work out distances, and she had no idea whether the First Gate was as close as it sounded. She knew it was marked by a veil of mist, and she couldn't see it.

To be on the safe side, Lirael drew both sword and pipes and took several steps towards Life, till she was close enough to feel its warmth at her back. She should cross now, she knew, but a daredevil curiosity gripped her and kept her there—the urge to see, albeit briefly, a denizen of Death.

When she did see the first signs of it, all her curiosity was gone in an instant, replaced by fear. For something was approaching under the river, not upon it, a vee of ripples heading straight for her, moving swiftly against the current. Something large and hidden, able to cloak itself against her senses. She hadn't felt its presence at all, and saw the ripples purely by chance, as a result of her own caution.

Instantly, she felt for Life again, but at the same time, the vee exploded into a leaping figure, a shape of fire and darkness. It held a bell, a bell that rang with power, fixing her on the very border of Life and Death.

The bell was Saraneth, Lirael somehow knew, recognizing it deep in her bones as the bell's fierce power fought against her straining muscles. But a raw Saraneth, one that was not partnered with Charter Magic, as in her pipes or an Abhorsen's bells. There was more power here, and less art. It had to be the bell of a Free Magic sorcerer. A necromancer!

She could feel the wielder's will behind the bell, seeking domination of her spirit, an implacable force of hatred beating down her own pathetic resistance. Now Lirael saw the wielder clearly, despite the steam that eddied around his body as if he were a hot iron plunged into the river.

It was Hedge, the necromancer from the vision the twins had shown her. She could feel the fires of Free Magic that burnt in him, defeating even the chill of Death.

"Kneel before your master!" commanded Hedge, striding towards her, the bell in one hand, a sword burning with dark, liquid flames in the other. His voice was harsh and cruel, the words infused with fire and smoke.

The necromancer's command struck at Lirael like a blow, and she felt her knees unlock, her legs beginning to crumple. Hedge already had her in his power, the deep commanding tone of Saraneth still ringing in her ears, echoing inside her head, a sound she couldn't dislodge from her mind.

He came still closer, the sword raised above his head, and she knew that it would soon fall upon her unprotected neck. Her own sword was in her hand, the Charter marks burning like golden suns as Nehima reacted angrily to the Free Magic menace that approached. But her sword arm was locked at the elbow by her enemy's will, held in place by the terrible power of the bell.

Desperately she tried to pour strength into her arm, to no

avail. Then she tried to reach into the Charter, to draw forth a spell to blast the necromancer with silver darts or red-gold fire.

"Kneel!" the necromancer commanded again, and she knelt, the cold river clutching at her stomach and breasts, welcoming her in its soon-to-be-permanent embrace. The muscles in her neck twitched and stood out in cords as she fought the compulsion to bend her head.

Then she realized that by giving in, just a little, she could bend her head down, enough so her lips could touch the panpipes held in her frozen left hand. So she submitted, too quickly, lips meeting silver with bloody force, not even knowing which pipe would sound. At the worst, it would be Astarael, and then she would take the necromancer with her into the deeper realms of Death.

She blew as hard as she could, forcing all that remained of her will into directing the clear note that cut through the echoing remnants of the necromancer's bell.

The pipe was Kibeth. The sound struck Hedge as he swung for a beheading blow. It caught his feet with joyful trickery, spinning him around completely. His sword-stroke swung wide, high above Lirael, and then Kibeth was walking and dancing him like a drunken fool, sending him cavorting towards the First Gate.

But even surprised by Kibeth, his will and Saraneth fought to hold Lirael as she tried to throw herself back into Life. Her arms and legs felt like clumsy sacks of earth, the river like quicksand, trying to suck her under. Desperately, she pushed to free herself, reaching towards Life, reaching for the day, for the Dog, for everything she loved.

Finally, as if a rope that held her snapped, Lirael pitched forward into sunlight and cool breezes, but not before the necromancer had shouted out his farewell, in words as cold and threatening as the river of Death itself.

"I know you! You cannot hide! I will—"

His last words were cut off as Lirael completely re-occupied her body, senses re-arranging themselves for the living world. As the Book had warned, there was ice and frost all over her, lining every fold of her clothing. There was even an icicle hanging from her nose. She broke it off, which hurt, and sneezed.

"What! What was that!" barked the Dog, who was practically under her feet. Clearly, she had sensed that Lirael had been attacked.

"A n-necromancer," said Lirael, shivering. "The one . . . the vision . . . that the Clayr showed me. Hedge. He . . . he . . . almost killed me!"

The Dog growled, low in her throat, and Lirael suddenly noticed that she had grown as tall as her own shoulder and now sported much larger and sharper teeth. "I knew I should have stayed with you, Mistress!"

"Yes, yes," mumbled Lirael. She still could hardly speak, her breath coming in little panicked pants. She knew the necromancer couldn't follow her back here—he would have to return to his own body in Life. Unfortunately, her little Kibeth pipe wouldn't have walked him far. He was easily powerful enough to come back and send Dead spirits through to pursue her. The bodiless ones.

"He'll send something after me. We've got to get out of here!"

The Dog growled again but didn't object as Lirael stumbled back across the stony island, intent on getting aboard *Finder* as quickly as possible. She circled behind Lirael, so every time the girl looked back nervously, there was the Dog, standing between her and danger.

A few minutes later, safe in the swift waters of the Ratterlin,

Lirael collapsed from the shock, lying down in the boat with just one hand lightly touching the rudder. *Finder* could be trusted to steer her own course.

"I would have bitten that necromancer's throat out," said the Dog, after letting Lirael gasp and shake for several minutes. "He'd have had cause to remember my teeth!"

"I don't think he would notice if you *did* rip his throat out," said Lirael, shivering. "He felt more Dead than alive. He said, 'I know you,'" she continued slowly, looking up at the sky, angling her face back to catch more of the sun, delighting in its blessed heat upon her still frosted lips and nose. "How could he know me?"

"Free Magic eats up necromancers," said the Dog, shrinking herself down to a less belligerent and more conversational size. "The power they seek to wield—the Free Magic they profess to master—ultimately devours them. That power recognizes your Blood. That's probably what he meant by 'I know you.'"

"I don't like the thought of anyone outside the Glacier knowing me," said Lirael, shuddering. "Knowing who I am. And that necromancer's probably with Nicholas now, in Life. So when I find Nicholas, I'll find the necromancer. Like a bug going to a spider to find a fly."

"Tomorrow's trouble," said the Dog, soothing her, not very convincingly. "At least we're done with today's. We're safe on the river."

Lirael nodded, thinking. Then she sat up and scratched the Dog under the chin and all around her ears.

"Dog," she said hesitantly, "there's Free Magic in you, maybe even more than the Charter Magic in your collar. Why don't you . . . why aren't you . . . why aren't you like the necromancer?"

The Dog sighed, with a meaty "oof" that made Lirael

wrinkle her nose. The hound tilted her head to one side, thinking before she answered.

"In the Beginning, all magic was Free Magic—unconstrained, raw, unchanneled. Then the Charter was created, which took most of the Free Magic and made it ordered, subject to structure, constrained by symbols. The Free Magic that remained separate from the Charter is the Free Magic of necromancy, of Stilken, Margrue, and Hish, of Analem and Gorger, and all the other fell creatures, constructs, and familiars. It is the random magic that persists outside the Charter.

"There is also the Free Magic that helped make the Charter but was not consumed by it," continued the Dog. "That is quite different from the Free Magic that would not join in the creation of the Charter."

"You speak of the Beginning," said Lirael, who wasn't at all sure she understood. "But could that be before the Charter? It doesn't have a Beginning—or an End."

"Everything has a Beginning," replied the Dog. "Including the Charter. I should know, since I was there at the birth of it, when the Seven chose to make the Charter and the Five gave themselves to the making. In a sense, you were there, too, Mistress. You are descended from the Five."

"The Five Great Charters?" asked Lirael, fascinated by this information. "I remember the rhyme about that. It must have been one of the first things we memorized as children."

She sat up even straighter, and clasped her hands behind her back, unconsciously assuming the recital position she'd learned as a child.

> *"Five Great Charters knit the land,*
> *Together linked, hand in hand.*
> *One in the people who wear the crown,*

Two in the folk who keep the Dead down,
Three and Five became stone and mortar,
Four sees all in frozen water."

"Yes," said the Dog. "A good rhyme for pups to learn. The Great Charters are the keystones of the Charter. The bloodlines, the Wall, and the Charter Stones all come from the original sacrifice of the Five, who poured their power into the men and women who were your ancestors. Some of those, in turn, passed that power into stone and mortar, when blood alone was judged to be too easily diluted or led astray."

"So if the Five were sort of . . . dissolved into the Charter, what happened to the other two?" asked Lirael, digesting this information with a frown. Everything she had read said the Charter had always existed and always would. "You said there were Seven who chose to make the Charter."

"It began with the Nine," replied the Dog quietly. "Nine who were most powerful, who possessed the conscious thought and foresight that raised them above all the tens of thousands of Free Magic beings that clamored and strove to exist upon the earth. Yet of the Nine, only Seven agreed to make the Charter. One chose to ignore the Seven's work but was finally bound to serve the Charter. The Ninth fought and was barely defeated."

"That's number eight and nine," said Lirael, counting on her fingers. "This would be much easier to understand if they had names instead of numbers. Anyway, you still haven't explained what happened to . . . um . . . six and seven. Why didn't they become part of the Great Charters?"

"They put a great deal of their power into the bloodlines, but not all their being," replied the Dog. "But I suspect they were perhaps less tired of conscious, individual existence. They wished to go on, in some form or another. I think they wanted to see what happened. And the Seven did have names. They are remembered in the bells and in the pipes you have in your belt. Each of those bells has something of the original power of the Seven, the power that existed before the Charter."

"You're not . . . you're not one of the Seven, are you?" asked Lirael, after a moment of anxiety-laden silence. She couldn't imagine that one of the creators of the Charter, no matter how much power it had given away, would condescend to be her friend. Or would continue to do so once its true loftiness had been established.

"I'm the Disreputable Dog," replied the Dog, licking Lirael's face. "Just a leftover from the Beginning, freely given to the Charter. And I'll always be your friend, Lirael. You know that."

"I guess I do," replied Lirael doubtfully. She hugged the Dog tight, her face pressed into the hound's warm neck. "I'll always be your friend, too."

The Dog let Lirael keep on hugging, but her ears were pricked, listening to the world around them. Her nose kept sniffing the air, trying to get more of the scent that had come back from Death with Lirael. A disturbing scent, one the Dog hoped was purely from her own imagination and long memory, because it was not the smell of just one human necromancer, no matter how powerful. It was much, much older, and much more frightening.

Lirael stopped hugging when the Dog's wet smell began to overcome her, and she moved back to take the tiller. *Finder* kept steering herself, but Lirael felt a surge of welcome recognition as Charter marks blossomed under her hand, warm and comforting after the chill of Death.

"We'll probably see the Sindle Ferry later today," remarked

Lirael, her brow furrowing as she recalled the maps she had rolled, unrolled, catalogued, and repaired in the Library. "We're making good time—we must have come twenty leagues already!"

"Towards danger," said the Dog, moving aft to flop down at Lirael's feet. "We mustn't forget that, Mistress."

Lirael nodded, thinking back to the necromancer and Death. It seemed unreal now, out in the sunshine, with the boat sailing so cheerfully down the river. But it had been all too real then. And if the necromancer's words were true, not only did he know her, he might know where she was going. Once she left the Ratterlin, she would be relatively easy prey for the necromancer's Dead servants.

"Perhaps I should make a Charter-skin soon," she said. "The barking owl. Just in case."

"Good idea," said the Dog, slurring. Her chin was propped on Lirael's foot, and she was drooling profusely. "By the way, did you see anything in the Dark Mirror?"

Lirael hesitated. She'd momentarily forgotten. The vision of the past had been put out of her mind by the necromancer's attack.

"Yes." The Dog waited for her to go on, but Lirael was silent. Finally, the hound raised her head and said, "So you are a Remembrancer now. The first in these last five hundred years, unless I am mistaken."

"I suppose I am," said Lirael, not meeting the Dog's eyes. She didn't want to be a Remembrancer, as the book called someone who Saw into the past. She wanted to See into the future.

"And what did you See?" prompted the Dog.

"My parents." Lirael blushed as she thought again of how close she had come to seeing her parents making love. "My father."

"Who was he?"

"I don't know," replied Lirael, frowning. "I would recognize a portrait, I think. Or the room that I saw. It doesn't really matter, anyway."

The Dog snorted, indicating that Lirael hadn't fooled her one bit. Obviously, it mattered a lot, but Lirael didn't want to talk about it.

"*You're* my family," said Lirael quickly, giving the Dog a quick hug. Then she stared deliberately ahead at the shining waters of the Ratterlin. The Dog really was her only family, even more than the Clayr she had lived with all her life.

They had shown she would never be truly one of them, she thought as she tightened her headscarf, remembering how the silk had felt against her eyes. Families did not blindfold their own children.

Chapter Thirty-Seven

A BATH IN THE RIVER

FOLLOWING SANAR AND Ryelle's advice, Lirael spent her first night away from the Clayr's Glacier anchored in the lee of a long, thin island in the very middle of the Ratterlin, with more than four hundred yards of swift, deep water on either side.

Soon after dawn, following a breakfast of oatmeal, an apple, a rather tough cinnamon cake, and several mouthfuls of clear river water, Lirael drew in the anchor, stowed it, and whistled for the Dog. She came swimming across from the island, where she'd performed her canine duty for the other dogs who might one day visit it.

They had just raised the sail and were beginning to reach before the wind when the Dog suddenly went stiff-legged and pointed across the bow, letting out a warning yip.

Lirael ducked her head down so she could see under the boom, her gaze following the line pointed by the Dog's fore-limb at some object two or three hundred yards downstream. At first, she couldn't make out what it was—something metal on the surface of the river, reflecting the morning sun. When she did recognize it, she had to peer more carefully to re-affirm her initial judgment.

"That looks like a metal bathtub," she said slowly. "With a man in it."

"It *is* a bathtub," said the Dog. "And a man. There's something else, too . . . you'd best nock an arrow, Mistress."

"He looks unconscious. Or dead," replied Lirael. "Shouldn't we just sail around?"

But she left the tiller to *Finder*, took out the bow, and quickly strung it. Then she loosened Nehima in its sheath and took an arrow from the quiver.

Finder seemed to share the Dog's desire for caution, for she turned away from a direct intercept. The bathtub was traveling much more slowly than they were, propelled only by the current. With the wind on her beam, *Finder* was considerably faster and could curve around in an arc to pass the bathtub and keep going.

Keeping going was what Lirael wanted to do. She didn't want to have anything to do with strangers before she absolutely had to. But then, she would have to deal with people sooner or later, and he did look as if he was in trouble. Surely he wouldn't have chosen to be out in the Ratterlin in a craft as unreliable as a metal bathtub?

Lirael frowned and tugged her scarf down lower over her forehead, so it shaded her face. When they were only fifty yards away, and about to pass the tub, she also nocked an arrow, but did not draw. The man was definitely unaware of *Finder's* approach, since he hadn't so much as twitched. He was on his back in the bath, with his arms hanging over the sides and his knees drawn up. Lirael could see the hilt of a sword at his side, and there was something across his chest—

"Bells! A necromancer!" exclaimed Lirael, drawing her bow. He didn't look like Hedge, but any necromancer was dangerous. Putting an arrow in him would simply be insurance. Unlike their Dead servants, necromancers had no trouble with running water. This one was probably pretending to be hurt, to lure her into an ambush.

She was just about to loose the arrow when the Dog suddenly barked, "Wait! he doesn't smell like a necromancer!"

Surprised, Lirael jerked, let go—and the arrow sped through the air, passing less than a foot above the man's head. If he'd sat up, it would have pierced his throat or eye, killing him instantly.

As the arrow arced downward to plop into the water well past the tub, a small white cat emerged from under the man's legs, climbed onto his chest, and yawned.

This provoked an immediate response from the Dog, who barked furiously and lunged at the water. Lirael only just managed to drop her bow and grab the hound's tail before the Dog went over the side.

The Dog's tail was waving happily, at such a speed Lirael had difficulty hanging on to it. Whether this was actual friendliness or excitement at the prospect of chasing a cat, Lirael didn't know.

All the noise finally woke the man in the tub. He sat up slowly, obviously dazed, the cat moving up to perch precariously on his shoulder. At first, he looked the wrong way for the source of the barking; then he turned, saw the boat—and instantly went for his sword.

Swiftly, Lirael picked up her bow and nocked another arrow. *Finder* turned into the wind so they slowed, giving Lirael a reasonably stable platform from which to shoot.

The cat spoke, words coming out amidst another yawn.

"What are you doing here?"

Lirael jumped in surprise but managed not to drop her arrow.

She was about to answer when she realized the cat was speaking to the Dog.

"Humph," replied the Dog. "I thought someone as slippery

as *you* would know the answer to that. What are you called now? And who is that sorry ragamuffin with you?"

"I am called Mogget," said the cat. "Most of the time. What name do you—"

"This sorry ragamuffin can speak for himself," interrupted the man angrily. "Who or what are you? And you, too, mistress! That's one of the Clayr's boats, isn't it? Did you steal it?"

Finder yawed at this insult, and Lirael tightened her grip on the bow, right hand creeping to the string. He was obviously a very arrogant ragamuffin, and younger than she was, to boot. And he was wearing a necromancer's bells! Apart from that, he was quite handsome, which was another black mark as far as she was concerned. The good-looking men were always the ones who came up to her in the Refectory, certain that she would never refuse their attentions.

"I am the Disreputable Dog," said the Dog, quite calmly. "Companion to Lirael, Daughter of the Clayr."

"So you got stolen as well," said Sam grumpily, hardly thinking about what he was saying. He hurt all over, and Mogget's presence on his shoulder was both extremely uncomfortable and annoying.

"I am Lirael, Daughter of the Clayr," pronounced Lirael, her anger overriding her familiar feeling of being an imposter. "Who or what are you? Besides insufferably rude?"

The man—boy, really—stared back at her, till the blush spread further across her face and Lirael bent her head, hiding under her hair and scarf. She knew well what he was thinking.

She couldn't possibly be a Daughter of the Clayr. The Clayr were all tall and blond and elegant. This girl . . . woman . . . was dark-haired and wore odd clothes. Her bright-red waistcoat was not at all like the star-dusted white robes of the Clayr he'd seen in Belisaere. And she lacked the aloof confidence of the seeresses, who had always made him nervous when he had met them by chance in the corridors of the Palace.

"You don't look like a Daughter of the Clayr," he said, paddling the bathtub a bit closer. The current was already taking him past *Finder*, and he had to battle just to keep in place. "But I guess I can take your word for it."

"Stop!" commanded Lirael, half drawing her bow. "Who are you? And why are you wearing the bells of a necromancer?"

Sam looked down at his chest. He'd forgotten he was wearing the bandolier. Now he was aware of how cold it was, how it pressed against his chest and made breathing difficult.

He unbuckled the bandolier as he tried to work out something inconclusive to say, but Mogget beat him to it.

"Well met, Mistress Lirael. This ragamuffin, as your servant so aptly described him, is His Highness Prince Sameth, the Abhorsen-in-Waiting. Hence the bells. But on to more serious matters. Could you please rescue us? Prince Sameth's personal vessel is not quite what I am used to, and he is eager to catch me a fish before my morning nap."

Lirael looked at the Dog questioningly. She knew who Prince Sameth was. But why on earth would the second child of King Touchstone and the Abhorsen Sabriel be floating in a bathtub in the middle of the Ratterlin, leagues from anywhere?

"He's a royal Prince, all right," said the Dog, quietly sniffing. "I can smell his Blood. He's wounded, too—it is making him irritable. Not much more than a pup, really. You'd best be careful of the other. The Mogget. I know him of old. He's the Abhorsen's servant all right, but he's Free Magic, of the bound variety. He doesn't serve of his own free will, and you must never loose his collar."

"I suppose we have to pick them up," said Lirael slowly,

hoping the Dog would contradict her. But the Dog simply stared back, looking amused. *Finder* finally settled the matter by moving her tiller a little, and the boat started to head slowly towards the bathtub.

Lirael sighed and put away the bow, but took care to draw her sword instead, in case the Dog was mistaken. What if this Prince Sameth was actually a necromancer, and not the Abhorsen-in-Waiting at all?

"Leave your sword by your side," Lirael called. "And you, Mogget, sit under the Prince's legs. When you're alongside, don't move until I tell you."

Sam didn't answer immediately. Lirael saw him whisper to the cat and realized that he was having a conversation similar to the one she'd had with the Dog.

"All right!" Sam shouted after listening to the cat, and he pushed his sword cautiously down to the bottom of the tub, with the bells. He looked feverish, Lirael thought as they drew closer; he was very flushed on the cheeks and around the eyes.

Mogget climbed down gracefully, disappearing below the rim of the bathtub. The makeshift vessel continued on its way, spinning in the current. *Finder* moved, too, tacking across the wind to come broadside.

Boat and bathtub met with a loud clang. Lirael was surprised by how low in the water the tub was—it hadn't seemed so submerged from a distance. The Prince scowled up at her, but true to his word, he didn't move.

Quickly, Lirael reached across with her left hand and touched the Charter mark on his forehead, her sword held ready to strike if the mark was false or corrupted. But her finger felt the familiar warmth of the true Charter, bright and strong. Despite what the Dog had told her, the Charter certainly seemed to go on forever, without Beginning or End.

Hesitantly, Sam stretched out his hand, too, obviously waiting for permission, with the sharp point of her sword so near. She nodded, and he touched her forehead with two fingers, the Charter mark there flashing brilliantly, brighter even than the sun on the river.

"Well, I guess you can get out of the bathtub," said Lirael, breaking the silence. She felt suddenly nervous again, having to share the boat with a stranger. What would she do if he wanted to talk all the time, or tried to kiss her or something? Not that he seemed to be in any shape to do much of anything. She put her sword down and reached out to help him up, wrinkling her nose. He smelt of blood and dirt and fear, and obviously hadn't washed for days.

"Thank you," muttered Sam, slithering over the gunwale, his legs cramped and useless. Lirael saw him bite his lip against the pain, but he didn't cry out. When his legs were swung over, he took a breath and said shakily, "Could . . . could you get my sword, and the bells and the saddlebags? I'm afraid I can hardly move."

Lirael quickly complied. She lifted the saddlebags out last. As they came free, the balance of the bathtub shifted, and one end went briefly underwater. For a second it righted itself, riding still lower in the river. Then a slight wave filled one end beyond recovery, and it flipped over, sinking like a strange silver fish into the clear water below.

"Farewell, brave vessel," whispered Sam, watching as it sank below the upper band of light into the darkness of the deep. He sat back and let out a sigh that was half pain and half relief.

Mogget had jumped as the tub filled and was now facing the Dog, so close their noses almost touched. Both just sat there, staring, but Lirael suspected they were communicating in some way unknown to their human "masters." It didn't look entirely friendly. Both of them had their backs up, and the Dog was growling, low and soft, the sound rolling out from deep in her chest.

Lirael busied herself turning *Finder* back downriver, ducking under the boom as it swung across. The boat hardly needed her help, but it was easier than talking. Once that was done, the silence grew oppressive. The two animals still stood nose-to-nose. Eventually, Lirael felt she had to say something. She wished she were back in the Library and could just write a note.

"What . . . um . . . happened to you?" she asked Sam, who had settled himself at full length in the bottom of the boat. "Why were you in a bathtub?"

"It's a long story," said Sam weakly. He tried to sit up to see her better, but his head dropped back and bumped on a thwart. "Ow! In the simple version, I guess you could say I was escaping from the attentions of the Dead, and the tub happened to be the best boat available."

"The Dead? Near here?" asked Lirael, shivering as she thought of her own encounter with Death. With the necromancer Hedge. She'd presumed that in Life he would be near the Red Lake, as he was in the vision. But that might not have actually happened yet. Perhaps Hedge was somewhere close, right now—

"Several leagues upstream, last night," said Sam, prodding the flesh around his wound with a finger. It was tender and felt tight against the trouser leg, a sure sign that the spell to contain infection had failed in the face of his weariness and over-exertion.

"That looks bad," said Lirael, who could see the dark stain of old blood showing through the cloth. "Did the necromancer do it?"

"Mmm?" asked Sam, who felt like he might pass out again. Pressing on the wound had been a big mistake. "There was no necromancer there, fortunately. The Dead were following set orders, and not being too smart about it. I got stabbed earlier."

Lirael thought for a moment, unsure what to tell him. But he was a royal Prince and the Abhorsen-in-Waiting.

"It's just that I fought a necromancer yesterday," she said.

"What!" exclaimed Sam, sitting up, despite a sudden wave of nausea. "A necromancer? Here?"

"Not exactly," said Lirael. "We were in Death. I don't know where he was physically."

Sam groaned and fell backwards again. This time Lirael saw it coming and just managed to catch his head.

"Thanks," muttered Sam. "Was . . . was he sort of thin and bald, with red armor plates at his elbows?"

"Yes," whispered Lirael. "His name is Hedge. He tried to cut my head off."

Sam made a sort of coughing noise and turned towards the gunwale, the muscles in his neck straining. Lirael just managed to get her hands free before he threw up over the side. He hung there for a few minutes after that, then feebly splashed his face with cold river water.

"Sorry," he said. "Nervous reaction, I suppose. Did you say you fought this necromancer in Death? But you're a Clayr. Clayr don't go into Death. I mean, nobody does, except necromancers and my mother."

"I do," mumbled Lirael back. She blushed again. "I'm . . . I'm a Remembrancer. I had to find out something there, something in the past."

"What's a Remembrancer? What's the past got to do with Death?" asked Sam. He felt delirious. Either Lirael was raving or he was somehow not able to understand what she was saying.

"I think," said the Dog, turning from her nose-to-nose communication with the cat, "that my mistress should tend to your wound, young Prince. Then we might all start at the beginning."

"That could take a while," said Mogget gloomily, searching for fish over the side. Whatever he'd been communicating with the Dog, their body language indicated that he'd come out second best.

"The necromancer," whispered Sam. "Did he burn you, too?"

"No," replied Lirael, puzzled. "Who did he burn?"

Now she was confused. But Sam didn't answer. His eyelids fluttered once, then closed.

"You'd best tend to his wound, Mistress," said the Dog.

Lirael sighed in exasperation, got out her knife, and began to cut Sam's trouser leg away. At the same time, she reached out to the Charter, pulling out the marks for a spell that would cleanse the wound and knit the tissue back together.

Explanations would obviously have to wait.

Chapter Thirty-Eight

THE BOOK OF THE DEAD

THE EXPLANATIONS HAD to wait almost the whole
day, because Sam didn't wake up until *Finder* gently
beached herself on a sandy spit, and Lirael began to set
up camp on the adjoining island. Over a dinner of grilled fish,
dried tomatoes, and biscuit, they told each other their stories.
Lirael was surprised by how easy it was to talk to him. It was
almost like talking to the Dog. Perhaps it was because he wasn't
a Clayr, she thought.

"So you've Seen Nicholas," said Sam heavily. "And he's
definitely with this necromancer, Hedge. Digging up some terrible Free Magic thing. I guess that must be the Lightning Trap
he wrote to me about. I was hoping—stupidly, I suppose—that
it was all a coincidence. That Nick wouldn't have anything to
do with the Enemy, that he was really going to the Red Lake
because he'd heard about something interesting."

"I didn't See it myself," Lirael said reluctantly, to forestall
any requests that she use her supposed Sight to find out more.
"I mean they showed it to me. It took a Watch of more than
fifteen hundred Clayr to See near the pit. But they didn't know
when it was . . . or will be. It might not have happened yet."

"I guess he hasn't been in the Kingdom for that long," said
Sam doubtingly. "But I would think he would have made it to
the Red Lake by now. And the digging you Saw might have
started without him. The Dead in the blue caps and scarves must

be Southerling refugees, the ones who came across the Wall more than a month ago."

"Well, according to the Clayr's other vision, I will find Nicholas at the Red Lake sometime soon," said Lirael. "But I don't want to go there unprepared. Not if Hedge is with him."

"This is getting worse by the day," said Sam, groaning and cradling his head in his hands. "We'll have to send a message to Ellimere. And, I don't know . . . get my parents back from Ancelstierre. Only then there're the Southerlings to worry about. Maybe Mother could come back and Dad could stay there—"

"I think the Clayr have already sent messages," said Lirael. "But they don't know as much as we do, so we should send some, too. Only we'll have to do something ourselves, won't we? It'll take too long for the King and the Abhorsen to even hear about this, let alone come back."

"I suppose so," said Sam, without enthusiasm. "I just wish Nick had waited for me at the Wall."

"He probably didn't have a choice," said the Dog, who was curled up at Lirael's feet, listening. Mogget lay nearby, his paws extended towards the dying remnants of the cooking fire, clean fishbones near his face. As soon as he'd eaten dinner, he'd fallen asleep, ignoring Sam and Lirael's conversation.

"I suppose so," agreed Sam as he absently looked at the scars on his wrists. "That necromancer, Hedge, must have . . . must have got hold of him when we were at the Perimeter. I never actually saw Nick after that. We just exchanged letters. I guess I'll just have to keep trying to find the dumb bastard."

"He looked sick," said Lirael, surprised by the feeling of concern that rose in her from the memory. He'd reached out his hand to her and said hello. . . . "Sick and confused. I think the Free Magic was affecting him, but he didn't realize what it was."

"Nick never really understood what it was like here, or accepted the idea that magic works," said Sam, staring into the embers. Nick had only got worse as he got older, always asking why. He'd never accepted anything that seemed to contradict his understanding of the forces of nature and the mechanics of how the world worked.

"I don't understand Ancelstierre," said Lirael. "I mean I've heard about it, but it might as well be another world."

"It is," said the Dog. "Or it's best to think of it that way."

"It always seemed somehow less real than here," said Sam, still staring at the fire, not really listening. He was watching the sparks fly up now, trying to count the number of them in each little flurry. "A really detailed dream, but sort of washed out, like a thin watercolor. Softer, somehow, even with their electric light and engines and everything. I guess it was because there was hardly any magic at school, because we were too far from the Wall. I could weave shadows and do tricks with light sometimes, but only when the wind blew from the north. Sometimes I felt like part of me was asleep, not being able to reach the Charter."

He fell silent, still staring at the embers. After a few minutes, Lirael spoke again. "Getting back to what we're going to do," she said hesitantly. "I was going to Qyrre, to get the constables or the Royal Guard there to escort me to Edge. But it seems that Hedge already knows about me—about us—so that can't be a very sensible thing to do. I mean I still have to get to the Red Lake, but not so openly. It would be stupid to just tie up at the Qyrre jetty and get out, wouldn't it?"

"Yes," agreed the Dog, looking up at her, proud that she had worked this out for herself. "There was a smell about Hedge, a smell of power strong enough for me to catch when Lirael escaped him. I think he is more than a necromancer. But whatever he is, he is clever, and has long prepared to move

against the Kingdom. He will have servants among the living as
well as the Dead."

Sameth didn't answer for a moment. He tore his gaze away
from the fire, frowning as he saw Mogget's sleeping form. Now
that Nicholas was definitely known to be in the clutches of the
Enemy, Sam didn't know what to do. Rescuing Nicholas had
seemed like a good idea back in the safety of his tower room—
simpler, uncomplicated.

"We can't go to Qyrre," he said. "I was thinking we
should go to the House—Abhorsen's House, I mean. I can send
message-hawks from there, and we can . . . uh . . . get stuff for
the journey. Mail hauberks. A better sword for me."

"And it would be safe," said the Dog, with a penetrating
look at Sam.

Sam looked away, unable to meet the Dog's eyes. Somehow
she knew his secret thoughts. Half of him said he would have to
go on. Half of him said that he couldn't. He felt sick with the
tension of it. Wherever he went, he could not escape being the
Abhorsen-in-Waiting, and all too soon he would be shown to
be an imposter.

"I think that's a good idea," said Lirael. "It's on the Long
Cliffs, isn't it? We can strike west from there, staying off the
roads. Are there any horses at the House? I can't ride, but I
could wear a Charter-skin while you—"

"My horse is dead," interrupted Sam, suddenly white-
faced. "I don't want another one!"

He got up abruptly and limped out into the darkness, staring at the Ratterlin, watching the silver ripples in its dark expanse.
He could hear Lirael and that Dog creature—which was too
much like Mogget for comfort—talking behind him, too low
to make out the words. But he knew they were talking about
him, and he felt ashamed.

"He's a spoilt brat!" whispered Lirael crossly. She wasn't

used to this sort of behavior. On her explorations she had done what she wanted, and in the Library there was strict discipline and a chain of command. Sam had provided useful information, but otherwise he seemed to be a nuisance. "I was just trying to make some sort of plan. Maybe we should leave him behind."

"He is troubled," acknowledged the Dog. "But he has also been through much that tested him beyond all expectation—and he is hurt and afraid. He will be better tomorrow, and in the days to come."

"I hope so," said Lirael. Now that she knew more about Nicholas, the Lightning Trap, and the attacks of the Dead upon Sam, she realized she would probably need all the help she could get. The entire Kingdom would need all the help it could get.

"It is his job, after all," she added. "Being the Abhorsen-in-Waiting. I should be safely back at the Glacier while he deals with Hedge and whatever else is out there!"

"If the Abhorsen and the King are correct about Hedge's plans, nowhere will be safe," said the Dog. "And all who bear the Blood must defend the Charter."

"Oh, Dog!" Lirael said plaintively, giving the hound a hug. "Why is everything so difficult?"

"It just is," said the Dog, woofling in her ear. "But sleep will make it seem easier. A new day will bring new sights and smells."

"How will that help?" grumbled Lirael. But she lay down on the ground, dragging her pack over to use as a pillow. It was too hot for a blanket, even with the slight breeze off the river. Hot and awfully humid, with mosquitoes and sand-flies into the bargain. Summer had not yet begun as far as the Kingdom's calendar was concerned, but the weather had paid no attention to human reckoning. And there was no sign of a cooling rainstorm.

Lirael swatted a mosquito, then turned her head as Sam

came back and rummaged in his saddlebag. He was getting something out—a bright, sparkling object. Lirael sat up as she saw it was a jeweled frog. A frog with wings.

"I'm sorry I behaved badly before," Sam mumbled, setting down the flying frog. "This will help with the mosquitoes."

Lirael didn't need to ask how. It became clear immediately as the frog executed a backwards somersault and used its tongue to collect two particularly large and blood-laden mosquitoes.

"Ingenious," said the Dog sleepily, lifting her head for a moment from the comfortable hole she'd scratched out to sleep in.

"I made it for my mother," said Sam, self-pity evident in his voice. "That's about the only thing I'm really good at. Making things."

Lirael nodded, watching the frog wreak havoc on the local insect population. It moved effortlessly, bronze wings beating as fast as a hummingbird's, making a soft sound like tightly closed shutters moving slightly in the wind.

"Mogget had to kill her," Sam said suddenly, looking back into the fire. "My horse, Sprout. I pushed her too hard. She foundered. I couldn't do the mercy stroke. Mogget had to cut her throat, to make sure the Dead didn't kill her and grow stronger."

"It doesn't sound like there was much choice," said Lirael uncomfortably. "I mean, there was nothing else you could have done."

Sam was silent, staring at the few red coals that remained, seeing the shapes and patterns of orange, black, and red. He could hear the Ratterlin's subdued roar all around, the wheezing breath of the sleeping Dog. He could practically feel Lirael sitting there, three or four steps away, waiting for him to say something.

"I should have done it," he whispered. "But I was afraid.

Afraid of Death. I always have been."

Lirael didn't say anything, feeling even more uncomfortable now. No one had ever shared something so personal with her before, least of all something like this! He was the Abhorsen's son, the Abhorsen-in-Waiting. It simply wasn't possible that he could be afraid of Death. That would be like a Clayr who was afraid of the Sight. That was beyond imagining.

"You're tired and wounded," she said finally. "You should rest. You'll feel better in the morning."

Sam turned to look at her but kept his head down, not meeting her gaze.

"You went into Death," muttered Sam. "Were you afraid?"

"Yes," acknowledged Lirael. "But I followed what it said in the book."

"The book?" asked Sam, shivering despite the heat. "*The Book of the Dead*?"

"No," replied Lirael. She'd never even heard of *The Book of the Dead*. "*The Book of Remembrance and Forgetting*. It deals with Death only because that's where a Remembrancer has to go to look into the past."

"Never heard of it," muttered Sam. He looked at his saddlebags as if they were bulging poison sacs. "I'm supposed to be studying *The Book of the Dead*, but I can't stand looking at it. I tried to leave it behind, but it followed me, with the bells. I . . . I can't get away from it, but I can't look at it, either. And now I'll probably need them both to save Nick. It's so bloody unfair. I never asked to be the Abhorsen-in-Waiting!"

I never asked for my mother to walk away from me when I was five, or to be a Clayr without the Sight, thought Lirael. He was young for his age, this Prince Sameth, and, as the Dog said, he was tired and wounded. Let him have his bout of self-pity. If he didn't snap out of it tomorrow, the Dog could bite him.

That had always worked on her.

So instead of saying what she thought, Lirael reached out to touch the bandolier lying at Sam's side.

"Do you mind if I look at the bells?" she asked. She could feel their power, even as they lay there quiescent. "How do you use them?"

"*The Book of the Dead* explains their use," he said reluctantly. "But you can't really practice with them. They can only be used in earnest. No! Don't . . . please don't take them out."

"I'll be careful," said Lirael, surprised at his reaction. He had gone pale, quite white in the darkness, and was shivering. "I do know a bit about them already, because they're like my pipes."

Sam shuffled back a few steps, the panic rising in him. If she dropped a bell or accidentally rang one, they might both be hurled into Death. He was afraid of that, desperately afraid. At the same time, he felt a sudden urge to let her take the bells, as if that might somehow break their connection with him.

"I suppose you can look at them," he said hesitantly. "If you really want to."

Lirael nodded thoughtfully, running her fingers over the smooth mahogany handles and the rich, beeswax-treated leather. She had a sudden urge to put on the bandolier and walk into Death to try the bells. Her little panpipes were a toy in comparison.

Sam watched her touch the bells and shivered, remembering how cold and heavy they had felt upon his chest. Lirael's scarf had fallen back, letting her long black hair tumble out. There was something about her face in the firelight, something about the way her eyes reflected the light, that made Sam feel odd. He had the sense that he'd seen her before. But that was impossible, as he'd never been to the Glacier, and she'd never left it until now.

"Could I also have a look at *The Book of the Dead*?" asked Lirael, unable to disguise the eagerness in her voice.

Sam stared at her, his mind paralyzed for a moment. "*The Book of the Dead* could d-d-destroy you," he said, his voice betraying him with a stutter. "It's not to be trifled with."

"I know," said Lirael. "I can't explain, but I feel that I must read it."

Sam considered. The Clayr were cousins of the royal line and the Abhorsen, so he supposed Lirael had the Bloodright. Enough not to get destroyed straightaway. She had also studied *The Book of Remembrance and Forgetting*, whatever that was, which seemed to have made her something of a necromancer, at least as far as traveling in Death was concerned. And her Charter mark was true and clear.

"It's there," he said roughly, pointing at the appropriate saddlebag. He hesitated, then backed away, till he was a good ten paces from the fire, closer to the river, with both the Dog and Mogget between him and Lirael—and the book. He lay down, purposefully looking away from Lirael. He didn't want to even see the book. His flying frog jumped after him and rapidly cleared the mosquitoes away from his makeshift bed.

Sam heard the straps of the saddlebags being opened behind his back. Then came the soft brilliance of a Charter light, the snap of silver clasps—and the ruffling of pages. There was no explosion, no sudden fire of destruction.

Sam let out his breath, closed his eyes, and willed himself to sleep. He would be at Abhorsen's House within a few days. Safe. He could stay there. Lirael could go on alone.

Except, his conscience said as he drifted off, Nicholas is *your* friend. It's *your* job to deal with necromancers. And it's *your* parents who would expect you to face the Enemy.

Chapter Thirty-Nine

HIGH BRIDGE

S AM FELT MUCH better the next morning, physically, at least. His leg was greatly improved by Lirael's healing magic. But mentally he felt very nervous about the responsibilities that once again weighed upon him.

Lirael, on the other hand, was physically exhausted but mentally very invigorated. She'd stayed up all night reading *The Book of the Dead*, finishing the last page just as the sun rose, its heat quickly banishing the last few cool hours of the night.

Much of the book was already lost to her. Lirael knew she'd read the whole thing, or had at least read every page she'd turned. But she had no sense of the totality of the text. *The Book of the Dead* would require many re-readings, she realized, as it could offer something new each time. In many ways, she felt it recognized her lack of knowledge, and had given her the bare minimum she was capable of understanding. The book had also raised more questions for her about Death, and the Dead, than it had answered. Or perhaps it had answered, but she would not remember until she needed to know.

Only the last page stayed fixed in her mind, the last page with its single line.

Does the walker choose the path, or the path choose the walker?

She thought about that question as she stuck her head in the river to try to wake herself up, and was still thinking about it as she retied her scarf and straightened her waistcoat. She was reluctant to part with the bells and *The Book of the Dead*, but she finally returned them to Sam's saddlebags as he finished his own morning ablutions farther downstream, behind some of the island's sparse foliage.

They didn't talk as they loaded the boat, not so much as a word about the book or the bells, or Sam's confession of the previous night. As Lirael raised *Finder*'s sail and they set off downriver again, the only sound was the flapping of the canvas as she slowly hauled in the mainsheet, accompanied by the rush of water under the keel. Everyone seemed to agree that it was too early for conversation. Especially Mogget. He hadn't even bothered to wake up and had had to be carried aboard by Sam.

It wasn't until they were well under way that Lirael passed around some of her plate-sized cinnamon cakes, breaking them into manageable hunks. The Dog ate hers in one and a half gulps, but Sam looked at his askance.

"Do I risk my teeth on it or just suck it to death?" he asked, with an attempt at a smile. Clearly he felt better, Lirael thought. It was better than the dismal self-pity of the night before.

"You could give it to me," suggested the Dog, without moving her gaze from the hand that held the cake.

"I don't think so," said Sam, taking a bite and making an effort to chew. Then he held out the uneaten half and said, with his mouth full, "But I'll trade you this half for a close look at your collar."

Before he finished speaking, the Dog lunged forward, gulped the cake, and put her chin on Sam's thigh, her neck in easy reach.

"Why do you want to look at the Dog's collar?" asked
Lirael.

"It has Charter marks I've never seen," replied Sam, reaching down to touch it. It looked like leather with Charter marks
set upon it. But as his fingers met the surface, Sam realized it
wasn't leather at all. It was nothing but Charter marks, a great
sea of marks, stretching into forever. He felt as if he could push
his whole hand into the collar, or dive in himself. And within
that great pool of magic, there were very few Charter marks that
he actually knew.

Reluctantly, he pulled his hand away, and then, on a whim,
scratched the Dog's head between the ears. She felt exactly as a
normal dog should, just as Mogget felt like a cat. But both were
intensely magical beings. Only Mogget's collar was a binding-
spell of great force, and the Dog's collar was something very different, almost like a part of the Charter itself. It had something
of the same feel as a Charter Stone.

"Excellent," sighed the Dog, responding to the scratching.
"But do my back as well, please."

Sam complied, and the Dog stretched out under his fingers,
luxuriating in the treatment. Lirael watched, suddenly struck
by the realization that she'd never before seen the Dog with
another person. The hound had always disappeared when any
other people were around.

"Some of the Charter marks in your collar are familiar,"
said Sam idly, as he scratched and watched the morning sun play
across the water. It was going to be another very hot day, and
he'd lost his hat. It must have come off when he fell down the
steps of the mill's landing stage.

The Dog didn't answer, merely wriggling to direct Sam's
scratching hand farther down her back.

"Only I can't think where I've seen them," continued
Sam, pausing to concentrate. He didn't know what the Charter

marks were for, but he had seen them somewhere else. Not in a grimoire or a Charter Stone, but on some object or something solid. "Not in Mogget's collar—those are quite different."

"You think too much," growled the Dog, though not angrily. "Just keep scratching. You can do under my chin as well."

"You're a very demanding Dog for a supposed servant of the Clayr," said Sam. He looked at Lirael and added, "Is she always like this?"

"Pardon?" asked Lirael, who had started thinking about *The Book of the Dead* again. It took an effort for her to pay attention to Sam, and for a moment she wished she were back in the Great Library, where no one spoke to her unless they had to.

Sam repeated his question, and Lirael looked at the Dog. "She's usually worse," she replied. "If it's not food she's after, it's scratching. She's incorrigible."

"That's why I'm the *Disreputable* Dog," said the Dog smugly, wagging her tail. "Not just the Dog. But you'd better stop scratching now, Prince Sameth."

"Why?"

"Because I can smell people," replied the Dog, forcing herself up. "Beyond the next bend."

Sam and Lirael looked, but couldn't see any sign of habitation or another vessel on the river. The Ratterlin had turned into a wide bend, and the riverbanks were rising into high bluffs of pinkish stone, obscuring the view ahead.

"I can hear roaring, too," added the Dog, who was now perched on the bow, her ears erect and quivering.

"Like rapids?" asked Lirael nervously. She trusted *Finder*, but didn't fancy shooting any waterfalls in her—or in any boat, for that matter.

Sam stood up next to her, keeping one hand on the boom for balance, and tried to see ahead. But whatever was there lay beyond the bend. He took another look at the riverbanks, noting that they'd risen up to become real cliffs, and that the river was getting narrower, and was perhaps only a few hundred yards wide ahead.

"It's okay," he said, and then, seeing her puzzlement at the Ancelstierran expression, he added, "I mean it's all right. We're coming to the High Bridge Gorge. The river gets a lot narrower, and faster, but not so bad that boats can't get through. And the river is lower than it should be at this time of year, so I bet it won't be too fast."

"Oh, High Bridge," said Lirael, with considerable relief. She'd read about High Bridge, and had even seen a hand-colored etching of it. "We actually sail under the town, don't we?"

Sam nodded, thinking. He'd been to the town of High Bridge only once, over a decade ago, with his parents. They'd reached it overland, not on the Ratterlin, but he did remember Touchstone pointing out the guardboats that patrolled upstream of the town, and in the pool beyond High Bridge, where the river widened again. They not only kept at least that part of the Ratterlin free of river pirates but also exacted tolls from traders. Ellimere had probably already given the river-guards orders to "escort" him ashore and return him to Belisaere.

Which would be one way of reaching safety, he thought, and it would make Ellimere responsible for whatever happened next. But he would have to face up to his fight with the constables, and it would mean a delay in any attempt to rescue Nick. And he had no doubt Lirael would choose to go on without him.

"We do, don't we?" repeated Lirael. "Sail under it?"

"What?" asked Sam, who was still wondering what would be the best thing for him to do. "Yes . . . yes, we do. Um, I'd better lie down under a blanket or something before we're in sight of the town."

"Why?" asked Lirael and the Dog at the same time.

"Because he's a truant Prince," yawned Mogget, walking up and stretching on his back paws to look ahead. "He ran away, and his sister wants him back for the Belisaere Festival, to play the Summer Fool or some such."

"The Bird of Dawning," corrected Sam with embarrassment as he got down into the scuppers, ready to hide.

"When you said you'd left Belisaere to look for Nicholas, I thought you meant you'd been sent by your parents!" exclaimed Lirael, unconsciously taking on the tone she used to scold the Dog. "The way I've been sent by the Clayr. You mean they don't even know what you're doing?"

"Er . . . no," replied Sam sheepishly. "Though Dad might have guessed that I've gone to meet Nick. If they know I've gone, that is. It depends where they are in Ancelstierre. But I'll explain when we send messages. The only problem is that Ellimere has probably ordered all the Guard and the Constabulary to send me back to Belisaere if they can."

"Great," said Lirael. "I was counting on your being useful if we did need to get help along the way. A royal Prince, I thought—"

"Well, I could still be useful—" Sam began to say, but at that moment they rounded the bend, and the Dog let out a warning bark. Sure enough, a guardboat was moored to a large buoy mid river—a long, slim galley of thirty-two oars in addition to its square-rigged sail. As *Finder* appeared round the bend, a sailor cast off from the buoy, and others raised the red sail, the golden tower of the royal service gleaming upon it.

Sam hunkered down still lower, pulling the blanket across his face. Something touched his cheek as he settled down, and he started, thinking it was a rat. Then he realized Mogget was slinking under the blanket, too.

"No sense in their wondering why an aristocratic cat would

share deck space with a mangy dog," whispered Mogget, close to Sam's ear under the stifling blanket. "I wonder if they'll do that old trick city guards do with hay wagons, when they suspect smuggling."

"What's that?" Sam whispered back, though he had the feeling he didn't want to know.

"They stick everything with spears to make sure there's nothing—or no one—hidden there," said Mogget absently. "Mind if I move under your arm?"

"They won't do that," said Sam, firmly. "They'll see this is one of the Clayr's boats."

"Will they? They might—but Lirael doesn't look like a Clayr, does she? You yourself suspected her of stealing this boat."

"Quiet down there," woofed the Dog, close by Sam's other ear. Then he felt her bulk settle in at his side—on top of the blanket. It moved again after that, as Lirael tugged on it so it looked like covered baggage rather than a body.

Nothing happened for at least ten minutes. Mogget seemed to go back to sleep, and the Dog rested more of her weight against Sam's side. Sam found that while all he could see was the underside of the blanket, he could hear all sorts of sounds he hadn't noticed before: the creak of the clinker-built hull, the splash of the bow wave, the faint hum of the rigging, and the clatter of the boom as they turned into the wind and stopped.

Then he heard another sound—the heavy splash of many oars moving in unison, and a voice calling the time. "With a will, and a way, that's a stroke and a lay, with a will, and way . . . oars up and in!"

There came a shout, so loud and close it almost made Sam flinch.

"What vessel, and where are you bound?"

"The Clayr's boat *Finder*," Lirael said, but her voice was lost in the rush of the river. She forced herself to shout, surprised by the strength of her own voice. "The Clayr's boat *Finder*. Bound for Qyrre."

"Oh, aye, I know *Finder*," replied the voice, less formal now. "And she obviously knows your hand, Mistress—so you may pass. Will you be stopping to climb up to town?"

"No," said Lirael. "I travel on urgent business for the Clayr."

"No doubt, no doubt," replied the guardboat commander, nodding at Lirael across the forty feet of water that separated the two vessels. "There's trouble brewing, for sure. You'd best beware of the riverbanks, for there have been reports of Dead creatures. Just like the old days, before the return of the King."

"I'll be careful," shouted Lirael. "Thank you for the warning, Captain. May I go on now?"

"Pass, friend," shouted the guard, waving his hand. At that motion, the oars dropped in again, the men straining at their benches. The steers-woman put the rudder over, and the guardboat drove hard away, bow slicing through the current. Lirael saw something metallic glisten under the water as the galley rose up, and she realized it was a long steel ram. The guardboat clearly had the means to sink any craft that didn't stop at its hail.

As they passed, one of the guards looked at Lirael strangely, and she saw his hand creeping to the string of his bow. But none of the others so much as looked at her, and after a moment, the strange guard turned away, leaving Lirael with a feeling of unease. For a moment, she felt she had smelled the metallic tang of Free Magic. She looked at the Dog, and saw that she was staring back at the same guard, all the hair on her back on end.

Sam listened to the steady swish of the oars as the galley drew away, and the receding voice of the cantor. "Are they gone?"

"Yes," said Lirael slowly. "But you'd better stay hidden. They're still in sight, and we're coming up to High Bridge now. And there was something not quite right about one of them. I caught the hint of Free Magic, as if it might not have been a man at all."

"It can't have been Free Magic," said Sam. "The river is flowing too strongly."

"Unlike the Dead, not all things of Free Magic turn back from running water," said Mogget. "Only those with common sense."

"The cat speaks truly," added the Disreputable Dog. "Running water is no bar to those of the Third Kindred, or anything infused with the essence of the Nine. I would not expect such things here, but I did smell something of that ilk aboard the guardboat, Prince Sameth. Something that had only the semblance of a man. Fortunately, it did not dare reveal its presence among so many. But we must be on our guard."

Sam sighed and fought back the temptation to peel the blanket aside just a little bit. It was very hard to lie in darkness going into possible danger. And he'd never seen High Bridge from the water, and it was supposed to be one of the most spectacular sights in the Kingdom.

Lirael certainly thought so. Despite the increasing current, she was content to let *Finder* steer, choosing to gape, instead.

High Bridge had originally been an enormous natural bridge of stone, resting upon the cliffs of the gorge, with the Ratterlin rushing under it four hundred forty feet below. Over the centuries, the natural grandeur of the bridge had been augmented by the human buildings upon it. The first of the buildings constructed there was a castle, built to take advantage of the protection offered by so much deep running water beneath it.

No Dead creatures could come against its walls, for they must also pass above the river's swift waters.

This had proved to be an enormous attraction during the years of the Interregnum, when the great majority of Charter Stones in the Kingdom were broken and the villages that depended upon them for safety destroyed, leaving the Dead and those in league with them free to do as they chose. Within a few years, the original castle had been surrounded by houses, inns, warehouses, windmills, forges, manufactories, stables, taverns, and all manner of other buildings. Many were actually dug down into the bridge itself, for the stone was several hundred feet thick. The bridge was more than a mile broad, too, though not very long, the distance between the eastern and western cliffs once being famously covered in a single bowshot by the archer Aylward Blackhair.

Lirael was staring up at this strange metropolis when she heard a woman's shout, seemingly from the figurehead at the front of the boat. At the same time *Finder*'s tiller shot out of her hand, pushing hard over to the left. Instantly, the boom swung violently across and the boat heeled over to the right, her starboard quarter almost in the river, spray and water foaming in across the side.

Sam found himself piled up against the starboard rail. Somehow both Mogget and the Dog had ended up on top of him, along with what felt like everything else. And water was pouring in on him in bucketloads.

Sam thrust his hands out of the blanket and clawed along the side of the boat, reaching out for the rail. But his hands went straight into rushing water, and Sam realized that *Finder* was heeled over so far she must be about to capsize. Desperately he struggled to free himself of Mogget, Dog, baggage, and blanket, at the same time as he shouted, "Lirael! Lirael! What's happening?"

Chapter Forty

UNDER THE BRIDGE

LIRAEL WAS TOO busy pulling herself back into the boat to answer. The boom had caught her on the shoulder, knocking her overboard before she even knew what was happening. Fortunately, she'd managed to grab the rail and hang on, looking up fearfully as *Finder*'s hull towered above her, so far over it seemed certain the boat would capsize—with Lirael underneath.

Then, as quickly as she'd heeled over, *Finder* righted herself, the sudden lurch helping Lirael fling herself back in, to end up in a terrible tangle of blanket, Sam, Dog, Mogget, lots of odds and ends, and sloshing water.

At the same time, *Finder* passed under High Bridge, moving out of sunlight into the strange, cool twilight, as the Ratterlin streamed into the vast tunnel made by the bridge of stone high overhead.

"What happened?" spluttered Sam when he finally got free of the wet blanket. Lirael was already by the tiller, completely drenched, her hand gripped around something projecting from the stern.

"I thought *Finder* had gone mad," said Lirael. "Till I saw this."

Sam shuffled back, cursing the blanket that was still tangled around his legs. It wasn't exactly dark under High Bridge, because light did come in from either end, but it was a strange light, like sun slowly breaking through fog, soft and diffused by the water. The Dog rushed over to look, too, but Mogget sniffed and padded to the bow, to begin the long process of licking himself dry.

The Dog saw what Lirael held before Sam did, and growled. There was a splintered hole through the port side of the stern, under the gunwale, where Lirael had been sitting before *Finder* had knocked her over with the boom. In her hand Lirael held the crossbow bolt that had made the hole. Its shaft was painted white, and it was fletched with raven feathers.

"It must have just missed you!" exclaimed Sam, as he put three of his fingers through the hole.

"Only thanks to *Finder*," said Lirael, stroking the tiller gently. "Look at what it did to my poor boat."

"It would have gone straight through you, even if you'd had armor on," said Sam grimly. "That's a war bolt—not a hunting quarrel. And a very good shot. Too good to be natural."

"They'll probably try again on the other side—or before," said Lirael, looking up with alarm at the stone high above them. "Are there any openings above us, do you know?"

"No idea," said Sam. He followed her gaze and could see only unbroken yellow stone. But the bridge was several hundred feet above them, and the light bad. There could be any number of dark openings he just couldn't see.

"I can't see any, Mistress," growled the Dog as she craned her head back, too. "But we'll be through in a few minutes, with this current."

"Do you know how to cast an arrow ward?" Sam asked Lirael. The current was indeed taking them along at a rapid rate, and the bright, sunlit arch that marked the other side of the bridge was getting closer all too quickly.

"No," said Lirael nervously. "I was probably supposed to. I

skipped fighting arts quite a lot."

"All right," Sam said. "Why don't we swap places? I'll sit here and steer, but with an arrow ward at my back. You get ready with your bow, prepared to shoot back. Mogget—you've got the best eyes—you spot for Lirael."

"The Horrible Hound, or whatever she calls herself, can do that," declared Mogget, from the bow. "I'm going back to sleep."

"But what if the ward doesn't work?" protested Lirael. "You're already wounded—"

"It'll work," said Sam, moving up, so Lirael had little choice but to get out of the way. "I used to practice with the Guard every day. Only a spelled arrow or bolt can get through."

"But it might be spelled," said Lirael, quickly re-stringing her bow with a dry string from a waxed packet. The black and white bolt had not carried any scent of magic, but that did not mean the next would be unspelled.

"It still has to be stronger than the ward," said Sam confidently—much more confidently than he actually felt. He had cast arrow wards many times, but never in an actual fight. Touchstone had taught him the spell when Sam was only six years old, and the arrows fired to test it were mere toys with cushioned heads made from the rags of old pajamas. Later, he had graduated to blunted arrows. He had never been tested against a war bolt that could punch through an inch of plate steel.

Sam sat by the tiller and turned to face the stern. Then he began to reach for the Charter marks he needed. He usually used his sword to trace the ward in the air, but he had been taught to use only his hands if need be, and that worked just as well.

Lirael saw his hands and fingers move swiftly and surely,

Charter marks beginning to glow in the air. They hung there, shining, just beyond the arc his fingertips were describing. Whatever else he might be, she thought, Sam was a very powerful Charter Mage. And he might be afraid of Death and the Dead, but he wasn't a coward. She wouldn't want to be sitting there with only a spell between her and the razored edges of a crossbow bolt traveling with killing speed. She shivered. If it were not for *Finder*, she would probably already be dead, or bleeding to death in the scuppers.

Lirael's stomach muscles tightened at that thought, and she paid careful attention to nocking her arrow. Whoever the hidden killer was, Lirael would try her best to make sure he didn't get more than one shot.

Sam finished describing the full circle of the arrow ward but remained crouched at the stern. His hands continued to move, drawing Charter marks that fled his fingers to join the glowing circle above and behind him.

"Have to keep it going," he said, panting. "Bit of a drawback. Get ready! We'll be out in a sec—"

They suddenly burst out into sunshine, and Sam instinctively shrank to present a smaller target.

Lirael, kneeling by the mast and looking up, was momentarily blinded. In that second, the assassin fired. The bolt flew true. Lirael screamed a warning, but the sound was still in her throat when the black-feathered quarrel hit the arrow ward—and vanished.

"Quick!" gasped Sam, the strain of maintaining the spell showing in his face and straining chest.

Lirael was already searching for the crossbowman. But there were many windows and openings up there, either in the stone of the Bridge itself or in the buildings that were built upon it. And there were people all over the place, too, in windows, on balconies, leaning over railings, swinging on platforms roped to plaster walls. . . . She couldn't even begin to find the shooter.

Then the Dog moved up next to Lirael, raised her head—and howled. It was an eerie, high tone that seemed to echo across the water, up the sides of the river gorge, and everywhere across the town itself. It sounded as if scores of wolves had suddenly appeared on the river, in the town, and all around.

Everywhere, people stopped moving and stared. Except in one window, about halfway up. Lirael saw someone there suddenly fling the shutters wide open, one hand still clutching a crossbow.

She drew and shot as he stood there, but her arrow was caught by an errant breeze and went wide, striking the wall above his head. As Lirael nocked another arrow, the assassin stood up in the window frame, precariously balanced on the sill.

The Dog drew breath and howled again. The assassin dropped his crossbow so he could jam his fingers in his ears. But even then he couldn't block out the terrible sound, and his legs moved of their own accord, stepping out into space. Desperately, he tried to hurl his upper body backwards into the room, but he seemed to have no control at all below the waist. A moment later, he fell, following the crossbow down four hundred feet into the water. He kept his fingers in his ears all the way down, and his legs kept moving even though there was nothing to tread but air.

The Dog stopped howling as the assassin's body hit the water, and both Sam and Lirael flinched as they felt him die. They watched the ripples spread till they met *Finder*'s wash and disappeared.

"What did you do?" asked Lirael, carefully replacing her bow. She'd never seen or felt anyone actually die before. She had only attended Farewells, with the death made distant, all wrapped up with ceremony and tradition.

"I made him walk," growled the Dog, sitting back on her haunches, a ridge of hair along her back stiff and angry. "He would have killed you if he could, Mistress."

Lirael nodded and gave the Dog a quick hug. Sam watched them warily. That howl was pure Free Magic, with no Charter Magic in it at all. The Dog seemed friendly and appeared to be devoted to Lirael, but he could not forget how dangerous she was. There was also something about the howl that reminded him of something, some magic he had experienced that he couldn't quite place.

At least Mogget's case was straightforward. He was a Free Magic creature, bound and safe while he wore the collar. The Dog appeared to be a free-willed blend of the two magics, which was completely beyond anything Sam had ever heard about. Not for the first time, he wished that his mother were here. Sabriel would know what the Dog was, he felt sure.

"We'd better swap places again," said Lirael urgently. "There's another guardboat ahead."

Sam quickly scrunched down, on the opposite side from the Dog, who looked at him and grinned, showing a very sharp, very white, and very large set of teeth. Sam forced himself to smile back, remembering the advice he'd been given about dogs when he was a boy. Never let them know you're afraid. . . .

"Ugh! There's a lot of water here," he complained as he lay down, squelching, and drew the sodden blanket towards him. "I should have bailed it out in the tunnel."

He was just about to draw the blanket over his face when he saw Mogget, still sunning and grooming himself on the bow.

"Mogget!" he commanded. "You should hide, too."

Mogget looked pointedly at the water swishing around Sam's legs and stuck out his small pink tongue.

"Too wet for me," he said. "Besides, the guardboat will stop us for sure. They will have been signaled from the town after this canine show-off's demonstration of vocal talents—though hopefully no one will recognize what that actually was. So you might as well sit up."

Sam groaned and sloshed upright. "You might have told me before I lay down," he said bitterly, picking up a tin cup and beginning to bail.

"It would be best if we can get past without being stopped," the Dog commented, sniffing the air. "There may be more enemies concealed aboard this guardboat, too."

"There's more room to maneuver up ahead," said Lirael. "But I don't know if it's enough to evade the guardboat."

The eastern side of the river was the main river-port for High Bridge. Twelve jetties of various lengths thrust out into the river, most of them cluttered with trading boats, whose masts made a forest of bare poles. Behind the jetties, there was a quay carved into the stone of the gorge, a long terrace cluttered with cargoes being readied to go aboard the boats or up to the town. Beyond the quay, there were several steep stairways that ran up the cliff-face to the town, in between the derrick cables that lifted up the multitude of boxes and chests, barrels and bales.

But the western side of the river was open, save for a few trading boats ahead of them downstream, and the one guardboat, which was already slipping its mooring. If they could get past the guardboat and keep ahead, there was nothing to stop them.

"They've got at least twenty archers on that boat," said Sam doubtfully. "Do you think we can just sail past?"

"I suppose it depends how many—if any—of them are agents of the Enemy," said Lirael as she hauled the mainsheet tighter, trimming the sail for more speed. "If they're real guards, they won't shoot at a royal Prince and a Daughter of the Clayr. Will they?"

"I suppose it's worth a try," muttered Sam, who couldn't think of an alternative plan. If the guards were real guards, the worst that would happen was that he would be returned to Belisaere. If they weren't, it would be best to stay as far away as possible. "What if the wind drops?"

"We'll whistle one up," said Lirael. "Are you much of a weather-worker?"

"Not by my mother's standards," replied Sam. Weather magic was mostly performed with whistled Charter marks, and he was no great whistler. "But I can probably raise a wind."

"This is not a brilliant plan, even by your mother's standards," commented Mogget, who was watching the guardboat raise its sail, obviously intent on an intercept. "Lirael doesn't look like a Daughter of the Clayr. Sameth looks like a scarecrow, not a royal Prince. And the commander of this guardboat may not recognize *Finder*. So even if they *are* all real guards, they probably will just feather us with arrows if we try to sail past. Personally, I don't want to be made into a pincushion."

"I don't think we have a choice," said Sam slowly. "If even two or three of them belong to the Enemy, they will attack. If we can conjure up enough of a wind, we might be able to stay out of bowshot anyway."

"Fine!" muttered Mogget. "Wet, cold, and full of holes. Another fun day on the river."

Lirael and Sam looked at each other. Lirael took a deep breath. Charter marks flowered in her mind, and she let them flow into her lungs and throat, circling there. Then she whistled, and the pure notes leapt up into the sky.

Answering the whistle, the river behind them darkened.

Ripples and white peaks sprang up across the water and streaked across towards *Finder* and her waiting sail.

A few seconds later, the wind hit. The boat heeled over and picked up speed, the rigging adding its own whistle at the sudden pressure. Mogget hissed his lack of appreciation and hastily sprang back from the bow as spray flew over where he'd been a moment before.

Still Lirael whistled, and Sam joined in, their combined weather spell weaving the wind behind *Finder*'s quarter, at the same time stripping it away from the guardboat, whose sail lay limp and airless.

But the guardboat had oars, and expert rowers. The cantor sped his call, and the oars dipped in faster rhythm as the galley rushed forward to intercept *Finder*, water suddenly foaming around its bow, the bright metal of the ram gleaming in the sun.

Chapter Forty-One

FREE MAGIC AND THE FLESH OF SWINE

THEY'LL BE WITHIN bowshot in a few minutes," warned Mogget gloomily, gauging with a jaundiced eye the distance to the galley, and then the proximity of the western shore. "I suppose we'll end up having to swim for our miserable lives."

Lirael and Sam exchanged glances of concern, reluctant to agree aloud with the cat. Despite their spell-woven wind and their current scudding run across the water, the galley was still too fast. They were as close as they dared to the shore, and were rapidly running out of river to maneuver in.

"I guess we'd better heave to and risk the presence of enemies among the guards," said Sam, who was acutely aware that he had already injured two constables. "I don't want any of us to get shot because they think we're smugglers or something, and I definitely don't want to hurt any guards. Once they find out I am who I am, I'll order them to let you go. And who knows? I might be lucky. Maybe Ellimere hasn't ordered my arrest after all."

"I don't know—" Lirael started to say, her voice anxious. There was still a slight chance they might get past. But she'd hardly said a word when the Dog barked in interruption.

"No! There are at least three or four Free Magic creatures aboard that boat! We mustn't stop!"

"Smells all right to me," said Mogget, shuddering as more

spray spumed in over the bow. "But then I don't have your famous nose. However, as I can see a half dozen archers getting ready to shoot, perhaps you actually can smell something."

Sam saw that Mogget was quite correct. The guardboat was angling to cross their path, but six archers were already formed up on the forward deck, arrows nocked. Obviously they intended to shoot first and make polite enquiries later.

"Are the archers human?" asked Sam quickly.

The Dog sniffed the air again before replying. "I cannot tell. I think most of them are. But the captain—the one with the plumed hat—has only the semblance of a man. It is a construct, made from Free Magic and the flesh of swine. That odor I cannot mistake."

"We have to show the human archers who they're shooting at!" Sam exclaimed. "I should have brought a shield with the royal blazon or something. They'd never dare shoot at us then, even if they're ordered to."

"Of course!" said Lirael, suddenly slapping herself on the forehead. "Here, take this!"

"What!" shouted Sam, throwing himself back to clutch at the tiller as Lirael let go. "What do I do? I don't know how to sail!"

"Don't worry, she steers herself," Lirael shouted back as she crawled forward to the storage box in the forepeak. It was a matter of only twelve feet, but Lirael found it hard going, since *Finder* was heeled over at a sharp angle and the boat kept leaping up and then coming down with a bone-jarring smack every few yards.

"Are you sure?" Sam shouted again. He could feel the pressure on the tiller, and he felt that only his white-knuckled grip was keeping them from veering sharply into the riverbank. Experimentally, he opened his fingers for a second, ready to grab hold again immediately. But nothing happened. *Finder* kept her course, the tiller barely moving. Sam sighed in relief, but his sigh became a choking cough as he saw a flight of arrows snap away from the guardboat—straight at him.

"Too far yet," said the Dog, casting a professional eye on the arrows' flight, and sure enough, the arrows plunged into the water a good fifty yards away.

"Not for long," grumbled Mogget. He jumped yet again to try to find a drier spot. He seemed to have found it near the mast when a slight twitch of the tiller—without Sam's cooperation—caught a small wave and neatly sloshed it in and over his back.

"I hate you!" hissed Mogget in the general direction of the boat's figurehead as the water drained away from his feet. "At least that rowboat looks dry. Why don't we just let ourselves be captured? We've got only the Dog's nose to say the captain is a construct."

"They're shooting at us, Mogget!" said Sam, who wasn't entirely sure whether Mogget was joking.

"There are two other constructs on board besides the captain," growled the Dog, whose nose was still vigorously sampling the air. She was getting bigger, Sam noticed, and fiercer-looking. Clearly she expected a fight, discounting whatever Lirael thought she was doing up at the bow.

"Got it!" exclaimed Lirael, as another flight of arrows sped towards them. This time, they splashed into the river no more than two arms' lengths away. Sam could probably have touched the closest one.

"What?" shouted Sam. He simultaneously reached into the Charter to begin making an arrow ward. Not that it would be much use against six archers at once. Not when he wasn't up to his full strength.

Lirael held up a large square of black cloth and let it flap into the breeze, revealing a brilliant silver star shining in the middle of it. The wind almost tore it from her grasp, but she clutched it to her chest and began to crawl back to the mast.

"*Finder*'s flag," she shouted as she pulled out a halyard and started to unscrew the pin in a shackle so it could be put through an eyelet in the banner. "I'll have it up in a minute."

"We don't have a minute!" screamed Sam, who could see the archers about to loose again. "Just hold it out!"

Lirael ignored him. Quickly she fitted the shackles at each end, screwing in the pins with what looked like deliberate slowness to Sam. He was about to lunge forward and grab the damned flag when Lirael suddenly let it go and pulled on the halyard—as five more arrows leapt towards them from the guardboat.

Finder reacted first, nudging the tiller over to turn the bow into the wind. Instantly, she lost speed, the sail flapping and clapping like maniacal applause. Sam ducked as she did it, and the tiller smacked him in the jaw, hard enough to make him think he'd been shot—at least for a moment. Then it swung back again, just missing him, as the boat returned to her original course.

But those few seconds of lost speed had been vital, Sam realized, as the arrows that should have struck them plunged into the water only a few feet ahead.

Then the great silver star of the Clayr billowed out from the mast, shining in the sun. Now there could be no doubt about whose boat this was, for the flag was not just a thing of cloth but, like *Finder* herself, was imbued with Charter Magic. Even in the darkest night, the starry banner of the Clayr would shine. In the bright day, it was almost blinding in its brilliance.

"They've stopped rowing," announced the Dog cheerily, as

the guardboat suddenly lost way in a confusing pick-up-sticks jumble of oars. Sam relaxed and let the beginnings of the arrow ward fade away, so he could start checking whether he'd lost any teeth.

"But two archers are still going to shoot," the Dog continued, making Sam groan and hurriedly try to reach for the Charter marks he'd just let go.

"Yes . . . no . . . the other four are overpowering them. The captain is shouting . . . it has revealed itself!"

Sam and Lirael looked back at the guardboat. It was a mess of struggling figures, accompanied by shouting, screaming, and the clash of weapons. In the middle of it, a column of white fire suddenly appeared, with a whoosh loud enough to make the Dog's ears crinkle back and to make the others flinch. The column roared up twelve feet or more, then slid sideways and arced over the side.

For a moment, Sam and Lirael thought it would sink and disappear, but it actually bounced off the river as if the water were springy grass. Then the column started to move towards them, and it began to transform itself into something else. Soon it was no longer a tall streak of white fire but a gigantic burning boar, complete with tusks. It ran after *Finder* in great splashing leaps, squealing as it ran, a sound that sent a wave of nausea through everyone who heard it.

Sam was the first to react. He picked up Lirael's bow and sent four arrows in quick succession into the thing that was fast catching up to them. All struck it head on, but they had no effect save for a sudden flurry of sparks. The arrows turned instantly into molten metal and ash.

Sam was reaching for another arrow when Lirael thrust her hand past him, and she screamed a spell over the wind. A golden net flew from her fingers, spreading wider and wider as it crossed the intervening water. It met the boar-thing as it jumped, wrapping it in ropes of yellow red fire that dampened the thing's white-hot brilliance. Boar and net came plunging down, and both disappeared under the surface of the river, cutting off the terrible squealing. As the waters of the Ratterlin closed over the boar, an enormous plume of steam shot up for at least a hundred feet. When it subsided, there was no sign of either net or Free Magic creature, save for many small pieces of what looked like long-decayed meat, morsels that even the ravenous seagulls overhead chose to avoid.

"Thank you," said Sam, after it became clear that nothing more was going to come from the guardboat or out of the depths. He knew the net-spell Lirael had used but hadn't thought it would work against something that looked so powerful.

"Mogget suggested it," said Lirael, who was clearly surprised both by that and by the fact that the spell had worked so well.

"While that kind of construct can move across running water, it is destroyed by total immersion," explained Mogget. "Slowing it for even a moment was enough."

He looked slyly at the Dog, and added, "So you see that this hound is not the only one who knows of such things. Now I really must have a little nap. I trust that some fish will be forthcoming when I wake?"

Sam nodded wearily, though he had no idea how he was going to catch any. He almost patted Mogget, as Lirael so often did the Dog. But something in the cat's green eyes made him pull his hand back before the motion was really begun.

"Sorry I didn't think of the flag earlier," said Lirael as they sped on. The spell-wind had lessened, but it still blew quite strongly at their backs. "There's a whole pile of stuff there I looked at for only a second when we first left the Glacier."

"I'm glad you remembered it when you did," said Sam, his words slightly muffled as he tested the operation of his jaw. It seemed to be only bruised, and he still had all his teeth. "And this wind will come in handy. We should get to the House by tomorrow morning."

"Abhorsen's House," Lirael said thoughtfully. "It's built on an island, isn't it? Just before the waterfall where the Ratterlin goes over the Long Cliffs?"

"Yes," replied Sam, thinking of that raging cascade and how grateful he was going to be to have its protection. Then it occurred to him that far from thinking of the waterfall as safety, Lirael was probably wondering how they would reach the House without going over the mighty falls and down to certain destruction.

"Don't worry about the waterfall," he explained. "There's a sort of channel behind the island, where the current isn't as strong. It goes back almost a league, so as long as you enter it at the right point and stay in it, there's no problem. The Wallmakers made it. They built the House, too. It's brilliant work—the channel, I mean. I tried to make a model of it once, using the waterfall and pools on the second terrace at home. The Palace. But I couldn't spell the current to split. . . ."

He stopped talking as he realized Lirael wasn't listening. She had an abstract expression on her face, and her eyes were focused over his shoulder, into the distance.

"I didn't realize I was that boring," he said with an annoyed smile. Sam wasn't used to pretty girls ignoring him. And Lirael was pretty, he suddenly realized, potentially even beautiful. He hadn't noticed before.

Lirael started, blinked, and said, "Sorry. I'm not used to . . . People don't talk to me much back home."

"You know, you'd look a lot better without that scarf," said

Sam. She really was attractive, though something about her face unsettled him. Where had he seen her? Perhaps she looked like one of the girls Ellimere had forced on him back in Belisaere. "You know, you remind me of someone. I don't suppose I could have met one of your sisters or something, could I? I don't remember ever seeing any dark-haired Clayr, though."

"I don't have any sisters," replied Lirael absently. "Only cousins. Lots and lots of cousins. And an aunt."

"You could change into one of my sister's dresses at the House. It'd give you a chance to get out of that waistcoat," said Sam. "Do you mind if I ask how old you are, Lirael?"

Lirael looked at him, puzzled at the question, till she saw the glint in his eye. She knew that look from the Lower Refectory. She looked away and pulled up her scarf, trying to think of something to say. If only Sam could have just stayed like the Dog, she thought. A comforting friend, without the complication of romantic interest. There had to be something she could do to completely discourage him, short of throwing up or otherwise making herself totally unattractive.

"I'm thirty-five," she said at last.

"Thirty-five!" exclaimed Sam, "I mean, I beg your pardon. You don't look . . . you seem much younger—"

"Ointments," said the Dog, sporting a wicked, one-sided grin that only Lirael could see. "Unguents. Oils from the North. Spells of seeming. My mistress works hard to keep her youth, Prince."

"Oh," said Sam, leaning back against the stern rail. Surreptitiously he looked at Lirael again, trying to see some lines he'd missed or something. But she really didn't look a day older than Ellimere. And she certainly didn't act like a much older woman. She wasn't all that confident or outgoing, for a start. Perhaps it was because she was a librarian, Sam thought, as he tried to make out what he thought was probably a very shapely form under the baggy waistcoat.

"Enough of that talk, Dog!" commanded Lirael, turning her head to hide her own smile from Sam. "Make yourself useful and keep an eye out for danger. I'm going to make myself useful by weaving a Charter-skin."

"Aye, aye, Mistress," growled the Dog. "I will keep watch."

The hound stretched and yawned, then jumped to the bow, sitting down right in the path of the spray, her mouth wide open and tongue lolling. How she stayed upright and steady was a mystery, Lirael thought, though she had the unpleasant notion that the Dog might have grown suckers on her bottom.

"Mad. Absolutely mad," said Mogget, as he watched the Dog get drenched. The cat had resumed his post near the mast and was once again licking himself dry. "But then, she always was."

"I heard that!" barked the Dog, without looking back.

"Of course you did," said Mogget, sighing, and he licked away at his collar. He looked up at Lirael, his green eyes twinkling with wickedness, and added, "I don't suppose I could trouble you to take off my collar so I can get properly dry?"

Lirael shook her head.

"Well, I suppose if the village idiot here wouldn't do it, there was no chance you would," grumbled Mogget, inclining his head at Sameth. "It's enough to make me wish I'd volunteered in the first place. Then I wouldn't be forced out all the time on these barbaric boat trips."

"What didn't you volunteer for?" asked Lirael curiously. But the little cat only smiled. A smile that had rather too much of the carnivorous hunter in it, Lirael thought. Then he twitched his head, Ranna tinkled, and he was asleep, sprawled out in the noonday sun.

"Be careful with Mogget," Sam warned, as Lirael succumbed to the temptation to scratch the cat's furry white belly. "He's nearly killed my mother in his unbound form. Three times, in fact, during the time she's been the Abhorsen."

Lirael pulled her hand back just as Mogget opened one eye and made an—apparently playful—swipe with one claw-extended paw.

"Go back to sleep," said the Dog from the bow, without looking around. She certainly seemed confident that Mogget would obey.

Mogget winked at Lirael, holding her gaze for a moment. Then that one sharp green eye closed, and he really did seem to fall asleep, Ranna tinkling at his neck.

"Well," Lirael said. "Time to make a Charter-skin."

"Do you mind if I watch?" asked Sam eagerly. "I've read about Charter-skins, but I thought the art was lost. Even Mother doesn't know how to make one. What shapes do you know?"

"I can make an ice otter, a russet bear, or a barking owl," replied Lirael, relieved to see that the spasm of romantic interest that had gripped Sam had passed. "You can watch if you like, but I don't know what you'll see. They're basically just very long and complex chains of Charter marks and joining-spells— and you have to hold them in your head all at the same time. So I won't be able to talk or explain or anything. And it will probably take me until sunset. Then I have to fold it exactly right so it can be used later."

"Fascinating," said Sam. "Have you tried putting the completed spell into an object? So that the whole chain of marks is there, ready to be pulled out when you need it, but it hasn't actually been cast?"

"No," replied Lirael. "I didn't know that it was possible."

"Well, it's difficult," explained Sam eagerly. "It's sort of like repairing a Charter Stone. I mean, you have to use some of your own blood to prepare whatever is going to hold the spell. Royal blood, that is, though Clayr or Abhorsen blood should work equally well. You need to be very careful, of course, because if you get it wrong . . . Anyway, let's see your Charter-skin first. What is it going to be?"

"A barking owl," replied Lirael, with a sense of foreboding. She didn't need the Sight to know that Sameth would like to ask an awful lot of questions. "And it'll take about four hours. Without," she added firmly, "any interruptions."

Chapter Forty-Two

SOUTHERLINGS AND A NECROMANCER

THE SUN WAS setting, sending a red light across the broad river. Despite Sam and Lirael's earlier weather spell, the wind had turned and was blowing strongly from the south. Even against the wind, *Finder* continued to make good time, tacking in long diagonals between the eastern and western shores.

As Lirael had expected, Sam hadn't been able to stop himself asking questions. But even with the interruptions she had managed to create the Charter-skin of a barking owl and fold it up properly for later use.

"That was fascinating," said Sam. "I'd like to learn how to make one myself."

"I've left *In the Skin of a Lyon* back at the Glacier," replied Lirael. "But you can have it if you ever go there. It belongs to the Library, but I expect you'd be allowed to borrow it."

Sam nodded. The prospect of him visiting the Clayr's Glacier seemed exceedingly remote. It was just another piece of a future that he couldn't imagine. All he could think of was reaching the safe haven of the House.

"Can we sail through the night?" he asked.

"Yes," replied Lirael. "If the Dog is prepared to stay up as lookout, to help *Finder*."

"I will," barked the Disreputable Dog. She had not shifted from her position at the bow. "The sooner we're there, the better. There is a foul scent on this wind, and the river is too deserted to be normal."

Sam and Lirael both looked around. They had been so intent on the Charter-skin that they hadn't noticed the complete absence of any other boats, though there were a number anchored close to the eastern shore.

"No one's followed us down from High Bridge, and we have passed only four craft coming from the south," said the Dog. "This cannot be normal for the Ratterlin."

"No," Sam agreed. "Whenever I've been on the river, there've always been lots of boats. Even in winter. We should have seen some of the wood barges at least, heading north."

"I haven't seen a single craft all day," said the Dog. "Which means that they have stopped somewhere, to take shelter. And the boats I've seen tied up have all been out on the jetties or moored to buoys. As far as they can get from the land."

"There must be more of the Dead, or those Free Magic constructs, all along the river," said Lirael.

"I knew Mother and Dad shouldn't have gone," said Sam. "If they'd known—"

"They would still have gone," interrupted Mogget with a yawn. He stretched, and tasted the air with his delicate pink tongue. "As per usual, trouble comes in several directions at once. I think some is coming our way, for I am afraid to say that the hound is correct. There *is* a reek on this breeze. Wake me if something unpleasant seems likely to occur."

With that, he settled back down again, curling into a tight white ball.

"I wonder what Mogget would call 'something unpleasant,'" muttered Sam nervously. He picked up his sword and drew it partially out of the scabbard, checking that the Charter marks he'd put there still flourished.

The Dog sniffed the air again as the boat came about, onto a port tack. Her nose quivered, and she raised her snout higher as the scent grew stronger.

"Free Magic," she said finally. "On the western shore."

"Where, exactly?" asked Lirael, shading her eyes with her hand. It was hard to see anything to the west, against the setting sun. All she could make out was tangled groves of willows between empty fields, a few makeshift jetties, and the semi-submerged stone walls of a large fish trap.

"I can't see," replied the Dog. "I can only smell. Somewhere downstream."

"I can't see anything, either," added Sam. "But if the Free Magic isn't on the river, we can just sail past."

"I can smell people, too," reported the Dog. "Frightened people."

Sam didn't say anything. Lirael glanced at him and saw that he was biting his lip.

"Could it be the necromancer?" Lirael asked. "Hedge?"

The Dog shrugged. "I cannot tell from here. The scent of Free Magic is strong, so it could be a necromancer. Or perhaps a Stilken or Hish."

Lirael swallowed nervously. She could bind a Stilken, since she had Nehima to help. And Sam, the Dog, and Mogget. But she didn't want to have to.

"I knew I should have read that book," muttered Sam. He didn't say which book.

They sat in silence for a minute, as *Finder* continued on her way towards the western shore. The sun was sinking fast now, more than half of its ruddy disc below the horizon. The stars were starting to become brighter as darkness fell.

"I suppose we'd better . . . we'd better take a look," Sam said at last, with obvious effort. He buckled on his sword, but made no move to pick up the bandolier of bells. Lirael looked at them and wished she could take them up, but they were not hers. It was up to Sam to decide what to do with them.

"If we tie up at that next jetty, will we be close?" Lirael asked the Dog. The hound nodded her head. Without needing orders, *Finder* turned towards the jetty.

"Wake up, Mogget!" said Sam, but he spoke softly. It had grown quiet on the river with the fall of night. He did not want his voice to carry over the soft burble of the current.

Mogget did not stir. Sam spoke again and scratched the cat's head, but Mogget continued to sleep.

"He'll wake when he needs to," said the Dog. She also spoke softly. "Prepare yourselves!"

Finder expertly slid up to the jetty as Lirael lowered the sail. Sam jumped ashore, his sword drawn, closely followed by the Dog.

Lirael joined them a moment later, Nehima bare, the Charter marks on the blade glowing in the twilight.

The Dog sniffed the air again and cocked one ear. All three stood still. Listening. Waiting.

Even the hungry gulls had stopped calling. There was no sound, save their own breathing and the rush of the river under the jetty.

Off in the distance, the silence was suddenly broken by a long-drawn-out scream. Then, as if that were a signal for noise to begin, it was followed by muffled shouts and more screams.

At the same time, Lirael and Sam both felt several people die. Though it was far away, they flinched at the shock of the deaths and then again as it was quickly repeated. There was something else there, too, that they could sense. Some power over Death.

"A necromancer!" blurted Sam. He took a step back.

"The bells," said Lirael, and she looked down at the boat. Mogget was awake now, his green eyes gleaming in the dark. He was perched upon the bell-bandolier.

"They're coming this way," announced the Dog calmly.

The shouts and screams grew closer. But Lirael and Sam still couldn't see anything beyond the line of willows. Then, fifty yards downstream, a man burst out of the trees and fell into the water. He went under at once but bobbed to the surface some distance out. He swam for a few strokes, then turned on his back to float, too weary or too hurt to keep swimming.

Behind him, a burnt and blackened corpse shambled to the water's edge and let out a horrible, gobbling cry as it saw its prey escape. Repelled by the swift flow of the river, the Dead Hand staggered back into the trees.

"Come on," said Lirael, though she could barely get out the words. She drew her panpipes and marched off. The Dog followed her. Sam hesitated, staring out into the darkness.

More people screamed and shouted beyond the trees. No words were clear, but Sam knew they were desperately afraid, and the shouts were for help.

He looked back at the bells. Mogget met his gaze, unblinking. "What are you waiting for?" asked the cat. "My permission?"

Sam shook his head. He felt paralyzed, unable to reach for the bells or to follow Lirael. She and the Dog were almost at the end of the jetty. He could sense the Dead nearby, less than a hundred yards away, and the necromancer with them.

He had to do something. He had to act. He had to prove to himself he wasn't a coward.

"I don't need the bells!" he shouted, and he ran down the jetty, his boots echoing on the wooden planks. He burst past the surprised Lirael and the Dog, and sprinted through the gap where the willows had been pruned back.

He was past the trees in an instant and out in a twilit pad-
dock. A Dead Hand rushed at him. He cut its legs away and
kicked it over, all in one fluid motion. Before it could rise, he
jumped over it and ran on.

The necromancer. He had to kill the necromancer, before
he could drag him into Death. He had to kill him as quickly as
he could.

A hot rage rose in him, banishing the fear. Sam growled
and ran on.

Lirael and the Dog emerged from the willows to see Sam
charge. The Dead Hand he'd cut down scrabbled towards them,
but Lirael had the panpipes ready at her lips. She chose Saraneth
and blew a strong, pure note, its commanding tones stopping
the Hand in its tracks. Without a pause, Lirael changed to
Kibeth, and a trill of dancing notes sent the corpse somersault-
ing backwards even as the Spirit inhabiting it was forced to walk
back into Death.

"It's gone," said the Dog, loping forward. Lirael ran, too,
but not with Sam's reckless abandon.

It was still light enough to see that thirty or forty Dead
Hands had surrounded a group of men, women, and children.
Obviously, they'd tried to reach the safety of the river, only to
fail at the very last. Now they had formed a ring with the children at the center, a last desperate defense.

Lirael could sense the Dead Hands . . . and something else,
something strange and much more powerful. It was only when
she saw Sam charge past the Hands and scream a challenge that
she realized that it had to be the necromancer.

The people were screaming, too, and shouting, and crying.
The Dead roared and screeched back, as they pulled their victims

down and ripped their throats out or rent them limb from limb. Makeshift clubs and sharpened branches struck at the Dead, but their wielders did not know how to use them to best effect, and they were heavily outnumbered.

Lirael looked across and saw the necromancer turn to face Sam. He raised his hands, and the hot metal smell of Free Magic suddenly filled the air. A moment later, a blinding, blue white spark exploded out, leaping across to strike the charging boy.

At the same time, the Dead Hands howled in triumph as they burst through the ranks of struggling men and women and into the inner circle of children.

Lirael turned her easy run into an all-out sprint. Whoever she tried to help, it looked like she would be too late.

Sam saw the necromancer raise his hands and saw the bronze of his face. Even as he threw himself to the side, his mind raced. A bronze face! Then this wasn't Hedge, but Chlorr of the Mask, the creature his mother had fought years ago!

The bolt sizzled past him, missing him by a few inches. Heat from its passage struck him, and the grass behind him burst into flame.

Sam slowed down as he reached into the Charter and pulled out four marks. He drew them with his free hand, fingers flashing too quickly to follow. A triangular silver blade suddenly materialized in his grip. Before it was even fully formed, Sam threw it.

The blade spun as it shot through the air. Chlorr easily ducked it, but the spinning blade turned a few paces beyond her and came shooting back.

Sam rushed forward as the blade struck the necromancer in the arm. He expected it to almost sever that limb, but there were only a burst of golden flame, a gout of white sparks, and a smoldering sleeve.

"Fool," said Chlorr, raising her sword. Her voice crawled

across his skin like a thousand tiny insects. Her breath stank of death and Free Magic. "You have no bells."

In that instant, Sam realized that Chlorr didn't have any bells, either. Nor were there any human eyes behind the mask. Pools of fire burnt there, and white smoke puffed from the mouth-hole.

Chlorr was no longer a necromancer. She was one of the Greater Dead. Sabriel *had* finished her as a living being.

But someone had brought her back.

"Run!" shouted Lirael. "Run!"

She stood between the last four survivors and those Dead Hands who had resisted the panpipes. Lirael had blown on Saraneth till her face was blue, but there had just been too many of them for her to deal with, the power of the pipes too slight. The Dead who were left didn't seem affected at all.

Worse still, the children wouldn't run. They were too shocked, incapable of doing anything, let alone understand what Lirael was shouting at them.

A Dead Hand lunged, and Lirael thrust at it. The Dog leapt at another, knocking it down. But a third, a low, loping thing with elongated jaws, got past them. It rushed at a small boy who could not stop screaming. The jaws closed, and the scream was instantly cut off.

Sobbing with fury and revulsion, Lirael spun around and hewed off the thing's head, Nehima showering silver sparks as it cut through. But even then the Dead Hand functioned, the spirit inside indifferent to any physical harm. She cut at it again and again, but Dead fingers still clutched its victim, and the head still gnashed its teeth.

Sam parried another blow from the thing that had once been Chlorr. Her strength was incredible, and once again he nearly lost his sword. His hand and wrist were numb, and the Charter marks he'd spelled so laboriously into the blade were slowly being destroyed by Chlorr's power. When they were gone, the blade would shatter—

He staggered back and glanced quickly around the field. He could just make out Lirael and the Dog, fighting with at least a half dozen Dead Hands. He'd heard the pipes before, the voices of Saraneth and Kibeth, though strangely different from the bells he knew. They had sent most of the spirits animating the Hands back into Death, but had had no effect upon Chlorr.

Chlorr struck again, hissing. Sam dodged. Desperately, he tried to think of what he could do. There had to be some spell, something that would at least hold her back long enough for him to get away. . . .

Lirael and the Dog struck together, smashing the last Dead Hand to the ground. Before it could get up, the Dog barked in its face. Instantly, it went limp, no more than a ghastly, misshapen corpse, the spirit banished.

"Thanks," gasped Lirael. She looked around her, at the grotesque forms of Dead Hands and the pathetic bodies of their victims. Desperately, she hoped to see even just one of the children. But there was no one standing except her and the Dog. There were bodies everywhere, sprawled on the blood-soaked ground. The cast-off remnants of the Dead Hands piled up with the slaughtered people.

Lirael closed her eyes, her sense of Death almost overpowering her. That sense confirmed what her eyes had already told her.

No one had survived.

She felt sick, the gorge rising in her throat. But as she bent forward to throw up, she suddenly heard Sam shouting.

She straightened up, opened her eyes, and looked around. She couldn't see Sam, but off in the distance there was a blaze of golden fire, interspersed with huge showers of white sparks. It might have been a fireworks display, but Lirael knew better.

Even so, it took her a few seconds to work out what Sam was shouting.

When it finally percolated into her stunned, shocked mind, all thought of throwing up disappeared. She jumped over the bodies of the Dead Hands and their victims and started to run.

Sam was shouting, "Help! Lirael! Dog! Mogget! Anyone! Help!"

Sam's sword had broken on the last exchange of blows. It had snapped off near the hilt, leaving him with a useless dead weight, devoid of magic.

Chlorr laughed. A laugh strange and distant behind her mask, as if it echoed from inside some far-off hall.

She had grown taller as she had stalked after Sam, visibly a thing of darkness under the rotting, splitting furs. Now she stood head and shoulders above him, white smoke drifting from her mouth as she raised her sword again. Red fire flowed along the blade, and flaming drops fell to the grass.

Sam threw the hilt at her face and jumped back, shouting, "Help! Lirael! Dog!"

The sword came down. Chlorr leapt forward as well, faster and farther than Sam had expected. The blade whisked past his nose. Shocked, he shouted again, "Mogget! Anyone! Help!"

Lirael saw the necromancer's sword of red fire come blazing down. Sam fell under the blow, and the red fire obscured Lirael's vision.

"Sam!" she screamed.

As she screamed, the Disreputable Dog sprang ahead, leaping in great bounds towards Sam and the necromancer.

For a panicked second, Lirael thought Sam had been killed. Then she saw him roll aside, untouched. The necromancer raised her sword again, and Lirael burst her lungs trying to get there in time to do something. But she could not. She was still forty or fifty yards away, and her mind was empty of all the spells that might have crossed the distance and distracted the enemy.

"Die!" whispered Chlorr, raising her sword two-handed above her head, the blade pointing straight down. Sam looked up at it and knew he could not get out of the way in time. She was too fast, too strong. He half raised his hand and tried to speak a Charter mark, but the only one that came to mind was something useless, some mark used in making his toys.

The blade came down.

Sam screamed.

The Disreputable Dog barked.

There was Charter Magic in the bark. It hit Chlorr as she struck. Her arms flashed gold and sizzled, white smoke gouting out of a thousand tiny holes. The blow that should have impaled Sam went awry, the sword sinking deep into the earth, so close that his hip was burnt by the flame.

All Chlorr's unnatural strength had gone into the blow. Now she struggled to free the weapon as the Dog advanced upon her, growling. The hound had grown and was now the size of a desert lion, with teeth and claws to match. Her collar shone with golden fire, the Charter marks shifting and joining in a wild dance.

The Dead creature let the sword go and backed away. Sam struggled to his feet as Chlorr drew back. He clenched his fists as he tried to calm himself, in preparation for casting a spell.

Lirael arrived a second later, completely out of breath. Gasping, she slowed to a walk and moved up behind the Dog.

Chlorr raised one shadowy fist, her fingernails elongating into thin blades of darkness. White smoke still eddied around her, but the holes in her arm had already closed.

She took one step forward, and the Dog barked again.

There was Free Magic power in this bark, reinforced with Charter-spells. Her collar shone even brighter, and Sam and Lirael had to half-close their eyes.

Chlorr flinched and raised her hands to shield her face. More white smoke poured out from behind her mask, and her body changed shape under the furs. She began to collapse in on herself, her clothes crumpling as the shadowflesh within leaked away.

"Curse you!" she shrieked.

The furs fell to the ground, and the bronze mask bounced on top of them. A shadow as dark and thick as ink flowed away from the Dog and Lirael, moving faster than any liquid ever spilled.

Lirael started to follow, but the Dog blocked her way.

"No," said the Dog. "Let it go. I have only forced it out of its shape. It is too powerful for me to send back into Death alone, or destroy."

"It was Chlorr," said Sam, white-faced and shivering. "Chlorr of the Mask. A necromancer my mother fought years ago."

"It is one of the Greater Dead now," said Mogget. "Back from beyond the Seventh or Eighth Gate."

Sam jumped several feet into the air. When he looked down, Mogget was sitting quite calmly near Chlorr's sword, as if he'd been there all the time.

"Where were you?" Sam asked.

"I've been looking around while you took care of things here," explained Mogget. "Chlorr has fled but will return. There are more Dead Hands less than two leagues to the west. A hundred of them at least, with Shadow Hands to lead them."

"A hundred!" exclaimed Sam as Lirael said, "Shadow Hands!"

"We'd better get back to the boat," said Sam. He looked at Chlorr's sword, quivering in the earth. No flames ran down it now, but the steel was as dark as ebony and etched with strange runes that wriggled and convulsed and made him feel nauseated.

"We should destroy this," he said. His head felt strangely fuzzy, and he found it difficult to think. "But . . . but I don't know how to do it quickly."

"What about all these people?" asked Lirael. She couldn't call them bodies. She still couldn't believe they were all dead. It had happened so quickly, in just a few frenzied minutes.

Sam looked across the field. There were more stars out now, and a slim crescent of a moon had risen. In the cool light he saw that many of the slain people wore blue hats or scarves. A scrap of blue material was caught in the claws of one of the Dead that Lirael had banished with her pipes.

"They're Southerlings," he said, surprised.

He walked over for a closer look at the nearest body, a fair-haired boy who couldn't have been more than sixteen. Sam's eyes showed more puzzlement than fear, as if he couldn't believe what was happening. "Southerling refugees. I guess they were trying to escape."

"Escape from what?" asked Lirael.

Before anyone could answer, a Dead creature howled in the distance. A moment later the howl was taken up by many desiccated, decaying throats.

"Chlorr has reached the Hands," said Mogget urgently. "We must leave now!"

The cat hurried away. Sam started to follow, but Lirael grabbed him by the arm.

"We can't just leave!" protested Lirael. "If we leave them, their bodies will get used—"

"We can't stay!" protested Sam. "You heard Mogget. There are too many to fight, and Chlorr will come back, too!"

"We have to do something!" Lirael said. She looked at the Dog. Surely the Dog would help her! They had to perform the cleansing rite on the bodies or bind them so they couldn't be used to house spirits brought from Death.

But the Dog shook her head. "There's no time," she said sadly.

"Sam can get the bells!" protested Lirael. "We have to—"

The hound nudged Lirael behind the knee, pushing her on. The girl stumbled forward, tears welling up in her eyes. Sam and Mogget were already well ahead, hurrying towards the willows.

"Hurry!" said the Dog anxiously, after a glance over her shoulder. She could hear the clicking of many bones and smell decaying flesh. The Dead were closing fast.

Lirael wept as she broke into a shambling jog. If only she could run faster, or knew how to use the panpipes better. She might have been able to save even one of the refugees.

One of the refugees. One *had* got away from the Dead.

"The man!" she exclaimed, breaking into a run. "The man in the river! We have to rescue him!"

Chapter Forty-Three

FAREWELL TO *FINDER*

EVEN WITH THE Dog's highly developed sense of smell and Mogget's unrivaled night vision, it took almost an hour to find the Southerling who'd managed to reach the river.

He was still floating on his back, but his face was barely above the surface, and he didn't seem to be breathing. But as Sam and Lirael pulled him in closer to the boat, he opened his eyes and groaned with pain.

"No, no," he whispered. "No."

"Hold him," whispered Lirael to Sam. She quickly reached into the Charter, drawing out several marks of healing. She spoke their names and cupped them in her hand. They glowed there, warm and comforting, as she sought any obvious wounds to place them for best effect. Once the spell was active, they could pull him out of the water.

There was a huge dark stain of dried blood on the man's neck. But when she moved her hand to it, he cried out and tried to escape from Sam's grasp.

"No! The evil!"

Lirael pulled her hand back, puzzled. It was obviously Charter Magic she was about to cast. The golden light was clear and bright, and there was no stench of Free Magic.

"He's a Southerling," whispered Sam. "They don't believe in magic, even the superstitions the Ancelstierrans believe in, let alone our magic. It must have been terrible for them when they crossed the Wall."

"Land across the Wall," sobbed the man. "He promised us land again. Farms to build, a place of our own . . ."

Lirael tried again to place the spell, but the man shrieked and fought against Sam's hold. The waves he made ducked his head under several times, till Lirael had to take her hand away and let the spell go, away into the night.

"He's dying," said Sam. He could feel the man's life ebbing away, feel the cold touch of Death reaching out to him.

"What can we do?" asked Lirael. "What—"

"All dead," said the man, coughing. Blood came out with the river-water, bright in the moonlight. "At the pit. They were dead, but still they did his bidding. Then the poison . . . I told Hral and Mortin not to drink . . . four families—"

"It's all right," said Sam soothingly, though his voice was nearly breaking. "They . . . they got away."

"We ran, and the Dead followed," whispered the Southerling. His eyes were bright, but they saw something other than Sam and Lirael. "Night and day we ran. They dislike the sun. Torbel hurt his ankle, and I couldn't . . . couldn't carry him."

Lirael reached across and stroked the man's head. He flinched at first, but relaxed as he saw no strange light in her hands.

"The farmer said the river," continued the dying man. "The river."

"You made it," said Sam. "This is the river. The Dead cannot cross running water."

"Ahh," sighed the man, and then he was gone, slipping away to that other river, the one that would carry him to the Ninth Gate and beyond.

Sam slowly let go. Lirael raised her hand. The water closed over the man's face, and *Finder* steered away.

"We couldn't save even one," whispered Lirael. "Not even *one*."

Sam didn't answer. He sat staring past her, out at the moon-lit river.

"Come here, Lirael," said the Dog gently, from her post at the bow. "Help me keep watch."

Lirael nodded, her lower lip trembling as she tried to keep herself from sobbing. She clambered over the thwarts and threw herself down next to the Dog, and hugged her as hard as she could. The Dog bore this without a word, and said nothing about the tears that spilled off onto her coat.

Eventually, Lirael's grip loosened, and she slid down. Sleep had claimed her, the kind of sleep that comes only after all strength is exhausted and battles won or lost.

The Dog shifted a little to make Lirael more comfortable and twisted her head to look behind her in a way no normal dog could twist. Sam was asleep, too, curled up in the stern, the tiller moving slightly above his head.

Mogget seemed to be asleep, at his customary post near the mast. But he opened one bright green eye as the Dog looked back.

"I saw it, too," said Mogget. "On the Greater Dead, that Chlorr."

"Yes," said the Dog, her voice troubled. "I trust you will have no trouble remembering where your loyalties lie?"

Mogget didn't answer. He slowly closed his eye, and a small and secret smile spread across his mouth.

All through the night, the Disreputable Dog sat at the bow, while Lirael tossed and turned beside her. They passed Qyrre in the early, silent hours of the morning, merely a white sail in the distance. Though it had been her original destination, *Finder* did not try to put in to the dock.

Lirael experienced a mild attack of panic when she awoke to the sound of a waterfall ahead. At this distance, it sounded like the buzz of many insects, and it took her a moment to figure out what it was. Once she did, she had a few anxious moments till she realized that *Finder* was traveling quite slowly compared to the tree branches, leaves, and other flotsam racing past on either side of them.

"We're in the channel, approaching Abhorsen's House," explained the Dog, as Lirael rubbed the sleep out of her eyes and stretched, in a futile effort to relieve her aches and kinks.

All the deaths of the night before seemed long ago. But not at all like a dream. Lirael knew that the face of the last Southerling, his look of relief as he finally knew he had escaped the Dead, would stay with her forever.

As she stretched, she looked at the huge mass of spray thrown up by the Ratterlin's fall over the Long Cliffs ahead. The river seemed to disappear into a great cloud that smothered the cliffs and the land beyond in a giant, undulating quilt of white. Then, just for a moment, the mist parted, and she saw a bright tower, its red-tiled, conical roof catching the sun. It looked like a mirage, shimmering in the cloud, but Lirael knew that she had come to Abhorsen's House at last.

As they drew closer, Lirael saw more red-tiled roofs emerge from the cloud, hinting at other buildings grouped around the tower. But she couldn't see more, because the whole island the House was built on was surrounded by a whitewashed stone wall that was at least forty feet high. Only the red tiles and some treetops were visible.

She heard Sam come forward from the stern, and he was soon next to her, looking ahead. By unspoken consent, they didn't talk about what had happened, though the silence was heavy between them.

Finally, desperate to say something, Sam took on the role of a tour guide.

"It doesn't look it, but the island is larger than a football field. Um, that's a game I used to play at school, in Ancelstierre. Anyway, the island is about three hundred yards long and a hundred yards wide. There's a garden and an orchard as well as the House itself—you can just see the blossoms on the peach trees, over on the right. Too early for fruit, though, unfortunately. The peaches here are fantastic, Charter knows why. The House isn't much compared to the Palace in size, but it is bigger than it looks, and there's a lot packed into it. Quite a bit different from your Glacier, I guess."

"I like it already," said Lirael, smiling, still looking ahead. There was the faint hint of a rainbow in the cloud, arching over the white walls, framing the House with a border of many colors.

"Just as well," muttered Mogget, as he appeared suddenly at Lirael's elbow. "Though you should be warned about the cooking."

"Cooking?" asked the Dog, licking her lips. "What's wrong with it?"

"Nothing," said Sam sternly. "The sendings are very good cooks."

"Do you have sendings for servants?" asked Lirael, who was curious about the difference between the Abhorsen's life and the Clayr's. "We do most of the work ourselves at the Glacier. Everyone has to take turns, especially with the cooking, though there are some people who specialize."

"No one apart from the family ever comes here," replied Sam. "I mean the extended family—those of the Blood, like the

Clayr. And no one has to do anything, really, because there are so many sendings, all eager to help. I think they get bored when the place is empty. Every Abhorsen makes a few sendings, so they kind of multiply. Some are hundreds of years old."

"Thousands," said Mogget. "And senile, most of them."

"Where do we land?" asked Lirael, ignoring Mogget's mutterings. She couldn't see any gate or landing spot in the northern wall.

"On the western side," said Sam, raising his voice to counter the increasing roar of the falls. "We skirt around the island, almost to the waterfall. There's a landing stage there for the House, and the stepping-stones across to the western tunnel. Look, you can see where the tunnel entrance is, up on the bank."

He pointed at a narrow ledge halfway up the western riverbank, a grey stone outcrop almost as high as the House. If there was a tunnel entrance there, Lirael couldn't see it through the mist, and it seemed perilously close to the waterfall.

"You mean there are stepping-stones across that?" exclaimed Lirael, pointing to the edges where the waters rushed over in a torrent that was at least two hundred yards wide, extremely deep and going at a speed Lirael couldn't even guess at. Worse than that, Sam had told her that the waterfall was more than a thousand feet high. If they were somehow drawn out of the channel, *Finder* would go over in seconds, and it was a very long way to fall.

"On both sides," shouted Sam. "They go to the riverbanks, and then there are tunnels that lead down to the bottom of the cliffs. Or you can keep going over the banks and stay on the plateau, if you want."

Lirael nodded and gulped, looking at the point where the stepping-stones must cross from the House to the western shore. She couldn't even see them under all the spray and the churning of the water. She hoped she wouldn't need to, and remembered the Charter-skin that was now safely rolled up in the bag that held *The Book of Remembrance and Forgetting*, ready to be put on. She could just fly across in the shape of a barking owl, screeching all the way.

A few minutes later, *Finder* was next to the whitewashed walls. Lirael looked up at them, drawing an imaginary line from the boat's mast to the top of the walls. Somehow, the walls looked even higher close up, and they had curious marks that even fresh whitewash couldn't conceal. The sort of stains left by a flood that had reached almost to the top.

Then they were at the wooden landing stage. *Finder* gently bumped against the heavy canvas fenders that hung there, but any sound from the bump was totally lost in the stomach-vibrating crash of the waterfall. Sam and Lirael quickly unloaded everything, gesturing to make themselves understood. The waterfall was too loud for them to hear even a shout, unless—as Sam demonstrated to Lirael—he was right against her ear, and then it hurt.

When everything was piled up on the landing stage, with Mogget perched on Lirael's pack and the Dog happily catching spray in her mouth, Lirael kissed *Finder*'s figurehead on the cheek and pushed the boat off the jetty. She thought she saw the carved face of the woman wink, and her lips curve up in a smile.

"Thank you," she mouthed, while Sam bowed at her side, showing his respect. *Finder* flapped her sail in answer, then swung about and began to move upstream. Sam, watching carefully, noted that the current in the channel had reversed and was moving north, against the flow of the river. Once again, he wondered how it was done and tried to think of how he could get to look at the Charter Stones that were sunk deep in the riverbed below. Perhaps Lirael would teach him how to make an ice-otter Charter-skin—

A touch at his arm broke his reverie, and he turned to pick up his saddlebags and sword. Then he led the way to the gate and pushed it open. As soon as they passed through, the noise of the waterfall practically ceased, so Lirael had to listen carefully to hear even a distant roar. She could hear birds in the trees instead, and many bees buzzing past on their way to the peach blossoms. The mist also parted above and around Abhorsen's House, for Lirael stood in sunshine, which quickly dried the spray that had fallen on her face and clothes.

There was a red-brick path ahead, bordered by a lawn and a line of shrubs with clumps of odd, stick-shaped yellow flowers. The path led to the front door of the House, which was painted a cheerful sky blue, bright against the whitewashed stone on either side of it. The House itself seemed normal enough. It was mainly one large building of three or four stories, in addition to the tower. It also had some sort of inner courtyard, too, because Lirael could see birds flying in and out. There were many windows, all quite large, and it exuded comfort and welcome. Clearly Abhorsen's House was not a fortification, relying on means other than architecture for its defense.

Lirael raised her arms to the sun and drank in the clear air, and the faint perfume from the gardens, of flowers and fertile soil and green growing things. She suddenly felt peaceful, and strangely at home, though it was so different from the enclosed tunnels and chambers of the Glacier. Even the gardens in the vast chambers there, with their painted ceilings and Charter-mark suns, could not begin to duplicate the vastness of the blue sky and the true sun.

She exhaled slowly and was about to drop her arms when she saw a small speck high above her. A moment later it was

joined by a dark cloud of many somewhat larger things. It took
Lirael a few seconds to realize that the smaller speck was a bird
that seemed to be diving straight at her, and the larger specks
were also birds—or things that flew like birds. At the same time
her Death sense twinged, and Sam cried out next to her.

"Gore Crows! They're after a message-hawk!"

"They're actually below it," said the Dog, her head craned
back. "It's trying to dive through!"

They watched anxiously as the message-hawk fell, zigzag-
ging slightly to try to avoid the Gore Crows. But there were
hundreds of them, and they spread across a wide area, so the
hawk had no choice but to try to smash through where they
were fewest. It selected its point and closed its wings, dropping
even faster, as if it were a stone thrown straight down.

"If it makes it through, they won't dare pursue," said Sam.
"Too close to the river, and the House."

"Go!" whispered Lirael, staring up at the hawk, willing it to
go even faster. It seemed to fall for ages, and she realized it must
have been very high indeed. Then all of a sudden it hit the black
cloud, and there was an explosion of feathers and Gore Crows
hurtling in all directions, while still more flew in. Lirael held her
breath. The hawk didn't re-appear. Still the Gore Crows flew
in, till there were so many in a small area that they began to
collide, and black, broken bodies began to fall.

"They got it," said Sam slowly. Then he shouted. A small
brown bird suddenly dropped out of the swirling mass of Gore
Crows. This time it fell seemingly out of control, lacking the
fierce direction and purpose they'd seen before. A few Gore
Crows broke off to pursue it, but they had gone only a little way
before they pulled up and sheered off, repelled by the force of
the river and the protective magics of the House.

The hawk fell further, as if it were dead or stunned. But

only forty or fifty feet above the garden, it suddenly spread its wings, breaking its fall just enough to swoop in and land at Lirael's feet. It lay there, feathered breast panting, and the marks of the Gore Crows' attacks obvious in its tattered plumage and bleeding head. But its yellow eyes were still lively, and it hopped easily enough onto Sam's wrist when he bent down and offered it a place on the cuff of his shirt.

"Message for Prince Sameth," it said, in a voice that was not any bird's. "Message."

"Yes, yes," said Sam soothingly, gently stroking its feathers back into place. "I am Prince Sameth. Tell me."

The bird cocked its head to one side and opened its beak. Lirael saw the hint of Charter marks there, and she suddenly understood that the bird carried a spell inside it, a spell that was probably cast upon it while it was still in its egg, to grow as it grew.

"Sameth, you idiot, I hope this finds you at the House," said the message-hawk, its voice changing again. Now it seemed to be a woman. From the tone of voice and the expression on Sam's face, Lirael guessed that it was his sister, Ellimere.

"Father and Mother are still in Ancelstierre. There is greater trouble there than they feared. Corolini is definitely under the influence of someone from the Old Kingdom, and his Our Country Party grows more influential in the Moot. More and more refugees are being moved nearer the Wall. There are also reports of Dead creatures all along the Ratterlin's western shores. I am calling up the Trained Bands and will be marching south to Barhedrin with them and the Guard within two weeks, to try to prevent any crossings. I don't know where you are, but Father says it is essential that you find Nicholas Sayre and return him to Ancelstierre at once, as Corolini claims we have kidnapped him to use as a hostage to influence the Chief

Minister. Mother sends her love. I hope you can do something really useful for a change—"

The voice suddenly stopped, having reached the limit of the message-hawk's rather tiny mind. The bird made a peeping sound and started to preen itself.

"Well, let's go in and get cleaned up," said Sam slowly, though he kept staring at the hawk as if it might speak again. "The sendings will look after you, Lirael. I guess we should talk about everything at dinner tonight?"

"Dinner!" exclaimed Lirael. "We'd better talk about it before then. It sounds like we should be off again straight-away."

"But we only just got here—"

"Yes," agreed Lirael. "But there're the Southerlings, and your friend Nicholas is in danger. It may be that every hour counts."

"Particularly since whoever controls Chlorr and the other Dead knows we're here," growled the Dog. "We must move quickly before we are besieged."

Sam didn't answer for a moment. "Okay," he said quickly. "I'll meet you for lunch in an hour, and we can . . . uh . . . work out what to do next."

He stalked off ahead, his limp suddenly becoming notice-ably worse, and pushed the front door open. Lirael followed more slowly, her hand loosely draped over the Dog's back. Mogget walked next to them for a few paces, then used the Dog's back to springboard himself onto Lirael's shoulder. She jumped as he landed, but relaxed as she realized he had sheathed his claws. The little cat carefully draped himself around her neck and then seemed to go to sleep.

"I'm so tired," Lirael said as they stepped over the thresh-old. "But we really can't wait, can we?"

"No," growled the Dog as she looked around the entrance

hall, sniffing. There was no sign of Sam, but a sending was retreating with the message-hawk on its gloved hand, and two other sendings were waiting at the foot of the main staircase. They wore long habits of light cream, with deep cowls covering their heads, hiding their lack of faces. Only their hands were visible, pale ghostly hands made of Charter marks, which occasionally sparkled as they moved.

One came forward and bowed deeply to Lirael, then beckoned to her to follow. The other went straight to the Disreputable Dog and took her by the collar. No words were spoken, but both the Dog and Mogget seemed to guess the sending's intentions. Mogget, despite appearing to be asleep, was the first to react. He leapt from Lirael's neck and ran through a cat door under the stairs, displaying a speed and liveliness Lirael hadn't seen before. The Dog was either less quick on the uptake or was less practiced in evading the attentions of the sendings of Abhorsen's House.

"A bath!" she yelped in indignation. "I'm not having a bath! I swam in the river only yesterday. I don't need a bath!"

"Yes you do," said Lirael, wrinkling her nose. She looked at the sending and added, "Please make sure she has one. With soap. And scrubbing."

"Can I at least have a bone afterwards?" asked the downcast Dog, looking back with pleading eyes as the sending led her away. Anyone would think she was going to prison, or worse, Lirael thought. But she couldn't help herself running over to kiss the hound on the nose.

"Of course you can have a bone, and a big lunch as well. I'm going to have a bath, too."

"It's different for dogs," said the Dog mournfully, as the sending opened a door to the inside courtyard. "We just don't like baths!"

"I do, though," whispered Lirael, looking down at her

sweat-stained clothing and running her fingers through her dirty hair. For the first time she noticed that there was blood on her as well. The blood of innocents. "A bath and clean clothes. That's what I need."

The sending bowed again and led her to the stairs. Lirael followed obediently, enjoying the different creaks in each step as they climbed. For the next hour, she thought, I will forget about everything.

But even as she followed the sending, she was thinking of the Southerlings who had tried so hard to escape. Escape the pit where their fellows had been killed and forced into servitude. The pit she had seen, with Nicholas standing alone on a hill of spoil, while a necromancer and his lightning-blackened corpses labored to dig up something that Lirael was sure should never again see the light of day.

Chapter Forty-Four

ABHORSEN'S HOUSE

WHEN LIRAEL CAME back downstairs, she was very clean indeed. The sending had proved to be a true believer in scrubbing and plenty of hot water—the latter supplied by hot springs, Lirael guessed, for the first few basins had been accompanied by a nasty sulphurous whiff, exactly as sometimes happened back in the Glacier.

The sending had put out rather fancy clothes for her, but Lirael had refused them. She put on her spare Librarian's outfit instead. She had worn the uniform for so long that she felt strange without it. At least in her red waistcoat she could feel something like a proper Clayr.

The sending was still trailing after her with a surcoat folded over its arm. It had been quite insistent that she try it on, and Lirael had been hard pressed to explain that waistcoats and surcoats simply didn't go together.

Another sending opened the double doors to the right of the stairs as she came down. The bronze knobs were turned by pale spell-hands, hands that stood out in stark relief against the dark oak as the sending pushed the door open. Then the sending moved aside and bowed its cowled head—and Lirael caught her first glimpse of the main hall. It took up at least half the ground floor, but it was not the size that immediately struck Lirael. She was seized with an intense feeling of déjà vu as she looked down the length of the hall to the great stained-glass window that showed the building of the Wall. And there was the long, brilliantly polished table laden with silver, and the high-backed chair.

Lirael had seen all of this before, in the Dark Mirror. Only then the chair had been occupied by the man who was her father.

"There you are," said Sam from behind her. "I'm sorry I'm late. I couldn't get the sendings to give me the right surcoat—they've dug up something odd. Must be getting senile, like Mogget said."

Lirael turned around and looked at his surcoat. It had the golden towers of the royal line, but they were quartered with a strange device she had never seen—some sort of trowel or spade, in silver.

"It's the Wallmakers' trowel," explained Sam. "But they've all been gone for centuries. A thousand years at least. . . . I say, I like your hair," he added as Lirael continued to stare at him. She wasn't wearing her headscarf. Her black hair was brushed and shining, and the waistcoat didn't really hide her slender form. She really was very attractive, but something about her now struck him as rather forbidding. Whom did she remind him of?

Sam pushed past the sending that was holding the door open, and was halfway to the table when he realized that Lirael hadn't moved. She was still standing in the doorway, staring at the table.

"What?" he asked.

Lirael couldn't speak. She beckoned to the sending that carried her surcoat. Lirael took it and unfolded it so she could see the blazon.

Then she folded the surcoat again, shut her eyes for a silent count of ten, unfolded it, and stared at it again.

"What is it?" asked Sam. "Are you all right?"

"I . . . I don't know how to say this," Lirael began, as she undid her waistcoat and handed it to the sending that appeared at her elbow. Sam started at her sudden undressing, but he was even more shocked when she put on her surcoat and slowly smoothed it out.

On the coat were the golden stars of the Clayr quartered with the silver keys of the Abhorsen.

"I must be half Abhorsen," said Lirael, in a tone that indicated she hardly believed it herself. "In fact, I think I'm your mother's half-sister. Your grandfather was my father. I mean, I'm your aunt. Half-aunt. Sorry."

Sam shut his eyes for several seconds. Then he opened them, trod like a sleepwalker over to a chair, and sat down. After a moment, Lirael sat down opposite him. Finally he spoke.

"My aunt? My mother's half-sister?" He paused. "Does she know?"

"I don't think so," muttered Lirael, suddenly anxious again. She hadn't really thought about the full ramifications of her birth. How would the famous Sabriel feel about the sudden appearance of a sister? "Surely not—or she would have found me long ago. I only worked it out myself by using the Dark Mirror. I wanted to see who my father was. I looked back and saw my parents in this very room. My father was sitting in that chair. They had only one night together, before he had to go away. I suppose that was the year he died."

"Can't have been," said Sam, shaking his head. "That was twenty years ago."

"Oh," said Lirael, blushing. "I lied. I'm only nineteen."

Sam looked at her as if any more revelations would turn his brain. "How did the sendings know to give you that surcoat?" he asked.

"I told them," said Mogget, his head popping up from a chair nearby. It was obvious that he'd been snoozing, because his fur was sticking up all on one side.

"How did you know?" asked Sam.

"I have served the Abhorsens for many centuries," said Mogget, preening. "So I tend to know what's what. Once I realized that Sam was not the Abhorsen-in-Waiting, I kept my eyes open for the real one to turn up, because the bells wouldn't have appeared unless her arrival was imminent. And I was here when Lirael's mother came to see Terciel—that is, the former Abhorsen. So it was rather elementary. Lirael was clearly both the former Abhorsen's daughter and the Abhorsen-in-Waiting the bells were meant for."

"You mean I'm not the Abhorsen-in-Waiting? She is?" asked Sam.

"But I can't be!" exclaimed Lirael. "I mean, I don't want to be. I'm a Clayr. I suppose I am a Remembrancer as well, but I am . . . I am a Daughter of the Clayr!"

She had shouted the last words, and they echoed through the hall.

"Complain all you like, but the Blood will out," said Mogget when the echoes faded. "You are the Abhorsen-in-Waiting, and you must take up the bells."

"Thank the Charter!" sighed Sam, and Lirael saw that there were tears in his eyes. "I mean, I was never going to be any good with them, anyway. You'll be a much better Abhorsen-in-Waiting, Lirael. Look at the way you went into Death with only those little pipes. And you fought Hedge and got away. All I managed to do was get burnt, and let him get to Nicholas."

"I am a Daughter of the Clayr," insisted Lirael, but her voice sounded weak even to her. She had wanted to know who her father was. But being the Abhorsen-in-Waiting, and one day—hopefully long distant—the Abhorsen, was a much more difficult thing to accept. Her life would be dedicated to hunting down and destroying or banishing the Dead. She would travel all over the Kingdom, instead of living the life of a Clayr within the confines of the Glacier.

"'Does the walker choose the path, or the path the walker?'" she whispered, as the final page from *The Book of the Dead* came shining into her mind. Then another thought struck her, and she went white.

"I'll never have the Sight, will I?" she said slowly. She was half Clayr, but it was the Abhorsen's blood that ran strongest in her veins. The gift she had longed for her entire life was finally and absolutely to be denied to her.

"No, you won't, Mistress," said the Dog calmly, as she came in behind Lirael and put her snout on Lirael's lap. "But it is your Clayr heritage that gives you the gift of Remembrance, for only a child of Abhorsen and Clayr can look into the past. You must grow in your own powers—for yourself, for the Kingdom, and for the Charter."

"I will never have the Sight," Lirael whispered again, very slowly. "I will never have the Sight. . . ." She clasped her arms around the neck of the strangely clean Dog, not even noticing that the hound smelled sweetly of soap, for the first and probably last time. But she did not cry. Her eyes were dry. She just felt very cold, unable to warm herself with the Dog's comforting heat.

Sam watched her shiver but did not shift from his chair. He felt as if he should go over and comfort her somehow, but didn't quite know how. It wasn't as if she were a young woman or a girl. She was an aunt, and he didn't know how to behave. Would she be offended if he tried to hug her?

"Is it . . . is the Sight really that important to you?" he asked hesitantly. "You see," he continued, twisting his linen napkin, "I feel . . . I feel amazingly relieved that I don't have to be the Abhorsen-in-Waiting. I never wanted the sense of Death, or to go into Death or any of it. And when I did, that time, when the necromancer . . . when he caught me . . . I wanted to die, because then it would be over. But I somehow got out, and I knew that I couldn't ever go into Death again. It was just everyone else expecting me to follow in Mother's footsteps, because Ellimere was so obviously going to be the Queen. I thought maybe it was the same for you. You know, all the other Clayr have the Sight, so that's the only thing that matters, even if you don't want it. It would be the only way to meet their expectations, like me being the Abhorsen-in-Waiting. Only I didn't want to be what they wanted, and you did. . . . I'm babbling, aren't I? Sorry."

"More than a hundred words in a row," remarked Mogget. "And most of them made sense. There is hope for you yet, Prince Sameth. Particularly since you are quite right. Lirael is so obviously an Abhorsen that wanting the Sight must be solely a peculiarity of her upbringing in that ridiculously cold mountain of theirs."

"I wanted to belong," said Lirael quietly, sitting up. It was only the shock of losing a childhood dream, she told herself. In a way, she'd known ever since she had been blindfolded before being allowed into the Observatory, or perhaps since Sanar and Ryelle had waved her farewell. She had known that her life would change, that she would never have the Sight, never be truly one of the Clayr. At least she had something else now, she told herself, trying to still the terrible sense of loss. Much better to be the Abhorsen-in-Waiting than a Sightless Clayr, a freak. If only her head could make her heart believe that was true.

"You belong here," said Mogget simply, waving one white

and pink paw around the Hall. "I am the oldest servant of the Abhorsens, and I feel it in my very marrow. The sendings likewise. Look at the way they cluster there, just to see you. Look at the Charter lights that burn brighter above you than anywhere else. This whole House—and its servants—welcome you, Lirael. So will the Abhorsen, and the King, and even your niece, Ellimere."

Lirael looked around, and sure enough, there was a great throng of sendings clustered around the door to the kitchen, filling the room beyond. At least a hundred of them, some so old and faded that their hands were barely visible—just suggestions of light and shadow. As she looked, they all bowed. Lirael bowed in return, feeling the tears she had held back flow freely down her cheeks.

"Mogget is correct," woofled the Dog, her chin securely resting on Lirael's thigh. "Your Blood has made you what you are, but you should remember that it is not just the high office of Abhorsen-in-Waiting you have gained. It is a family you have found, and all will welcome you."

"Absolutely!" exclaimed Sam, jumping up with sudden excitement. "I can't wait to see Ellimere's face when she hears I've found our aunt! Mother will love it, too. I think she's always been a bit disappointed with me as Abhorsen-in-Waiting. And Dad doesn't have any living relatives, because he was imprisoned for so long as a figurehead down in Hole Hallow. It'll be great! We can have a welcoming party for you—"

"Aren't you forgetting something?" interrupted Mogget, with a very sarcastic meow. He continued, "There is the little matter of your friend Nicholas, and the Southerling refugees, and the necromancer Hedge, and whatever they're digging up near the Red Lake."

Sam stopped speaking as if he had been physically gagged,

and sat back down, all his enthusiasm erased by a few short words.

"Yes," said Lirael heavily. "That is what we should be concerning ourselves with. We have to work out what to do. That's more important than anything else."

"Except lunch, because no one can plan on an empty stomach," interrupted Mogget, loudly seconded by a hungry bark from the Dog.

"I suppose we do have to eat," agreed Sam, signaling to the sendings to begin serving the luncheon.

"Shouldn't we send the messages first, to your parents and Ellimere?" asked Lirael, though now that she could smell the tasty aromas coming from the kitchen, food did seem to be of prime importance.

"Yes, we should," agreed Sam. "Only I'm not sure exactly what to say."

"Everything we have to, I suppose," said Lirael. It was an effort to get her thoughts together. She kept looking down at the silver keys on her surcoat and feeling dizzy and sort of sick. "We need to make sure that Princess Ellimere and your parents know what we know, particularly that Hedge is digging up something best left buried, something of Free Magic, and that Nick is his captive, and Chlorr has been brought back as a Greater Dead spirit. And we should tell them that we're going to find and rescue Nick and stop whatever the Enemy plans to do."

"I suppose so," agreed Sam half-heartedly. He looked down at the plate the sending had just put in front of him, but his attention was clearly not on the poached salmon. "It's only . . . if I'm not the Abhorsen-in-Waiting, I'm not really going to be able to do much. I was thinking of staying here."

Silence greeted his words. Lirael stared at him, but he wouldn't meet her gaze. Mogget kept eating calmly, while the

Dog let out a soft growl that vibrated through Lirael's leg. Lirael looked at Sam, wondering what she could say. Even now she wished she could write a note, push it across the table, and go away to her room. But she was no longer a Second Assistant Librarian of the Great Library of the Clayr. Those days were gone, vanished with everything else that had defined her previous existence and identity. Even her librarian's waistcoat had been spirited away by the sendings.

She was the Abhorsen-in-Waiting. That was her job now, Lirael thought, and she must do it properly. She would not fail in the future, as she had failed the Southerlings on the banks of the Ratterlin.

"You can't, Sameth. It isn't just rescuing your friend Nicholas. Think about what Hedge is trying to do. He's planning to kill two hundred thousand people and unleash every spirit in Death upon the Kingdom! Whatever he's digging up must be part of that. I can't even begin to face it all alone, Sam. I need your help. The Kingdom needs your help. You may not be the Abhorsen-in-Waiting anymore, but you are still a Prince of the Kingdom. You cannot just sit here and do nothing."

"I'm . . . I'm afraid of Death," sobbed Sam, holding up his burnt wrists so Lirael could see the scars there, scarlet burns against the lighter skin. "I'm afraid of Hedge. I . . . I can't face him again."

"I'm afraid, too," Lirael said quietly. "Of Death and Hedge and probably a thousand other things. But I'd rather be afraid and do something than just sit and wait for terrible things to happen."

"Hear, hear," said the Dog, raising her head. "It's always better to be doing, Prince. Besides, you don't smell like a coward—so you can't be one."

"You didn't hide from the crossbowman at High Bridge," added Lirael. "Or the construct when it came across the water.

That was brave. And I'm sure that whatever we face won't be as bad as you think."

"It will probably be worse," said Mogget cheerfully. He seemed to be enjoying Sam's humiliation. "But think of how much worse it would be to sit here, not knowing. Until the Dead choke the Ratterlin and Hedge walks across the dry bed of the river to batter down the door."

Sam shook his head and muttered something about his parents. Obviously he didn't want to believe Mogget's predictions of doom and was still clutching at straws.

"The Enemy has set many pieces in motion," Mogget said. "The King and the Abhorsen seek to counter whatever brews in Ancelstierre. They must succeed in stopping the Southerlings from crossing the Wall, but surely that is only part of the Enemy's plans—and because it is the most obvious, perhaps the least of them."

Sam stared down at the table. All his hunger was gone. Finally he looked up. "Lirael," he said, "do you think I'm a coward?"

"No."

"Then I guess I'm not," said Sam, his voice growing stronger. "Though I am still afraid."

"So you'll come with me? To find Nicholas, and Hedge?"

Sam nodded. He didn't trust himself to speak.

Silence fell in the hall, as they all thought of what lay ahead. Everything had changed, transformed by history and fate and truth. Neither Sam nor Lirael were who they had been, only a little while before. Now they both wondered what all this meant, and where their new lives would lead them.

And where—and how soon—those new lives might end.

Epilogue

Dear Sam,

I am writing to you local-style, with a quill pen and some wretchedly thick paper that soaks up the ink like a sponge. My fountain pen has clogged irreparably, and the paper I brought with me has succumbed to some sort of rot. A fungus, I think.

Your Old Kingdom is certainly inimicable to the products of Ancelstierre. Clearly the level of moisture in the air and the proliferation of local fungi is as abrasive as conditions in the tropics, though I would not have expected it from the latitude.

I have had to cancel most of my planned experiments, due to problems with equipment and some quite alarming experimental errors on my part, invalidating the results. I put this down to the illness I have suffered from ever since I crossed the Wall. Some sort of fever that greatly weakens me and has encouraged hallucinatory episodes.

Hedge, the man I hired in Bain, has proved to be a great asset. Not only did he help me pinpoint the location of the Lightning Trap from all the local rumors and superstitious ramblings, but he has overseen the excavation with commendable zeal.

We had quite a lot of trouble hiring local workers

at first, till Hedge hit upon the idea of recruiting from
what I understand to be a lazaret or leper colony of
sorts. The workers from there are quite able-bodied
but shockingly disfigured, and they smell atrocious.
In daylight, they go about completely muffled in
cloaks and swaddling rags, and they seem much more
comfortable after dark. Hedge calls them the Night
Crew, and I must agree this is an appropriate name.
He assures me the disease is not readily contagious,
but I avoid all physical contact, to be on the safe side.
It is interesting that they share the same preference for
blue hats and scarves as the Southerlings.

   The Lightning Trap is as fascinating as I expected.
When we first found it, I observed lightning striking
a small hillock or mound more than twice every hour
for several hours, with thunderstorms overhead on an
almost daily basis. Now, as we get closer to the true
object that is buried underneath, the lightning comes
even more frequently, and there is a constant storm
overhead.

   From what I have read and—you will laugh at
me for this, because it is most uncharacteristic—from
what I have dreamt, I believe that the Lightning Trap
itself is composed of two hemispheres of a previously
unknown metal, buried some twenty or thirty
fathoms below the mound, which we found to be
completely artificial and very difficult to break into,
with all sorts of odd building materials. Including
bone, if you can believe it. Now the excavation goes
much faster, and I expect we shall make our discovery
within a few days.

   I had planned to go on to Belisaere at that point,

to meet you, leaving the experiment in abeyance for a few weeks. But the state of my health is such that a return to Ancelstierre seems prudent, away from this inclement air.

I will take the hemispheres with me, having procured suitable import licenses from Uncle Edward. I believe they are unusually dense and heavy, but I expect to be able to ship them from the Red Lake downriver to the sea, and from there to a little place north of Nolhaven on the west coast. There is a deserted timber mill there, which I have procured for use as an experimental station. Timothy Wallach— one of my fellow students at Sunbere, though he is in Fourth Year—should already be there, setting up the Lightning Farm I have designed to feed power into the hemispheres.

It is indeed pleasant to have private means and powerful relatives, isn't it? It would be very hard to get things done without them. Mind you, I expect my father will be quite cross when he discovers I have spent a whole quarter's allowance on hundreds of lightning rods and miles of extra-heavy copper wire!

But it will all be worth it when I get the Lightning Trap to my experimental station. I am sure that I will be quickly able to prove that the hemispheres can store incalculable amounts of electrical energy, all drawn from storms. Once I have solved the riddle of extracting that power again, I shall need only to replicate them on a smaller scale, and we shall have a new source of limitless, inexpensive power! Sayre's Super Batteries will power the cities and industries of the future!

As you can see, my dreams are as large as my seriously enlarged head. I need you to come and shrink it, Sam, with some criticism of my person or abilities!

In fact, I hope you will be able to come and see my Lightning Farm in all its glory. Do try, if it is at all possible, though I know you dislike crossing the Wall. I understand from my last conversation with Uncle Edward that your parents are already in Ancelstierre, discussing Corolini's plans to settle the Southerling refugees in your deserted lands near the Wall. Perhaps you could tie in a visit to them with a side trip to see my work?

In any case, I look forward to seeing you before too long, and I remain your loyal friend,

Nicholas Sayre

Nick put the pen down and blew on the paper. Not that it needed it, he thought, looking at the blurred lines where the ink had spread, making a mockery of his penmanship.

"Hedge!" he called, sitting back to quell a wave of dizziness and nausea. These fits often came over him now, especially after concentrating on something. His hair was falling out, too, and his gums were sore. But it couldn't be scurvy, for his diet was varied and he drank a glass of fresh lime juice every day.

He was about to call for Hedge again when the man appeared at the tent door. Barbarously clad, as usual, but the man was very efficient. As you would expect from a former sergeant in the Crossing Point Scouts.

"I have a letter to go to my friend Prince Sameth," said Nick, folding the paper several times and sealing it with a blob of wax straight from the candle and a thumbprint. "Can you see it gets sent by messenger or whatever they have here? Send someone to Edge, if necessary."

"Don't worry, Master," replied Hedge, smiling his enigmatic smile. "I'll see it's taken care of."

"Good," mumbled Nick. It was too hot again, and the lotion he'd brought to repel insects was not working. He'd have to ask Hedge again to do whatever it was he did to keep them at bay . . . but first there was the ever-present question—the status of the pit.

"How goes the digging?" Nick asked. "How deep?"

"Twenty-two fathoms by my measure," replied Hedge, with great enthusiasm. "We will soon be there."

"And the barge is ready?" asked Nick, forcing himself to keep upright. He really wanted to lie down, as the room started to spin and the light began to gain a strange redness that he knew was only in his own eyes.

"I need to recruit some sailors," said Hedge. "The Night Crew fear water, because of their . . . affliction. But I expect my new recruits to arrive any day. Everything is taken care of, Master," he added, as Nick didn't reply. But he was looking at the young man's chest, not at his eyes. Nick stared back at him, unseeing, his breath coming in ragged gasps. Somewhere deep inside, he knew that he was fainting, as he so often did in front of Hedge. A damnable weakness he could not control.

Hedge waited, licking his lips nervously. Nick's head swayed forward and back. He groaned, his eyelids flickering. Then he sat up, bolt straight in his chair.

Nick had indeed fainted, and there was something else behind his eyes, some other intelligence that had lain dormant. It suddenly sang now, accompanied by fumes of acrid white smoke that coiled out of Nick's nose and throat.

"I'll sing you a song of the long ago—
    Seven shine the shiners, oh!
What did the Seven do way back when?
    Why, they wove the Charter then!

Five for the warp, from beginning to end.
Two for the woof, to make and mend.
That's the Seven, but what of the Nine—
What of the two who chose not to shine?
The Eighth did hide, hide all away,
But the Seven caught him and made him pay.
The Ninth was strong and fought with might,
But lone Orannis was put out of the light,
Broken in two and buried under hill,
Forever to lie there, wishing us ill."

There was silence for a moment after the song, then the voice whispered the last two lines again.

"Broken in two and buried under hill, Forever to lie there, wishing us ill'. . . . *But it is not my song, Hedge. The world spins on without my song. Life that knows not my lash crawls unbidden wherever it will go. Creation runs amok, without the balance of destruction—and my dreams of fire are only dreams. But soon the world will fall asleep, and it will be my dream that all will dream, my song that will fill every ear. Is it not so, my faithful Hedge?"*

Whatever spoke did not wait for Hedge to answer. It went on immediately, in a different, harsher tone, no longer singing. "Destroy the letter. Send more Dead to Chlorr and make sure that they slay the Prince, for he must not come here. Walk in Death yourself, and keep watch for the spying Daughter of the Clayr, and kill her if she is seen again. Dig faster, for I . . . must . . . be . . . whole . . . again!"

The last words were shouted with a force that threw Hedge against the rotting canvas of the tent, to burst out into the night. He looked back through the rent, fearful of worse, but whatever had spoken through Nick was gone. Only an unconscious, sick young man remained, blood slowly trickling from both nostrils.

"I hear you, Lord," *whispered Hedge.* "And as always, I obey."

Turn the page for sneak peeks at

ABHORSEN,

ACROSS THE WALL,

and

CLARIEL

ABHORSEN

NICK WOKE TO THUNDER and lightning. As always in recent times, he was disoriented and dizzy. He could feel the ground moving unsteadily beneath him, and it took him a moment to realize that he was being carried on a stretcher. There were two men at each end, marching along with their burden. Normal men, or normal enough. Not the leprous pit workers Hedge called the Night Crew.

"Where are we?" he asked. His voice was hoarse, and he tasted blood. Hesitantly he touched his lips, and he felt the dried blood caked there. "I'd like a drink of water."

"Master!" shouted one of the men. "He's awake!"

Nick tried to sit up, but he didn't have the strength. All he could see above was thunderclouds and lightning, which was striking down somewhere ahead. The hemispheres! It all came back to him now. He had to make sure the hemispheres were safe!

"The hemispheres!" he shouted, pain spiking in his throat.

"They're safe," said a familiar voice. Hedge suddenly towered above him. He's got taller, Nick thought irrationally. Thinner, too. Sort of stretched out, like a toffee being fought over by two children. And he had seemed to be balding before, and now he had hair. Or was it shadow, curling across his forehead?

Nick shut his eyes. He couldn't think where he was or how he had got here. Obviously he was still sick, more seriously ill than before, or they wouldn't have to carry him.

"Where are we?" Nick asked weakly. He opened his eyes again, but he couldn't see Hedge, though the man answered from somewhere close by.

"We are about to cross the Wall," replied Hedge, and he

laughed. It was an unpleasant laugh. But Nick couldn't help laughing, too. He didn't know why, and he couldn't make himself stop till he choked and had to.

Beyond Hedge's laugh and the constant boom of thunder, there was another noise. Nick couldn't identify it at first. He kept listening as his stretcher bearers stolidly carried him forward, till at last he thought he knew what it was. The audience at a football game or a cricket match. Shouting and yelling at a win. Though the Wall would be an odd place to have a game. Perhaps the soldiers at the Perimeter played, he thought.

Five minutes later Nick could hear screaming in the crowd noise, and he knew it was no football game. He tried to sit up again, only to be pressed back down by a hand that he knew was Hedge's, though it was black and burnt-looking, and there were red flames where the fingernails should be.

Hallucinations, Nick thought desperately. Hallucinations.

"We must cross quickly," said Hedge, instructing the stretcher bearers. "The Dead can keep the passage for only a few more minutes. As soon as the hemispheres are through, we will run."

"Yes, sir," chorused the stretcher bearers.

Nick wondered what Hedge was talking about. They were passing between two lines of his strange, afflicted laborers now. Nick tried not to look at them, at the decaying flesh held together by torn blue rags. Fortunately, he couldn't see their ravaged faces. They were all facing away, like some sort of back-to-front honor guard, and they had linked their arms.

"The hemispheres are across the Wall!"

Nick didn't know who spoke. The voice was strange and echoing, and it made him feel unclean. But the words had an immediate effect. The stretcher bearers began to run, bouncing Nick up and down. He gripped the sides and, on the peak of one of the bounces, used its extra momentum to sit up and look around.

They were running into a tunnel through the Wall that separated the Old Kingdom and Ancelstierre. A low, arched tunnel cut through the stone. It was packed with the Night Crew from beginning to end, great lines of them with their arms linked and only a very narrow passage in between the lines. Every man and woman was glowing with golden light, but as Nick got closer, he saw that the glow was from thousands of tiny golden flames, which were spreading and joining, and the people farther inside the wall were actually on fire.

Nick cried out in horror as they entered the tunnel. There was fire everywhere, strange golden fire that burnt without smoke. Though the Night Crew were being consumed by it, they did not attempt to flee, or cry out, or do anything to stop it. Even worse than that, Nick realized that as individuals were consumed by the fire, others would step into their places. Hundreds and hundreds of blue-clad men and women were pouring in from the far side, to maintain the lines.

Hedge was struggling ahead, Nick saw. But it was not exactly Hedge. It was more a Hedge-shaped thing of darkness, limned with red fire that fought against the gold. Every step he took was clearly an effort, and the gold flames seemed almost a physical force that was trying to prevent his crossing through the tunnel in the Wall.

Suddenly a whole group of the Night Crew ahead blazed, like candles collapsing into a final pool of wax, and disappeared completely. Before the people on either side could relink arms or new Night Crew rush in, the golden fire took advantage of the gap and roared out all the way across the tunnel. The stretcher bearers saw it, and they swore and screamed, but they kept on running. They hit the fire like swimmers running from

the shore into surf, diving through it. But though the stretcher
and its bearers made it through, Nick was plucked off the
stretcher by the fire, wrapped in flame, and tumbled down onto
the stone floor of the tunnel.

With the golden fire came a piercing cold pain in his heart,
as if an icicle had been thrust through his chest. But it also
brought a sudden clarity to his mind, and sharper senses. He
could see individual symbols in the flames and the stones, symbols that moved and changed and formed in new combinations.
These were the Charter marks he'd heard about, Nick realized.
The magic of Sameth . . . and Lirael.

Everything that had happened recently rushed back into his
head. He remembered Lirael and the winged dog. The flight
from his tent. Hiding in the reeds. His conversation with Lirael.
He had promised her that he would do whatever he could to
stop Hedge.

The flames beat at Nick's chest but did not burn his skin.
They tried to attack what was in him, to force the shard from
his body. But it was a power beyond the magic of the Wall, and
that power chose to re-assert itself even as Nick tried to embrace
the Charter fire, grabbing at flames and even attempting to swal-
low flickers of golden light.

White sparks spewed out of Nick's mouth, nose, and ears,
and his body suddenly uncurled, went ramrod straight, and
flipped upright, elbows and knees vertically locked. Like some
inflexible doll, Nick tottered forward, the golden flames raging
at every step. Deep within his own mind he knew what was
happening, but he was only an observer. He had no power over
his own muscles. The shard had control, though it didn't know
how to make him walk properly.

Joints locked, Nick lumbered on, past countless ranks of
burning Night Crew, as more and more of them poured into

the tunnel from the far end. Many of them hardly looked like Night Crew at all but could almost be normal men and women, their skin and hair fresh and alive. Only their eyes proclaimed their difference, and somewhere deep inside, Nick knew that they were dead, not just sick. Like their more putrescent brethren, these new arrivals also wore blue caps or scarves.

Ahead of him Hedge burst out of the tunnel and turned back to gesture at Nick. He felt the gesture like a physical grasp, dragging him forward even faster. The golden fire reached out to him everywhere it could, but there were too many Night Crew, too many burning bodies. The fire could not reach Nicholas, and finally he staggered out of the tunnel, away from the golden flames.

He had crossed the Wall and was in Ancelstierre. Or rather in the No Man's Land between the Wall and the Perimeter. Normally this would be a quiet, empty place of raw earth and barbed wire, made somehow peaceful by the soft whisper of the wind flutes that Nick had always presumed to be some sort of weird decoration or memorial. Now it was wreathed in fog, fog eerily underlit by the low, red glow of the setting sun and flashes of lightning. The fog thinned in places as it rolled inexorably south, revealing scenes of awful carnage. The white mass was like the curtain of a horror show, briefly drawing back to show piles of corpses, bodies everywhere, bodies hanging on the wire and piled on the ground. They were all blue capped and blue scarved, and Nick finally recognized that they were slain Southerling refugees, and that in some horrible way, that was who Hedge's Night Crew had also been.

Lightning crackled above him, and thunder rumbled. Fog billowed apart, and Nick caught a glimpse of the hemispheres a little way ahead, roped onto the huge sleds that Nick knew had been waiting for them when they off-loaded the barges at the Redmouth. But he couldn't remember that happening, or anything between talking to Lirael in the reed boat and his awakening just before crossing the Wall. The hemispheres had been dragged here, obviously by the men who were dragging them now. Normal men, or at least not the Night Crew. Men dressed in strange, ragged combinations of Ancelstierran Army uniforms and Old Kingdom clothes, khaki tunics contrasting with hunting leathers, bright colored breeches, and rusty mail.

The force that had propelled him through the tunnel suddenly retreated, and Nick fell at Hedge's feet. The necromancer was at least seven feet tall now, and the red flames burning around his flesh and in his eye sockets were brighter and more intense. For the first time, Nick was frightened of him, and he wondered why he hadn't been all along. But he was too weak to do anything but crouch at Hedge's feet and clutch at his chest, where the pain still throbbed.

"Soon," said Hedge, his voice rumbling like the thunder. "Soon our master will be free."

Nick found himself nodding enthusiastically and was as frightened by this as he was by Hedge. He was already drifting back into that dreamy state where all he could think about was the hemispheres and his Lightning Farm, and what had to be done—

"No," whispered Nick. What must *not* be done. He didn't know what was happening, and until he did know, he wasn't going to do anything. "No!"

Hedge recognized that Nick spoke with an independent voice. He grinned, and fire flickered in his throat. He lifted Nick up like a baby and cradled him to his chest, against the bandolier of bells.

"Your part is nearly done, Nicholas Sayre," he said, and his breath was hot like steam and smelled of decay. "You were never more than an imperfect host, though your uncle and father have proved to be more helpful than even I could have hoped, albeit unwittingly."

Nick could only stare up at the burning eyes. Already he had forgotten everything that had come back to him in the tunnel. In Hedge's eyes he saw the silver hemispheres, the lightning, the joining that he knew once again was the single high purpose of his own short life.

"The hemispheres," he whispered, almost ritually. "The hemispheres must be joined."

"Soon, Master, soon," crooned Hedge. He stalked over to the waiting bearers and laid Nicholas down on the stretcher, stroking his chest just above his heart with a blackened, still-burning hand. What little was left of Nick's Ancelstierran shirt dissolved at Hedge's touch, showing bare skin that was blue with deep bruising. "Soon!"

Nick watched dully as Hedge walked away. No independent thought was left to him. Only the burning vision of the hemispheres and their ultimate joining. He tried to sit up to look at them but didn't have the strength, and in any case the fog was thickening once again. Wearied by the effort, Nick's hands fell to the ground on either side of the stretcher, and one finger touched a piece of debris that sent a strange feeling through his arm. A sharp pain and a gentle, healing warmth.

He tried to close his hand on the object, but his fingers refused. With considerable effort Nick rolled over to see exactly what it was. He peered down from the stretcher and saw it was a piece of broken wood, a fragment of one of the smashed wind flutes, like the one whose stump he could see a few feet away. The fragment was still infused with Charter marks, which flowed over and through the wood. As Nick watched them, something stirred in the recesses of his mind. For a moment he remembered who he really was once more, and recalled the promise he had given to Lirael.

His right hand would not obey him, so Nicholas leaned over even more and tried to pick up the wooden fragment with his left hand. He succeeded for a few seconds, but even his left hand was no longer his to command. His fingers opened, and the piece of the wind flute fell on the stretcher, between Nick's left arm and his body, not quite touching on either side.

Hedge did not walk far from Nicholas. He strode through the fog, which parted before him, straight to the largest pile of Southerling corpses. They had been killed by the Dead that Hedge had raised earlier that day from the temporary cemeteries around the camps. He was amused by the notion of using Southerling Dead to kill Southerlings. They had also killed the soldiers in the quaintly named Western Strongpoint, and the sailors in the lighthouse.

Hedge had crossed the Wall three times that day. Once to set the initial attacks in motion in Ancelstierre, which was no great task; second to go back to prepare the crossing of the hemispheres, which was much more difficult; and the third time with the hemispheres and Nicholas. He would never need to cross again, he knew, for the Wall would be one of the first things his master would destroy, along with all other works of the despised Charter.

All that remained to be done here was to go into Death and compel as many spirits as he could find to return and inhabit these bodies. Though Forwin Mill was less than twenty miles away and they should be able to reach it by morning, Hedge knew the Ancelstierran Army would attempt to prevent their breaking out of the Perimeter. He needed Dead Hands to fight the Army, and most of the ones he'd brought from the north and those created earlier that day in the Southerling camp cemeteries had been consumed in the crossing of the Wall, used up in order to get the hemispheres across.

Hedge drew two bells from his bandolier. Saraneth, for compulsion. Mosrael, to wake the spirits who slumbered here in No Man's Land, now freed from the chains of the hated Abhorsen's wind toys. He would use Mosrael to rouse as many as possible, though use of that bell would send him far into Death himself. Then he would come back through the gates and precincts, using Saraneth to drive any other spirits he could find into Life.

There would be plenty of bodies for all.

But before he could begin, he sensed something coming through the darkness. Ever careful, Hedge put Mosrael away, lest it sound of its own accord, and drew his sword instead, whispering the words that set the dark flames running down the blade.

He knew who it was, but he did not trust even the bounds and charms he had laid upon her. Chlorr was one of the Greater Dead now. In Life she had come under the sway of the Destroyer, but in Death she was somewhat beyond that control. Hedge had forced her obedience by other means, and as always with a necromancer's control over such a spirit, this obedience could be tenuous.

Chlorr appeared as a shape of darkness that was only vaguely human, with misshapen appendages upon a bulky torso that suggested two arms, two legs, and a head. Deep fires burned where eyes should be, though the fires were too large and too widely set apart. Chlorr had crossed the Wall with Hedge the first time and had led the surprise attack on the Ancelstierran Army garrison, in their Western Strongpoint. They had not expected an assault from the south. Chlorr had reaped many lives and was all the more powerful for it. Hedge watched her warily and kept a firm grip on Saraneth. The bells did not like to serve necromancers, and even a bell that an Abhorsen would find steady had to be shown who was master at all times.

Chlorr bowed, somewhat ironically in Hedge's estimation. Then she spoke, a misshapen mouth forming in the cloud of darkness. The words were a gibberish, slurred and broken. Hedge frowned and raised his sword. The mouth firmed up, and a tongue of blood-red fire flickered from side to side in the hideous maw.

"Your pardon, Master," said Chlorr. "Many soldiers are coming on a road from the south, riding horses. Some are Charter mages, though they are not adept. I slew those who came first, but there are many more behind, so I returned to warn my master."

"Good," said Hedge. "I am about to prepare a new host of Dead, which I will send to you when they are ready. For now, gather here all the Hands that you can and attack these soldiers. The Charter Mages in particular must be slain. Nothing must delay our lord!"

Chlorr bent her great, shapeless head. Then she reached back behind her and dragged forward a man who had been hidden by the fog and her dark bulk. He was a thin, little man, his coat ripped off his back to show a classic clerk's white shirt, complete with sleeve protectors. She held him by the neck just with two huge fingers, and he was almost dead from terror and lack of air. He fell to his knees in front of Hedge, gasping for breath and sobbing.

"This is yours, or so he says," said Chlorr. Then she strode off, her hands reaching out to touch any Dead Hands that were close by. As she touched them, they shuddered and jerked, then slowly began to follow her. But there were surprisingly

few Hands left, and none at all in the tunnel through the Wall.
Chlorr was careful not to go near the brooding mass of stone
that still shimmered every now and then with golden light.
Even she did not take crossing the Wall lightly, and possibly
could not have done it without Hedge's help and the sacrifice
of many lesser Dead.

"Who?" demanded Hedge.

"I'm . . . I'm Deputy Leader Geanner," sobbed the man.
He proffered an envelope. "Mister Corolini's assistant. I've
brought you the treaty letter . . . the permission to cross . . . to
cross the Wall—"

Hedge took the envelope, which burst into flame as he
touched it and was consumed, grey flakes of ash falling from his
blackened hand.

"I do not need permission," whispered Hedge. "From
anyone."

"I've also come for the . . . the fourth payment, as agreed,"
continued Geanner, staring up at Hedge. "We have done all
you asked."

"All?" asked Hedge. "The King and the Abhorsen?"

"D . . . d . . . dead," gasped Geanner. "Bombed and burnt
in Corvere. There was nothing left."

"The camps near Forwin Mill?"

"Our people will open the gates at dawn, as instructed. The
handbills have been printed, with translations in Azhdik and
Chellanian. They will believe the promises, I'm sure."

across the wall

THERE WAS A KNOCK on the door. Nick hastily put the dagger back in its sheath.

"Yes!" he called. The sheathed dagger was still in his hand. For a moment he considered exchanging it for the slim .32 automatic pistol in his suitcase's outer pocket. But he decided against it when the person at the door called out to him.

"Nicholas Sayre?"

It was a woman's voice. A young woman's voice, with the hint of a laugh in it. Not a servant. Perhaps one of the beautiful young women he'd seen arrive. Probably a not very successful actor or singer, the usual adornments of typical country house parties.

"Yes. Who is it?"

"Tesrya. Don't say you don't remember me. Perhaps a glimpse will remind you. Let me in. I've got a bottle of champagne. I thought we might have a drink before dinner."

Nick didn't remember her, but that didn't mean anything. He knew she would have singled him out from the seating plan for dinner, homing in on the surname Sayre. He supposed he should at least tell her to go away to her face. Courtesy to women, even fortune hunters, had been drummed into him all his life.

"Just one drink?"

Nick hesitated, then tucked the sheathed dagger down the inside of his trousers, at the hip. He held his foot against the door in case he needed to shut it in a hurry; then he turned the key and opened it a fraction.

He had the promised glimpse. Pale, melancholy eyes in a very white face, a forced smile from too-red lips. But there were also two hooded men there. One threw his shoulder against the door to keep it open. The other grabbed Nick by the hair and pushed a pad the size of a small pillow against his face.

Nick tried not to breathe as he threw himself backward, losing some hair in the process, but the sickly-sweet smell of chloroform was already in his mouth and nose. The two men gave him no time to recover his balance. One pushed him back to the foot of the bed, while the other got his right arm in a wrestling hold. Nick struck out with his left, but his fist wouldn't go where he wanted it to. His arm felt like a rubbery length of pipe, the elbow gone soft.

Nick kept flailing, but the pad was back on his mouth and nose, and all his senses started to shatter into little pieces like a broken mosaic. He couldn't make sense of what he saw and heard and felt, and all he could smell was a sickly scent like a cheap perfume badly imitating the scent of flowers.

In another few seconds, he was unconscious.

Nicholas Sayre returned to his senses very slowly. It was like waking up drunk after a party, his mind still clouded and a hangover building in his head and stomach. It was dark, and he was disoriented. He tried to move and for a frightened instant thought he was paralyzed. Then he felt restraints at his wrists and thighs and ankles and a hard surface under his head and back. He was tied to a table, or perhaps a hard bench.

"Ah, the mind wakes," said a voice in the darkness. Nick thought for a second, his clouded mind slowly processing the sound. He knew that voice. Dorrance.

"Would you like to see what is happening?" asked Dorrance. Nick heard him take a few steps, heard the click of a rotary electric switch. Harsh light came with the click, so bright that Nick had to screw his eyes shut, tears instantly welling up in the corners.

"Look, Mr. Sayre. Look at your most useful work."

Nick slowly opened his eyes. At first all he could see was a naked, very bright electric globe swinging directly above his head. Blinking to clear the tears, he looked to one side. Dorrance was there, leaning against a concrete wall. He smiled and pointed to the other side, his hand held close against his chest, fist clenched, index finger extended.

Nick rolled his head and then recoiled, straining against the ropes that bound his ankles, thighs, and wrists to a steel operating table with raised rails.

The creature from the case was right next to him. No longer in the case, but stretched out on an adjacent table ten inches lower than Nick's. It was not tied up. There was a red rubber tube running from one of Nick's wrists to a metal stand next to the creature's head. The tube ended an inch above the monster's slightly open mouth. Blood was dripping from the tube, small dark blobs falling in between its jet black teeth.

Nick's blood.

Nick struggled furiously for another second, panic building in every muscle. The ropes did not give at all, and the tube was not dislodged. Then, his strength exhausted, he stopped.

"You need not be concerned, Mr. Nicholas Sayre," said Dorrance. He moved around to look at the creature, gently tapping Nick's slippered feet as he passed. "I am taking only a pint. This will all just be a nightmare in the morning, half remembered, with a dozen men swearing to your conspicuous consumption of brandy."

As he spoke, the light above him suddenly flared into white-hot brilliance. Then, with a bang, the bulb exploded into powder and the room went dark. Nick blinked, the afterimage of the filament burning a white line across the room. But even with that, he could see another light. Two violet sparks that were faint at first but became brighter and more intense.

Nick recognized them instantly as the creature's eyes. At the same time, he smelled a sudden, acrid odor, which got stronger and stronger, coating the back of his mouth and making his nostrils burn. A metallic stench that he knew only too well.

The smell of Free Magic.

The violet eyes moved suddenly, jerking up. Nick felt the rubber hose suddenly pulled from his wrist and the wet sensation of blood dripping down his hand.

He still couldn't see anything save the creature's eyes. They moved again, very quickly, as the thing stood up and crossed the room. It ignored Nick, though he struggled violently against his bonds as it went past. He couldn't see what happened next, but something . . . or someone . . . was hurled against his table, the impact rocking it almost to the point of toppling over.

"No!" shouted Dorrance. "Don't go out! I'll bring you blood! Whatever kind you need—"

There was a tearing sound, and flickering light suddenly filled the room. Nick saw the creature silhouetted in the doorway, holding the heavy door it had just ripped from its steel hinges. It threw this aside and strode out into the corridor, lifting its head back to emit a hissing shriek that was so high-pitched, it made Nick's ears ring.

Dorrance staggered after it for a moment, then returned and flung open a cabinet on the wall. As he picked up the telephone handset inside, the lights in the corridor fizzed and went out.

Nick heard the dial spin three times. Then Dorrance swore and tapped the receiver before dialing again. This time the phone worked, and he spoke very quickly.

"Hello? Lackridge? Can you hear me? Yes . . . ignore the crackle. Is Hodgeman there? Tell him 'Situation Dora.' All the fire doors must be barred and the exit grilles activated. No, tell him now. . . . 'Dora' . . .Yes, yes. It worked, all too well. She's completely active, and I heard Her clearly for the first time, speaking directly into my head, not as a dreaming voice. Sayre's blood was too rich, and there's something wrong with it. She needs to dilute it with normal blood. . . . What? Active! Running around! Of course you're in danger! She doesn't care whose blood. . . . We need to keep Her in the tunnels; then I'll find someone . . . one of the servants. Just get on with it!"

Nick kept silent, but he remembered the dagger at his hip. If he could bend his hand back and reach it, he might be able to unsheath it enough to work the rope against the blade. If he didn't bleed to death first.

"So, Mr. Sayre," said Dorrance in the darkness. "Why would your blood be different from that of any other bearer of the Charter Mark? It causes me some distress to think I have given Her the wrong sort. Not to mention the difficulty that now arises from Her desire to wash Her drink down."

"I don't know," Nick whispered after a moment's hesitation. He'd thought of pretending to be unconscious, but Dorrance would certainly test that.

In the distance, electric bells began a harsh, insistent clangor. At first none sounded in the corridor outside, then one stuttered into life. At the same time, the light beyond the door flickered on, off, and on again, before giving up in a shower of sparks that plunged the room back into total darkness.

Something touched Nick's feet. He flinched, taking off some skin against the ropes. A few seconds later there was a click near his head, a whiff of kerosene; and a four-inch flame suddenly shed some light on the scene. Dorrance lifted his cigarette lighter and set it on a head-high shelf, still burning.

He took a bandage from the same shelf and started to wind

it around Nick's wrist.

"Waste not, want not," said Dorrance. "Even if your blood is tainted, it has succeeded beyond my dearest hopes. I have long dreamed of waking Her."

"It, you mean," croaked Nick.

Dorrance tied off the bandage, then suddenly slapped Nick's face hard with the back of his hand.

"You are not worthy to speak of Her! She is a goddess! A goddess! She should never have been sent away! My father was a fool! Fortunately I am not!"

Nick chose silence once more, and waited for another blow. But it didn't come. Dorrance took a deep breath, then bent under the table. Nick craned his head to see what he was doing but could hear only the rattle of metal on metal.

The man emerged holding two sets of old-style handcuffs, the kind whose cuffs were screwed in rather than key locked. He quickly handcuffed Nick's left wrist to the metal rail of the bed, then did the same with the second set to his right wrist.

"It has been politic to play the disbeliever about your Charter Magic," he said as he screwed the handcuffs tight. "But She has told me different in my dreams, and if She can rise so far from the Wall, perhaps your magic will also serve you . . . and ropes do burn or fray so easily. Rest here, young Nicholas. My mistress may soon need a second drink, whether the taste disagrees with Her or not."

CLARIEL

THE HOUSE WAS one of the best in Belisaere, high on the eastern slope of Beshill. It boasted five floors, each with a broad balcony facing east, and on top there was a pleasant roof garden which delivered a view over the lesser houses on the slope below, and past them across the red roofs of the buildings that clustered closely on the valley floor on either side of the Winter Road. Beyond the houses was the seven-tiered Great Eastern Aqueduct and its lesser companion, the city wall. The eastern wall had its feet almost in the water; beyond it lay the glittering expanse of the Sea of Saere, now dotted with those slower, straggling fishing boats that were coming late to Fish Harbor, hours after the rest of the fleet had returned to unload their catch with the dawn.

Clariel stood at the intricately carved marble railing on the edge of the roof garden, with the sun on her face and the cool sea breeze ruffling her shorn-at-the-neck jet-black hair, and wondered why she couldn't like the view, the house, or indeed, the whole city of Belisaere.

She was seventeen years old, two months shy of being eighteen, and up until their arrival in the city three days before had lived her entire life in the much smaller town of Estwael in the far northwest of the Old Kingdom, and more important to her in recent years, in and about the Great Forest that surrounded Estwael.

But Estwael and the Great Forest had been left behind, despite Clariel's entreaties to her parents. She'd asked to remain, to become a Borderer, one of the wardens who patrolled the forests and woods of the kingdom. But her parents refused, and anyway the Borderers did not recruit youths, as Sergeant Penreth in Estwael had told Clariel numerous times, though always with a matter-of-fact kindness, for they were long acquaintances, if not friends. Nor would her parents accept any of her various other reasons for being allowed to stay behind.

Typically, Clariel's mother, Jaciel, had simply ignored her daughter's request, refusing to even discuss the matter. Jaciel's mind was rarely focused on her family. A goldsmith of rare talent, all her attention was typically on whatever beautiful gold or silver object she was currently making, or on the one that was taking shape in her head.

Harven, Clariel's father and manager of all practical matters in their family life, had patiently explained to his daughter that besides being too young to join the Borderers it was very likely that in a year she would not want to anyway. He had then added insult to injury by telling Clariel the move to Belisaere was as much for her benefit as it was for her mother, who had been accorded the honor of being invited to join the High Guild of Goldsmiths in the capital.

There would be many more opportunities for her in Belisaere, Clariel had been told repeatedly. She could be apprenticed herself, straight into a High Guild or one of the Great Companies. There might be a business the family could buy for her. Or she might make an advantageous marriage.

But none of these "opportunities" interested Clariel, and she knew they never would have left Estwael just for her benefit. Any advantage she might receive would be entirely incidental to her mother's desire for a much larger workshop, a greater variety of better metals, gems, and other materials to work with, and an increased labor force, doubtlessly including at least half a dozen more pimply apprentices who would try to look down the front of Clariel's dress at dinner.

A meaningful cough behind her made Clariel turn around. Her father smiled at her, the weak smile that she knew was a harbinger of bad news. It had made frequent appearances in the last few months, the smile. When people first met Harven they would think him strong, until his mouth turned up. He had a weak, giving-in smile. He was a goldsmith too, but was not particularly gifted in the actual craft. He was much better at managing the business of his wife's work.

"Have you come to tell me that by some stroke of good fortune I am to be allowed to go home?" asked Clariel.

"This is our home now," said Harven.

"It doesn't feel like it," said Clariel. She looked over the railing again, across all the white stone buildings with their red tiled roofs, and then back again at the ornamental shrubs in the terra-cotta boxes that made up their own roof garden, shrubs with pale bark and small, weak-looking yellow leaves. "There is nothing green here. I haven't seen a single proper tree. Everything is ordered, and tamed, and put between walls. And there are too many people."

"There are lots of big trees in the gardens on Palace Hill," said Harven. "We just can't see them from here."

Clariel nodded glumly. A few trees too distant to be seen, across miles and miles of houses and workshops and other buildings, and thousands and thousands of people, rather proved her point, she thought.

"Did you come to tell me something?" she asked, knowing that he had, and she wasn't going to like whatever it was. His smile gave that away.

"Ah, your mother had a meeting with Guildmaster Kilp yestereve, and he made her aware of an opportunity for you that she . . . we desire you to take up."

"An opportunity?" asked Clariel, her heart sinking. "For me?"

"Yes, an opportunity," continued her father, raising his

hands and lifting his shoulders to emphasize what a good opportunity he was about to reveal. "The Goldsmiths, the Merchant Venturers, the Spicers, the Northwestern Trading Company . . . all the High Guilds and most of the great companies, they send their children to the Belisaere Select Academy—"

"A school?" interrupted Clariel. "I've been to school! And I'm not a child!"

Clariel had indeed attended school in Estwael, from the age of eight to fourteen, and had been taught how to calculate using an abacus; keep accounts; write formal letters; supervise servants; ride in the great hunt with hounds and hawks; fight with dagger, sword, and bow; and play the psalter, zittern, and reed pipe.

She had also been been baptized with the forehead Charter mark shortly after her birth and taught the rudiments of Charter Magic, that highly organized and difficult sorcery that drew upon the endless array of symbols that collectively made up the magical Charter that described, contained, and connected all things upon, below, above, within, and beyond the world.

Indeed, it would have been very surprising if she had not been taught Charter Magic, given she was a granddaughter of the Abhorsen. The Abhorsen, chief of the family of the same name, both an office and a bloodline, descended from the remnants of the ancient powers who had made the Charter, codifying and ordering the Free Magic that had once been such a threat to all living things in its arbitrary and selfish nature.

The Abhorsens, like their cousins in the Royal Family and also the glacier-dwelling, future-gazing Clayr, were as deeply a part of the foundations and beginnings of the Charter as the more physical underpinnings: the Great Charter Stones beneath the royal palace in Belisaere; the Wall that defined the borders of the Old Kingdom to the south; and the Great Rift to the north.

In addition to the dame school in the town, Clariel had

attended another, more informal educational institution, largely without her parents' knowledge. Since she'd turned twelve Clariel visited her aunt Lemmin whenever she had a day free. Lemmin was an herbalist who lived on the fringe of the forest, in a comfortable house surrounded by her enormous, high-walled garden. Her parents assumed that Clariel stayed within those walls. But her visits to her relative rarely encompassed more than a hug and a greeting, for with her aunt's good-natured connivance, Clariel would go on out through the forest door, out to follow the Borderers into the deeper woods, or to join the hunters from the lodge. From them all she had learned the habits of animals, the nature of trees, and how to track, and hunt, and snare, to forage, to gut and skin, and make and mend, and live in the wild.

The wild . . . that was where she should be, Clariel thought. Not imprisoned here behind a great maze of walls, roped in by the vast net of streets, caught up in the thrashings of the multitudes of people likewise trapped—

"It's not like your old school," her father said, interrupting Clariel's thoughts. "It is a new thing, that they call a polishing . . . no, I mean finishing . . . a finishing school. And it's not for children as such . . . it's for the young men and women who are children of the senior Guild members. You'll meet the best people in the city and learn how to mix with them."

"I don't want to meet the 'best people' in the city!" protested Clariel. "I don't particularly want to meet anyone. I'm quite happy by myself. Or at least, I was, back home. Besides, who is going to help you?"

Clariel had assisted her father for several days each week for a long time, working on all the aspects of being a goldsmith that Jaciel ignored, which included money-changing, some minor loans and financial dealings, and the administration of the workshop, particularly the detailed accounts of the raw materials bought, how they were used, what they were made into, and how much profit they returned when sold. She had liked doing this, mostly because she was left alone, and it had been quiet and peaceful in Harven's old study, a high tower room with tall windows that gave a wonderful view of the forested hills that surrounded Estwael. It also only took her a dozen hours a week, leaving her plenty of time to wander in the green world beyond the town.

"The Guild is sending me a senior apprentice," said Harven. "One who is suited for the . . . less . . . ah . . . someone with the . . ."

"With an eye for numbers and good penmanship?" suggested Clariel. She knew that her father felt diminished by his lack of talent in the actual craft of goldsmithing, though he tried to hide it. He had not made anything himself for years, probably because he could not come even close to his wife's genius, though he always lamented how the business took up all of his time, leaving nothing for the craft.

"Yes," said Harven. "Though I expect I will still need your help, Clarrie, only not as much."

"Or at all, from the sound of it," said Clariel. "How much time do I have to spend at this school?"

"Three days a week, until the Autumn Festival," said Harven. "And it's only mornings, from the ninth hour until noon."

"I suppose I can survive that," said Clariel. It was already several weeks past midsummer, though the days were still long and the nights warm. "But what happens after the Autumn Festival? Can I go home then?"

Harven looked down at the sharp-pointed, gilded toes of his red leather shoes, fine footwear for the consort of the city's newest and probably most talented High Goldsmith. Along with the smile, looking at his shoes was a well-known telltale. He had a habit of shoe-gazing when he was about to lie to his daughter, or wanted to avoid directly answering a question.

"Let us see what paths appear," he mumbled.

Clariel looked away from him, up at a lone silver gull flying toward Fish Harbor, going to join the flocks that endlessly circled and bickered there, mirroring the people below.

She knew what her father wasn't saying. Her parents were hoping she would find someone who wanted to marry her, or more likely, wanted to marry into the family of Jaciel High Goldsmith. An apprentice from a Guild family, or one of these "best people" from the school. This would solve the problem of a daughter who didn't want to be a goldsmith herself, or take up any of the other crafts or businesses deemed suitable.

But Clariel didn't want to marry anyone. She had once or twice—no more—wondered if she was naturally a singleton, like the russet martens who only came together for the brief-est mating season and then went their own way. Or her own aunt Lemmin, for that matter, who chose to live entirely alone, though happily for Clariel could stand visitors provided they amused themselves.

They had talked about solitude and self-sufficiency once, Lemmin and her niece, soon after Clariel had first chosen to lie with a young man and had found herself quite separate from the experience, and not caring one way or another about repeating the act itself or the emotional dance that went with it.

"Perhaps I don't like men," Clariel had said to her aunt, who was pulling garlic bulbs and delighting in her crop. "Though I can't say I have those feelings for women, either."

"You're young," Lemmin had replied, sniffing a particularly grand clump of garlic. "It's probably too early to tell, one way or another. The most important thing is to be true to yourself, however you feel, and not try to feel or behave differently because you think you should, or someone has told you how you must feel. But do think about it. Unexamined feelings lead to all kinds of trouble."

Clariel examined her feelings once again, and found them unchanged. What she desperately wanted to do was get out of the city and, since the Borderers wouldn't let her join them, purchase a hunting lodge or forester's hut outside Estwael, to go hunting and fishing and just *live* in the quiet, cool, shaded world of the forest valleys and the heather-clad hills that she loved. But that would require her parents' permission, and money, and she had neither of these things.

At least not until she worked out how to get them . . .

"There is one other matter," said Harven cautiously. He was gazing over the railing now himself, which was a slight improvement from staring at his shoes, though he still wouldn't look her in the eye. "Well, a few other matters."

Clariel lost sight of the seagull, who had joined the flock and been absorbed by it, all individuality gone in an instant.

"Yes?"

"This school . . . uh, the Academy . . . it doesn't teach Charter Magic."

"And this means?" asked Clariel, encouraging the bad news out. Her father's smile was spreading across his face again, so obviously there was more unpleasantness to come.

"Apparently it's not the fashion these days, or something," muttered Harven. "The best people don't practice Charter Magic, they hire people to do it for them, if absolutely necessary."

"These 'best people' sound rather lazy and stupid," observed Clariel. "Do they get awfully fat from not doing *anything* for themselves?"

She herself was slim, and up until relatively recently, could easily pass for a boy. She still could, with a bit of preparation and the right clothes. It was quite useful, and had made it easier to follow the truffle-hunting pigs, tickle trout in the Wael River, hunt the small puzzle deer, or do any of the things that she liked but weren't proper for a well-brought-up child of the merchant elite. She thought this potential for deception might come in handy in Belisaere as well. Particularly for leaving the city.

"No, don't be silly," said Harven. "In any case, your mother wants you to further your Charter Magic studies—"

"Why?" asked Clariel. "She never wanted me to before. Is it something to do with grandfather?"

Her mother was a Charter Mage, and certainly used her magic in her goldsmithing, but she made no display of it outside her workshop. This was presumably because she was estranged from her family, the Abhorsens, and the Abhorsens were very much a living embodiment of some aspects of the Charter and tended to be powerful Charter Mages. In fact, Jaciel's father was the current Abhorsen, but Clariel had never met him, because of a never-spoken-about rift that had occurred when Jaciel was young.

"Possibly, possibly," muttered Harven, which suggested to his knowing daughter that it probably *didn't* have anything to do with the Abhorsens. But he seized upon it as a possible explanation to her, adding, "The Abhorsen or the Abhorsen-in-Waiting do come to Belisaere upon occasion, there are ceremonies and so on, so we might well have to meet either your grandfather or your aunt—"

"My aunt is the Abhorsen-in-Waiting?" asked Clariel. "I didn't even know Mother *had* a sister!"

Her parents never talked about Jaciel's family, so this was all interesting information. She hardly knew anything about the Abhorsens really, apart from the childhood rhyme everyone learned about the Charter:

> *Five Great Charters knit the land*
> *Together linked, hand in hand*
> *One in the people who wear the crown*
> *Two in the folk who keep the Dead down*
> *Three and Five became stone and mortar*
> *Four sees all in frozen water*

The Abhorsens were the "folk who keep the Dead down," which as far as Clariel knew meant they hunted down necromancers, and banished Dead spirits that had somehow returned from Death to Life.

Abhorsens could walk in Death themselves and like necromancers used Free Magic bells to command and compel the Dead, though the Abhorsens' bells were somehow not Free Magic as such but bound to the Charter.

Not that the Abhorsens did much keeping the Dead down in the present era, as far as Clariel knew. She'd never heard of the Dead causing any trouble in her lifetime. Nor for that matter did the Clayr, the fourth of the Great Charter bloodlines, seem to see very much into the future. If they did, they kept it to themselves, just as they kept themselves remote in their glacier-sheltered fortress far to the north. Even the King, head of those "who wear the crown" didn't do much ruling anymore, though Clariel had never really been interested in who ultimately was in charge of the various institutions that effectively managed the kingdom.

Abhorsens, Clayr, the King: they all seemed to be relics of a bygone past, just as the "stone and mortar" of the rhyme meant very little in the present day. This referred to the Wall to the south, to Clariel merely a curious landmark she'd heard about but never seen; and to the Great Charter stones she knew only as they were depicted in a mummer's play: big grey man-size puppets painted with gold representations of Charter marks. In Estwael they had become part of a comic turn in the Midsummer Festival, tall rocks that crashed into each other, fell over, got up again, and then repeated the whole process numerous times to gales of laughter.

"Of course you knew about your mother's sister," said Harven, as if they talked about Jaciel's family all the time, instead of never. "Anyway, we may be seeing her or your grandfather, and then there's the King, who is your mother's second cousin after all, and they all are . . . well . . . you know, very big on Charter Magic."

"I thought you said the 'best people' don't do Charter Magic anymore because it's too much like hard work or they'll get their fingers scorched black or something. Are the King and the Abhorsens not the best people?"

"Don't be silly," said Harven. "They're more . . . more kind of separate, particularly these days. Out of the way. Modern times, you know, and different ways and means, things change . . ."

"What *are* you talking about, Father?" asked Clariel.

"You are to have lessons in Charter Magic," rallied Harven, getting back to the subject at hand. "We have arranged for you to take afternoon lessons with a Magister Kargrin, whose house is on the hill below us, possibly you can see it from here, I believe it is quite distinctive—"

Clariel looked over the railing. There were hundreds of houses on the western slope of Beshill, and many more beyond, all crowded together.

"Where?" she asked.

"Somewhere downhill," replied Harven, waving vaguely. "The house with the sign of the hedgepig on the street of the Cormorant . . . anyway, your guard will lead you there—"

"My guard?"

"I thought I told you about the guards already?"

"No you did not," replied Clariel sternly. "What guards?"

"The Guild has sent us some guards, for the house and the workshop, and also to . . . look after us. The family."

"Why do we need guards?"

"I don't think we need them particularly," said Harven, but he was looking at his shoes again. "It's just something they do here. In any case, one will be guarding you. To and from the Academy, and so forth. His name is . . . um . . . well, it's slipped my mind for a moment. He's waiting to meet you downstairs. Also your mother wants Valannie to help you with your clothes."

"What's wrong with my clothes?" asked Clariel. She was wearing what she wore most ordinary days in Estwael, basically her own version of a Borderer's uniform: a short-sleeved doeskin jerkin over a knee-length woolen robe with long sleeves dyed a pale green with an inch of linen trim at the wrists and neck; woolen stockings and knee-high boots of pig leather, made from the first boar Clariel had hunted and killed herself, when she was fourteen.

Admittedly, leather and wool was a little too heavy to be comfortable in Belisaere. The sun was hotter and the winds warmer here by the sea, compared to Estwael, which was situated in a high valley and surrounded by the wooded hills of the Great Forest. There was a term used disparagingly in other parts of the kingdom—when it was unseasonably cold, they called such days an "Estwael Summer."

"Women wear different things here," said Harven. "Valannie

will help you buy whatever you need."

Valannie was Clariel's new maid. She had been waiting for them at the new house, and like it, had been provided by the Guild rather than being hired by the family. Jaciel didn't care about choosing her own servants, particularly since Valannie was immediately competent and useful. But Clariel had refused her help as much as possible so far. She was determined to do without a maid, since she could not have the help of her old nurse, Kraille, who had chosen to retire to her son's farm outside Estwael, rather than brave the horrors of the city.

"So you need to come down," said Harven.

Clariel nodded, without speaking.

"I'm sorry, Clarrie," said her father. "But it will all be for the best. You'll see."

"I hope so," said Clariel bleakly. "You go, Father. I'll be down in a minute."

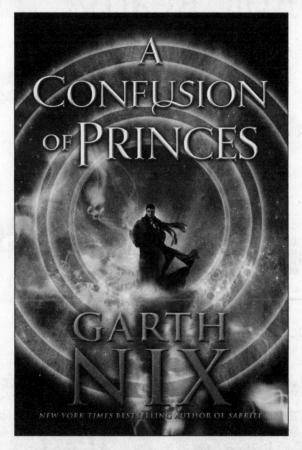